STUART CL

"*Project U.L.F.* is a flat ou... ence-fiction adventure in a long time."

- MyShelf.com

"Books like this simply validate my love of science fiction. Not only are his characters realistic and interesting, but the storyline is extremely engaging. From the time I first sat down to read, straight through to the end, I was captivated...Clark's vivid depiction of the deadly planet and imaginative creatures brought the book to life."

- SciFi Chick

"Attention all science-fiction fans, there is a new writing talent on the horizon. Clark has created a remarkable world filled with unusual and dangerous flora and fauna in a future that still hasn't learned the evil of power and greed. The adventure is fast-paced, the characters are authentic and multi-dimensional, and the alien lifeforms are creatively drawn and very surprising.

"Clark charts the science fiction waters well, crafting an enjoyable tale."

- Press & Sun Bulletin

"With realistic creatures just alien enough to be intimidating, the reader feels the threat the adventurers face on a moment to moment basis. Clark's narrative is smooth, uncluttered and edited well."

- Front Street Reviews

"Clark offers the reader an exciting story told from the point-of-view of different characters...the strange creatures he describes and the conflicts among the team members keep the pages turning."

- SFRevu

"Captivating from the first page, Project U.L.F. is a story that is not bogged down by technical literature, but filled with terminology suited for thc genre. Science fiction fans will find it easy to read and unable to put the novel down until you reach its entirety."

- Book Pleasures

Also by Stuart Clark

Project U.L.F.

Project U.L.F.: Reacquisition

PROJECT U•L•F
REACQUISITION

BY

Stuart Clark

HOLLISTON, MASSACHUSETTS

PROJECT U.L.F. REACQUISITION

This book is a work of fiction. Names, characters, places and incidents are products of the author's imagination or are used fictitiously. Any resemblance to actual events, locations or persons, living or deceased, is entirely coincidental.

Cover Art by Henning Ludvigsen

First printing, February 2010
10 9 8 7 6 5 4 3 2 1

ISBN # 0-9787782-8-6
ISBN-13 # 9780978778286
LCCN # 2009934477

Silver Leaf Books, LLC
P.O. Box 6460
Holliston, MA 01746
+1-888-823-6450

Visit our web site at www.SilverLeafBooks.com

For Karen

ACKNOWLEDGMENTS

There are a number of people who I would like to thank for their assistance in the creation of this novel. The very good friends who read the manuscript and offered honest criticism on where it could be improved, namely Helen Arsicot and her father Don Ritchie, Lucy Pesaro and Laura Blanton.

Dan Managlia, my brother-in-law and resident Chicagoan, for his comments and insights.

All the folks at Silver Leaf Books for their continued support, especially Brett Fried and my editor, Alison Novak.

Henning Ludvigsen, my cover artist, for another wonderful piece of artwork

And last but not least, my family, for their love and support.

PROJECT U·L·F
REACQUISITION

To Frank,

Lock all your doors!

Best Wishes

Your friend

Stuart Clark

12·08·12

It is just like man's vanity and impertinence to call an animal dumb because it is dumb to his dull perceptions

- Mark Twain

PROLOGUE

Marty felt the wheels of the hover vehicle thud into place beneath him as he skillfully piloted it down to the street from the skytrack. He took pride in the fact that he nearly always made a soft landing, especially tonight with Michelle sitting next to him.

She beamed at him, "Nice job."

"Thanks." He touched an illuminated panel, shutting down the vehicle's turbine and switching to the regular engine and began to drive Michelle the last few blocks home. He smiled. It felt like the smile had never left his face all night.

The headlights picked out the features of the road ahead, the small camera embedded in the roof relaying the scene to the two people inside via an image projected onto a virtual windshield.

Marty looked over at Michelle again and she caught his glance. "What?"

"Just you," he said.

They had been friends since junior high and sweethearts since high school. She had been the only girl he had ever dated, the only girl he had ever wanted to date. Tonight he had cemented that relationship by proposing to her and she had accepted. They would be together forever.

"You're funny," she said. "Cute, but funny." She reached across and laid a hand lovingly on his thigh. He looked down, saw the diamond solitaire he had given her just hours earlier glinting in the darkness and smiled to himself again.

"Hey, big boy," she teased, "What do you say we take a little detour, y'know, fool around a little bit?" Her hand moved further up his leg. Marty squirmed a little in his seat. "C'mon. Don't you think tonight deserves a little celebration?" The insinuation was clear.

"Hey, come on, Michelle, ease off, will ya?"

"What are you afraid of? I'm only playing. I'm not going to bite you." Her hand moved further north.

"'Chelle. Come on!" he snapped. "Not while I'm driving."

She huffed and pulled her arm back, folding it across her chest. "You're no fun at all."

"Aw come on," he looked across at her, "Don't be like that. There'll be plenty of time for that. It's just I'm driving. If anything happens it could get us both..."

Michelle threw her hands onto the dashboard, her elbows locked, her eyes widening in horror. Marty had just enough time to look up and see a humanoid figure standing in the road in front of them.

Instinctively he stamped on the brakes, locking all four wheels and sending the vehicle into a long skid. He braced himself, but just at the moment of impact, the figure went up over the roof and disappeared out of sight.

For what seemed like eternity, the vehicle continued on its graceful slide and then abruptly came to a halt, skewed across the street.

For a moment they sat there in stunned silence. Marty blew out a breath and let his head fall back on the seat. His hands still gripped the steering controls tightly. He rolled his head to the side. He knew just by looking at her that Michelle was about to cry.

"Hey, baby, it's okay. I mean, you're okay, right?"

She nodded, blinking away the first of the tears.

"Well that's good. That's good. And I'm okay. So we're okay."

She nodded silently again.

He blew out another breath and ran a hand through his hair. "What the hell was that?"

"I don't know." Michelle's voice shook with emotion.

"I'm going to go check it out. Stay here, okay?"

She grabbed his arm with both hands. "No, Marty! No! Let's

just go home. I just want to go home."

"It'll be all right, honey, just stay here. I'll be right back. You'll see. Driver's door," Marty commanded. The door popped out from the chassis and pivoted upward on its forward hinge. Cool night air rushed in. He stepped out and his breath plumed in the darkness.

There was nothing in the street behind them. No sign of what it was that they had almost hit. No indication that anything had happened apart from two snaking lines of black on the asphalt and the fading smell of burnt rubber in the air. Marty started walking back to where the skid marks began, his eyes scanning right and left along the street. Nothing. No sign of anything.

He stopped at the end of the tracks, scuffing them with the tip of his sneaker as if trying to erase the whole event. He looked further back down the street, put his hands on his hips and shook his head, not finding an explanation for what had just happened.

He took a deep breath. "Weird."

The hover vehicle's door popped behind him and he turned to see Michelle getting out. "Come on, Marty. It's getting cold in here. Whatever it was, it's gone. Let's just go."

It was then that the creature landed between them.

It rose slowly from its forced crouch until it stood at its full eight feet in height. Yellow, rabid eyes burnt into Marty. "Oh, my God," he said under his breath. Michelle screamed.

"Mi…" He tried to speak but his throat would give no voice to his words. "Mi…Get in the car Michelle." She continued to scream hysterically. "Michelle! Just get in the car!"

It took a step towards him. A large, hairy, padded foot fell soundlessly on the road. It was covered in hair, more like a coat than fur. Short brown hair which covered it from its feet to the tufts on its short, pointed ears. It snarled at Marty, the lips on the black muzzle pulling back to reveal a wicked set of canines.

Marty backed away from it, but it took another step towards him. It spread its arms out wide, arms with paws that seemed disproportionately large. For the first time Marty could see that a small membrane of skin connected the arms to the body from the elbow up, and on the back of each elbow was a small, gripping claw. To his horror, he watched as three razor-sharp claws extended and retracted on each paw as if being made ready for use.

"Marty!" Michelle sobbed. "Don't leave me here!"

"It's all right, honey," he shouted back. "I'm not leaving. Just stay calm. Everything will be okay."

With lightning speed the creature dropped to all fours and with three giant bounds was on Marty before he could even react. Once again it reared up on its back legs, extended its claws and with a single vicious swipe took Marty's head clean off. The decapitated body crumpled to the road in a heap.

Michelle cupped her hands to her mouth and gasped. "Oh, my God!" she whispered to herself and then again, "Oh my God! Oh my God! Oh my God!"

She didn't hesitate to get back in the hover vehicle now, climbing in quickly and frantically pulling the door down behind her. Once inside, she clambered across to the driver's side, the seat that Marty had occupied only minutes before, and desperately reached out to pull the door down, fearing that at any moment whatever it was that had just killed him would appear right there and end her life too. She grabbed the handle and pulled the door closed.

"Oh my God! Oh my God! Oh my God!" Her hands shook uncontrollably. She had to get away from here. The engine was still running. That was good. "Think, Michelle, think," she told herself. The restraint! She reached around and grabbed the slender belt, pulling it over her shoulder. She tried to buckle it but her shaking hands would not allow her to. She let it zip back into place. Restraint? What the hell was she thinking? Just go!

She put the car into gear and lurched away and then for some reason, whether it was out of guilt for leaving Marty or just morbid curiosity, she turned the car back around.

Caught in the headlights, the creature was already crouched

over Marty's body. As she watched, appalled, it looked up at her. Its nose was already painted red with blood.

"No!" she screamed. "Get the hell away from him!" Without thinking she grabbed the accelerator lever and pushed it forward. The car lurched into life once again, shooting forward and throwing her back in the seat. She drove straight at the thing hunched over Marty, arms locked in grim determination, tears streaking down her face. As she bore down on it she saw the yellow eyes, bright in the headlights. Haunting. Crazy. And then just as before, right at the last second, the creature sprang up and out of the way.

The vehicle hit Marty's body, bucked wildly and threw Michelle out of her seat. Her head hit the roof and she fought to maintain control, but it was too late. With a crunch of metal, Michelle crashed into another vehicle parked on the street. A small cloud of steam started rising from the crumpled hood.

She brought a hand up to her face and sobbed uncontrollably, thinking about what she had just done. This whole situation was like some horrible nightmare.

A thud brought her back to her senses. She looked behind her. It was obvious from the dent that something heavy had landed on the roof. Before she could even react, three blades ripped through the ceiling next to her head. She screamed again as the claws pulled backwards with a tortured screeching, slicing open the vehicle's roof with ease.

"Driver's door!" Michelle screamed, but the door remained in place, damaged electronics from the impact rendering the voice activated system inoperative.

She fumbled blindly for the manual door latch, watching in horror as the thing tried to reach her, systematically ripping the roof apart. Finally, she found it.

Michelle ran. She didn't get very far.

CHAPTER 1

It was just after 4:00 AM when Chris Gault pulled his hover vehicle up to the staff entrance at Chicago's Interplanetary Zoological Park. He was surprised that the security guard was not at his post, but shrugged it off. The man was probably doing a quick check of the nearby perimeter fence. It wasn't unheard of. Besides, they had other security measures.

He turned to his left and opened his eyes wide, submitting to the retinal scan. The barrier rose obediently in front of him.

He pulled the vehicle up in his designated bay, shut off the engine and yawned. He was lagged and he knew it. Chris had just got back from an expedition four days ago and he still hadn't got back in synch with local time.

He hated lag. He also hated the fact that he seemed to suffer from it more than most people. Getting over cryosleep was one thing, lag was a whole other world of hurt. Some people barely suffered from it at all. Others had their own methods or superstitions or crazy ways of dealing with it. Chris just suffered with it for a week or more.

He'd been awake since 1:20 AM. Then he'd just tossed and turned and watched the digits on the clock tick by as they teased him with their progress. He couldn't stand it anymore so he had decided to go to work. He needed to keep his mind active. Better to be doing anything than nothing—and there was always something that needed doing at the IZP.

Chris got out of his car and walked through the double doors into the main building of the IZP. Things were different at the zoo these days. It was a shadow of its former self. The buildings looked dilapidated and old, as if the very concrete had grown tired and weary. There hadn't been any money spent here in years.

Part of that could be attributed to the Managing Director, Stephen Gruber. Prior to having the top job, Gruber had been the zoo's chief financial officer, and as such, he had kept a tight hold on the purse strings. He was a bean counter, a miser, and he didn't pay out for anything unless it was absolutely necessary. Now that he had the final say, it was difficult to get anything past Gruber. He hadn't greenlighted any new projects in a long time.

It wasn't all Gruber's fault, though. Admissions were down. For some reason they weren't discovering new star systems as frequently as they used to. Consequently there were fewer expeditions. Fewer expeditions meant fewer new captured life forms, and fewer new life forms meant fewer new exhibits. The zoo just wasn't popular any more, and in this day and age of 3D holo-videos where you could literally bring an animal to life in the middle of your living room, it was understandable.

As a result the U.L.F. division, the department specializing in the acquirement of the unidentified life forms, had gone from a staff of two hundred and fifty people to just under a hundred in the space of a few years, and about a fifth of the remainder had already submitted resignations. Right now a bunch of new intakes were being trained, but how long their careers would last was anyone's guess. To be honest, Chris was worried about his job. Gone were the good old days when his friend Wyatt ran the department.

He missed Wyatt. They were still friends and saw each other occasionally, Chris was, after all, godfather to Wyatt's son Alex, but Chris wished he had longer to get to know the man in a professional capacity. As it was, their relationship had been forged briefly in the most extreme conditions, when both men had been pushed to their very limits.

Chris had been just a kid back then, and even now was still relatively young, but he'd grown up fast. He sighed. That was all in the past.

Still, at least the zoo had the baby puglion. Born two months ago, the six-foot long infant was drawing some crowds and bringing in some much-needed revenue. A visit to the new arrival should be his first call.

He pressed his thumb against a sensor pad and another set of doors slid open. He stepped through and into a large room where walls were lined with racks of impressive-looking equipment. This was the U.L.F. department's storeroom.

It wasn't one of the elaborate-looking traps that Chris was after, nor a weapon, body armor or restraining equipment. Just a simple flashlight. He spied one in a crate on the floor and picked it up, flicking it on and peering in to its face to make sure its lux emitter still worked. You couldn't take anything for granted in this place anymore. Satisfied, he started on a very early morning round.

* * * * *

The puglion compound was located in the bottom of Reptile Mountain, at least a half-mile walk from the ULF administration buildings. The impressive structure was the centerpiece of the IZP, erupting from the earth like a huge volcano. It was totally fabricated and hollow inside but even Chris had to admit, it looked quite authentic.

The Chicago night air was chilly and he shrugged off a shiver as his body acclimatized to the cold. His exhaled breaths expired in brief, wispy clouds.

The puglion swamp accounted for the entire ground level of Reptile Mountain. Above that, and accessible only by elevator, were the offices of the zoo's senior staff and the boardroom.

Puglions were large aliens, known to grow to thirty feet in

length in the wild. Here at the zoo, the two adults were twenty and eighteen feet long, stunted by the size of their artificial environment. They would never grow to their full potential, but as they had proved, they were mature enough to breed.

They were nasty, vicious, reptilian creatures captured from the bogs of Dachon-three. They had been difficult to trap, even more difficult to transport. They wouldn't be going out for any more puglions, that was for sure, which was why it was good that they now had a youngster.

Beyond the zoo's distant perimeter wall the occasional hum of a hover vehicle could be heard, but otherwise it was quiet. Chris's footfalls sounded incredibly loud against the concrete. It *was* quiet. Eerily quiet.

Chris's stomach tightened in a knot. A veteran of numerous expeditions now, Chris was finely attuned to his surroundings, even when back home on Earth. Like most trappers, he had an innate sixth sense that kicked in when all was not as it should be. It was an instinct that had served him well in the past, and he was not going to ignore it now. He slowed his pace.

Cautiously, he turned onto another of the zoo's walkways. On the track ahead a dark form huddled on the ground. Even though his eyes had adjusted to the dim light, Chris could not make out what it was. He flicked on the flashlight and aimed it at the black silhouette. The light revealed one thing; whatever it was, it was actually black. There were no distinguishing marks on the form to identify it.

Chris approached warily, passing the light beam over the object's full length. As he got closer he spotted a flash of white. He squinted to bring it into sharper focus and recognized it almost immediately. The heel of an old sneaker. This first piece of information now revealed what he had been unable to see before. A human form, laid on the ground in a fetal position with its back to him, dressed from head to toe in black, except for the white footwear. He sighed with relief. At least now he knew what he was dealing with.

"Hey!" Chris called. "What are you doing here? This is state property. You know you shouldn't be here." There was no response.

It wasn't the first time something like this had happened. Security was supposed to go around the entire zoo after closing time to ensure that everyone had left. That didn't just mean the grounds but also the indoor exhibits. The reptile houses and tropical exhibits were heated buildings and zookeepers had reported finding some of Chicago's vagrants bedded down in them from time to time when they opened up in the morning. It hadn't happened in a long time but that didn't mean that security couldn't get lax.

What about this guy, though? He was out on a walkway in the middle of the night. Was he drunk?

"Hey!" Chris called again. "Did you hear me? You can't be here." Again there was no response.

Keeping the beam of the flashlight trained on the figure, Chris approached slowly. When he was closer, he crouched and placed the flashlight on the ground. There was still no sign that the individual even knew that he was there.

Now he could see that the stranger was crouched into a tight ball. Not only that, but he or she was wearing a balaclava-style hood. He reached out and touched the shoulder. The body flinched at the contact.

"Hey. Who are you? What are you doing here?" He gave the shoulder a gentle shake. The figure groaned in response. Chris was getting angry now. "Buddy, look, I'm not fooling around with you. You're in a lot of trouble right now. You can either talk to me or tell your story to a cop. I don't care which it is. So which is it going to be?"

Again, nothing.

"All right. You want to play it that way, that's fine." Chris grabbed the shoulder and pulled it towards him, trying to pull the figure onto its back. He wasn't ready for the blood-curdling scream.

He jumped backwards and fell hard on his rump, not able to find balance on his feet. The figure rolled slowly towards him and for the first time he saw the hands clenched tightly over the stomach, soaked in blood.

"Jesus. What happened to you?"

Two terrified eyes regarded him through holes in the hood. "Help me."

Coming quickly to his senses, Chris picked himself up and rushed to the masked figure's side. He grabbed one of the hands and tried to pull it away but the intruder resisted. "I'm a trained medic," he said, "I can help you, but you have to let me see the wound."

He felt the arm relax under his grip, moved it away and then did the same with the other. Already he didn't like what he saw. The figure's black jacket was unzipped and underneath, a black top, shredded by three diagonal slashes, glistened with moisture. The color was masked by the shirt and the darkness but he didn't need to see color to know what it was.

He reached down and pulled the shirt out of the pants to get a better look at the wounds underneath. The masked man groaned in protest.

"Sorry, but I've got to do this."

Under the shirt, the man's flesh bore three matching slashes. All had punctured deeply. From experience, Chris knew that much more damage had been done than the three wounds suggested. The guy had lost a lot of blood. His damaged innards were being held in by ribbons of skin. This was bad. This was really bad.

Chris touched the com-link hanging over his ear. "Security. I have an intruder down in yellow section, walkway three. I need immediate medical assistance and an evac HV down here right now!" He paused, waiting for the reply. There was nothing, just the indifferent hiss of static. "Dammit!"

"You won't get a reply," the intruder managed. "It's our fault. It's all our fault."

Chris ran through scenarios in his head. Even if help arrived the chances of this guy making it were already nose-diving. The best thing he could do was make him comfortable. Quickly he took off his jacket and then his sweater. Carefully Chris stuffed the sweater under the masked man's bloody shirt and replaced his arms over his stomach. "Here, hold this tight against you."

The man did as he was told, grunting with the effort and the pain.

Chris moved to the man's head and pulled off the balaclava. He took a sharp intake of breath. Chris himself was young, but he was looking at a kid. The youngster regarded him with guilty, knowing eyes.

Carefully Chris propped him up, cradling his head and shoulders in his arms. "It's okay. Help will be here in a minute. You'll be okay." he lied.

"My friend?" The kid asked. "What about my friend?"

"I don't know, but let's not worry about that right now. Let's get you sorted out."

"But it went after him after it attacked me."

"What did?"

"The thing. The thing that came out of the enclosure."

Chris's stomach knotted again. "What did you do?"

"I'm sorry. We had no idea. It's our fault. It's all our fault."

"Tell me what you did."

"I don't want to die."

"No one's going to die." The comment galvanized Chris into action again. Again he touched the com-link. "Security. I need immediate medical assistance in yellow section, walkway three. Respond, please."

"I'm so cold."

"Oh no you don't. Stay with me now, you hear?"

"Just make sure my friend's okay."

"Okay, I'll do that, just as soon as you're taken care of."

Suddenly, as if remembering something, the kid grabbed at Chris's arm. "You have to stop it!"

"Stop what?"

"We had no idea! You have to understand that!" The kid was getting hysterical.

"Okay! Okay! Calm down. Relax. We can figure it, out whatever it is."

"Oh God! It's our fault. It's all our fault! You have to stop it. The...the..." The kid slumped back into Chris's arms. "So cold.... so cold." He took three quick breaths and lolled his head over to look at Chris one last time. He managed two whispered words as a final long breath escaped past his lips. "I'm sorry."

"Goddammit!" Chris cursed under his breath. Damn security. Where the hell was everybody?

Chris placed the kid's head back on the ground carefully and with as much dignity as he could manage. He picked himself up and for the first time since removing his sweater felt the cold again. Giving himself a cursory look over he could see that he was covered in blood. The kid's blood. He felt nauseous.

There was only one alien Chris knew that would make a wound like that. The mantor. Mantors were formidable creatures and they liked nothing more than chasing down prey. If the kid had an accomplice and he had run, then Chris doubted that had ended happily either. If you stood and faced the mantor it would open you up with its razor sharp claws. If you ran then it would bring you down. Either way, you didn't stand a chance.

Chris started out for the mantor enclosure. To most people this would seem like madness, but he had good reason to go. If the mantor was loose, as he suspected, they were in trouble. Real trouble. Recapturing it was not a job to be taken lightly and certainly not one he would attempt on his own, but beyond that, he had to protect himself.

Each of the aliens had a keeper and each keeper had his own

equipment to protect him from his charge, should he need to enter the cage. Chris headed off for the keeper's station.

He hadn't gone far when he came across the second body. Decapitated. A crumpled heap by the side of the path. He took a furtive look around, listening for any signs of danger, and hurried on.

He knew he was coming at the enclosure from the wrong side. He would have to walk around the perimeter of it to reach the keeper's quarters. He went left around the viewing rail, thinking that would be the quicker option, and immediately spied the breach in the cage.

Between the viewing rail and the cage was a deep grassy moat that separated the public from the electrified enclosure. The two intruders had obviously climbed the rail, navigated the moat and set to work cutting a hole in the wire mesh. A large pair of industrial bolt cutters with rubber-insulated handles was discarded on the grass near where a large oval-shaped portion of the cage was bent outward.

Chris could only take a guess what had happened, but he figured that the two had started cutting a hole in the cage. Once they were through a few wires they'd probably done enough damage to short out the whole cage. Whether it was the noise they were making, or electrical arcing, something had attracted the mantor. They had run then, struggling to get back out of the moat and over the viewing rail. It was, after all, meant to make escape difficult. But escape they had, if not for long.

The mantor would have been going berserk in the cage and maybe it had tried to reach them, distant as they were, and discovered that the wire fence was no longer electrified. After that, it began testing the fence for weak spots and eventually found the area that they had started to cut and finished the job for them. Once the mantor was loose they had no chance.

Chris reached the keeper's quarters and placed his thumb on the sensor pad he found there. The door slid open for him. He stepped inside and watched the door close again before allowing himself a sigh of relief. He was safe, for now at least.

He looked up at the items hanging up on the wall. It was rudimentary stuff, nothing akin to the equipment the ULF trappers used, but it was specialized for one animal and one animal only, and for that it served its purpose.

He began putting it on. A pair of armor-plated chaps that strapped around his thighs, a large breastplate that hung over his shoulders and buckled neatly behind his back, and a thick titanium helmet with a long neck guard and a visor which, when slid down into place, gave him two narrow eye slits to peer through.

He reached up to the wall again and brought down a large round object, the "smiter," as it was known to staff. It was primarily for warding off attacks but with enough weight behind it and in the right circumstances it could be used effectively to stun an aggressive animal into submission. He reached through the straps on its back with his left arm and tightened it into place with his right hand.

Finally, he took the last item down from the wall. An eight-foot long tazer fork. To the casual observer it looked like nothing more than a very large cocktail fork, but it was much more dangerous than that. On contact, a huge electrical current would surge between the two prongs and through the tissues of any intended target, immobilizing it temporarily in a fit of painful muscle spasms. Chris jabbed it against the floor and was rewarded with an arcing blue spark and a puff of smoke. The mantor wasn't the smartest creature he'd known but it had a healthy respect for pain.

Prepared now for whatever awaited him outside, Chris opened the door and stepped back out into the park, a 25th century knight ready for battle.

He had no intention of facing the mantor. He had seen what it could do firsthand. The equipment was solely for his own protection if the alien was still around.

Chris thought back to his conversation with the kid. You have to stop it, he had said. Stop what? The mantor? He should really call the cops and report the break-in and the resulting danger to the public, but the only way he could do that was via a call to security through his com-link, and they weren't answering. He was off to security to see what those clowns were up to.

* * * * *

Upon entering the main security building, Chris immediately discarded the helmet and tazer fork, tossing them aside with no regard for where they fell. Anger coursed through him. He'd been playing scenarios in his head all the way here and he knew one thing for sure; someone was going to get a dressing-down.

He didn't know what he expected to find when he stepped through the double doors and into the main command area, but he was ready for almost anything. People slouching in chairs, feet up on consoles, comms not being monitored. Whatever was going on, he was going to give them a piece of his mind.

He never expected to find it deserted.

Chris slowed as he entered the room. This was crazy. Something was very wrong.

In front of him was a long arcing console that spanned the length of the curved room. Six empty chairs stood next to it. In front of that, slightly lower down, was a second similar console and again, six empty seats. A shift of twelve men was supposed to be working here.

On the opposite wall, a huge screen displayed a schematic of the whole zoo. Each color-coded section was lit in its corresponding color. Each lit section indicated that all shields, barriers, locks and electric fields were operating effectively. He quickly recognized the dark area in the yellow section as corresponding to the mantor's enclosure.

Down both sides and along the bottom of the large map were dozens of video feeds from cameras all over the zoo. Chris scanned them quickly. In two places the feeds were out. He didn't need the knot in his stomach to tell him that wasn't normal.

Chris paced the length of the long arcing desk. Lights blinked everywhere. At the far end of the desk were a mug and a half-eaten sandwich. He placed a hand against the mug. The contents were still warm. Whatever had happened here, he hadn't long missed it.

He turned around. Above the door through which he had entered was a whole second floor accessible by a curved, iron-railed metal stairway at either end of the room. He couldn't see beyond the gallery that jutted out above his head. He wasn't about to go up there, either. There could still be danger.

"Hello!" he called. "Is there anybody there? Can anybody hear me?"

There was a thump and a muffled cry, but it came from close by. A door, just off to his left.

Chris moved swiftly to the door, placing his head close to it. "Hello. Can you hear me? Is everyone all right?"

There was an answer but he couldn't make it out.

"Hold on. I'll get you out of there." Chris went to put his thumb on the biometric sensor but it was gone, smashed away, leaving only a bundle of exposed wires. "Oh, great." He was glad he knew a thing or two about wiring. "Hold on," he said again. "This is going to take a little while."

Grabbing two of the wires, he touched the exposed ends together experimentally. Sparks flashed and Chris recoiled quickly, shaking his stinging hands. "Okay. Not those two," he muttered to himself.

He tried again. This time no sparks, but no movement from the door either. By trial-and-error he managed to eliminate wires until he found the two he needed. On contact, the door slid open and immediately, three hooded, bound men fell out and onto the floor. Behind them, others, also bound and hooded, staggered out. Chris looked in at the remainder. Eleven men had been locked in a room barely the size of a broom cupboard.

Quickly, Chris pulled the hood off the nearest man. Underneath the hood the man's mouth had been taped. Chris grabbed one end of the tape and yanked it off.

"Thank God you found us!" the guard blurted.

"What happened here?" Chris asked.

"There were six of them. Armed. We don't know where they came from or how they got in. We had no warning."

"But how is that possible?"

The guard offered up his bound wrists.

"Sorry. Let me get that for you." Chris pulled out a pocket knife and began to cut the rope away.

"I don't know. The only unusual thing that happened was that a section of the perimeter wall went down. Briefly, though, and then it came back up." The guard's hands came apart and he began to rub the stiffness out of his wrists. "Thank you."

Chris gave him the knife. "Here. Help your friends." Chris then set about taking the hoods from the others and removing the tape from their mouths while the first guard cut their bonds. "Go on," he said.

"We sent a man to go check it out. Shortly after that, two sets of feeds went down."

"Almost simultaneously," a second guard chipped in.

"I was about to go investigate myself," the first guard continued, and that's when they came in. Six of 'em. All wearing masks. No warning, just straight through the door."

"What did they want?"

"Didn't say. Didn't say much of anything. Just ordered us over here up against the wall. Four of them kept us under the gun while the other two tied us, taped us and then shoved us in here." He indicated the small room with a backward tick of his head.

"What then?"

"That was it. We couldn't get out. They left us alone."

"Did you hear anything?"

"No."

"Anyone?"

The ten other men all shook their heads.

"I heard them leave," said one. "They hardly spoke while they were here but I definitely heard them leave."

"How long ago?"

"Fifteen. Maybe twenty minutes."

Others nodded their agreement.

"What happened to the man you sent out?" Chris asked the first guard.

"Dunno. He hasn't come back, that's for sure."

"We need to find him. He could be in real danger."

"Why, what's happened?" Another asked.

"The mantor's loose."

All eleven men looked shocked, some muttering curses under their breaths.

Chris looked up at the wall, where the second set of cameras was out. "What's that?" He asked, gesturing with his head.

One of the guards walked over to the side of the desk, leaning towards the wall and squinting a little to make out the feeds around the blank area. "That's Reptile Mountain," he said. "That's the puglion enclosure."

"Great," Chris said under his breath. "Today just keeps getting better."

He stood and looked at the others assembled around him. "Okay, I need you to go back to your stations. Check that everything is as it should be. I'm going to go back out there and try to find your co-worker."

"Do you want some of us to come with you?" the first guard asked.

"No. No need to put more people at risk. I'll be okay." He bunched his hand into a fist and rapped on his body armor with his knuckles. "At least I should be," he said, with the best grin he could manage.

The other man smiled sympathetically and nodded. "Okay

then. Be careful."

Chris nodded and turned for the door. "Oh, and someone call the cops too." Some of the security guards were already settling in behind their desks. He had barely gone five more paces when another voice spoke.

"Er, sir. You might want to come take a look at this."

Chris didn't like the tone of the voice. He turned on a dime and was next to the man in a second. The other man was staring down at his monitor, paneled flush into the desk. The display was flashing a horizontal red bar that almost spanned the screen. Below the bar it read: *Downloading 99%*. And then the blinking stopped and a new message appeared.

Download Complete.

There was a second when nothing happened. It was as if time stood still. Literally nothing happened. Nobody even breathed. And then a new message appeared.

Executing.

Chris's attention was suddenly caught by the huge screen above him. Almost instantly, large parts of the map started disappearing, color being replaced by black. Enclosures, buildings, then entire sections blinked out. Security and safeguards in every part of the zoo were being overridden. A nightmare was unfolding in front of him and he was powerless to stop it.

Chris watched as every area in the zoo vanished and then, finally, the aquarium failed. He looked at the now totally blank screen in horror. "Oh shit."

CHAPTER 2

The aquarium was at the northernmost tip of the IZP. An aquarium of one shape or another had occupied this spot in Chicago for centuries and had been its own separate entity until Chicago's city zoo had become the IZP. In the boom years that followed the IZP grew, expanding north until it butted up against the aquarium and at that point it just made sense to merge the two and make the IZP the largest zoo on Earth.

It was ideally located. East of the city and perched right on the banks of Lake Michigan. A body of water so vast it was tidal.

Like most aquariums, the majority of the exhibits were housed in self-contained tanks, but for the larger warm-blooded aquatic aliens, the lake was their home.

She didn't know it, but she was the big draw here. She cruised through the cold, dark water with a casual sway, bioluminescence lighting her wake. On one side of her enclosure were five large windows through which any given day's crowds would stare and point at her. Occasionally, when her need for oxygen grew large, she would gape her enormous mouth and throw out her bottom jaw forcing hundreds of gallons of water over huge gills and showing a frightening array of teeth. It always drew gasps from the onlookers. The deep, silty bottom sloped away and into the teasing depths of the lake, a realm that was foreign and forbidden to her.

Dotted all over her massive head were tens of thousands of ampullae, receptors that picked up the tiny electric fields generated by all living things. By her prey. Superbly evolved, she could detect things hidden within rocks or buried deep in the mud, but she was agitated here. Her neurons fired constantly, aggravated by the containment field that limited her movements. What they were doing to her was close to torture and she preferred to stay near the viewing windows where the electric current was less painful to her. It was no coincidence that it had been designed that way.

When the aquarium failed she was instantly aware of the changing electric field, or rather, lack of one. The invisible boundary was gone and the murky depths called to her. With two flicks of her massive tail she disappeared farther into the lake.

* * * * *

Officer Ed Wood was just buying a cup of tea and some doughnuts when the call came in on the police net. He held his hand up to his face and pushed the com-link further into his ear.

"All patrol units, please be advised we have an eight-three-three criminal trespass at the IZP. All available units please respond."

"Ten-four, control. This is Officer Wood, badge number Bravo three-nine-five-seven-four responding. Go ahead." Wood grabbed his tea in one hand and swept up the bag of doughnuts in his other arm, acknowledging the cashier with a raised Styrofoam cup and nod of his head as he exited the store.

"This is control. What's your ten-twenty, Officer Wood?"

Wood took a quick look around. "I'm on the corner of thirtieth and Lowe. About two miles away from the location."

"Ten-four, Wood. Proceed. Code two. Be informed, two suspects found dead at scene. Be on lookout for other suspects in vicinity. Potentially six other males dressed in black. Caller requests you report to staff entrance at IZP where you will be met. Specifically instructs that you do not exit your vehicle. Exercise extreme caution."

"Ten four, control."

Wood climbed into his black and white, put his tea in the gyroscopic holder and threw the bag of doughnuts on the passenger seat. Any guy on the force had his share of unusual stories and this one sounded like it might be his latest. He switched on his headlights and then the emergency lights and pulled away.

* * * * *

Chris was back out in the park again, running now towards the original security post he had passed on his way in this morning. The cops would be on their way and that was where they had been told to go, but Chris also wanted to check that nothing had happened to the security guard who was supposed to have been there.

He was wearing the helmet again now and his ragged breathing echoed around inside the small chamber, sounding incredibly loud in his ears. His vision was limited by the two slits he had to look through. The only other things going for him right now were that the enclosures had only just failed and that it was early in the morning. Most of the aliens would still be asleep and not even be aware that at any time they could all run, walk or fly straight out of their enclosures.

Chris thought back to the conversation with the dying kid. He'd known. He'd known about everything. He'd known that Chris would not be able to get through to security when he was trying to save his life. He'd known about the download and what it was going to do. *You have to stop it,* he had said. Chris realized now that he hadn't just meant the mantor.

The only thing he hadn't known was just how dangerous the aliens in the IZP were. *We had no idea.* No. He was right about that.

This wasn't about a couple of crazy pranksters whose stunt had gone tragically wrong. This had been planned. But who would do such a thing?

Chris rounded the main building and saw the security post in front of him. Above the brick, the tinted glass window showed an empty gatehouse. Chris slowed to a walk, his shoulders slumped in defeat.

* * * * *

Detective Superintendent Ed Lieberwits hadn't even had chance to greet the dawn himself when the shrill tone of his telelink interrupted his sleep. This was what you got for working in Chicago's homicide department. Perk of the job.

He leaned over the bed and reached out from under the covers, searching with his hand for the answer button. After a frustrating few seconds he realized it was no use. He was going to have to open his eyes. He pushed himself up in bed, squinting in the half-light and then rubbing the sleep from his eyes. He didn't need to look at a clock to know it was way too early. The link rang persistently.

"All right!" he said angrily. "All right," he muttered again. He answered the call and the screen blinked into life, too bright for his ill-adjusted eyes. For the second time in as many minutes, Lieberwits was squinting again.

A cop appeared on the small screen; nobody he recognized, just a regular beat cop from one of the downtown precincts. He was calling from somewhere outside. "Sorry to wake you, Detective, they said you should be called."

Lieberwits waved him off. No need for apologies or pleasantries now, it was too late for that. Just get to the meat of the matter. "What you got for me?"

"Double homicide. One Caucasian male. One Caucasian female. You should come take a look."

"Where are you?"

"Palmer Street. Figured you might like to know so you can get down here before the newshounds get a whiff of it."

"Yeah, thanks," Lieberwits said. "I'll be there as soon as I can."

Lieberwits hung up the link and then rubbed his face with the palms of his hands, letting out a tired sigh. Truth was, double homicides were so common in Chicago these days they barely made column inches on the news net. What made this one so special?

* * * * *

Officer Wood was not quite ready for what greeted him when he arrived at the IZP. He pulled his patrol vehicle around in a lazy arc and the swath of headlight picked out a single figure approaching the entrance from the other side.

Wood brought his vehicle to a stop and then watched, stunned, as what looked like some kind of medieval gladiator approached. He stifled a laugh. The boys back at Central were going to love this. He touched the exit pad and watched as the door pivoted upward on its front hinge. The armored figure rushed towards him. "No! No! Don't get out of the car!"

Wood was a little startled. He was half out of the vehicle. "Is there a problem, sir?" He was still trying to hold back a grin.

"Just close the door and I'll tell you all about it."

"Are you under the influence of stims or alcohol? Is this some kind of joke, sir?"

The helmeted figure flicked up his visor. Underneath there was a deadly serious face. "At five fifteen in the morning? You think I have nothing better to do?"

"I don't know, sir, you tell me."

Chris was in no mood for some patronizing cop routine. "Look," he said, putting both hands out to ease the brewing tension. "I can explain everything but I really need you to get back in the car. It's for your own safety."

Wood stood there for a moment pondering the proposal, trailing leg still half in his vehicle, then shrugged and sat back down. The door swung back down into place and sealed. Outside, Chris rapped on the exterior with a gauntlet. Wood opened the virtual window a half inch.

"I know this must look stupid to you," Chris began, "But we have a serious situation here. At least eight people have broken into the zoo and overridden all our security systems." Wood gave him a blank look. "One of our aliens is loose and it's dangerous. Lethally dangerous. Two of the intruders already found that out. Any of our other exhibits could escape at any time and trust me, you don't want to meet most of those either. That's what all this stuff is for." Chris gestured to his body armor.

"Listen, there's a service road runs from here right round to our security building. The guards there were bound and gagged by six masked men. They'll probably be able to tell you more than me. Let me get in and I can show you the way."

"What about those two?" Wood asked.

Chris turned. Behind him in the gatehouse two heads had appeared.

* * * * *

"Left here," Chris instructed. Wood complied with the direction. Behind them, beyond the five-inch thick acrylic, the two security guards were jabbering animatedly. Their voices came through on the speakers.

"So I got to the perimeter wall and was just searching the area when I heard the scream."

"Yeah, that first scream was awful. I never want to hear a scream like that again as long as I live. That's when I left the gatehouse and went to investigate."

"Well, me too, I left the perimeter and started towards it but when I heard that second scream, that was it, I was done. They don't pay me enough to deal with shit like that."

"Right."

"Then what did you do?" Wood asked.

"Well, I knew that the gatehouse was closer than coming back here to the main building, so I got on the link and told them that was where I was going. Nothing. That's when I knew something really screwy was going on and when I got to the gatehouse, even Dave here was gone."

"I was on my way back because at that point I knew there wasn't much I could do out in the park and honestly, I didn't want to be out there anymore. I got a wife and three kids, you know," Dave offered by way of explanation. "Anyway, that's when I heard it. That unearthly howl. And that's when I started running."

"Yeah, he came out of those trees like a bat out of hell. Scared the crap out of me, he did. I nearly shot the damn fool."

"So Brian and me, we got back into the gatehouse and tried to raise control but they weren't answering."

"You didn't call the police?" Chris asked.

"We were going to but that's when it appeared."

"The mantor?"

"Yeah," Brian said. Both men suddenly went very quiet and then Dave spoke up again.

"It saw us and it tried to get to us. It was scary. I've never been so grateful for bullet proof glass. It sniffed around for a while after that. Felt like forever. And then it just disappeared into the night. We stayed in hiding just in case it was still around. Pulled the link under the desk and called 911 but our connection to the network was down. We couldn't do anything."

Chris looked at Wood and shrugged his shoulders. Thank God for security.

The control building loomed into view in front of them and Wood brought the car to a halt. The four men bundled out and ran to the nearest door. Instinctively Chris went to place his thumb on the biometric sensor. Wood gave him a puzzled look. "If everything you've said is true, you shouldn't need to do that." He grabbed the handle and pulled. The door opened easily. "Thought so."

They stepped inside and into a long corridor. "How many people did you say you had in here?" Wood asked.

"With these two, thirteen," Chris replied

"Okay. I need to call this in. Get some more patrol units down here. Get some more people to take statements from the victims."

"Do me a favor, would you?" Chris asked.

"What's that?"

"Make sure they have body armor and weapons."

* * * * *

Lieberwits walked towards the crime scene. Two large police trucks were pulled up nearby and three patrol units were parked along the other side of the street. Their flashing red and blue lights brought the area vividly to life. A web of red, pencil-thin laser lines cordoned off the carnage in the street.

He palmed his holo-ID to the cop standing guard and then noticed it was the same man who had called him. The cop tipped his hat, "Detective," and then deactivated the barrier.

Lieberwits stepped through. "What have we got here?"

"A mess."

"I can see that." Lieberwits surveyed the area. Tire tracks scored the road. Ahead of him a body lay in the street, covered with a white sheet. A dark stain spoiled both the shroud and the asphalt nearby. Beyond the corpse an HV sat in a crumpled wreck, concertinaed against another, the driver's door hanging open. The occasional whisper of steam still escaped from the hood.

"Jesus," Lieberwits said. "What the hell happened to that?" The roof looked like it had been set upon with a gigantic can opener. The cop shook his head, not able to offer an explanation. "Any witnesses?"

"No. Just the neighbor who found the bodies. Early riser."

Lieberwits looked over at the apartment buildings. A distraught-looking woman was being interviewed by an officer who made notes on a unit strapped to his wrist. She adjusted a flimsy-looking bathrobe around herself and hugged it close with folded arms. She shivered. Lieberwits suspected it wasn't just from the cold.

"Have we identified the victims?"

"Only the male," the officer said, pulling a tablet out of a back pocket. He licked the tip of a finger and touched the screen. "One Marty White."

"Family been informed?"

"We've got someone on that right now. Kinda hoping they can help us identify Jane Doe over there."

Lieberwits looked over to where the cop had indicated. A team of white-suited forensics was huddled around another body on the ground. A pair of female legs protruded from the crowd, one stockinged foot shoeless, the other wearing a broken heel.

"She was running," the cop explained without waiting for the question.

Lieberwits looked back at the HV. "Do you blame her?"

From the group one man emerged and came towards them. He pulled off bloodied rubber gloves, folding them inside each other casually but with practiced care. Lieberwits recognized him. He was a regular at crime scenes. It seemed the respect was mutual. "Well, detective," the other man began. "I don't think your presence here is required. Sorry to have disturbed you so early in the morning."

Lieberwits frowned. "What do you mean?"

"I mean," said the technician with a hint of smugness, "that there was no murder committed here this evening. Not murder as we know it." Lieberwits snorted his amusement and then regained his composure when his smile was not returned. "The female victim was mauled."

"Mauled?" He couldn't believe what he was hearing. "What do you mean, mauled?"

The technician rolled his eyes and sighed as if Lieberwits was already starting to bore him. "I mean this was an animal attack."

Lieberwits looked back at the HV. "You're telling me an animal did that?" he protested, pointing.

"That I don't know. What I do know is that your victim... sorry, victims, were attacked by an animal. Everything is consistent with that conclusion. Ragged, torn wounds and some..." He stopped, hesitant to continue.

"Some *what*?" Lieberwits demanded.

The technician glanced at the police officer as if searching for permission to continue and then looked back at Lieberwits. "Some consumption," he finished.

Lieberwits retched, covering his mouth with his hand. He was glad he had passed on breakfast.

The three men were interrupted by the broadcast link in the nearby mobile tactical unit. A voice came through on the network. Lieberwits was grateful for the sudden distraction.

"*Control, this is Officer Wood confirming an eight-three-three at the IZP.*" Lieberwits's ears pricked up at the mention of the zoo. He'd been there five years earlier investigating a murder-suicide case that had been swept under the carpet by his superiors. He recognized the code number. Someone had broken into the zoo. The call now had his full attention.

"*Request back-up. Please ensure all responding units are armed and armored. We have one escaped animal, potentially more. Please also be on the lookout for six male suspects dressed in black. Armed, considered dangerous.*"

Lieberwits cast his attention back to the young officer. "Well, you guys look like you have the area secure, and seeing as how this doesn't seem to warrant my presence I'll be on my way. You can take care of the details, right?"

The cop nodded with a shrug, "Guess so."

"Thanks for filling me in. Keep up the *excellent* work." Lieberwits gave the forensic technician a shake of the hand. The other man's face said it all. *Told you so.*

Lieberwits walked back to his car, climbed in and started the engine. He looked through the virtual windshield. Across downtown Chicago, amidst the line of skyscrapers, a band of pale blue was starting to climb into the night sky. The day was just beginning, and Lieberwits had a hunch it was going to be a long one.

* * * * *

Chris felt a wave of relief wash over him when Bobby answered her telelink. "Oh, thank God."

Roberta "Bobby" Keele was one of Chris's closest friends in the ULF department. They were team members; she, an expedition leader first and trapper second, he also with a double role as trapper and medic. With their wealth of ULF experience they made a formidable team and the fourteen other members of their expedition squad knew that they were lucky to be working with these two individuals, but beyond that, their loyalty to each other went much, much deeper. They had each saved the other's life.

"Chris?" Bobby clumsily brushed the mass of curls out of her face with her hands. She blinked comically at him on the screen. "It is you!" She looked at something off screen. "Chris, do you know what time it is? Where the hell are you, anyway?"

"I'm at work...the IZP. Listen Bobby, there's no time. Something's happened."

"What? What is it?"

"Someone's broken in here. Someone who knew enough to override the security systems."

Bobby was clearly shocked. "The exhibits?"

"Able to walk free any time they like. I know for a fact that the mantor is loose. The aquarium is down too."

"Jesus Christ," Bobby said under her breath. "Who else knows about this?"

"The cops are already here but they're not equipped to deal with this."

"Okay, you handle that. I'll call the rest of the team." She hung up on him but he didn't mind. The fact that she instinctively knew the purpose of the call and what was required calmed him a little.

At least now he had an ally.

* * * * *

"Okay, we have comms back on line," the young security guard announced proudly.

"What about everything else?" Chris snapped.

The smile evaporated from the other man's face and Chris immediately felt guilty for stealing the moment away from him. "I'm sorry. You did a good job."

"It's okay. This was a relatively easy fix. Hardware. They just ripped out some boards. The other stuff...." He shook his head. "That's software, sir. I don't even know what they did."

Chris's mouth set in a thin line. He'd guessed as much. He put a comforting hand on the young guard's arm. The guy had done his best. He tapped his com-link. "Test. Security. Test. Test," and heard his voice play back to him over the room's talk-back system.

Across the room, Wood stopped his conversation and listened intently to an incoming transmit. "Ten four, control." He looked up at Chris. "The first of the backup units are arriving. You want to escort them in?"

"Let's do it." Chris looked at the remaining men in the room. "All right, now let's all stay in touch, okay?" With that, he and Wood were gone.

* * * * *

When they arrived at the staff entrance there were six patrollers waiting for them, each with two cops in them. Chris popped the door on Wood's car and was about to put the helmet back on when something caught his eye. He watched woefully as, high above, nine winged aliens made good on their bid for freedom.

He cursed under his breath. He had always had his doubts about the safety of containment fields. They were supposed to be more humane and less stressful to the alien exhibits. An invisible electric barrier supposedly gave the captives the perception they had a certain freedom; no bars to mark their prison walls. The intelligent aliens knew it was there, of course. They sensed it. You could see it in their eyes. It creeped Chris out. You could only look at those eyes for so long before you knew there was something going on in that foreign brain. The dumb ones? Well, they soon learned.

The public had loved the advent of containment fields. Now they had a completely unobstructed view of exotic life from across the universe. Problem was, now that the containment fields were down there was no physical barrier to stop the exhibits from escaping. Anything and everything in the zoo was now free the minute it decided to walk or take wing.

He shook his head. Why hadn't they just used good old-fashioned cages? Then again, what good would that have done? Even the mantor, one of their few caged exhibits, was loose. This was a colossal debacle. A catastrophe that Chicago wasn't prepared for. How could it be?

He looked at the six cars in front of him and then back at Wood, busy talking on his com-link. What good were the cops? What good was anyone in this situation?

He was about to get out of the car when Wood reached across and stopped him.

"What is it?"

"We've got someone using our frequency. Says he's a detective. Say's he's out by the main entrance."

"He's what?"

"He's waiting out by the main entrance."

"What does he want?"

"Says he has some information. About an animal attack earlier this morning. He heard about the break-in and decided to come by."

"We have to get him away from there. He's in real danger. Tell these guys to wait here. We'll be back and they can follow us in. But let's get over there right now!"

* * * * *

Lieberwits was out of his car and peering through the large wrought-iron gates of the main entrance when Chris and Officer Wood pulled up. He was blissfully unaware of the danger he was in and turned at the sound of the approaching vehicle.

Two doors popped wide and swung up and from one a young man leaned out and regarded him with a stern look.

"Ah! Do you work here?"

"Get in the car!" Chris shouted.

Lieberwits was taken aback. "Now listen here, sonny!"

"Sir, I don't have time for this. If you want to talk to me, we talk in the car. Right now I have aliens roaming free and more getting loose the more time we waste. So please, get in the car!"

Lieberwits shrugged and did as he was told.

* * * * *

The seven vehicles followed each other down the service road like a giant metallic serpent. Chris had asked them all to turn off their emergency lights. Some of the aliens in the zoo were known to be attracted to flashing lights; in fact it was an entrapment technique they had used on numerous occasions. The last thing he needed right now was an alien life form splattered all over the front of a cop car.

They reached the security building and Chris shepherded all of the cops and Lieberwits inside. They had been discussing Lieberwits's "crime" scene on the way in. Chris was sure the mantor was responsible.

"Where did you say this was again?"

"Over on Palmer street in Cragin."

"It's got that far already?"

"Don't ask me, sonny. You seem to think that it's your beastie that's done it. I'm just telling you what I saw and where it was."

The mantor was moving fast. They needed people on the ground, out there, tracking these things down right now.

Chris and Lieberwits pushed open the double doors to the main control area. As if in answer to Chris's thoughts, a man dressed head-to-foot in green fatigues stood with his back to them, talking to one of the security guards. Even from behind, Chris recognized him immediately.

"Swarovski! Thank God!"

Pete Swarovski turned at the sound of his name. His face cracked into a broad grin and his eyes sparkled with life. "Hey man, what happened? I swear everything was working when I left!"

Chris smiled. Swarovski had a wisecrack for everything. They clasped hands in a gesture of unity. "You got here quick!"

"Came as soon as I got the call. I was up already."

"You lagged too?"

"Yeah. It's killing me, man. I was just watching some awful holo-flick. You should see the crap they put on the networks early in the morning."

"Tell me about it."

The smile dropped from Swarovski's features. "What's going on here? Bobby sounded really freaked out. It sounds serious."

"It is. The whole zoo and the aquarium are down. All the security is out. All the containment fields are inoperative."

"That's bad."

Chris nodded. He didn't need reminding. Remembering himself, he turned to introduce Lieberwits, who was gawking at the huge wall opposite, mouth agape, wondering at the technology.

"Pete, this is Detective Superintendent Ed Lieberwits. It sounds like he's witnessed one of our exhibits' handiwork."

Swarovski shook Lieberwits's hand. Lieberwits was sure he heard a bone crack. He forced a smile all the same. "Pleasure."

"Detective." It was Wood, calling from the other side of the room. He was standing with the guard Chris had first freed. Lieberwits walked over to join them. "I'm assuming you'll be taking charge here, seeing as how you're the highest rank among us."

Lieberwits hadn't really thought about it. "Er, yes. Yes I will."

"This man can tell you everything that happened up until the moment when I got the call."

The security guard recounted his story again, Lieberwits interrupting him occasionally to be sure of the fine detail. When he was finished, the three of them stood in silence for a moment.

"Well, obviously it was pretty well orchestrated," Lieberwits said.

"But who would do it? And why?" asked the guard.

"I don't know. That's what we intend to find out." Lieberwits turned to Wood. "Were you the first officer on the scene?"

"Yes, sir."

"I could use your help. Can I commandeer your services for a while…" Lieberwits strained to see his badge "…Wood, is it?"

"Yes, sir. I guess so, sir."

"You got a first name, Wood?"

"Yes, sir. Edward, sir."

Lieberwits sniggered. "Your parents have a sense of humor?"

"What do you mean, sir?"

"Ed-Ward. Ed Wood. Edward Wood. What the hell kind of a name is that?"

Wood shrugged. "So what, you're a comedian now?"

"C'mon. That's funny!" Lieberwits gave him a playful punch on the arm.

"The first hundred times. Maybe."

Lieberwits pulled a face. "C'mon. You're with me and you know what they say?"

"What's that?"

"Two Ed's are better than one!"

Wood sighed. "You are a comedian."

The two of them started for the exit, but just at that moment the double doors imploded into the room and seven people marched in, all dressed in the same green fatigues as Swarovski. At the front of the group was a woman, a mass of auburn curls tumbling down from her head. "Nobody's going anywhere until we get these systems back on-line," she ordered with a voice that seemed too big for her body. Chris smiled. Bobby had arrived.

* * * * *

The control room was buzzing now with a roughly equal mixture of security guards, cops and ULF team members. Chris and Bobby had moved to the upper gallery and looked down over the scene. The cops were interviewing the guards, the ULF guys were scattered around, some taking seats, others scrutinizing the monitors to see what exactly was going on in the park outside. All of them waiting for instruction and clearly eager to get to work. Every now and then, another member of their team would arrive and they would all welcome the new arrival with handshakes and back slaps. They were close to their full complement of sixteen.

Bobby leant with her elbows on the gallery rail. "What's our situation, Chris? How many staff do we have available to deal with this?"

"Three teams are out on assignment already. The fourth just set out on a new expedition. They're two weeks into hyperdrive flight. They're billions of miles from here. We could have them turn around, but……"

Bobby held her head in her hands. "We're the only team here?" she asked, despairingly.

"Afraid so."

"We're exhausted. How are we supposed to cope with this?"

"I don't know. But we have to. We have to get people out there on the streets."

"We can't coordinate this. None of the ULF admin staff have the experience for this kind of thing."

Chris thought for a second, then looked up to find Bobby looking back at him, the same flicker of an idea mirrored in her eyes. They needed someone here at the zoo. Someone who could coordinate their movements across the city. Someone with managerial experience. Someone with ULF experience, too. Someone who knew the inherent dangers of what they were about to do.

They both knew who they had to call.

Wyatt.

CHAPTER 3

Harry McGlade looked out into the mist that hung in a low cloud over the lake. Despite there being little wind there was a chill in the air and his breath clouded in front of him. Harry was definitely a fair-weather fisherman and he thought for a moment about turning back, but the forecast had been good. Once the sun came up and burnt away the mist it was supposed to be a bright, sunny day. The kind of day a man could waste away in a little boat and warm tired, old bones. Besides, Harry had a new rig that he was desperate to put to the test. He couldn't bear the thought of putting it off any longer.

Harry walked down the small pontoon at the water's edge, rod clutched in one hand, tackle box in the other. He passed a number of small yachts, dinghies and water gliders, until at last he came to his own boat. A classic small rowboat.

For a long time now, Harry had borne the brunt of many a joke from other boat owners. The annual mooring fees alone had to cost more than his boat was worth, and he only used it for half the year at best. What kind of fool was he? But what did they know? They didn't understand that out there, on the lake, Harry spent his happiest moments. A man, alone with his thoughts, away from the crazy city of Chicago with nothing but the sounds of the water lapping against the wooden sides of his vessel and the wind singing a siren's song as it cut past the line of his rod. That, to Harry, was priceless.

He pulled the boat into the pontoon by its mooring line and when it was alongside, stepped down into the tiny vessel. The maneuver lacked the grace of youth and Harry wobbled before landing hard on his backside on the crossbeam that served as a seat. He placed the tackle box in the well of the boat and then checked his rod, ensuring that his small tumble hadn't damaged his gear. Everything looked good. One barbed end of the treble hook that hung from the tailpiece of the colorful lure was hooked around the first eyelet of the rod. From the nose of the lure, attached to a small brass ring, a twenty-inch wire trace ran up to an expertly tied knot. The thirty-pound breaking strain line was reeled tight, preventing any catching or snagging. Everything was still in place.

There was little chance a fish would snap a line that strong and no way anything would bite through the wire trace. Yes, Harry was going to land himself a big one today, one that would no doubt be bigger by the time he made it back to the bar tonight, and bigger still on each recounting of the tale.

Harry cast off the rope from the pontoon, struggled back to his seat and collected an oar from each side of the boat. With some effort, he managed to put the oars in their clasps and then, with some deft strokes, skillfully piloted the small vessel away from the deck. Once in open water, Harry began to heave on both oars and quickly disappeared into the mist.

* * * * *

Kate Dorren was already awake when the telelink call came. Her young son, Alex, was having trouble sleeping and had been up half the night. Her husband had just returned from a brief shipping trip to the Mars colony and was asleep, practically comatose, in their bedroom, oblivious to their son's needs. She didn't mind. Wyatt had been working hard lately. He was exhausted.

Kate placed Alex on the bed and answered the bedside telelink unit. She watched as the small screen came to life.

Initially, she was pleased to see Chris; after all he was a friend to them both. "Hey..." she began, but then she remembered the time and the words stuck in her throat. Immediately she knew something was wrong. This wasn't a social call. "Chris. What is it? What's wrong?"

"Hi Kate, sorry to call you so early..." Chris seemed reluctant to continue, or at least reluctant to carry on the conversation with her. "Is Wyatt there?"

Kate thought about quizzing him further. She could sense that something was wrong. The mere fact that Chris wanted to speak directly with Wyatt was proof enough of that. She gave Wyatt a gentle nudge. He stirred from his sleep.

"What? What is it?"

"Wyatt, it's Chris on the link. He says he wants to talk to you."

Wyatt turned over in the bed and struggled to rouse himself from sleep. He shared a brief look with Kate, and both of them knew what the other was thinking. Kate stood, picked Alex up from the bed and heaved him up to her chest. She wrapped a single arm around him and with a backward glance removed herself from the room and the conversation she was not supposed to hear.

After a moment Wyatt managed to look across to Kate's side of the bed and the bright screen. "Hey buddy, what's up?"

"Wyatt, we've got a situation down here."

"Why? What's wrong?"

"Somebody's broken into the zoo. All of our systems are down."

Wyatt was suddenly awake. He moved swiftly to the other side of the bed, allowing his legs to swing out and down so that he was sitting and giving the telelink his full attention.

"Bobby's here, as is the rest of our team, but there's nothing we can do right now. All of the containment fields are down and there's no point in us going out there to catch any of the exhibits since we have no way of containing them once they are caught. Besides, the highest concentration of loose aliens is going to be right here at the zoo. We don't want to be walking out into that kind of shitstorm."

"What do you want me to do?" Wyatt knew this was a call for help.

"We need you. Here at the zoo. Once all the systems are back up we need to get out and get the exhibits back but we need someone with your knowledge to coordinate the effort."

"How many teams do you have?" Wyatt asked.

"Just us."

"Jesus, Chris. That's insane!"

"It's all we have to work with, Wyatt, and we don't have a choice. We need to get these things back or people all over the city are going to have a very bad day." He paused. "We've survived worse, Wyatt. Remember?"

Wyatt did remember but right now he was thinking. He perched on the edge of the bed, running his hands through his hair. "Is Travis still in charge of training the new recruits?"

"Yeah, but we haven't had many of them lately. He does have a squad in training, though."

"Get Travis. I'll be there as soon as I can."

"Okay. When you get here, come straight to the main security building, and be careful on your way in. We haven't had a chance to do an inventory of the exhibits yet. We have no idea what's loose."

Wyatt nodded grimly.

"Sorry, Wyatt," Chris added.

"It's okay. It's not your fault."

Chris nodded as if deep in thought. He did look genuinely sorry.

Wyatt hung up the link and immediately went to the closet. As he moved to press the touch pad he was aware of a presence on the other side of the bedroom door. Kate had been listening in.

"I guess you heard all that," he said to the door. There was no reply. He nudged the door with his foot and it slowly swung open.

Kate leaned against the wall, hugging Alex to her. A single tear had begun to run down her cheek.

"I have to go."

"I know you do," she said quietly. "I had hoped this was all over, though. Isn't that what you had said to me? That you were giving this all up?"

The guilt hit him in the back of the throat and spread like a tumor. The IZP had been his life once. But that was the problem—"had been" were the operative words. Wyatt had been the head of the ULF department before he had met Kate and she, seeing the risks he had taken and the nightmare they had both endured, had asked him to give it up. Now he had a new life with her and their baby son, and a new job as a shuttle pilot with her father's freight forwarding firm—but he was about to drop everything and put himself in harm's way again at the first call for help.

Kate didn't understand what the zoo meant to him. He had explained it to her, of course, but she would never really understand. It had been a lifeline to him. It had provided a chance for him to get his life back. How could he turn his back on something like that? Especially now, when they were calling him for help.

"They need me now." He pulled on a shirt.

"Your son needs you, Wyatt…and he, if nothing else, should remind you of what's at risk. He bears the names of our friends who didn't make it."

"Aw, come on. Don't be like that."

"Don't be like what?"

"Don't be making this personal," Wyatt moaned. "Anyway, it's not like that."

Kate gave him a look that suggested he should explain further.

"They want me to coordinate things. I'll be working out of the zoo."

"Really?" A light flickered in her puffy eyes.

"Really. Now look, I know he needs me around more…"

Kate shot Wyatt another glance.

"...and you do too. I'm just trying to support us, that's all. It just takes me away a lot of the time. Right now, though, all of Chicago's sons and daughters need me too, because if I don't help sort out this mess then everybody is at risk. I know what those aliens are capable of." Wyatt pulled on a pair of pants and buckled a belt around them. He ruffled the small amount of hair on Alex's head. "Isn't that right, son?" Alex gurgled an attempt at a response and Wyatt and Kate both smiled, sharing a moment. Wyatt leaned over and gave Kate a light kiss on the forehead.

"I'm sorry for giving you a hard time," Kate said. "I just worry about you."

"That's okay," Wyatt said, attempting a smile. "You're my wife. That's your job." He pulled a pair of shoes from the hallway closet and stepped into them, gave Kate and Alex one last brief hug and opened the door to leave.

"Be careful," Kate said, wiping away her stray tear and attempting a brave face.

"You too. Lock and bolt this door after I leave and close all the windows. They have no idea what's out there yet."

Kate nodded her understanding.

Wyatt turned and closed the door behind him.

* * * * *

Wyatt pulled their hover vehicle round the front of the apartment building and immediately configured it for flight. The turbine whined and the car lifted off the street, the wheels rolling under the axles and locking into the body.

He wrenched his joystick to the right and the HV banked and pulled away. Flying like this in the city was highly illegal; he should be using the skytrack, but it was an emergency and if he got the attention of a few cops that might not be a bad thing. They needed all the help they could get and he could lead them directly to the IZP.

* * * * *

Stephen Gruber gazed out of the window of his penthouse apartment. He grabbed the thin end of his tie and pulled, fixing the knot at his neck while admiring the view. He actually had one of the best views of the city from here—but he paid a high price for it. No, that wasn't strictly true. The IZP paid a high price for it. Then again, that wasn't quite accurate either; the IZP and its "generous sponsors" paid a high price for it.

The sun was creeping up over the horizon, turning Lake Michigan into a vat of gold. The image always brought a smile to Gruber's lips. If only it were actually gold.

It would have been a perfect view except that Trump Tower stood between the city's behemoth buildings and the lake. Dwarfed by the rest of the skyline, Trump Tower stood decrepit and derelict, an eyesore to the rest of the city. It was a miracle it was still standing after five hundred years and it should have been torn down a century ago, but it was old and there were those who fought to maintain it, who thought that antiquities should be preserved. Gruber had no time for such sentimentality.

Gruber's personal com-link buzzed, interrupting his thoughts. He huffed, fishing around in the pocket of his pants before pulling the small gadget out. He glanced at the caller ID briefly before flicking it open. "Yes?"

"It's done." The voice was smooth and slick.

"What is?"

"You don't remember? We discussed it at length."

"What? When? No, wait! You said I'd get a call before anything happened. What the fuck happened?" Gruber yelled.

"Calm down, Stephen."

"Calm down! Do I sound calm to you? Do I? Why wasn't I informed of this before now?"

"Relax, Stephen." The voice never changed from its calming lilt. "We took care of everything. We're taking care of everything.

No one will blame you for what's happened. We'll make an announcement shortly. The public will be informed, and then be better able, to a degree, to protect themselves."

"I was supposed to be the first call," Gruber said, more petulant now than hysterical. "I didn't think I'd be finding out about it after the fact."

"You know how it goes," the cool voice said again. "Plans change."

The link beeped once, indicating that the other man had hung up. Gruber pulled it away from his ear and looked at it in disbelief. He slammed it shut and gripped it tightly in his fist. "Fuck!"

* * * * *

The lure had been a good investment. Harry was glad he'd listened to his pals in the bait-and-tackle shop—it was working well. He was only on his seventh cast and already two decent-sized fish lay in the bottom of the boat, gasping their last.

Harry wound the last few feet of line in and the lure came up from the depths, skipped across the surface and swung out of the water towards him. In one motion, he swung the rod around his head and flicked it forward, listening with pleasure as the line buzzed through the eyes of the rod and the lure was cast out again, landing in the distance with a splash.

Harry waited a while, allowing enough time for the lure to sink to a decent depth before slowly starting to reel it in again. He wound casually. Easy.

Suddenly the line went taut. It was solid, like Harry had snagged something. As he yanked the rod upward it bent it over like a serpent ready to strike. He tried the same thing again. Nothing. He tried yanking sideways, first one way and then the other. Again, nothing. Solid as a rock.

He didn't want to snap the rig but he couldn't get it loose. That was the problem with those treble hooks, once they got stuck into something they were a bitch to get free. Harry was just resigning himself to the fact that he would have to buy another one of those lures when the ratchet on his reel starting clicking. Slowly. Very slowly, line was being pulled off his reel.

Harry felt his heart start to race. He sat himself back down and brought the rod into his lap. "Yes," Harry whispered, just in case he might scare away his catch of the day, "Come to me, my beauty."

* * * * *

There was a tangible sense of relief at security command and control when Wyatt walked in. Chris sensed the other man's presence long before he saw him. It was like a weight had been lifted from the room.

Chris looked over the gallery balcony. "Wyatt! Up here."

Wyatt made his way to the stairway, stopping briefly to exchange hellos with some of the ULF team, who shook his hand and told him they were grateful to see him. Some of them had been around long enough to remember him.

Once he'd made it upstairs, he grasped Chris's hand in much the same fashion that Swarovski had earlier and then gave Bobby a light kiss, more a formality than a friendly greeting. "How are you doing, Bobby?"

"I've had better days," she commented, dryly.

"Thanks for coming," said Chris. "You made good time."

"Yeah. I tried my best to attract some police attention and get us some help but nobody bit." Wyatt looked down into the lower level and the plethora of blue uniforms that mingled with the ULF staff and the zoo's own security team. "I know why now. They're all in here."

Chris managed a faint smile.

"What happened?"

Chris recounted the whole story from the beginning. When he

was finished he looked at Wyatt. "So what do we do now?"

Wyatt looked around at the surroundings. "Can we set up an operations center here?"

"I guess. What do you need?"

"I'll want a tactical map and display of the city and I'll need a headset tapped into your com-link and ULF frequencies." Wyatt looked around him again as if judging the space he had to work with. "Is there a working terminal in the room?"

"Not here," Chris said, "but there are some down the corridor in some of the offices."

"Okay. Let's worry about that later. I want some monitors in here, each one tuned to one of the news networks. We'll need all the help we can get, and while I admit the journos can be a pain in the ass sometimes, we can use them to our advantage. If there's something going down anywhere in the city, they'll probably know about it earlier than most. We can use them to be our eyes and ears out there.

"We need to call the cops, I mean really call the cops and inform them of what's going on, get all their resources out in the field. The Home Guard and the local Earth Alliance bases too, let's get everyone with arms and armor out there—and let's not just call locally, let's tell the whole city, state and also the services in the neighboring states. We're gonna try and lock down this city, and if that fails, we'll have to lock down neighboring counties. Failing that, we'll have to lock down the state."

Chris nodded his understanding, "What do we tell them?"

"We tell them that if they encounter anything their primary objective is to capture or contain it. Failing that, shoot to kill."

Chris and Bobby both hung their heads in disappointment. It was the words they hadn't wanted to hear but needed to be said. They'd all gone face-to-face with some of these aliens; they all knew what they were capable of. The cops and army forces had to be able to defend themselves.

Wyatt saw their sadness. "I know it's hard," he said. "These jokers thought they were doing these aliens a favor by setting them loose. In reality, all they did was condemn them. Now most of them are going to end up dying or being destroyed. That's not our fault."

His resolve hardened again. "Let's put a call in to the mayor's office too. Get some kind of official statement out so the press can deal with them and not with us. We don't need a public relations disaster on top of this.

"Links too," Wyatt continued. "I'll need some telelinks in here and all links in the zoo forwarded here. If anyone calls in with any information I want them coming straight to me. What's our status with the containment fields?"

"The security guys are working on it right now," Chris said. "Hold on, I'll check." Chris walked over the gallery balcony again and called up the security guard who had got the comms back online earlier. The young man rushed up the stairs to join them.

"Sir?"

"What's the update on the security systems?" Chris asked.

The security guard shrugged and sighed. He looked embarrassed at his lack of news. "We really can't tell you anything, sir. We don't know what they did or how the software they downloaded into our systems is actually working. We haven't even got the faintest idea how to go about fixing what they've undone."

"What are our options?" Wyatt asked.

The young guard looked at him as if noticing him for the first time. "Well, right now, it doesn't look like we have a lot of choice. Not if you want this all back on-line as soon as possible. What we're looking at is a hard reset of the whole security network, and then bringing every component live, one piece at a time."

"How long will that take?"

"Two hours, at least, possibly more."

Wyatt winced. That was ugly. Two hours during which time any alien in the zoo could walk free. "What about a software fix?"

"Like I said, sir," the young security guard said, spreading his hands and shrugging, "You're guess is as good as mine. Could be hours, could be days. We just don't know what the software is doing and with no working terminals in here, we can't even get started on a fix yet."

All of a sudden, Plan A was starting to sound a whole lot more attractive. "Shut down the system," Wyatt said.

"On whose authority, sir?"

"Mine."

"But…?"

Chris began to shepherd the security guard away. "Trust me," he said, "He knows what he's doing."

"Excuse me."

Wyatt turned quickly at the interruption. A man in a long raincoat and hat stood before him, a cop standing behind him.

"I'm sorry," Wyatt said. "Can I help you?"

Lieberwits flashed his holo-ID. Wyatt barely gave it a glance. "I'm Detective Lieberwits. This is Officer Wood. We'll be leading the investigation into what happened here this morning."

"Great. Thanks." Wyatt said, but his smile was insincere. "There's really nothing you can do right now, detective. You certainly can't leave here until the zoo is safe."

"No. We noticed. So while we seem to be limited in what we can do in terms of police work right now, we wondered if there was anything we could do to assist you, Mister…?"

"Dorren. Sorry, Wyatt Dorren." There. It was done. Pleasantries over, Wyatt stopped and thought for a moment. "Actually, there is something you could do for me. Bobby!"

Bobby looked up at him.

"Bobby, could you take Detective Lieberwits and Officer Wood here down the hall and find a working terminal? I need you to call up the zoo's directory. We need to call all the zookeepers and the ULF admin staff and get them in here. Tell them all to go to the staff entrance and wait in their vehicles for an escort. Then we need to call all non-essential staff, all the other office workers and cleaners, and tell them to stay home. No, not just stay home, stay home and bolt their doors. We need to keep them away. Have these guys help you with the calls."

Bobby nodded. "Sure. That's great, Wyatt, but they're not the only people we need to keep away. What about the public?"

Wyatt hadn't even thought about it. He looked at his watch. 8:40. The zoo opened at 9:00 AM.

* * * * *

Tyrone Bailey stood by the large wrought-iron gates that marked the entrance to the zoo. He'd been looking forward to this day for months, ever since his parents had told him they would take him for his sixth birthday.

Above the gates, a metal arch spanned from one huge gatepost to the other, two bars of iron describing a perfect semicircle. Between them, more iron was intricately sculpted into lettering to form three words. Tyrone craned his neck back and peered up at the archway, cupping his hands around the peak of his new Chicago Grizzlies cap, the city's resident Powerdisc team. The cap was a present too, as was the Grizzlies team shirt that was so horribly oversized for him it hung out from under his jacket and nearly reached his knees

"Can you read it, Ty?" his father asked, crouching down next to him.

"Int...Inter..."

"Interplanetary Zoological Park," his father finished for him. "It's the zoo! We made it, Ty! We told you we'd come for your birthday."

Behind them, Tyrone's mother smiled, pleased that the three of them would finally get to share a day out.

"What's your favorite alien, Ty? What do you want to go and see first?" his father asked.

"The baby puglion!"

"Really? Not the canjo or the ranagok? I thought when we looked at the holos at home you liked the ranagok."

"The baby puglion! The baby puglion!" Tyrone was working himself into a frenzy, but his father wasn't hearing him anymore. From where he crouched, Anton Bailey had a perfect view straight along the front perimeter wall of the IZP. Twenty yards away a large but slender black leg had reached over the wall and, he could only assume, a large black body was about to follow. For a moment, he couldn't believe what he was seeing.

Anton looked around; there was nowhere to run. The only other thing in sight was a hover vehicle, parked or abandoned, in the pick-up and drop-off spot at the end of the entrance walkway a hundred yards away. They wouldn't reach that in time, and besides, it was probably locked. Their only chance was to try and hide in the neatly manicured hedges that lined the paved promenade.

"Dina! The hedge! Quickly, now!"

She looked at him as if he were mad. It was only when he indicated over his shoulder with a backward jerk of his thumb that she saw it for the first time. She took a sharp intake of breath and brought her hands to her mouth, as if the former had caused the latter.

Three legs, a head and thorax had now appeared over the wall. Antennae waved in the air and a pair of emotionless black eyes looked upon a strange new world for the first time.

"Go!" Anton ordered her, turning around and sweeping up Tyrone in one arm, dragging the youngster away from the danger.

Immediately Tyrone began to cry and wail.

"Shhh, Tyrone. It's okay."

"My cap! My Grizzlies' cap!"

Anton turned to find that he had swept up little Tyrone so violently in his haste to get him away, that the boy's cap had come off his head and now lay on the paved walkway outside the zoo gates.

For a second he toyed with the idea of returning to retrieve it, and then he looked at the creature that was now stepping away from the wall, carrying a huge abdomen behind it.

"My cap!" Tyrone complained again. And the creature swung its head around and locked its eyes on them.

"I'll get you another one, son. I promise." Anton turned and ran, forcing his way through the hedge, which raked his arms and legs through his clothing, while trying his best to protect Tyrone from the very same. When they were through, the three of them crouched down and peered back out at the entrance through the leafy growth.

The alien was big. It was eight feet long and stood six feet high. Jet black in color, it supported its head, thorax and abdomen on eight strong but slender legs. The legs were covered in thick hairs and ended, not in feet, but in two soft pads of flesh that seemed to suck themselves to the ground.

It stepped over the opposing hedge with ease, and headed straight for their position.

"Dad! What is it?" Tyrone whimpered in fear.

"Shhh." Anton said quietly, bringing a finger to his lips for emphasis. "We'll be okay, son," he whispered. Regardless, he pulled his son close and cupped his other hand over the youngster's mouth.

The creature stopped, its head swiveling around with an unnatural quickness and ease. It was as though it were looking at its own feet, examining the unfamiliar surface it found itself on. It brought its forelimbs up over its head, cleaning its expressionless eyes with quick strokes.

The three humans on the other side of the hedge held their breath. As they watched, the alien cocked its head quickly, its attention caught by something else. The sounds of the metropolis. Agonizingly slowly, it seemed, the creature turned away from them and headed for the city, away from the IZP.

Anton released his grip on his son and breathed a large, misplaced, sigh of relief. Tyrone, thinking the danger had passed, shot through the bushes to retrieve the cap.

"Tyrone!" his father hissed. "Tyrone! Get back here!" But it was too late.

Tyrone stooped to pick up the cap, examined it briefly and brushed off some imaginary dirt before placing it back on his head. He turned to return to his parents—and there it was.

It stood taller now, rearing up on its four back legs, so that its head and thorax towered above the small child. The two front legs were held close in to the body, threatening to lash out at any moment. The next pair of legs flailed and clawed the air.

Tyrone tried to go one way but the creature moved to intercept him with a wicked, predatory movement. The other way proved no different. With nothing left to do, Tyrone, rooted to the spot, began to cry.

Anton and Dina watched, powerless, as the drama unfolded in front of them. From their position, they could see the back end of the alien, see its abdomen, bloated and swollen, pulsating as if there was something else alive in there. As they watched, the creature dropped its threatening stance and returned to standing on all eight legs.

Tyrone was paralyzed with fear. The alien brought its head down close to his. So close that he could smell it. It was foul and foreign. He wet his pants and whimpered. With a turn of its head, the alien brought an eye to bear on the young human and stared at him for a long time. Mandibles moved constantly, as if the creature was mouthing its own internal monologue, contemplating what to do. Then finally, once again, it turned and walked away.

Anton peered through the hedge at his son, not wanting to move yet, not wanting to attract the alien back. Through Tyrone's open jacket, he could see his son's shirt. The shirt of Tyrone's favorite player. Ibsen. Lucky number seven.

Tyrone would never know it, but had he been bigger he would have been killed.

* * * * *

When the security staff shut off the power all the monitors went out and the whole room was momentarily plunged into darkness. As his eyes adjusted to the lack of light, Wyatt looked over at the display wall. Where the schematic had been was now blank wall, and the monitor screens now formed a double track of gray rectangles around three sides. For a second, Wyatt felt like he was being watched by a giant pupil with an iris of compound eyes. It sent a shiver down his spine.

The hum of power was gone. The silence was disturbing.

It was probably this that made Stephen Gruber's entrance all the more startling. Gruber threw the doors open with such force that they clattered against the wall, sending a resounding bang around the whole room. "What the hell is going on here?" Gruber demanded, just as the lights came back up. Coincidence or not, Wyatt couldn't help thinking that Gruber had enough ire and nervous energy, that if someone had the means to harness it, he alone could light up most of the eastern seaboard. His face was a red, contorted mask of fury.

Some members of the ULF team were in the upper gallery, installing Wyatt's requested hardware. Bobby had left the two cops to make the necessary calls and now, halfway up the stairs, she struggled with one end of a large monitor that she had acquired from one of the offices down the hall. The other end was dwarfed by the goliath hands of Sean McAphee. McAphee could probably have carried the thing by himself.

Gruber came up the stairway, taking the steps two at a time and barging past the two of them. "What the hell is going on here?" he bellowed again. He pulled a colored handkerchief out of his lapel pocket and dabbed his sweating brow frantically. "Who's responsible for this debacle? Who are all these people?" he said to no one in particular, gesticulating wildly around the room.

"Most of them are your staff!" Wyatt said. "And the others,

those boys in blue, they're the local law enforcers, otherwise known as the police." There was more than a hint of sarcasm in Wyatt's voice.

Gruber turned on him, ready to unleash the fury that raged inside him, but he stopped short and a wave of recognition passed across his face before the frown returned. "What the hell is he doing here?" he said, pointing, the question directed at no one in particular.

"He's here to coordinate the reacquisition effort, sir," Chris said. "We need someone here at the zoo to provide a central point of operations. Wyatt's experience both in a managerial role and as a ULF staff member made him the obvious choice."

"Who authorized this?" Gruber couldn't argue with the reasoning, he was just going to chip away at whatever he could.

"I did," Bobby lied, placing the monitor on the floor and then standing to look Gruber in the face. "As the only ULF expedition leader here right now and the most senior member of staff, I took all means and appropriate action necessary to contain the situation. Wyatt is invaluable to us."

Wyatt couldn't help but be impressed at how vocal his friends were in his defense.

"Are you questioning my judgment?" Bobby leaned in close to Gruber so her face was just inches from his. He seemed to visibly shrink next to her, the wind taken completely out of his sails. Bobby was formidable. One didn't want her as an enemy.

"All right, then," Gruber managed under duress. "But you're not staff here," he said, pointing a finger at Wyatt. "You're not getting paid for this."

Wyatt was stunned. "Did you really just say that to me?" He looked across at Bobby. "Did he really just say that to me?" Bobby just shrugged and shook her head in disgust.

Wyatt couldn't tell if Gruber blushed, his face was already so red with anger, but he was sure he saw a flicker of embarrassment pass across the other man's features, realizing his misguided priorities had just been laid bare in front of the entire room. "Doesn't surprise me, though," Wyatt continued. "You always were a miserable tight-ass."

"What did you say to me?"

But Wyatt was already waving him off with the back of his hand, partly to ward off the question, but partly to dismiss him outright. He'd forgotten how much Gruber had irritated him when he had been at the zoo. Funny how five years worth of absence seemed to have been made up for in a matter of seconds.

"There! That's it." Delaney, another of the ULF team, finished wiring up one of the monitors, the wafer-thin glass screen coming to life. "News One" he said, and the channel flicked to one of Chicago's 24/7 news networks.

A strap with the words "Breaking News" covered the bottom third of the image, and a news anchor, clearly distracted by something, quickly faced front and to camera again. "This just in…" he began. "We are getting reports that there has been a breach of security at the Interplanetary Zoological Park. We're being told that the mayor's office is about to make an announcement."

The picture cut to a microphone-adorned lectern. On its front was the emblem of the mayoral office and the words City of Chicago. As yet there was no sign of the mayor.

Wyatt looked across at Bobby. "Did you call already?"

"I did," Gruber snapped. "When I saw the first news reports this morning, I immediately called the mayor and told him what was going on. I told him I'd get here as soon as I could and keep him astride of developments."

Wyatt looked at his watch. It was 9:20AM. "What time were you originally intending to get here, then?" The comment earned him a sideways look of contempt.

The mayor was now approaching the lectern. Journalists, off–camera, now began shouting and calling to him, all trying to get his attention. The mayor raised a hand to his mouth and coughed once, politely clearing his throat.

"Citizens of Chicago," he began. "It has been brought to our attention that at some time in the early hours of this morning, there was a breach of security at the city's much loved and famous landmark, the Interplanetary Zoological Park. We do not have specific details at this time, nor do we know the nature of any, if any, imminent threat. However, the zoo will be closed to visitors for the foreseeable future and we urge you to be vigilant and take whatever precautions necessary to protect you and yours as you go about your day-to-day activities. We will make further announcements as the information becomes available to us."

The sea of reporters burst into chatter, all desperate to get in another question, to eke another nugget of information out of the man, but it was clear that was all they were going to get. The mayor was already leaving and returning to his office.

"That's it?" Bobby asked, amazed. "He didn't tell us anything."

"Ignorance is bliss, Bobby." Delaney replied

"For you, maybe."

"Come on Bobby, you gotta admit, that dude is slick. Cool as a cucumber. He says exactly the right thing at exactly the right time and he's got a voice like liquid chocolate. Smooth as. I'd believe anything he said."

"Nice, Delaney. You should take up poetry." Bobby retorted. "Y'know, that's your problem," she added as an afterthought, "You would believe anything. You'd even believe me if I told you they'd taken the word gullible out of the dictionary."

"Have they?" Delaney looked deadly serious, as if this was news to him, and then his face cracked into a broad grin.

"Knock it off! We've got work to do."

* * * * *

"Yes, hello, ma'am, this is Officer Wood with the Chicago City Police Department...I'm sorry, what's that...? No. No, ma'am, nobody's died. I'm just calling to tell you…I'm sorry? No. No. I don't know who that is, ma'am. Listen, I'm calling to tell you not to come into work today…Pardon? No. You haven't been fired. There's a problem here at the zoo, we need you to stay home for your own safety…say again? No, nothing like that, just a security issue…No. Nobody's been shot. Okay…Okay, ma'am. Don't you worry, now. Have a nice day." Wood tapped the link on his ear, terminating the call.

Lieberwits looked at him and raised an eyebrow in vague amusement. "Sounded like fun."

"Do we have to tell them we're cops? You tell people you're a cop and they immediately think that their kid's got into trouble or worse, been kidnapped or killed. What is wrong with people? Why does everybody assume the worst?"

Lieberwits sighed. "Sign of the times. Not a lot of good in the world these days."

Wood snorted out a laugh. "Yeah. Take a look out the window." He put his elbow on the desk and cradled the top of his head in his hand. Sighing, he absentmindedly rubbed one eye with the heel of his palm. "Who'd do it, detective? Who'd be crazy enough to do something like this?"

"Oh, there's plenty of crazies out there, but this was planned, this was the work of an organization. Activists. Some of them are so fanatical they've lost sight of their goals, their actions far removed from the original vision." Lieberwits paused, looking blankly into space as if he was remembering something. "There's plenty of them…these groups," he continued. "The alien rights folks." He counted them off on his fingers. "The Alien Protection League; the Federation for Representation and Equality of Extra Terrestrials, that's FREE E.T. to you; the Alien Liberation Front; E.T. No Home…"

"E.T. No Home? Really?"

"No, you idiot, that was a joke." Lieberwits shook his head. "Separately, they're pretty harmless, just a bunch of tree-hugging fools with an axe to grind. Together, they could really amount to something, but they aren't that smart." Lieberwits thought for a moment, clasping his chin between thumb and forefinger. "God forbid those clowns ever get together and actually coordinate something. Now that would be really bad."

"You don't think this is bad?" Wood looked at him, eyebrows raised.

Lieberwits shrugged.

"Seriously, though, you think it's an alien rights group that did this?"

"I'm not sure, but when they let us out of here it's as good a place as any to start."

* * * * *

The line continued to pull slowly off Harry's reel. The ratchet click marked its steady progress like a metronome. He should probably set the hooks, Harry thought. All the yanking on the rod that he'd done before should have done it, but it wouldn't hurt just to be sure.

Harry leaned forward slowly and tightened the clutch on his reel. The clicking stopped, the top of his rod started bending in response.

Harry took a deep breath, readying himself for the fight he knew was coming, and then yanked the rod upward, hard.

For a split-second nothing happened, but then line started screaming off the reel, the ratchet roaring in protest. Harry was shocked. He hadn't expected this. The inanimate rod was now a wild thing in his hands. He looked down at his reel. Line was spooling off it, zipping off so fast that he could see each layer being torn away. He would have to stop that. He only had a finite amount of line.

He tightened the clutch a bit more but it had practically no effect. The ratchet still shrieked at the force it was being subjected to.

And then suddenly it stopped.

Harry looked around. It was dead calm, and without the noise of the reel, the silence was deafening. Slowly, he began to reel in whatever it was had taken the lure. Again, it was solid, like he was hauling a dead weight through the water, and then he couldn't reel any more as whatever it was started moving slowly away from him.

A small bow wave began to form at the rear of the boat. Harry and his boat were being towed through the water. The line whined in complaint.

Panicked, Harry started winding as fast as he could. He just wanted to get this thing out of the water, to end this charade.

The boat was moving swiftly through the water now, the rear end sinking deeper. The bow wave was getting so large that water was now beginning to spill into the back of the boat. Harry struggled to move away from it, using one hand to steady himself, the other still holding the rod that had taken on a life of its own.

Abruptly, the line went slack.

Harry sat back down in the boat, his face ashen. The small boat rocked gently in the water, drifting slowly, the bow wave now dissipating away from the vessel in a set of spreading, concentric circles. Cautiously he reeled in his line, thankful when the start of the wire trace began appearing out of the water. As it had done before, the lure skipped across the surface and swung in toward him. He reached out and caught it with his free hand.

The lure was mangled beyond recognition. More surprising was that all hooks on both set of trebles had been completely straightened out.

Harry let out of whistle of exclamation. "Holy cow. I must have hooked a monster." A second later, Harry found out exactly how right he was.

The water to Harry's right erupted, soaking him immediately. He dropped everything in fright, not caring where it landed, and quickly rubbed the spray out of his eyes, aware that something was close by. He looked up and his breath caught in his throat. It was, he realized, going to be the last breath he was ever going to take.

She towered over him. Twenty feet of her had breached clear out of the water, yet still more of her remained below the dark surface of the lake. For a moment, she hung there, frozen in time, an inhuman eye staring with an indifferent gaze, and then she fell, coming down across the wooden boat and smashing it to smithereens.

It would be many hours before small parts of Harry McGlade's boat washed up on the shore.

* * * * *

Travis Jacks was a big man. At six feet and four inches, he was head and shoulders above almost everyone in the room with the exception of Sean McAphee. The pair of them might have been separated at birth.

Despite the initial impression of his size, Jacks was remarkably thin for his height. His was a tall, lanky frame that barely seemed to fill his standard issue clothing. His dark, shoulder-length hair fell from his head in untidy waves and thick stubble covered his face; not quite a beard, but also more established than just a few days growth. His blue eyes twinkled with a childlike wonder and seemed to ask questions of everything they looked at.

He approached the large table that now stood in the center of the upper gallery. From each end a four-foot high metal pole rose out of the surface and now, projected between the two poles, a detailed map of Chicago hung in the air. Travis could see Wyatt standing on the other side of the map, eyes scanning the city blocks, scrutinizing it like a chess player might a board.

Travis leant across the table and shoved his hand through the image. "Hey, Wyatt. It's good to have you back."

Wyatt jumped, surprised to see what appeared to be a disembodied hand coming through the map at him. He'd forgotten how massive Jacks's hands were, and then remembered that he'd always thought that Jacks would have made a good Powerdisc player. That hand in a mitt, combined with Jacks's size—nothing would have gotten past him. It would be wrong to assume weakness from Jacks's wiry frame; his hands exuded strength and power.

Wyatt took the hand and shook it, focusing beyond the map to see Travis for the first time. "I wish it could be under better circumstances. You know why you're here, I take it?"

Jacks withdrew the hand. It disappeared through the map like a drowning victim slipping under water. "Yeah. I caught the news on the way in. Chris explained everything."

"I need your help, Travis. Not just you. You and your boys. Do you think they're ready for something like this?"

Jacks laughed. "No way, Wyatt! They're four months in. They're barely out of basic!"

"We still offer on-the-job training, don't we?"

"Yeah. After a year."

"Well, consider this as that, just premature," Wyatt said with a grin, trying to win Travis over with humor.

"Wyatt, this is deadly serious."

"I know. I wouldn't be asking if it wasn't." The smile had gone.

"What you're asking of me…To put these kids in harm's way, because that's what they are, Wyatt, they're just kids…It doesn't even bear thinking about."

"Like I said, I wouldn't be asking if I didn't have to. I need more people out there in the field."

"But that's crazy. We know what these things do on their home worlds. We know their habitats—that's what my guys are training for. But we have no idea how our equipment is going to perform out there. We have no idea how half of these things are going to behave in that environment. It's not desert or jungle or snow out there, Wyatt, it's concrete and steel. We're not prepared for that."

"I never said we were." Wyatt let the words hang in the air for a moment. "But the people of Chicago need us, Travis."

Travis stepped back from the table and the display and folded his arms across his chest, then brought his right hand up to stroke his stubble as he thought. He shook his head and sighed, a big sigh, as if the questions that were being asked of him were too difficult and he didn't have an answer for them; and then, for the first time, he really looked at the map.

A small red dot pulsated on the graphic, hemorrhaging outwards and into the city, the IZP at its center. "What's that?"

"Based on information given to us this morning about what we believe to be an attack, that dot plots the possible range of the mantor from the IZP"

"Jesus, Wyatt." Travis shook his head again. "This really isn't up for negotiation, is it?"

Wyatt didn't need to answer. "Can you call your boys in?"

"Tell them their training schedule's been revised?" Travis said with a faint smile, trying to reciprocate Wyatt's humor from earlier. Wyatt nodded once, acknowledging the gesture. "Let me go make some calls."

Travis turned to leave and then turned back. "I tell you this, though, if they all make it through this, I want you there personally on graduation day."

"That I can do."

* * * * *

The young pilot brought the aircraft round on its final heading, describing the third leg of a large triangular route. He'd recently gotten his private license and was just clocking some flight time, renting this small four-seater Gryphon for a couple of hours.

He liked Gryphons. He'd trained in one and immediately taken to the aircraft, finding it intuitive and a joy to fly. Not only that, but the two slimline thrusters that hung below the wings were extremely quiet, giving anyone in the aircraft the sensation of gliding rather than flying.

He had left Chicago's O'Hare skyport early, as the sun was just starting to show itself to the city, and set out on a southwesterly heading, away from the blinding glare. After forty minutes, he had turned southeast and continued on and now, he had made his final turn and was on a north-northeast heading back to the skyport and the westerly landing strips reserved for small aircraft.

He nudged the joystick forward and pointed the Gryphon's nose toward the earth, making a steady descent until he reached four thousand feet, where he leveled the aircraft out for final approach and called in his landing request. He didn't like landings; they were his least favorite part of flying and so the practice was good. He took a deep breath and readied himself.

An enormous bang disrupted his concentration and numerous displays on the console all suddenly dropped to red. The aircraft began to shake violently and lurched to the left, the joystick now unresponsive and fighting his efforts to retain control. Everything suggested a problem with the right thruster, a bird strike perhaps. It wouldn't be the first time, this close to the skyport. He should have killed the left thruster instantly and attempted to glide his crippled aircraft home, but at only four thousand feet and with a hundred other checks and procedures running through his head he didn't react quickly enough, and the left thruster won out over his battle with the controls. The Gryphon was now in a flat spin and falling fast.

"Mayday! Mayday!" he screamed into his link. He looked out the window to his right, expecting to see blood or feathers or both on his wing. "Mayd…" He never finished calling in his plea for help, so stunned was he at seeing green goo smeared all over his wing.

The Gryphon hit ground and exploded in a fireball.

* * * * *

Delaney held the last monitor as Chris mounted it in place. There were five now, hanging from a bracket in the ceiling in a neat row. Each one playing a different news channel. Each news channel, unfortunately, playing the same news story.

Chris stepped down from the chair he had been standing on and took a look around the upper gallery of security's command and control. It was an impressive scene. In the space of about an hour, the sixteen men of and women of his ULF squad had turned a basically empty room into an ops center worthy of a battleship cruiser.

Behind Wyatt stood a long table, along which were seven chairs. Seven links were fixed on the tabletop, ready to be manned by some of the admin staff that had been called in and were about to be escorted up to the building from the staff entrance. Chris gestured to the table with a nod of his head. Wyatt looked behind him.

"Do you think that will be enough?"

As if on cue, three of the links began trilling simultaneously.

Wyatt shot Chris a look. "No," he said sarcastically, suggesting Chris was the dumb one.

Wyatt snatched up the nearest link. "Hello. Wyatt Dorren. IZP."

"Hello. Is that the zoo?" It was a young woman's voice, but there was an edge to it that Wyatt didn't like. It was something he had heard too many times before. A voice laced with fear. "There's something in my apartment."

Wyatt looked back at Chris. It had begun.

CHAPTER 4

Of the other two link calls, one was a journalist, whom Chris redirected to the mayor's office, and the other was, coincidentally, the mayor's office.

Wyatt hung up his call. *Who is it?* he mouthed to Chris.

"Mayor's office."

"Put them through to Gruber. He seems to be their best buddy right now. I think he's in one of the offices down the hall."

"No. They want to talk to you. They want to send somebody down here."

Wyatt frowned.

"What do I tell them?" Chris asked.

"Tell them if he's brave enough, sure, someone can come down."

Chris paraphrased the message and terminated the connection.

Travis climbed the stairs and stepped into the upper gallery level. He looked tired. Weary. As if his shouldering of some of the burden of Chicago's newest disaster was already taking a heavy toll on him. "Okay," he said to Wyatt. "I've called all my guys. They're all on their way in."

"Good, I'll take care of them once they get here. In the meantime I've got something for you." Wyatt handed Travis a piece of paper with an address scribbled on it. "I need you to check it out."

Travis looked at the paper with a frown. "What's this?"

"Some woman who called. Says there's something in her apartment. Probably just an attention seeker. Saw something on the news about the zoo and decided to use it to her advantage."

"It's close, I mean, that address is just a few city blocks from here."

"Yeah, I know, which is why I think it's worth checking out, but I don't think it's anything to worry about. I think you can handle it on your own. Her link number is there. It might come in useful in tracking her down if this all turns out to be a hoax. Still, don't take any risks. Take all your gear with you."

Travis nodded, turned and left.

Wyatt turned to Chris. "We need to send a couple of guys out to escort the rest of the staff up here. Who do you want to nominate?"

Chris didn't even need to think about it. "Swarovski! Shady! Get up here!"

Swarovski strode over to another ULF team member and practically yanked him out of one of the chairs. Together they made their way up to the upper gallery to stand before Chris and Wyatt.

"Got a job for you guys," Chris said.

"Good," Swarovski replied. "I was starting to get cabin fever down there."

Wyatt looked at him, Swarovski wasn't lying, his hands played nervously by his sides. Judging by the looks of him, Swarovski's partner wasn't doing much better. Mike "Shady" Shades was a short man, probably only five feet four inches, but that wasn't the most noticeable thing about him. If Swarovski looked tetchy, this guy just looked downright nervous. His eyes darted around constantly. It seemed they barely stopped long enough to focus on anything. It gave the impression that he was a distinctly shady character. It was that and his surname that gave him his rather unfortunate moniker. "Shady" was the kind of guy who people avoided sitting next to in a skytrack carriage; they'd go and find another seat. That said, Shady was also the best point man in the ULF department. Out in the field, if there was anything to see,

Shady saw it. He didn't miss a thing.

Wyatt leaned forward on the table. "We have a number of essential staff coming in to help with this effort," he began. "They will all be arriving at the staff entrance and we need you to be there to protect them and escort them in."

'That's it?" Swarovski shrugged, as if what was being asked of him was a walk in the park. Shady nodded eagerly, like a dog that had just been asked if it wanted to go for a walk in the park.

"That's it," Wyatt straightened. "But I don't want you guys just driving down there in a hover vehicle. If you guys are locked up in an HV then you won't be providing any protection to these people. I want you to take one of the zookeeper's carts."

Swarovski and Shady gave each other a sideways look. Wyatt caught it. "I know you think that's crazy, but it's the only way you can have your weapons to hand and get a clear shot off if anything comes at you or any of the staff."

Swarovski shrugged again. "Hey, man, you're the boss."

* * * * *

Travis Jacks pulled up outside the apartment building and checked the address one final time. He glanced out of the virtual window and spied the number above the entrance foyer. 522. This was the place. He sighed, preparing himself for what might be in store, and popped the trunk of the HV with a voice command. He climbed out and took a brief look around. This didn't seem like the kind of place where an alien would go unnoticed. People seemed to be going about their business as usual. Men in suits left buildings and headed for work. A young mother pushed an infant in an anti-grav child seat, and an elderly couple chatted on the street corner. Everything seemed so normal. Didn't these people watch the news?

Maybe Wyatt was right. Maybe this was a hoax. He was beginning to feel extremely self-conscious as he started unloading his gear from the back of the HV, drawing worried looks from passers-by. He strapped the holster of his quad-sys gun to his leg, buckling it around his thigh and just above his knee, preferring not to lift the weapon out of his vehicle just yet. He buckled a large knife to his belt and then placed his round, open-faced helmet on his head and fastened it under his chin. Finally, he pulled the large gun out of his trunk and slid it into its holster along his right side. People averted their eyes and hurried on.

Travis turned and walked towards the apartment building, the HV's trunk slowly closing behind him as it detected his fading heat signature. He wanted to be out of the street as quickly as possible.

He entered the lobby and the watchman took one look at him and dove behind his desk. "It's okay. I'm not going to hurt you." If the man heard him, he chose not to respond. "I'm here to help." Again, no response. Travis shook his head and headed for the elevators.

A set of illuminated numbers marked the elevator's steady progress back to lobby level. Travis looked at his blurred and warped reflection in the large gold metal elevator doors. He could sympathize with the watchman. If he'd seen someone of his size kitted out with all the weapons he had, he probably would have dived behind the desk too.

The elevator's arrival was accompanied by the chiming of a bell, so antiquated it was laughable. The doors parted with a slow rumble and Travis stepped inside.

He hit the button for the fifth floor. A woman's voice, silky smooth, came through the speakers. "*You have selected the fifth floor*," it said in sultry tones. Travis wondered if the building's artificial intelligence program would be quite so relaxed if it knew it had an alien on its premises.

The doors to the elevator closed and Travis used the few moments of privacy to check his weapon, taking out the clip to ensure it was full before slotting it back into the gun and banging it home. He reached over his shoulder and grabbed the ends of four small clubs, which jutted out of his small backpack. They were attached together by a ball of cord, which he tucked into the barrel of the grenade-launching section of his weapon, then pushed the four narrow ends of the clubs into four small sockets arranged around the barrel, shoving until he heard them click home. He looked up at the small concealed camera located in the corner of the compartment and could imagine the watchman looking at him, frantically calling the cops, thinking that he'd let some weapon-obsessed psycho killer into the building.

The ridiculous bell chimed again and the doors parted. Cautiously, Travis stepped into the hallway.

* * * * *

The zoo cart did its best to speed along the access road, but speed was not its selling point. Swarovski had the power pedal of the cart pressed firmly to the floor. The electric motor buzzed like a hyperactive bug.

"Now I know why I'm not a zookeeper," Swarovski complained. "Never in my life did I think I'd be driving a turbocharged hair dryer."

Shady sat next to him, half-leaning out of the open side of the cart with his gun in his hand, its butt resting on his thigh. His eyes scanned the zoo grounds as they passed by. "Just shut up and drive, Swarovski," he said with a grin, "I'd rather be out here than still cooped up in that room."

Shady was right; it was good to be outside and feel the crisp air on his face.

* * * * *

Travis walked slowly along the corridor, his booted feet falling quietly on the carpeted floor. He held the large quad-sys gun in his right hand; butt in the crook of his elbow, barrel pointed toward the narrow ceiling. He reached into his pocket with his free hand and pulled out the small folded piece of paper, rubbing it against his pants to open it. With a final flick of his hand, the paper opened up and he read the address to himself again. Travis eyed the numbers on the doors as he passed by, making sure he was heading in the right direction. 5C…5D. He looked farther up the corridor towards his target door. 5G.

Travis could feel the adrenaline starting to pump. His pulse began to throb in his temples. Cautiously he approached the door to apartment 5G. He reached to press the button that would activate the visitor spyhole camera and stopped himself. The door was slightly ajar.

Instinctively, Travis looked at the apartment's keypad. It wasn't damaged and didn't look like it had been tampered with. Nobody had broken in. There was no sign of forced entry. Which could mean only one thing; the door had been opened from the inside.

"Visor. Thermal imaging camera," Travis said quietly into his helmet's in-built microphone. Instantly, a dark visor came down over his eyes. The helmet's tiny, front-facing thermal imaging camera went live and projected its feed onto the visor's heads-up display and over Travis's right eye. Through his left eye, Travis could see as usual.

His brain now did what his eyes couldn't do and took the two visual feeds and overlaid them onto one another. Now the physical environment was also being described in vivid fluorescent colors.

Three orange lines streaked along the entire length of the ceiling. Hot water pipes, hidden behind the drop paneling. Along the floor, a series of gray-blue smudges blemished the carpet. Invisible to the human eye, the heat-sensing camera had picked up the footprints of someone who had passed this way just minutes before.

Travis surveyed the corridor further. Now he really wasn't sure if this was a hoax or if somebody was just trying to lure him into some kind of trap. If they were waiting out here for him, the thermal imaging camera would pick up their body heat. He didn't think any of the alien exhibits at the zoo could open doors, but it wouldn't hurt to be careful. If there had indeed been an alien at this location, just the fact that the door was open meant that it could now be loose somewhere else in the building, and it could be close by. If someone, or something, was out in the corridor, he would see them, but there was nothing. It was clean.

* * * * *

Swarovski pulled the keeper's cart up to the staff entrance security gatehouse. Beyond the barrier a number of hover vehicles waited, their engines idling.

"Wait here, Shady," Swarovski said, "I'm gonna go check them out. Make sure they're all kosher. Know what I mean?"

Shady nodded, "Yeah. Don't need to be letting in some journalist for the inside scoop."

"Exactly. Give me a minute. Just keep your eyes peeled."

"Don't worry, Pete, I've got your back."

Swarovski walked away from the cart and around the barrier, indicating to the driver of the first vehicle that they should lower their virtual window so he could talk to them. Shady stepped out of the cart and headed in the opposite direction, gun carried in both hands across his chest. He moved around the back of the gatehouse, and looked up the grass bank towards the trees that marked the perimeter of the zoo's exhibition grounds. Almost immediately he got the uncomfortable feeling that he was being watched.

* * * * *

Lieberwits pulled the com-link from his ear and sighed. "Well, that's the last of them."

Wood rubbed his face with his hands, desperately trying to stifle a yawn. He checked his watch. His "shift" had supposedly finished two hours ago but given what was going on around them, going off-shift now seemed to be nothing more than an interesting idea.

"C'mon," Lieberwits said, "I'm sure I saw a replicator down the hallway. What do you say we go and get a coffee or something and then find out when we can expect to be allowed out of this place?"

"Okay," Wood managed through another yawn, before composing himself. "Shame," he said thoughtfully, "I've got a bag of doughnuts in the car."

"Oh yeah? Jelly or glazed?"

"Glazed."

"That is a shame." Lieberwits agreed.

* * * * *

Travis knocked lightly on the door. "Hello? Hello. Is there anybody home?" There was no answer. He looked at the piece of paper still in his hand. The link number was there. Wyatt had said to call.

He read the number out loud into his microphone and watched the digits appear on his heads-up display, then heard his headset connect to the city network and dial the number. After a short delay, he could hear the link in the apartment ringing. It sounded distant.

"Hello?" It was a young woman.

"Hello. Ma'am. I'm from the zoo. I believe you called us."

"Yes, yes. Oh, thank God."

"Ma'am, are you aware that the door to your apartment is open?"

"Yes. I left it open for you. I'm sorry but I can't come to the door. It's in here. I don't know what it is but it's in here."

"Okay, ma'am. Calm down. I'm here to help." Travis put the muzzle of his gun against the door and pushed gently. The door swung inward easily and bumped gently against the wall. A long hallway led into the apartment.

Travis stepped through the doorway. As he did so, the feed from his thermal imaging camera distorted and broke up momentarily. Travis could only guess that it was some kind of interference, probably steel supporting joints over the doorframe breaking up his signal. He took a step further into the apartment and his visor display returned to normal.

"Ma'am?"

"Yes?"

"What exactly is it you think is in your apartment?"

"I don't know. I just know it's not...right. That's why I called the zoo."

"Do you know what it looks like, just so I can get an idea of what I'm dealing with here?"

"No, I'm sorry. I haven't seen it."

"Excuse me?" Travis stopped dead in his tracks.

"I...I haven't seen it."

"You called me out here on the premise that you have something in your apartment and you haven't even seen it?" Travis's patience was wearing thin. "Listen, lady, I don't know if you've seen the news this morning, but we have more important things to deal with. I suggest you call for an exterminator droid if you have a pest problem."

"No! Please! Don't leave!" There was an urgency in her voice that bordered on panic. Travis sighed. "I can help you catch this thing," she added.

"Really? How are you going to do that?"

"Just stay on the link with me. I can direct you to where it is."

"Ma'am, I don't even know where *you* are."

"I'm in the room just off to your right."

Further up the hallway, there was a door on the right hand

side. It was closed. Travis approached it slowly and reached for the door handle.

"Don't! It's locked."

Travis hesitated, his hand inches away from closing around the handle. He stepped back from the door. "Well, are you coming out?"

"Not until you get rid of the thing that's in my apartment!"

"Ma'am, how do you even know that it's still in your apartment?"

"The same way I know you were just about to try the door handle."

For a moment there was silence between them. Travis stood in the hallway, his gun now dropped to his side as he stood there in thought, trying to make sense of the situation evolving around him. Then her voice came again. "And no, that wasn't a lucky guess."

"What are you, a mind reader?"

"Something like that."

"No, seriously. What's going on here?"

"You wouldn't believe it. Anyway, you'll find out soon enough. Now, are you going to help me get rid of this thing or was calling the zoo and getting you out here *my* mistake?"

Travis sighed again. He brought the gun up again, cradling the barrel in his left hand and stepped further into the apartment. "Nice place," he said, more to himself than to anyone.

"Thanks."

"I can't guarantee it will stay that way if you really have one of our critters in here."

* * * * *

Shady looked behind him, through the glass of the gatehouse, and saw Swarovski conversing with the driver of the first vehicle. It seemed Swarovski was done, since he smiled and nodded and moved towards the second HV waiting in line.

A slight breeze caught the trees, sending branches into slow oscillations and causing the leaves to rustle. It was a gentle sound, like someone playing carefully with tissue paper. It was almost loud enough to cover the other sound, but Shady's trained ears picked up on it immediately. A low, guttural, purr.

Shady turned back towards the trees slowly and brought his weapon to bear on them. He knew the alien that made that sound; he'd had the misfortune of capturing some of them. If what he thought he'd heard was really out in those trees then he and Pete were in trouble. Shady began to slowly back away along the other side of the gatehouse toward its single door.

"Pete!" he hissed, as loud as he could, never taking his eyes off the trees. "Pete!" he said again, glancing quickly over his shoulder. Swarovski was out of earshot, talking now to the driver of the third vehicle. Shady swallowed nervously and flicked off the safety catch of his weapon.

For as much as Shady just wanted to get in the gatehouse and shut the door, he couldn't. He would have to go past the door and around the front of the small hut to get Swarovski's attention. He wondered if he did that, whether they would have enough time. He didn't know how far away they were, and his visor and thermal imaging camera were useless to him because the foot of the arbor was over the crest of the hill, and the camera couldn't detect heat sources through the mound of earth. He had no idea where they were, he just knew that if he could hear them, they had to be close.

Shady glanced over his shoulder. Swarovski was moving on again. He cursed under his breath. He was now at the front of the gatehouse after circumnavigating the entire structure. "Pete!" he shouted, but it was no good. If he was facing the trees, Swarovski was never going to hear him. Shady turned and shouted. "Swarovski! Get your ass over here!"

Swarovski looked up, surprise registering on his features. He said something that looked like an apology to the driver of the vehicle and began to walk back towards Shady's position. As he approached, Swarovski's face dropped. Shady watched him draw his gun and break into a run and then turned to see all hell breaking loose.

A pack of gashoks were charging down the hill towards their position. There were at least ten of them, probably more. Shady wasn't counting, he just knew they were hopelessly outnumbered.

Shady opened fire, his weapon roaring to life in his hands.

"Go for the alpha male!" Swarovski was yelling behind him. "Take out the alpha male!"

Shady wasn't concerned with the alpha male. His attention was focused purely on the large female that was bearing down on him, all snarls and canines.

Gashoks were opportunistic pack hunters. Covered in shaggy tan fur, they ran on four legs and would eat anything that moved. A canine-like snout was filled with teeth that could crush bone. They preyed on the weak and the wounded, stole food from other creatures and if numbers allowed, like now, they weren't afraid to ambush.

The gashoks had been studied extensively in captivity. There was a clear hierarchy in their enclosure. One alpha male led the whole pack and had sired all of the infants that had been born at the zoo. Without an alpha male, the pack would be in disarray. However, the females were bigger, and when with cubs, inherently more aggressive than the males, who only really fought over issues of dominance when the females came into heat.

Shady was now looking down his barrel at the largest of the females. Bullets ripped into her and her snarling became a yelp as she tumbled and rolled, and then finally lay still. He moved towards the gatehouse door. Swarovski had come alongside him, able to join him for the first time and add more gunfire to his own. Swarovski's eyes scanned the aliens that continued to charge towards them, not slowed by the loss of one of their clan, looking to single out the alpha male. Shady fired randomly into the air, his other hand desperately trying to punch in the secure keycode for the door.

"Cover me!" Swarovski said. "Forget the door!"

"What?"

"Just give me some covering fire." Swarovski dropped into a crouch, putting the butt of his weapon against his shoulder and adopting a sharp-shooting position.

"Screw it!" Shady gave up on the door and gave his full attention to the approaching pack. They must have easily covered half the distance to the gatehouse in a matter of seconds. Two of their number lay dead, at least a dozen more still continued the attack. At that rate, Shady didn't like their chances much.

Swarovski was focused, his gun tracking one animal. Shady adopted the same tactic, bringing his gun up and looking down the sight. He was going to have to pick them off as quickly as he could, one at a time. Shady squeezed off a couple of rounds and saw the head of another gashok explode in a cloud of red. He searched around and located another animal, letting loose a couple of stray bullets.

Swarovski hadn't fired, his gun still steady in his hands. "Come on," he whispered under his breath. "Come on."

Shady fired again, wounding another alien, then saw the muzzle of Swarovski's gun flash with fire and heard a yelp.

"Go!" Swarovski ordered. "Get in the gatehouse!"

"But..."

"Just do it!"

Shady dropped his weapon to its shoulder strap. Already, he could sense a change. The gashoks' attack had halted almost instantly, their charge slowing to a canter as they became aware of a subtle change in their pack dynamic. Some sensed disarray among their group. Others sensed a new opportunity.

He punched the key code in completely and heard the lock give, then the two of them dove inside the gatehouse and turned to watch the scene outside.

"What happened?" Shady asked.

"I wounded the alpha male," Swarovski replied. "I didn't want to kill him, that might not have stopped them, but now, some of the juvenile males sense his weakness. See?"

Shady looked out of the window. Already, three or four of the younger male aliens had begun to close in on the old male, circling him with malicious intent as he struggled to stand on a crippled front leg. Swarovski's bullet had caught him in the left shoulder, and the wound bled profusely. The females paced warily beyond the circling males, waiting to see the outcome of the brewing confrontation. A new alpha male could easily turn and kill the cubs of another, ensuring only his progeny populated the next generation.

The old male began to run, limping on its front leg and heading straight for the gatehouse and the only visible escape route. Slowly, the juvenile males began to give chase, sensing his weakness and a long-awaited opportunity. The females followed.

In moments, the entire pack had passed by the gatehouse, the humans forgotten, as they chased their old patriarch out through the staff gates and through the assembled hover vehicles and their terrified occupants. Soon, they were all gone.

"What do you think will happen to them?" Shady asked.

"I don't know. Hopefully the juvenile males will be too preoccupied with trying to assert their dominance to pose any great risk to the public. While they're doing that, we can recapture them. But the old male, if they don't kill him, and he becomes an outcast, he could be a real problem. He's wounded. Alone. He could become one of the most dangerous aliens out there." Swarovski looked out of the windows at the hover vehicles still parked outside. He couldn't imagine what was going through the minds of the people sitting in them. "What do you say we just get these people up to the building and check them out when we get there?"

"Agreed."

* * * * *

Lieberwits slurped loudly at the steaming cup as he and Officer Wood walked along the hallway. His leather shoes click-clacked on the polished floor as they made their way back from the replicator towards the main control center.

"Shame they shut down their system," Lieberwits mused. "I guess that will have wiped all traces of where that program was downloaded from."

"Shouldn't have," said Wood. "But if these guys are as organized as they appear to be, I doubt they'll have left anything that's traceable behind anyway. My guess is they just registered a memory key on the city network, got in here, accessed that network address and downloaded the file."

"People can do that?"

"Yeah, it's easy. Wake up, grandpa. What century are you living in?"

"Never did like computers," Lieberwits offered as an excuse.

Wood was already off on another train of thought. "I'd also guess that whatever media that file was on was preloaded with some kind of timed virus or worm, so it will effectively self-destruct. Either that, or whoever did this will trigger it remotely. Even if we do trace the network address, I doubt we'll find anything there now, and if we do, it'll be corrupt and useless to us."

Lieberwits nodded thoughtfully even though Wood might as well have been speaking a foreign language to him.

The pair of them turned off the hallway and into the main control room. As they entered through the double doors a brief cheer went up.

"They must have missed us," Lieberwits said with a smile.

Wyatt heard the cheer from the upper gallery and looked over the railing to find out for himself what there was to cheer about when all around him the world seemed to be falling apart. The guards and ULF staff were all looking at the large schematic on the wall. Wyatt glanced at it and saw the red section, the southeast quadrant of the zoo, lit up again. Some of the security team clapped while others congratulated each other on their minor success. The ULF team just seemed to get more impatient. Chris noticed it too.

"They just want to get out there."

Wyatt nodded his understanding. "They'll get their chance."

* * * * *

The living room was sparsely but tastefully decorated. Not minimalistic, but not cluttered either. A small two-seater sofa lay flush with the wall to his right; at its far end, a small glass coffee table hosted a vase with a collection of fresh calla lilies. A large pair of sliding doors across from him gave access to the small balcony and fire escape. One of the doors was open, and the vertical ribbon blinds swung awkwardly in the breeze that came through the room. Immediately to his left, a small hallway ran down to two more doors, presumably the apartment's second bedroom and bathroom. The left-hand wall of the living room, where the unit's wallscreen was hidden, was huge. In the far left-hand corner, an arched pass-through window and then an archway gave a glimpse of the kitchen.

Travis stepped further into the living room, noticing that his size twelve boots were leaving imprints in the deep pile of the cream carpet.

"Don't worry," she said over the link

He frowned. Another lucky guess, or was there something going on here that he just wasn't understanding? "You really think you can help me, don't you?"

"Yes." She sounded hurt that he questioned it.

"Ma'am, I'm fully trained and equipped to handle this situation. I really think it best if you just leave this to me." Travis turned and walked down the small hallway to the left.

"It's not down there," she said.

Travis shook his head and continued on regardless. Cautiously, he gripped the handle of the first door. He brought his gun up, pointing it at the ceiling so it was flush with his body, and carefully released the safety catch with his thumb. He took a deep breath, steadying his nerve, and then threw the door open, dropping to one knee and snapping the gun down, then jerking it around to follow where his eyes searched. "Clear," he said to himself under his breath.

The bedroom was neat and tidy too. No sign of any kind of disturbance. Travis stepped into the room and again, the feed to his visor broke up as he stepped through the arch of the door. He tapped the helmet experimentally, but it did no good; only when he was fully through the door did his camera feed and vision return to normal.

A double bed with a wrought-iron headboard and brass fixtures dominated the room. At one side of the bed was a small wooden table and against the right wall stood a matching wooden dresser. The door to a closet stood open, fully showing its interior. Travis gave it a cursory once-over, to ensure nothing had taken up residence among the clothing, carefully pushing each hanger down the rail with the muzzle of his gun. He was surprised to find himself taking more than a passing interest in the woman's choice of clothes. She intrigued him, this woman. He shook his head, snapping himself out of his momentary lapse of concentration. Satisfied that there was no danger, Travis left the room and focused on the second door across the hallway.

Again, the room was empty. This time it was a small bathroom, decked out in light blue as if to make the water feel more at home. There was a strong smell of lavender mixed with a cocktail of other fragrances from perfumes and more aromatic soaps than one person could use, all strategically placed around the room in glass vases and dishes. Travis cursed his equipment; for some reason, the interference in here was particularly bad. That only left one more place to check, the kitchen.

A second door on the other side of the bathroom gave access to the kitchen beyond, but Travis chose not to use it. He would tackle the kitchen from the living room where he could at least peer through the archway first rather than charging in blind. Travis closed the door behind him and walked back towards the living area.

He heard her sigh over the link. A sigh of frustration. "Okay, so there's nothing down here. I just have to be sure." Her silence was as good an insult as any.

Travis walked back into the living room, making sure to go well into the room before turning to his left and towards the kitchen. If there was anything in there he wanted a visual on it long before he got close to it. He approached cautiously, crouching down to peer through the pass-through and into the kitchen beyond, swaying to his left and right to get a full picture of the layout. The room was well-lit and counter tops ran along either side of the kitchen towards the back wall. Along the left side, glass-fronted cabinets displayed glasses and chinaware. On the opposite wall lay wooden-fronted counterparts with brass colored handles.

A small island stood in the middle of the small space. An open tub of instant pancake mix stood on it, the handle of a spoon poking out of its top. There was also a glass bowl in which some of the sandy-colored batter had already been made. Above the island, pots and pans hung from a rack that itself hung from a heavy-duty chain attached to a hook in the ceiling.

A large display cabinet stood in the center of the far wall. This too contained china, but items that looked more like they were fixtures rather than everyday kitchenware. There were plates with exquisite blue patterning and a china tea set on which all the handles had an elaborate notch on which to rest one's thumb. Interspersed among the cups and saucers were some china figurines. Little, fragile people, guarding little, fragile things.

To the right of the cabinet, just beyond where the right countertop ended, there was a tiny table and two small chairs. To the left, the kitchen disappeared around a corner, no doubt to the door that gave access to the bathroom from this side.

It all looked very normal. Very safe. Regardless, Travis's heart was thumping in his chest. His nerves weren't helped when she spoke to him again. "You're close."

Travis approached the archway. Interference buzzed in his headset and his visor clouded with static snow. "Jesus, what the hell did they make this building out of?" he muttered under his breath.

"What?" her voice sounded garbled and inhuman through the distortion.

"Nothing." *So much for not charging in blind*, he thought.

"It's right there," she said. "Right there."

"There's nothing here," Travis argued. The muzzle of his gun was already through the archway and protruding into the kitchen. Travis knew he was going to have to just bite the bullet and step through if he wanted to maintain uninterrupted contact with her and be able to get a decent signal on his visor.

He took the step. Immediately she shouted. "Left!"

Travis turned his head quickly. He wasn't properly through the archway yet and the video feed to his visor was still poor but there was enough for him to see a heat source, a red ball, thus far hidden from view, dropping towards him from the corner of the kitchen.

He tried to bring his gun around, but the thing was too fast and cannoned into him, landing on his head and shoulders. Thirty pounds of vicious, thrashing alien took him completely by surprise.

The impact knocked him off-balance, the accompanying shock causing all of his muscles to tense, including his trigger finger. The four spring-loaded clubs now flew out of their chambers like rockets, flying apart on diverging paths and tearing the ball of cord apart behind them into a huge mesh net. Two of the clubs flew low, thudding into the kitchen counter and bouncing to rest, the other two went high, crashing through the glass cabinets and shattering dozens of glasses in an explosion of noise. One fell, onto the counter top, the other remaining lodged in the wall cabinet. Half the kitchen was now draped in what looked like a giant damaged cobweb. The net was useless. Its target was now climbing all over Travis's head, trying to wreak havoc on his helmet with tiny but razor-sharp claws.

Travis reached up with his free hand to grab the thing, to try and pull it off him. His hand closed around the tail and he felt a fire in his palm as a set of serrated, modified scales ripped into his skin. He felt warm moisture in his hand and knew it was his own blood. Ignoring the pain, Travis yanked the thing off him and threw it by its tail across the room, sending it crashing into the hanging pots and pans, the creature then dropping onto the island and upending the glass bowl, sending pancake batter everywhere.

"Visor," Travis said again, and the black eye cover slid up and away, back into the helmet. Travis didn't care for the visor any more. The electrical interference from the building and the other assembled appliances in the kitchen made it as good as useless to him.

The alien righted itself on the kitchen island with an agility that suggested it had not been hurt by its fall. Tiny clawed feet scrabbled for some kind of purchase on the marble counter top, and a small pair of wings, thus far folded back against the body, flapped to give the creature its balance as it made to renew its attack on Travis. Travis brought up his gun quickly and the creature thought better of it, giving an impressive show of teeth before diving off to the right just as the weapon chugged into life.

The can of pancake mix erupted as stray bullets tore into it, obscuring everything in the room and blinding Travis. His eyes watered and blinked involuntarily, irritated by the dust that clouded in the kitchen. He could barely keep them open.

Travis could hear the alien at the far end of the kitchen. He could hear its raspy breathing and the occasional crunch of broken glass or china as it shifted around. He had no idea what it was doing; whether it was having similar difficulties or whether it was just biding its time, waiting, literally, for the dust to settle.

"Where is it?" Travis said. A minute ago he had mocked her. Now he was totally reliant on her. There was no answer. "Where is it?" He tried to blink away the pain in his eyes.

"Hang on! Give me a minute!"

"I don't have a minute!"

There was a pause and then she said, "Far corner, beneath the table. I sense fear. It's afraid. It's hiding."

Travis fumbled blindly for the edge of the island, found it and then used it to guide himself around the left side of the kitchen, shattered glass crunching underfoot. Reaching the opposite corner of the island, he raised his gun to point it at the corner table, struggling to see it through squinting, burning eyes, and then he strafed the whole area with a hail of bullets. "What now? What do you sense now?"

"Nothing," she said quietly. "It's gone." She sounded almost sad.

Travis let the gun drop, slumped his shoulders and sighed. He felt his way around the corner and to the bathroom door, opened it and entered, then blindly filled the basin with water and began to bathe his eyes.

Cupping a last handful of water to his face, Travis peered above his hands and looked at his reflection in the mirror. His helmet and fatigues were covered in a fine yellow dust of pancake mix. The same dust clung to his stubble and gave him a somewhat elderly look. Water streaked his face and his eyes looked sore and were rimmed with red. Considering he'd only been up for a few hours, he looked like shit.

He examined the palm of his hand. The wound was deep but clean. It wasn't bleeding much but it hurt like hell. He should probably go find out what had attacked him. He might need some anti-venom.

Travis walked back into the kitchen. It was hard to believe it was the same place he'd looked at just minutes before. There was a sickly smell in the air, like something sweet had just started to burn. The merger of pancake mix and weapons discharge wasn't a pleasant combination. There wasn't a single intact pane of glass in any cabinet in the room. In addition to that, there weren't any surviving glasses either. Fragments of glass and china were everywhere and a fine yellow dust shrouded everything.

In the corner, the table and chairs were riddled with holes. Beneath them, what was left of a limleng lay in a pool of its own blood, the small, leathery wings on its back splayed awkwardly under the body. Limlengs weren't poisonous, but they were vicious when cornered. Travis was sorry he had to find out the hard way. He'd fully intended to catch it, but he'd been given no choice. He checked his wounded hand again. He'd just have to go and get a shot and make sure it didn't get infected.

Travis left the kitchen and headed toward the first room where the woman waited. As he approached, he could already hear her unlocking the door. She stepped out into the hallway and seemed to look straight through him. "Thank you," she said.

"I wouldn't thank me if I were you, you haven't seen what I did to your kitchen. Anyway, I should thank you. I was wrong to doubt you. Miss…?"

"Swift. Helen Swift. And what should I call you?"

"Travis…Jacks." He offered her his free hand, then remembered it was badly cut and withdrew it, but she never acknowledged it and continued to gaze with indifference as if looking at something far beyond him. He brought his hand up again, and waved it slowly past her face. She didn't flinch. She didn't even blink.

"Yes, Mister Jacks, I'm blind."

Travis pulled his hand back quickly, embarrassed. "But how…?"

"It means my other senses are more acute. I'm more attuned to my environment. These things of yours, Mister Jacks…"

"Please. It's Travis."

"Travis, some of these things are sentient beings. They are intelligent. They have thoughts and feelings and emotions, not like human thoughts and feelings, but…comparable."

"Is that why you were sad that it had to be killed?"

"Yes. And so were you. I sensed that from you. You have a respect for these creatures too."

Travis nodded.

"It's hard to explain, but I can feel their presence, just as easily as I sense your confusion right now, your fear."

"I'm not afraid," Travis protested too quickly.

She smiled at his pride. "But you are, and that's okay. It's okay to fear what you don't understand."

Travis looked at her for a moment. She was an enigma. On the outside she looked as delicate and fragile as one of the figurines that had stood in the kitchen, yet she had used her disability to develop a great gift and an inner strength that was palpable. It was ironic that he should feel totally exposed in front of a blind woman.

"Helen. Would you mind coming with me? There's someone I'd like you to meet."

CHAPTER 5

They hadn't spoken much on the ride back. The engine of the hover vehicle hummed quietly and gave them both a sense of peace and normality after everything that had just happened. Besides, Travis had no idea what to say to her. He felt guilty that he had doubted her. She had probably been doubted her whole life, doubted by people who had immediately made assumptions based on her obvious lack of sight. His guilt was compounded by his newly found knowledge of her heightened awareness. The fact that she could doubtless sense his discomfort made him more uneasy in her presence.

He turned a corner and straightened the HV, looking across at her to check that she was all right. She sat with her elbow on the door handle, her hand curled under her chin, supporting her head as she appeared to gaze out of the virtual window.

Travis had to admit she was pretty. Her neat, brown, bobbed hair curled slightly towards her neck and framed her face perfectly. Above the cuff of her blouse, her slender forearm rose to a delicate wrist and hand, the pale skin giving her an ethereal quality. Her thin fingers drooped from her hand like the first buds of spring and Travis wondered what it would be like to feel their touch. As he looked at her a smile touched the corner of Helen's lips and he brought himself up short, wondering if she was reading his mind at that precise moment.

"You needn't worry," she said.

"About what?" he said, defensively.

"Feeling guilty. You're not the first person to misjudge me and I'm sure you won't be the last. I don't hold it against you."

Travis said nothing for a moment, then attempted to steer the conversation on. "I couldn't help noticing that you had some pretty nice stuff in your wardrobe." He glanced across at her once more. She was dressed immaculately.

"What do you mean?"

"Well, you had some really pretty clothes."

"And that surprises you, does it?"

"Well…yeah," Travis began. "I mean…well…it's…well…it's not something I'd expect." He was floundering now and wishing he had never opened his mouth. Just his insinuation, he realized, was insulting, and Helen was insulted.

She turned towards him, her eyes not falling on him but looking somewhere out in space. "Mister Jacks…"

"Please, it's Travis."

"Mister Jacks," she said again, not allowing him to disarm her so easily, "Just because I'm blind doesn't mean that I don't take pride in my appearance, or keep my apartment clean, or do anything differently from you. I am exactly like you, or anyone else for that matter. I'm just blind. That's all."

Travis hung his head, ashamed of himself. This wasn't going well at all.

"A moment ago you were feeling guilty because you had misjudged me. Then you just went and did exactly the same thing again."

"I know. I'm sorry. That was a dumb thing to say."

"What is it? What's bothering you?"

Travis didn't want to admit it for fear of offending her again. "I've just never been around a blind person before, I guess. I don't know what to say to you or how to help you."

"You want to help me?"

"Yes."

"Well then the best thing you can do is drop all your preconceived ideas and notions of how a blind person should be. Then we can move forward."

"Okay."

She remained facing him for a moment, as if ascertaining for herself whether he was going to be true to his word and then, seemingly satisfied; she adopted her previous position and appeared to gaze out of the virtual window again. Silence returned between the two of them.

After a moment Travis spoke up again. "Anyway, you're not like anyone else."

"How's that?"

"You have a talent." Travis said. "A pretty freaky one at that." He looked over at her once more and she was smiling.

* * * * *

Wyatt looked up at the bank of five monitors suspended from the ceiling. Two of the news networks were now covering a story about a suspicious light aircraft crash about five miles south of O'Hare skyport. Could it have anything to do with their situation? Wyatt thought about it. There were certainly creatures that could have covered that distance in the time that had elapsed since the zoo's systems failed. He looked away from the screens and shook his head to rid himself of the images. He didn't want to think about it.

He cast his attention once more to the city map. The large pulsating dot seemed to be growing frighteningly fast, but now there were new marks on the map. Threads of blue were starting to form. All along the Wisconsin state line, a solid line of blue could be seen. Similar threads ran between Rockford and Davis Junction, Rochelle and Shabbona Grove, Marseilles and Gardner and Kankakee and Hopkins Park. These were the areas that had been locked down, where the local police departments, Home Guard and Earth Alliance troops had managed to close down all the roads. Soon, hopefully, there would be one confluent circle of blue to enclose the red dot that bled outward at speed. It would have to be soon if they hoped to contain the mantor.

There was another cheer and Wyatt looked toward the large schematic again. Now the yellow section, the southwest quadrant of the zoo, was lit up again. Slowly, the systems were coming live.

"I know what I must do!"

Wyatt looked over at the disturbance. Gruber was stomping his way up the stairs to the upper gallery.

"I'm going to city hall," Gruber announced.

Wyatt looked at him, eyebrows raised in question.

"To make a statement, of course." Gruber explained as if it was obvious. "To put the public at ease. They need to know that we are doing everything possible to ensure their safety. Right now there's been no announcement from the zoo at all. Only the mayor's office."

"That's because no one can get out." Wyatt pointed out to him. "In case you hadn't noticed, it's a free-for-all out there."

Gruber looked at the colored schematic. "Well the systems are coming back up. I'll take my chances. Besides, my HV is parked right outside, and anyway, somebody's got to do the responsible thing," he huffed. "Certainly doesn't look like it's going to be you." It was a cheap shot.

"I'm not employed here, remember?"

Gruber's cheeks flushed with color. He turned on his heel and left. Wyatt gave a curt two-finger salute to his back. "Good luck," he said. "And good riddance," he muttered afterwards.

Wyatt glanced over at the gallery rail. The young cop and the detective were staring at him with bemused looks on their faces, cups that they had been nursing for the last ten minutes still in their hands. "Shouldn't be long now," he said. "The systems are coming back up. We'll get you out of here." The pair nodded solemnly, as if stunned by what they had just seen and then returned their attention to the giant colored wall and all the technology of the room.

* * * * *

Travis was just about to reach for the door to the security building when Gruber burst through on his way out, forcing him to instinctively pull Helen out of the way. "Hey! Easy, sir!" Travis shouted. If Gruber heard him he did not acknowledge him. He simply climbed into his vehicle, started the engine and sped away.

Travis reached for the door again, holding it open with one hand while offering his other arm to Helen. She rested a hand on his forearm. It looked so tiny on the enormous sleeve of his jacket. She seemed so fragile, and yet in the short time that he had known her, he had realized that appearance was deceptive.

* * * * *

Swarovski scanned the ID and looked up into the face of the man brandishing it, scrutinizing him with a squint as if trying to imagine the man in front of him once looking like the mug shot that had appeared on the card reader's screen.

Swarovski and Shady stood in front of the two large doors of the security building's canteen, two lines of people in front of them, queuing up to get their clearance checked. Behind them, a filthy-looking mop slotted through the handles of the two doors barred anyone's exit.

Swarovski nodded once, satisfied, and then indicated with his eyes that the man should go and join the other keepers who were gathered around a handful of tables on one side of the room. He looked at them differently now. He pitied them somewhat, knowing that they had to ride around in those ridiculous carts all day. It was like sacrificing part of your manhood. They'd be here for a while, those guys. They wouldn't be going out into the zoo until all the containment fields were back up and the ULF team had gone through and done a preliminary sweep.

On the other side of the room was a small gathering of men and women—the admin staff that Wyatt would soon be putting to work. They would take them upstairs as soon as they had checked everybody out.

"Excuse me!"

Shady looked up from his reader at the interruption. A small, officious- looking man in a suit and tie was pushing in at the front of the line.

"Wait your turn please, sir," Shady said, a faint hint of anger in his voice. "We'll get to you in good time. We're processing everyone just as fast as we can."

"I can't wait. I *demand* to be seen now."

Shady stared at him for a moment, silently fuming. "As I said, sir, you'll be dealt with in turn."

"I demand to see Wyatt Dorren right now!"

"Who are you?"

"Dwight Goddard!" the man said indignantly, as if Shady should know.

"You got ID?"

"Of course I've got ID!" Goddard huffed and reached into his inside pocket, pulling out a small bar-coded plastic card. He handed it to Shady, who inserted it into the top of his reader. Goddard's details came up on the screen of the small hand held unit. Just from the formatting of the personal information, Shady could tell instantly that Goddard wasn't one of theirs. He wasn't IZP staff.

"Pete, we've got an impostor!"

Goddard's face only had a moment to register surprise before Swarovski's hands were on him and he was being manhandled back into the canteen and away from the doors.

"Hey! What is this? What's the meaning of this!" A moment later Goddard was being intimately acquainted with the surface of a canteen table, one arm locked behind his back.

"Who are you? What do you want?" Swarovski demanded of him.

"I told you who I am," Goddard managed through pain and gritted teeth. "I'm with the mayor's office! Read my ID. It's all there!"

Shady looked at the reader again, then at Swarovski. "He's right. He's from the mayor's office."

"What are you doing here?"

"I'm here to see Wyatt Dorren. He said himself it would be okay for me to come. I thought you'd be expecting me."

"Nope." Swarovski said. "Don't know nothing about you. Never heard of you."

"So what?" Goddard said into the table. "You're going to keep me in an arm lock for the rest of the day?"

Swarovski looked at Shady, who just shrugged, and then he slowly released his grip on Goddard. Goddard pushed himself up from the table and brushed himself down. "Thank you," he said sarcastically as he straightened his tie. Swarovski continued to eye him with suspicion.

"Well. Now that's all sorted out, will you take me to see him?"

"Nope." Swarovski said again. "Not until we've checked everybody in. You'll wait here like everyone else."

Goddard stared at him for a moment, exasperated, then sat down in a huff. This was one argument he wasn't going to win.

Swarovski returned his attention to the room. All eyes looked at him, shock registering on the faces. "Is there anyone else here who shouldn't be here?" he asked.

Everyone shook their heads vehemently.

* * * * *

Travis held open one of the large double doors to the security command center and allowed Helen through. Taking an arm, he steered her towards one of the curved sets of stairs and then gently helped her navigate the flight of steps.

Wyatt looked up at their arrival. *What now?* he thought to himself. Why Travis had brought the woman here was a mystery to him. More to the point, Travis looked a mess.

Travis guided Helen towards the gallery balcony and then took her hand and helped her locate the balcony rail. "Wait here," he said to her. She nodded her understanding. He turned and headed towards Wyatt.

Wyatt watched him approach. "You were supposed to help her. Not bring her back."

"It's complicated." Travis replied, heaving his gun up and putting it down noisily on one end of the table that the city map hovered over.

"What the hell happened to you?"

"Again, a long story," Travis said. "But she was right. She did have one of our aliens in her apartment."

"What was it?"

"A limleng".

"Where is it?"

"It's dead."

"You couldn't catch it?"

Travis held up his hand by way of explanation. An angry, weeping red line crossed his palm. "I tried."

"Oooh." Wyatt winced. "You should get that looked at."

"I will. But I need to talk to you…" Travis glanced over his shoulder at Helen who appeared to be gazing directly at them "… about her."

"What about her?"

Travis swallowed nervously, preparing himself for what he had to tell Wyatt and how ridiculous it sounded. A couple of hours ago he would have dismissed it himself. "She has some skill, Wyatt…some talent. I don't know what you'd call it, but I think she can help."

"Help?" Wyatt looked at her. "Help how?"

"Hear me out, will you? I know it sounds crazy, but she can detect things that you and I can't. She can see where things are. No, not see..." Travis rubbed his forehead, frustrated that he wasn't doing Helen's gift any justice and annoyed at himself for his totally inappropriate choice of word. "She can help us," he said flatly. "I know it."

Wyatt leaned over. "Travis," he said quietly. "You know I have a lot of respect for you." Travis nodded. "But seriously, this is a little too much. I mean, look at her. She's blind."

"But not deaf."

The two men both looked up to see Helen walking towards them.

"Don't you know it's rude to talk about someone behind their back?" she said.

"How...?" Wyatt couldn't fathom it. She must have heard their conversation over all the noise of the room from over twenty feet away.

Helen continued to walk purposefully towards them. "As your associate was trying to explain to you, albeit badly, I am finely attuned to my environment. That in itself is not necessarily a gift, more a necessity—a result of my disability." She was close to the table now and her steps faltered a little, as if her admission of her affliction had suddenly caused it to affect her. She put a hand out low in front of her and searched the air with it, looking for the edge of the table she knew was there. When her hand located it, she stepped closer and then stood straight again, regaining her posture and composure. "However, as I explained to Mister Jacks earlier," she continued. "I do have an ability to detect sentient life forms. Some, in fact most, of your aliens are sentient. I can help you find them."

"She could be useful to us, Wyatt. Our equipment is going to be affected by all kinds of interference out there."

"And in case you're wondering how I knew the table was

there, I can sense where you and Mister Jacks are standing right now. It makes no sense for the two of you to be conducting a conversation and stand so far apart unless there was a physical barrier between the two of you."

"Lucky guess, then?" Wyatt asked.

"You could think of it that way." She smiled at Wyatt's skepticism. "I like to regard it as an educated assumption based on years of experience."

Just then a steady stream of people began ascending the stairs to the upper gallery. Bringing up the rear were Swarovski and Shady, Swarovski manhandling up the steps a smaller man who occasionally turned to protest at his treatment.

Helen never turned toward the interruption, just continued to stare at Wyatt with her unseeing eyes. "Getting a little crowded in here, isn't it?" she asked.

Wyatt looked at Travis. "See?" Travis said, indicating Helen with his hands. "See?"

Swarovski approached the three of them, then shoved his charge forward with such force that it looked like he had just belched the other man up. The smaller man straightened his suit and gave Swarovski a disapproving glance over his shoulder.

"Mister Dorren?" he asked, extending a hand. "Wyatt.... Dorren?"

"That's me," Wyatt said, shaking the hand and eyeing the other man suspiciously. "And you are?"

"Dwight Goddard. From the mayor's office."

"Oh," Wyatt said. "I see. I can assure you, Mister Goddard, that we are doing everything in our power to bring this situation under control."

"Whoa! Easy!" Goddard said, attempting humor. "I'm not here to judge you, Mister Dorren. I am here on behalf of the mayor to offer you our help."

"Help? What kind of help?"

"Well, I'm sure you're aware of the need to deal with this

situation swiftly. The sooner the escaped exhibits are captured, the sooner Chicago's populace is safe and everyone is happy again."

"That goes without saying. What are you suggesting?"

"Well, a swift response requires bodies on the ground. We can help you with personnel. Put some more feet on the street."

Wyatt laughed. "I appreciate the offer, but it's not as easy as that. The ULF trappers here at the zoo are highly trained to deal with the alien exhibits. It's not something just anybody can do."

"I know that, Mister Dorren…may I call you Wyatt?" Goddard smiled but didn't wait for an answer. "We know that, Wyatt, which is why the personnel we are offering you are really being volunteered by us."

"What do you mean?"

"Well, let's just say it's a program. One I understand you are familiar with."

"Convicts?" Wyatt asked in disbelief.

"Exactly. Convicts. It will give you more men to deal with the crisis we have on our hands and, well, if one or two get lost along the way, then it's no great loss, is it?"

"Are you crazy?"

"On the contrary. It seems like a perfect solution." Goddard looked at Wyatt as if expecting some kind of recognition. When none was forthcoming he asked, "Is there a problem?"

"Yes, there's a problem," Wyatt began. "Which hare-brained bureaucrat came up with that idea?" Wyatt's temper flared. "Do you not think we have enough chaos on the streets of Chicago right now without setting loose the most dangerous elements of society? What the hell makes you think that they'll even do what you ask? They'll just run." He walked around the table to look Goddard in the eye. "Even if we could control them and use them, you want to send them out onto the streets and arm them with one of these?" Wyatt snatched up Travis's quad-sys gun and brought it around to bear on Goddard.

Goddard stared in alarm down the barrel hanging just inches

below his nose and flinched away. “I…I…Well, I thought it was a good idea.”

“It sucks. Get out of here. Get out of my sight.” Wyatt turned and threw the gun back down on the table with a clatter. Goddard just stood rooted to the spot, the look of absolute shock still on his face.

Wyatt walked back around the table to study the map again, then looked beyond the projection to see Goddard still standing there. “You heard me. Get him the hell out of here!”

Swarovski’s big hands clamped down on Goddard’s shoulders and a look of surprise registered on the smaller man’s features. Swarovski practically picked Goddard up and carried him back towards the stairs and the exit that he was going to be inevitably kicked out of. All around the upper gallery, the assembled people stared at Wyatt in shock.

“What?” he shouted at them.

Lieberwits turned away and returned his attention to the far wall, and the schematic that was nearing completion. He looked down into the lower gallery and could see the ULF staff now getting prepared for the next phase of the operation, all of them in green fatigues donning helmets, packing traps and holstering weapons. Men and women stood around in pairs performing buddy checks on each other.

Lieberwits was glad that he was going to be getting out of there soon. These zoo people were packing enough hardware to start another world war, and based on what he’d seen from the man in charge, they seemed to have pretty short fuses too. It wasn’t a good combination.

He felt under his jacket and located the small plasma pistol in its holster under his left arm, to reassure himself that he had the means to protect himself from anyone or anything that might now be roaming around Chicago’s streets. Instead he just felt wholly inadequate.

In the lower gallery, Chris folded a net and placed it in the side pocket of a backpack. He fastened the quick release clasp over it and gave the back of the pack a friendly pat. "That's it, you're all set."

The owner of the pack turned to face him. "Thanks," Jennifer said.

Jenny DeVreaux was Bobby's team's second medic, along with Chris. A medical student out of California, Jenny had actually moved to Chicago to actively seek a position at the IZP.

There had been a few raised eyebrows at the zoo when Jenny had first been hired and assigned as a medic to the ULF department. She was a small woman and the medic backpacks were significantly larger and heavier than the regular trapper backpacks, solely due to the additional medical supplies and comms equipment they had to carry. But Jenny had never complained. In fact, Chris could barely recall a day when he hadn't seen Jenny with a smile on her face. She just loved the work.

Chris liked Jenny. Along with Bobby, she brought a much-needed element of class and feminine calm to their testosterone-charged squad. She had cool blue eyes and shoulder-length blonde hair that stuck out from under her helmet in tufts. And of course, there was the ever-present smile. Looking at her now, it was hard to believe she was readying herself to walk out into chaos.

Swarovski walked back into the room after getting rid of the mayor's man. He rubbed his hands like he was trying to wipe them clean, as if just touching Goddard had soiled him somehow.

Chris looked around the rest of their squad: Bobby, Shady, McAphee, Delaney, Baducci, Kent, Hernandez, Fairchilds, Hamilton, Javits, Cooke, Radchovek and Mason. All suited and booted. All ready to go. All now looking towards the schematic. A silence descended on the room and for a moment, even the links stopped ringing.

One quadrant of the zoo remained in darkness.

From the corner of his eye, Chris saw Wyatt come to the balcony above him. He stopped there, arms locked out straight in front of him, hands gripping the rail tightly. The tension in the room was manifest.

The final quadrant flickered twice and then lit up as it came online. One final cheer erupted from the security team and the noise of activity returned instantly. It was as if the whole room had exhaled as one.

"Okay, roll call and comms check," Bobby shouted. Each member of the squad spoke their name into their helmet's built-in link. Satisfied, Bobby looked up at Wyatt. "You copy?"

He nodded. "Copy."

Wyatt looked over to Lieberwits and Wood. "You two. Go with these guys. They'll escort you to your vehicle and then to the staff entrance. You're getting out of here."

Lieberwits nodded and approached Wyatt. "We'll be in touch if we find out anything. We'll catch whoever did this."

Wyatt shook his hand. "Yeah, and we'll catch everything else."

Lieberwits smiled, then descended the stairs with Wood in tow.

Wyatt looked over the balcony once more at the ULF team. "Okay, ladies," he began, "And ladies," he said again, looking at Bobby and Jenny. "Let's get this show on the road."

CHAPTER 6

Wood's black and white patroller cruised down the service road flanked by the sixteen members of the ULF team. From inside, the only sound Wood and Lieberwits could hear over the quiet hum of the engine was the *clump-clump* of the squad's boots as they double-timed it along the paved road. Lieberwits glanced out of the passenger's virtual window at the man dressed all in green fatigues marching next to the vehicle. He was a big man, not only tall but clearly muscular beneath the loose fitting jacket and pants. Underneath his helmet and visor, what was visible of his face wore an expression of grim determination. As he ran, he carried his large weapon across his chest, left hand supporting the barrel up near his left shoulder, right hand gripping the butt, forefinger coiled loosely over the trigger, thumb ready to flick off the safety catch.

It was really only now, looking at the team of men and women escorting them along the road, that the full gravity of the situation hit Lieberwits. In the control room, surrounded by technology that he never hoped to understand, the whole episode had seemed somewhat surreal, described in flashing lights and multi-colored displays. But now, watching these men and women with their packs and their weapons, the seriousness of it hit home. Everything had been defined in terms that he now understood. People on the street with weapons. That was a language that Lieberwits knew well and it was never good. These people carried some of the largest guns he had ever seen outside of the military and that made his stomach clench involuntarily. Strangely, only now did he begin to wonder about the nature of the aliens that had been let loose into the city. He found that it scared him.

Wood brought the vehicle to a sudden halt, interrupting Lieberwits's train of thought. A woman from the ULF squad, the one they called Bobby, gave orders to two of the others, who nodded once and ran up the grassy incline next to them. Once they reached the crest of the rise, they squatted and brought their guns up in readiness. Satisfied that her lookouts were set, Bobby approached the vehicle and rapped on the virtual window next to Lieberwits's head. Wood obliged her by pressing a button on his armrest console and cracking Lieberwits's window open an inch.

"This is as far as we go with you," she said, "Once you get beyond the gatehouse you're on your own."

Lieberwits nodded. "Thanks."

Bobby acknowledged the gratitude with a nod. "You should be safe as long as you stay inside your car. If you do happen to see anything, don't get out of the car, don't try and do anything, just call it in and we'll handle it. Okay?"

"You got it." Lieberwits forced a smile. The virtual window closed and the vehicle slowly pulled away, passed by the gatehouse and disappeared out of sight.

Bobby returned her attention to the ULF squad. They huddled around her.

"Okay. I'm splitting us up into two teams of eight. One team takes the southwest quadrant, the rest will come with me, skirt the southern perimeter wall and then move north through the southeast quadrant.

"Swarovski. You're in charge of the second team. Take Shady and Jenny, Delaney, Baducci and Cookie and the other two on the hill. Hold your position until we're set and then we'll move in unison through the park."

Swarovski nodded, acknowledging his charge.

"The rest of you are with me. Remember guys, the name of the game is containment. You come across anything big, don't try and be heroes. Call it in and we'll come help. Other than that, do what you have to do to protect yourselves."

The insinuation was clear. Swarovski flicked the safety catch of his weapon off in response. Bobby caught it and shot him a look but Swarovski's visor was already down and she could not see his eyes behind the tinted glass.

"Sorry," he said. "But I don't want to be caught with my pants down again."

Bobby nodded. Swarovski was difficult to read sometimes, but he wouldn't do anything foolish or impulsive. She took a last look around the assembled faces. "Okay, people, let's move."

* * * * *

Wood pulled the black and white up next to Lieberwits's parked HV.

"What are you going to do now?" Lieberwits asked.

"Are you kidding me?" Wood looked at him with surprise. "I'm going home to bed. I've been up thirty-two hours now. I'm getting me some sleep."

"Okay."

"How 'bout you?"

"I'm going to go back to the station. There's a few people I want to look up. I can use the database there."

"You can't do that on your wrist unit?"

"What wrist unit?"

"Jeez. What do we need to do to drag you into this century? I'm surprised they haven't kicked you off the force."

"Not yet, sonny."

"Yeah, I noticed. How come?"

"'Cause I'm good." Lieberwits gave a wry grin. "The old dog's got some life in him yet." Lieberwits peered out of the virtual windshield. "You think it's safe out there?"

Wood shrugged, past caring. "What's safe anymore?"

Lieberwits gave him a sideways look, "Gee, thanks. That's reassuring."

Wood took a look around, taking the question more seriously. "Dunno. But I don't see anything out there. You've got a plasma pistol though, right? Tell me that you at least carry a gun."

"Yeah. I may be old school, but I'm not stupid."

"Thank God," Wood sighed.

"Okay. How do I get hold of you later?"

"Just call into the police network and ask for me, they'll have it patched through to my com-link."

"Okay. I'll do that. I'll let you know what I find out."

"Good luck." Wood said.

"Good night," Lieberwits replied.

Wood looked outside again. It was broad daylight. "Yeah. Something like that."

Lieberwits raised the door and then bolted for his own vehicle.

* * * * *

Swarovski was crouched motionless on the top of the rise, looking stoically back into the zoo. There had been nothing immediately visible in the twenty minutes since he and his team had fanned out along the ridge, but thermal imaging cameras had detected movement off in the distance. Swarovski looked to his right and left, seeing the seven people in his charge, all of them showing the same, measured composure. He trusted every one of them with his life.

The voice in his headset startled him. It was Bobby. "Swarovski. You copy?"

"Roger. You're loud and clear. You guys in position?"

"Roger."

"Anything interesting happen along the way?"

"So far, so good. All clear. Is your team ready to go?"

"Roger. We're all set."

"Okay. Overlapping formation as we discussed. Wyatt, you copy?"

In the security control room, Wyatt adjusted his headset. "I read you, Bobby. Let's keep it tight out there."

"Roger that."

Bobby looked back at her team of eight lined up in single file behind her. Chris brought up the rear. She signaled to them that they were ready to go and nodded to Chris, who peeled off the back, ran past her and set himself twenty feet in front of her. Mason then followed suit, positioning himself twenty feet in front of Chris, setting himself, gun raised and scanning the surroundings, providing cover for the next team member running quietly to the front of their line. And so it went on. Quietly they progressed into the park. Across the zoo, in the southwest quadrant, Swarovski and his team were doing the same.

* * * * *

Lieberwits exited the elevator on the fifth floor of the downtown police headquarters and headed for his office. He had barely gone twenty paces when a voice boomed out over the entire floor.

"Lieberwits! Get in here. Now!"

That was the thing with Captain Harrod. Nothing got past him. Literally.

"Cap?" Lieberwits poked his head around the door of Harrod's office and feigned innocence.

Harrod never looked up from his desk interface. "Come in. Close the door behind you. Take a seat."

He did as he was asked, then sat in silence as Harrod continued with his work. He knew what was coming. Harrod was just making him sweat a bit. Harrod had been on the force since before most of the division were born. He knew the methods that worked on the perps. No reason not to apply them to his own staff. After all, they were all human, it was just psychology.

Lieberwits watched him from across the desk. Harrod was a short, stocky man with a full head of silver-gray hair. Despite his stature, he wore his authority like a badge. Even sitting behind his desk he seemed to be omnipresent in his office, some would say in the entire department.

Harrod finished typing and paused for a moment, either to make sure his work was done or preparing himself for what was coming next, before leaning back in his chair. Lieberwits couldn't help noticing, as always, that Harrod's uniform looked a size too small. He'd always wondered whether that was just the Captain being unable to accept that the years behind a desk had not been kind to him or whether it was the dogged aggressiveness that had got Harrod to the top, now bottled up and physically manifesting itself, looking for some kind of release.

Harrod's stomach struggled against the buttons on his tunic. As if conscious of it, he laid his hands over his belly, clasping his fingers together and allowing his free thumbs to tap an unheard rhythm. He sighed, once, loudly, then pursed his lips as if deep in thought before speaking.

"What the hell is going on here?"

"I..."

"When I left here last night," Harrod cut him off. "All was good in the world. Kids were going home with their parents. People were getting home from work. Everyone slept safely in their beds.

"This morning I come in to this!" Harrod gestured to the large flat holo-screen that projected in the corner of his office. Lieberwits glanced at it. The sound was muted but a news anchor was clearly covering a story about the IZP, a picture of the main gates of the zoo behind her.

"I wake up to find my city is being overrun by lethal aliens!"

Funny how now there was a crisis everyone was staking their

claim on the city, Lieberwits thought. Most people pointed fingers or wanted nothing to do with the city's problems. Now there was a great opportunity to be the hero of the hour and score some political hit points.

"You wanna hear it?" Harrod's façade of calm control was slowly eroding away. Lieberwits shook his head. "No, seriously. You wanna hear it?"

Lieberwits shook his head again. "I know what it's about."

"I know you know," Harrod snapped, slamming his hand down on the desk. "You know why I know you know? Because when I got the alert from Central this morning and told them to put someone on it, they informed me that we already had somebody on it, and when I asked who that somebody was they told me Detective Superintendent Ed Lieberwits."

Harrod slumped back in his chair. "Detective Superintendent Ed Lieberwits," he said again slowly, regarding Lieberwits coolly, as if confirming that the very same sat before him. "Mind telling me how you managed to end up at the IZP at oh-six-hundred this morning?"

"Look, Cap," Lieberwits began. "It was a fluke. I got called out to a suspected double homicide. Turns out it was an animal attack but unlike anything anyone had ever seen before. It was that, that led me to the zoo."

Harrod regarded him through narrowed eyes, as if trying to detect a lie, but found no deception in the words. Lieberwits was a good guy. He knew it. He saw a lot of himself in the other man, although he would never admit it to him. But he also knew that Lieberwits had another agenda as far as the IZP was concerned. "Bit too much of a coincidence that this should land right in your lap, isn't it?"

Lieberwits knew better than to play Harrod for a fool. He shrugged.

"Everyone knows you've got that case file, you know?" Harrod continued, "From what went on there before."

He sighed. "Only reason you haven't been hauled over the coals for it is because nobody else can be bothered to hunt through the rest of the crap in your office to find it—and besides, you're the only person around here that deals in paperwork anymore. So what is it, Lieberwits? What is it that's got you so interested in the place?"

"There's history there, Cap." Lieberwits said. "What if these two things are somehow connected? I'd be the best person on the case."

Harrod raised his eyebrows. Maybe Lieberwits was right.

"I was the first detective on the scene at the last incident," Lieberwits continued. "And by coincidence I was the first one there again this time."

"What? You're telling me this was fated?" Harrod asked, a hint of amusement in his voice.

Lieberwits shrugged. "Maybe."

Harrod laughed out loud. "Give me a break."

"You asked me what interests me about the place?" Lieberwits's tone sobered Harrod quickly. "I'll tell you. Nothing. There's nothing about the place that interests me. But I'll tell you what does interest me. The truth. That's why I became a cop."

"You don't think the investigation uncovered the truth?"

"Absolutely not!" Lieberwits said angrily. "The whole thing was a whitewash."

"But it was, what, five, six years ago now?" Harrod asked.

"I know what I saw there, and the report didn't match up with what I saw."

"Most people would have been glad not to have had to deal with it and yet you went after it like a terrier. Still do, in fact."

"Because of something like this. If we don't know the truth about what happened then, and these things are connected, how many possible leads are we going to miss?"

The two men sat in silence for a moment, regarding each other across the desk and contemplating one another's words. Lieberwits broke the deadlock. "You have to let me take it, Cap. I know the history. I'm the best man to find out if something was, maybe still is, going on there. Besides, I'm a damn good cop, and you know it."

Harrod rubbed his chin with a hand. Thoughtful. "All right," he said finally. "You can stay on the case."

"Thank you, Captain." Lieberwits was already rising out of his chair.

"But Lieberwits…" Harrod stopped him, his voice stern. "…if I so much as get a glimpse of your ugly mug on television or your investigation brings my police department under any kind of scrutiny or disgrace, I'll come down so hard on your sorry ass you'll wish you'd never been born."

Lieberwits acknowledged that he'd understood with a nod, turned and exited Harrod's office.

* * * * *

The old gashok turned the corner and limped into the alleyway. He was lucky to have escaped with his life.

Initially, he had fled the zoo, chased by the pack that for years he had led and many of which he had sired. He did not feel the pain from his injury then, the adrenaline coursing through his system had numbed the hurt, but he knew that he was wounded and he knew that the others knew it too. The younger males had immediately sensed his weakness; smelled his blood on the air—and seen the opportunity to seize power for themselves.

He knew if he could run for long enough that he would be safe. The chasing pack would care less about usurping the old leader, clearly wounded, failing and soon to be outcast, and would turn their attention to establishing the new order. The infighting would begin and he would be forgotten and more importantly, safe.

He had bounded along on all four legs as best he could, aided by fear and his body's natural pain relief until the interest in him had waned. But now, in this side alley, with the adrenaline gone and nothing but pain replacing it, the Gashok knew that its injury was severe and potentially life threatening.

The gashok hopped forward with its right front leg. The left leg was useless and lifted off the ground to protect the injured limb. The paw curled back rigid, set against the pain. Blood oozed from the gashok's ruined shoulder, and now the occasional drop fell from the soaked fur around the injured area. The bullet had torn through its shoulder blade, shattering the bony plate and tearing open a gaping exit wound as it had deflected off the bone and out of the animal's back.

The gashok gingerly laid itself down between two large, wheeled trash containers, whimpering slightly as the injured limb touched the ground. It licked its wound, doing the only thing it knew how to do. The wound could be cleaned, but it was never going to heal.

As it lay there in the alley, trying to fight the pain, the old gashok slowly became aware of a scent on the air. A foreign smell, unlike any odor it had encountered before. Regardless, the aroma on the air caused the creature's stomach to tighten and its mouth to salivate. It had been a long time since the gashok had eaten and with a struggle it raised itself back onto its feet and moved to investigate the smell that was carried on the air from farther down the alley.

The old gashok was hungry. Only now he was wounded, and that made him infinitely more dangerous than before.

* * * * *

"Got it!"

Wyatt heard the voice of Zacharias "Zee" Kent in his headset, now the point man in Bobby's squad. "Good work, Zee!"

"Thank you, sir."

The two squads slowly working their way into the zoo had

bagged a few of the escaped exhibits, but they were small, slow-moving aliens, probably as bemused at being outside of their enclosures as the humans that were now finding them.

"Hey. This guy was small fry. Easy."

"Yeah, well just because we're playing at home, don't get complacent out there. All of you should be treating it like a proper day in the field. In fact, more so. Outside of their home worlds, we have no idea how our exhibits are going to behave, where they're going to hide, what they're going to do. Chances are they're going to be afraid and that means you need to be especially careful."

"Well it doesn't look like anything big that escaped is still here in the zoo." Zee replied.

"Not yet anyway," Wyatt corrected him. "You still have a lot of ground to cover."

Wyatt looked up at his schematic of the city. Zee's observations, whilst they were hardly surprising, were troubling. The insinuation was that most of the larger, faster, and almost by default, more dangerous aliens were outside the zoo's perimeter and disappearing into the city.

Behind him, what had begun as occasional trills was now a constant ringing as the com links became hot with incoming calls of sightings. Wyatt turned to look at the team of admin staff manning the links, taking the information and logging the sightings which then appeared as yellow dots on Wyatt's hovering map, pustules on an already wounded city.

For a moment he felt panic rising within him. He was daunted by the almost impossible task his few friends faced, and horrified at the danger the public was being exposed to.

Below him, in the lower gallery, Travis was briefing his team of rookies, telling them as much as Wyatt could tell him. Wyatt hadn't dispatched them yet for two reasons; one—he wanted to make sure the zoo itself was secure and; two—he wanted to know where the real dangers were in the city. They might be a team of rookies but they were sixteen strong and his veterans would mostly be working as two teams of eight as they had elected to do for the sweep.

A range of emotions showed on the rookies' faces. Some were clearly eager to get out there and put into practice what little they had learned. Others looked scared, not ready for the challenges ahead, and a few had the same look of horror and revulsion that Wyatt had first felt when he had heard the news and which now rose again like bile inside of him. A voice interrupted his thoughts.

"Sir?" It was one of the link operators.

"Huh?"

"Sir, I have a call for you."

"Okay. Put it through." Wyatt heard his link click as the line got switched. "Hello?"

"Hi."

"Kate?" Her call could not have been timelier. It was the friendliest voice he had heard all day. He reached down and activated the wrist unit of his link, seeing Kate's face fill its small screen. His foreboding gave way to relief on seeing her. "How are you doing?"

"Er, I think it's me that asks that question, isn't it?"

Wyatt smiled. "It's already been a long day."

Kate smiled sympathetically. "What's the situation there?"

"Well, we have all of the zoo's systems back up. Bobby and Chris and the rest of the guys are just going through the zoo now to recapture anything they can find within the grounds and to get an idea of what's still here and what's loose. Other than that, nobody's really gone anywhere."

"It doesn't sound good on the news."

"Haven't you noticed, nothing ever sounds good on the news?"

"Have you eaten?"

"Not really."

"Wyatt!" She chastised him.

"There are some replicators somewhere in this building, but you know what it's like, never tastes as good as the real thing."

She nodded. "No takeout pizza then?"

"Nah. I'm too afraid the delivery guy would end up as an extra topping. I don't want to pay for that."

Kate laughed out loud. Wyatt smiled at seeing her happy again. "How do you do that?" she asked.

"Do what?"

"Make me laugh when things are so miserable."

"Divine wit, or years of practice. One or the other."

Kate smiled again. "Listen. I was thinking, I'd like to get Alex out of the city. Maybe take him to my parents' place until this whole thing blows over. What do you think?"

"It's a good idea," Wyatt said, "But I want you to be safe and it's not safe right now." He returned his attention to the map. A solid blue line now encircled the red blot on the city. The police and the military had done a great job at deploying their forces. The perimeter they had set up was large and encompassed many suburbs outside the city, but it looked like they had the city contained. Now they would begin to close the net and as they moved in, so the communities they swept through would be granted the right to go about their business as normal. "It's a matter of time, though." Wyatt added. "I'll call you when I think it's okay for you to move. Even then, you may have to take a bit of a detour to get over to your folks."

Kate nodded. "Okay, then."

"Okay. Listen. I gotta go. There's a lot going on here, I just can't...."

"I know. I get it. I didn't mean to disturb you. Just wanted to let you know what I was thinking."

"Okay. Love you."

"Love you too. Be careful."

"I will be. Like I said, I'll call you later."

"Okay. Bye."

"Bye."

Kate's image disappeared and Wyatt let his hand fall. He

paused for a moment, trying to hold on to the conversation, maintain a grasp on normality, and then with a sigh, he returned to the table, casting his eyes over the streets and suburbs of Chicago, knowing that what was described so easily before him in shape and color was in fact the beginning of chaos on the city's streets.

* * * * *

There was one thing missing from Wyatt's map. In truth there were many things missing from Wyatt's map—they were also missing from the zoo. But there was one yellow dot that Wyatt was desperate to see which still hadn't been called in. It was the absence of this particular yellow dot that was keeping Wyatt from sending out Travis and his team. The mantor.

The fact was that the mantor had been seen, the sighting just had not been reported. Grace Watkins had been in her bathroom rifling through her medicine cabinet to assemble the cocktail of medicaments that enabled her old and frail body to continue, when something heavy had landed on the fire escape outside the bathroom window, causing her to start. With a shaking hand, she had managed to close the mirrored door of the cabinet. Even before she forced herself to look towards the window she was aware of a presence. A silhouette blocked the light that normally streamed through the window at this time of day and cast shadows across the small room.

Grace looked towards the form and her breath caught in her throat. She had no words to describe the thing outside. A creature unlike anything she had seen before. A creature that snapped and snarled just beyond her window.

She had the briefest of moments when she thought to herself that she would never forget those rabid, burning yellow eyes and then that thought was erased as intense pain seared through her chest and down her left arm causing her another sharp intake of breath.

Her world seemed to slow then, her head turning as she sought something to grab for she knew she was falling. She watched her hand swipe feebly for the faucets on the small basin, but she missed and sent four open bottles of pills scattering over the tiled floor. Moments later Grace too was lying on the floor, struggling for breath as the heart attack raked her body with spasms of pain. Finally she lay still.

Ironically, despite all of her ailments, Grace Watkins had never had a weak heart.

* * * * *

Lieberwits walked into his office and threw his hat over the old coat stand that occupied the corner behind his desk. "Screen. News channel five," Lieberwits said, and just as in Harrod's office, a flat panel holo-screen flickered into life in the corner. Lieberwits liked some background noise as he thought and worked and news channel five was good at getting the scoop on most news stories before anyone else.

As usual, Lieberwits's desk was buried in a mountain of paperwork. Loose leaves of paper and piles of manila folders full to capacity and threatening to snap hopelessly inadequate rubber bands bound around them.

Like most people, Lieberwits had his own filing system. Sometimes it worked, sometimes it didn't, but today he knew exactly where the file he was looking for was. He hadn't opened it in a while, but this particular manila folder had been somewhere on his desk for the past few years. Lieberwits pulled the folder out from under its stack, making a lunge to stop the five others on top from spilling over. Satisfied that everything was once again strategically balanced, he flopped the folder down on the center of his desk and cast his eyes over the case number printed in bold black. It was a number he knew well.

Five years ago Lieberwits had been called out to a shooting at the IZP. The case had been strange for a number of reasons. Firstly, shootings on private properties such as the IZP were rare; secondly, the weapon used at the scene was an old 22nd century, six cylinder revolver—almost an antique; and thirdly, the incident had involved two people of senior rank, Douglas Mannheim, the managing director of the IZP at the time and a General Kurt Leonardson, head of the Continuing Search for Extraterrestrial Intelligence or CSETI.

The case had been closed. Billed as murder/suicide. Mannheim had been found slumped over his desk, half his head blown away by a supposedly self-inflicted gunshot wound. Leonardson had been found sprawled on rocks below Mannheim's office, having supposedly fallen through the office window after reeling from a single bullet strike to the shoulder. But what Lieberwits had seen at the scene of the crime made no sense in light of the report's findings. For starters, there were spots of blood on the carpet in Mannheim's office that due to their shape and size had to have come from a bleeding, dripping wound. Those same blood spots had been typed and matched to Leonardson. Leonardson could not have been reeling and flailing, according to the case file. Also, if Leonardson's wound had been fatal, he would have dropped and died where he stood. He would never have made it as far as the windows, let alone fallen through them, and they would have found him dead on the floor of Mannheim's office.

For five years now Lieberwits had been devoting all his spare time and energy into joining the dots. Those two men, Mannheim and Leonardson, were connected by something more than just the shootings. There was something unsavory going on at the IZP. He was sure of it.

* * * * *

Wyatt looked at his watch. It was approaching 2:00 PM. They had four more hours of daylight—five at best—after which reacquisition would become much more difficult and many of the aliens would use the cover of darkness to slip deeper into the city and find suburban habitats to their liking.

He returned his attention to the map. He frowned at it, willing the mantor to show itself, when his concentration was interrupted by a familiar, if irritating, voice. Gruber. Wyatt looked up at his bank of monitors. Gruber's face appeared on all of them. He was at city hall, talking to a frenzy of press. Wyatt muted all but one of the screens.

"...and I apologize. What happened this morning at the IZP was totally beyond our control. I can only urge the public to be vigilant and do as I do, which is to put our faith in the excellent ULF teams employed by the zoo, who are, as we speak, deployed and in the process of re-capturing any aliens that have gotten loose from this random act of vandalism."

Teams? *Teams?* At best, Wyatt was working with a team and a half. Where were these teams Gruber was talking about?

His statement obviously over, Gruber then faced a barrage of questions.

"What should people do if they see an alien on the streets?" One reporter asked.

"Just call us at the zoo on the number you see on the screen. Our excellently trained staff will be happy to help you and we'll have somebody there to take care of it as soon as we can. Our ULF personnel are highly trained to deal with these situations, so leave it to us, and you'll be in safe hands."

Wyatt snorted in amusement. Gruber had some gall. He was making them out to be heroes before the finger of blame could be pointed and accuse them of being incompetent fools. They weren't heroes. They were damage limitation and that was the long and the short of it.

"How many aliens are loose?" Another asked.

"Erm, right now we don't have an accurate figure but we believe the impact to have been minimal."

"Huh?" Wyatt couldn't believe what he was hearing.

"Finally, ladies and gentlemen," Gruber continued. "May I suggest, when the zoo re-opens, that you all come by and view our wonderful alien specimens in a *safe*, secure environment?"

Wyatt shook his head in disbelief. Gruber was incorrigible. He was actually using this crisis to drum up some publicity. Wyatt muted the last monitor in disgust.

* * * * *

Lieberwits had just seen the same news report and turned the screen off with an order. For a moment he sat there, trying to digest what he had just heard. If he had been a layman, like Joe Public, he might have bought that whole story, but he had witnessed an alien's handiwork already and he had been there this morning. He had seen every system in the zoo fail and he had heard those very same "highly trained ULF personnel" air their fears in front of him and watched them as they had strapped on enough firepower to bring a small country to its knees. He doubted if the impact of the break-in had been "minimal."

It sounded like bullshit. It smelled like bullshit. And if Lieberwits was sure of one thing: if it sounded like bullshit and smelled like bullshit then it was probably bullshit.

He recalled Gruber's face from the broadcast and committed it to memory. He didn't like these zoo people.

Lieberwits shook his head to rid himself of the thought. Personal feelings didn't answer the question of who had broken into the IZP this morning. If, as he suspected, it had been some alien liberation crazies, then Lieberwits knew a good place to start.

He accessed CORE, the police department's Central Operations and Research Entity, and typed in some search terms. Moments later he was rewarded with a data file and a mug shot. On seeing the familiar face he smiled to himself. Andy Komicki was long overdue for a visit.

CHAPTER 7

The need for quiet had limited the two teams' radio contact and so, despite being aware that they were converging on each other's position, Swarovski's team was startled when Troy Hamilton stepped out from their right and onto the path in front of them.

Instantly all of Swarovski's team dropped to one knee and simultaneously raised their weapons to bear on the figure of Hamilton. He turned to them, arms raised, his gun still in his right hand. "Easy fellas," he said with a disarming smile. "*Homo sapiens.*"

Swarovski let his head drop and breathed a sigh of relief. Behind him, Baducci was not quite so relaxed. "Jesus, Hamilton!" he hissed, through gritted teeth, "You almost got your fucking head blown off."

Hamilton looked at him with raised eyebrows. "Whoa! Whoa! Whoa! Nothing happened. Nobody got hurt. We're all friends, right?" He glanced at Swarovski, then back at Baducci. "Right?"

Baducci went to move towards Hamilton. It was obvious Hamilton's casual indifference to the situation grated on his every nerve, but Swarovski held him back with a hand. "Let it go," he said.

Behind Hamilton, the rest of Bobby's squad stepped out from the adjoining path. Bobby gave Baducci a look, like a mother would a child that should know better, and Baducci reluctantly accepted that he would have to personally deal with his nervous tension rather than unleash it on Hamilton

"All right," Bobby said. "Two quadrants *clear*." She etched quotation marks in the air with her free hand to emphasize such status was potentially only a fleeting thing.

"Now this," Swarovski said, indicating their next objective with a forward jerk of his head.

Bobby turned to see what Swarovski was talking about. In the evening twilight, Reptile Mountain loomed above them, a black peak that, just by its very presence, seemed threatening.

"Looks nicer in the daytime, doesn't it?" Swarovski said. Bobby had to agree. She looked at her watch. Regardless of how long it took to secure the puglions, if indeed they needed securing, when the two teams went north of Reptile Mountain and diverged again into the northeast and northwest quadrants, they would be doing so in the dark. That was not something she was looking forward to. "Come on," she said to everyone. "Let's go."

* * * * *

The old gashok padded unsteadily along the dark alleyway. After evading his old pack, he had fled south and west and now found himself in Chicago's Chinatown district, in an alley behind Wentworth Avenue.

There was very little light here. No fluorescence to punctuate the darkness. No neon green or blue, like that which adorned the windows of the plethora of Chinese restaurants that lined the street, enticing customers in to taste their fare. Instead, the alley was simply home to large, wheeled trash containers and ever-present puddles of water, their contents so stagnant that it seemed even the atmosphere didn't want to claim them back.

There was life here though, amidst the darkness. The occasional movement among the detritus, or a glint of light as tiny eyes looked out from the blackest recesses of the alleyway. However, it was not this that had drawn the gashok farther into the alley. Those eyes and the skittering noises occasionally heard belonged to creatures too small to attract his interest and too fast for him to catch. The rats were already scurrying down the alley away from him, fleeing into the darkness, for they recognized a large predator in their midst.

What little light there was came from the open doors of the kitchens that backed out onto the alley. The sound of utensils against woks and hissing oil was clearly audible, though distant. The smell of Chinese food was heavy in the air.

* * * * *

The chef had just finished chopping his last batch of vegetables and placed the large santoku knife down on the surface next to him. He returned his attention to the wok, tossing its contents with a well-practiced yet casual flick of the wrist. He wiped his hands on his apron and then his brow with the back of a forearm. Theirs was one of the few traditional places on the street - still using the naked flame to cook. The heat of the burners always made the kitchen blisteringly hot and he was grateful for the occasional breeze that wafted in through the back door. He turned his face towards that breeze—and froze.

Coming through the door and down the three steps into the kitchen was a particularly nasty-looking animal. He had heard on the news about the break-in at the zoo, but never in his wildest dreams had he thought that it might affect him—especially here at work. That stuff just happened to somebody else. The old gashok saw him and immediately peeled back its lips in a snarl, a low, guttural growl emanating from its throat.

The chef immediately snatched up his knife, holding it in front of him in a trembling hand as if it were a talisman to ward off the evil that was now approaching. Then his eyes caught the gaping wound in the alien's shoulder and he got his first inkling of what was going on.

He remembered that the few man-eating tigers of his native

Asia were thought to be old, wounded animals striking out at humans because they were easy prey. This creature, too, was clearly a predator. Its impressive display of teeth had already proved that to him and its wound did not make it any less dangerous—and now it was looking for an easy meal.

In an instant he decided that this was a confrontation that he should avoid at all costs. He turned and ran, barreling through the swinging double doors out of the kitchen and, brandishing his knife, screamed all the way through the restaurant.

There was a series of loud crashes from the kitchen and three of the waiters ran to see what had struck such fear into their chef. Flinging open the doors, they had enough time to catch a glimpse of a tail as something ran back into the night, leaving them to survey the rest of the scene.

The kitchen was totally ransacked. The free-standing shelves had all been knocked over, the first tipping into the second and creating a domino effect throughout the kitchen. Now raw ingredients lay scattered all over the floor amidst utensils and pans and bowls. Grains of rice poured from an industrial-sized bag that had been tossed onto one of the surfaces and split, falling in an ever decreasing stream onto the tiled floor with the sound of a light rain, and a single bowl span in a wobbling, circular path, each cycle becoming a smaller and faster version of its predecessor until it finally came to a stop.

The only things missing were three crispy fried duck.

* * * * *

Hernandez placed his back against the wall next to the entrance of Reptile Mountain and snatched a quick glance inside through one of the square windows set in each of the double doors. He panted heavily. The short run to the base of the structure had been hard work with a fully laden pack.

There was nothing beyond the doors except a small antechamber which led into the heart of Reptile Mountain by way of another set of doors. Beyond those was the puglions' enclosure.

If the puglions had gotten free it was unlikely that they would have made it through the inward swinging doors and into the small room; the entryway was designed like that as a safety measure, but better to be safe than sorry. "It's clear," Hernandez said. He felt a collective sigh of relief from the rest of the team lined up behind him.

At the news, the others all peeled themselves off the wall and gathered around.

"What's the plan?" Shady asked, looking at Bobby and Swarovski in turn.

"We need some kind of strategy," Bobby said. "We're not all going to fit in that room with full kit, so we're going to need to stagger our entry."

"What about the door on the north side?" Swarovski asked. There was a second, identical anteroom on the north face of Reptile Mountain, directly opposite from where they stood now. "We could split up again. I'll take my squad over there and we could synchronize our entry."

Bobby pulled a face. "I don't want to do that. To walk around there from here would take maybe twenty minutes." She looked up at the darkening sky. "We don't know what we're going to find inside. It might be a cakewalk, then again, it might not be. Either way, we're going to be heading north in the dark. I don't want to waste time if we don't have to."

Swarovski shrugged.

"But we will split up. One team of eight goes in first, the second group follows."

"What do we do if those things are loose?" Fairchilds asked.

"If they are," Bobby said seriously, "and the containment field is back up, then we've got problems."

The team shared uneasy glances. They understood the implications of Bobby's words.

Reptile Mountain was not only home, but one huge arena for the puglions. Once the team passed through the anteroom, they would find themselves on a walkway that ran the circumference of the huge domed interior to the entry/exit on the north side, but the majority of the inside of Reptile Mountain was dominated by the puglion swamp.

At the center of the swamp, a single column stood which housed the elevators and stairwell that led to the executive offices high above. This was accessible by a sunken walkway that, at the push of a button hidden in the wall, would rise up from the swamp and allow passage to the central column.

An invisible domed containment field protected visitors from the lethal aliens, and the same containment field would adapt and alter its shape to accommodate the walkway and allow safe passage for those crossing the swamp. But the containment field, like most others in the zoo, was non-discriminatory. It would keep the puglions in, but it would also keep anything out. If one, or all, of the puglions had decided to climb out of the swamp while the systems were down and they had remained out when the containment field came back up, then they would effectively be trapped on the walkway—and that was something the team wouldn't know until they walked in there.

"Assuming they are loose," Radchovek began, "What the hell are we going to use to get them back in the swamp? Our splay nets are useless against animals that size and we don't want to shoot them if we can help it."

"I never met an animal that wasn't afraid of fire," Delaney said, matter-of-factly. "Terrestrial or otherwise. Nothing likes fire."

Bobby nodded, confirming Delaney's assertion.

"Flamethrowers it is. Everyone lock your weapons in, and remember, we're not trying to burn these things, just keep them at bay and shepherd them back in to the swamp if we need to. Hold on a minute, though." Bobby spoke into her helmet's built-in com-link. "Wyatt? You copy?"

In the security control room, Wyatt heard Bobby come through on his link. "I hear you, Bobby. What's up?"

"We're about to head in to Reptile Mountain but we need an extra set of eyes. We're blind until we walk in. You guys got any visual on the puglions before we go in there?"

Wyatt looked down into the lower gallery. "Hey you!" he said to a guard manning one of the stations in the long desk. The young man looked up at him. "Is there any way we can pull up the feeds from the cameras in Reptile Mountain?" The guard nodded, then indicated that Wyatt should look up at the wall.

The large schematic of the zoo disappeared and in its place the video feed from one of the small monitors was duplicated in larger scale. The resolution of the picture suffered from being projected in such large dimensions, but it was enough for Wyatt to make out the details, to see a part of the walkway and the swamp that dominated the room.

"Does that thing move?" Wyatt asked. The guard nodded, and to demonstrate, rubbed a finger over his desk interface, panning the camera. Wyatt watched as the scene slid slowly from left to right, The place looked clear, but it was difficult to know otherwise; the puglions weren't performing monkeys, they stayed submerged in the swamp most of the time.

"There!" Wyatt said quickly. There was some motion in the image. "Can you zoom in on that?"

This time the guard did not humor Wyatt with a response, just did as he was asked.

The picture wasn't very clear but there was a swirl in the swamp and then, what was unmistakably the back of a puglion broke the surface. Even at the low resolution Wyatt could see the characteristic bony plates standing up on the exposed back of the scaly creature.

"Bobby, I've got one in the swamp, but that's all I see right now."

"Copy that."

"Give me five minutes. We'll monitor the situation and report back."

"Roger. But we're losing light. We don't have a lot of time."

"I understand that. Stand by."

The guard continued to search the inside of Reptile Mountain. There did not appear to be anything on the visitor walkway, but there was no way of knowing if another of the puglions would show itself in the swamp. After five minutes, Wyatt called Bobby back. "Bobby. We don't see anything else in there. We could wait another half hour and not see anything. What's your appraisal of the situation?"

"We don't have much choice, Wyatt. I say we go. We need to get the zoo secure before we head out into the city. The time we waste here just delays us getting out there."

"Okay," Wyatt said reluctantly. "Just be careful. Stay in contact."

"Just be our eyes." Bobby said.

"Roger."

Bobby turned back to the team. "Okay, we're going in. My team goes in first. Pete, your guys follow us in."

Swarovski nodded.

"Okay. All set?" Bobby scanned the eyes of the entire squad. The looks she got in return told her they were ready for what lay beyond the doors. "Okay, let's go."

Bobby pulled the outer door open and allowed the seven others in her small squad to run in to the anteroom. Once inside they stood sandwiched between the two sets of doors, facing each other, four along each wall.

"You said flamethrowers, right?" Mason asked.

Bobby nodded from across the small room.

There was a small click and then a tiny flame appeared at the muzzle of Mason's raised weapon, the spark that would ignite the liquid fuel visible in the small cylinder mounted on top of the gun.

"That's what I thought," he added with a wry smile. Mason looked at the others. Seven other tiny flames had now joined his own.

"You ready?" Bobby asked.

"As I'll ever be."

"Okay. Let's do it."

Danny Mason kicked open the right-hand door and ran through, his gun held at waist height. He spun left, eyes scanning the visitor walkway. He didn't even get the chance to look right.

A huge clubbed tail caught Mason in the middle of his back, launching him through the air and into the containment field. On contact, the protective barrier crackled and sparked, sending fingers of fluorescent blue arcing across its invisible dome. Repelled by a ferocious amount of force, Mason landed on the walkway in a crumpled heap, groaning and writhing in pain.

Chris had been readying himself to follow Mason in when he heard the thump. Without thinking he barreled through the door to help his teammate and nearly had his head taken off as the puglion's tail swung back towards him.

With lightning-fast reflexes, Chris ducked and threw himself into a break-fall, rolling forward and then righting himself to end in a crouch. The tail missed his head by inches and smashed into the heavy metal door, two bony spikes on the side of the lethal club denting it severely.

Chris fired, sending a plume of flame towards the alien. He squinted against the searing heat. The flame was so intense and bright it seemed to suck all the light from the surroundings. He could hear the puglion shifting and hissing behind the orange wall of fire. "Man down! Man down! Get in here now!" he yelled into his link over the roar of the flame.

Chris released his trigger and the finger of flame evaporated. He blinked quickly, allowing his eyes to adjust to the light and saw the adult puglion on the walkway in front of him. It had turned to face him now, the club tail swinging high above the alien's back, readying itself for another opportunity to strike.

Chris eyed it warily. As if a long snout full of blunt snapping teeth weren't dangerous enough, the tail itself could be lethal—a meaty ball of flesh adorned with four long bony spikes, two jutting out from each side. The alien lunged and snapped at him and despite his better judgment, Chris inched forward. He fired his weapon again, sending another burst of flame in the creature's direction and the puglion backed away.

The door to his right flew open and Bobby and the rest of their team came in.

"It was waiting for us!" Chris shouted to the others. "Mason's hurt bad! Swarovski, get Jenny in here now!"

Outside, Swarovski's team began to pour into the anteroom.

Next to Chris, Javitz fired a second stream of flame toward the puglion, providing the others with cover and forcing the large alien to back away. Now a steady stream of ULF personnel were running into the enclosure. Chris saw Jenny come through the door. "Left! Left! Left!" He shouted at her. "Cookie! Get over here and fill in for me."

Cook ran to Chris and fired his own weapon in the direction of the puglion allowing Chris to drop back.

"Wyatt!" Bobby called through to security. "Wyatt, you gotta get this containment field down."

Wyatt had heard the chaos through his headset and now at the bottom of his screen he could see the clubbed tail, swinging with malicious intent. "What's going on there?" he asked, and then to the security guard "How come we didn't see it?"

The guard looked back at him. "The camera has a blind spot, right below where it's mounted."

"And where's that?"

"Right next to the entryway. Right next to the door."

Wyatt rolled his eyes.

"Never thought it would be an issue before, sir."

"Wyatt!" Bobby's voice came through on his headset again. "We've got one of the adults loose and on the walkway."

Was it possible that the puglion was that intelligent? Wyatt wondered. Could it have known to wait by the doorway for someone coming in? It would have seen thousands of people passing by every day walking in and out of those doors. Had it lain in wait and just gotten lucky by finding the one place the monitor couldn't see it? "Can we take down that field?"

"Sure," said the guard, "You just gotta tell me when."

Wyatt adjusted the microphone on his headset, more out of habit than anything else. "Bobby, we can take that field down, but you've got to give the order. I'm not just going to take it down without your say-so. There are two more of those things in there. I don't need to add to your problems."

"Copy that. Agreed. Stand by."

Chris ran to where Mason lay on the floor, Jenny now crouched beside him. She'd already cut off his pack and was now pulling bandages out of her own. Mason was seriously hurt. The right side of his face and his right hand were badly burnt where he'd been thrown onto the containment field. The skin was already blistering - red and angry. Even more disturbing was the dark stain on his right side and the crimson pool that was slowly spreading out from underneath him. He only needed to look at Chris's face to form his own diagnosis. "Bastard thing got me pretty good, didn't it?" he managed through gritted teeth.

"Save your breath, Mason!" Jenny ordered next to him, cutting away his jacket. "You're gonna need it."

"Wyatt," Chris called through to control, "We're going to need an emergency evacuation from Reptile Mountain, south entrance, ASAP."

"How bad is it?" Mason struggled to lift his head and see his own wounds, his face reddening with the effort.

Jenny knew better than to sugar-coat it. They were all straight talkers. "It's pretty bad. Put it this way, I think your tour of duty is over, soldier."

Mason's entire body slumped as the hope drained out of it. "Godammit! No!" he managed through the pain. He blinked away tears of anger and frustration.

"Hey," Chris said, gently laying a hand on his arm. "Worrying about what might be isn't going to do any of us any good. We just need to get you out of here." Mason nodded, accepting his fate. "Besides," he added with a faint smile, "We can use you on another day."

Behind them there were intermittent roars as Cook, Javitz and now Hernandez fired short bursts of flame towards the agitated puglion, forcing it back. They were keeping it at bay, but Bobby didn't like what she was seeing. The large alien was not even attempting to get back into the swamp.

"Hey guys!" she called, gathering the remaining free members of the squad around her. "We've got a problem."

"No shit." Delaney remarked.

"Hey, if I want sarcasm I'll ask for it!" she snapped. Delaney hung his head. "Problem is, that puglion has learned that it's trapped on the walkway. It's making no move to get back into the swamp. We're not going to get it back in this way."

"What do you suggest?" Hamilton asked.

"I need three guys to go around the other side to box it in. Make the swamp its only option."

"Bobby, that's going to take us a while," Shady said. "I mean, even inside, this is still a big place."

Shady was right. To traipse the entire circumference of the enclosure would take at least ten minutes even if they were double-timing it.

"I don't see we have a choice. I'm not taking this containment field down in the hope that creature figures it out for itself and risk its mate coming out to join us." She looked up to where the puglion snapped angrily at the three other men. "Besides, those guys can hold it off until you get there. We just need them to keep the door clear so we can get Mason out of here. Shady, Zee, Hamilton. You guys up for it?"

The three men nodded their agreement, and then set off at a run around the walkway, their packs bucking heavily on their backs.

Chris looked up at the sound of the three approaching men.

"You take care of him now, y'hear?" Zee said as he ran past. "We trained together."

"I've got it." Jenny said. Her hands were covered in Mason's blood. Mason now lay on his side next to her. The spine from the puglion's tail had punctured the skin and torn a ragged hole in his lower back, narrowly missing one of his kidneys. She had cleaned the wound and taped a large square bandage in place, but even that was now showing a patch of red at its center where the wound bled profusely. Jenny looked up at Chris. "Okay, he's good to go." Chris nodded.

Together they sat Mason up and then, taking an arm each, they put their heads beneath his shoulders to bolster his weight before lifting him to a standing position. Mason grimaced with the pain.

"Come on," Chris said, "We're getting you out of here."

The three of them headed for the door. Mason used the leg on his good side to initially help them along, but he was weak from shock and loss of blood and eventually gave in, sagging into their arms and allowing his feet to drag along behind as the two carried him out.

Bobby's eyes flitted between the three men struggling with the alien and the three others running round the enclosure to join the fight. Their progress seemed painfully slow. "Wyatt, stand by with that order."

"Copy that." In control, Wyatt was now in the lower gallery, standing behind the security guard whose left hand hovered over one of a hundred different lit touchpads in readiness. With his right hand he controlled the camera, tracking the progress of the three men racing around the walkway. "Come on. Come on." Wyatt muttered under his breath.

Hernandez, Cook and Javitz continued to tussle with the puglion, slowly but continuously pushing it back along the walkway and towards the other three men now closing in on it.

After what seemed like an eternity, Shady, Zee and Hamilton were finally getting into position. "Wyatt! Take the field down now!" Bobby ordered.

Wyatt nodded to the guard, who touched the desk's glass interface. The keypad's small light winked out. "It's down."

Like the other men, Shady, Zee and Hamilton stood three abreast the walkway and then simultaneously fired another wall of flame towards the reptilian alien.

Nobody was prepared for what happened next.

Unaware that it had been cornered, the puglion was startled. It reared up and rounded on its new attackers in a single movement with frightening speed. The low slung tail whipped around behind it and caught Hernandez a glancing blow but still with enough force to propel him and his pack off the walkway and twenty-five feet into the swamp. Clearly, the containment field was down.

Hernandez hit the filthy water with an almighty splash and disappeared from view. "Hernandez!" Bobby called out, but he had been pulled under the black surface by his heavy backpack and only thing to mark his passing were the large concentric waves radiating from his entry point. Bobby looked up at the five other men standing around the puglion, momentarily stunned by what had occurred. "Don't let that thing back in the water!" she yelled at them, but it was too late.

The alien, realizing that nothing now barred its way, scrambled for the water, practically launching itself off the walkway and disappearing in a shower of spray.

"Where is he?" Radchovek yelled. "Where the hell is he?"

"I don't know." Bobby called back, "But someone get that damn walkway up!"

Delaney ran back to the entrance and found the hidden button. Almost immediately after he pressed it, two rows of bubbles appeared, running from the walkway across the swamp and to the central column. From out of the bubbles, two steel handrails appeared and climbed slowly into the air, and then finally a steel mesh walkway rose out of the black water. Bobby leapt onto it, her boots clanking loudly on the narrow metal bridge as she began running across the span. "Hernandez!" she yelled again.

On the monitors in security, Wyatt could see her standing on the walkway. "Bobby, that containment field is still down."

"I know that!" She snapped, well aware of the danger she had put herself in. With no active containment field, she might as well have been wearing a sign around her neck that read "Fresh Meat." But if her predicament was bad, Hernandez's was infinitely worse. Assuming he was still alive, of course.

As if in answer to her doubts, Hernandez appeared at the surface like a breaching whale, startling them all. He drew in a huge breath with a gasp before falling back down with a splash. He stayed there for a moment, gulping in huge draughts of air.

"Hernandez! Are you all right?" Bobby called.

"Yeah. Y…yeah….Just got a bit winded…Just need to…catch my breath." He managed between gasps.

"You don't have time to catch your breath," Bobby informed him, unhitching a coil of rope from her belt.

"I had to…ditch my pack, it was…it was pulling me under."

"Don't worry about it. C'mon. You gotta get out of there."

Hernandez turned and started kicking in Bobby's direction.

"Where is it?" Hamilton yelled. They all scanned the surface of the swamp, searching for some sign of the puglions and to ascertain exactly what kind of danger Hernandez was in.

"There!" Cook pointed. Out in the middle of the swamp, about twenty yards away from Hernandez, a set of dorsal spines broke the surface in a graceful arc and then disappeared beneath the black water. It was obvious the alien was closing in.

"Get him out of there, Bobby!" Radchovek called out to her. "Get him the hell out of there!"

Hernandez put on a visible spurt and Bobby threw the line of rope out to him "Here. Grab this!" she yelled.

"Shit! There's the other one!" Zee shouted. Everyone looked to where he pointed. A second scaly back broke the surface near the central column. The second creature was moving in a direction perpendicular to the first. Hernandez caught the movement off to his right and for the first time felt a genuine fear.

He lunged for Bobby's rope, a pristine white lifeline lying across the surface of the black swamp, and just managed to get a hand on it. "I've got it!" he said. "Pull me in!"

Bobby knew the two puglions were homing in on Hernandez.

She would have to be strong to get him in before the two reptilian aliens covered the distance to him. “Hold on!” she called.

She took up the slack and then began hauling in the rope. Hernandez kicked his feet to aid her in her task and speed his removal from the swamp, but it wasn’t easy going. In some places the swamp was more stagnant water than anything else. In other places, it had the consistency of mud - and it was mud that Hernandez was now in.

Bobby pulled hard on the rope, trying desperately to free Hernandez from the gripping suction but instead the rope came free, flying out of Hernandez’s slippery hands. “I can’t hold it!” he wailed.

“Keep moving, godammit!” Delaney yelled. The puglions had not surfaced again but the shifting surface belied their presence. They were closing in fast.

Bobby was rapidly recoiling the rope in her hands, mindless of the muck that covered it, getting ready to cast it out to Hernandez again. “Wyatt,” she said calmly and quietly into her helmet mic. “You’d better be ready to get this field up.”

In the security building, Wyatt and the entire team were watching the whole drama unfold in front of them on the giant screen. “Whenever you give the order, Bobby, we’ll have that thing back up.”

“You’d better be on the money with this or people are going to die.”

Wyatt looked down at the young guard, his eyes glued to the screen, mouth agape. He swallowed nervously and Wyatt noticed that the hand that now hovered over the desktop was visibly shaking.

“Here!” Bobby shouted, throwing out the rope once more. The line fell within an arm’s length of Hernandez, who reached out and put his hand over it, before executing two circles with his forearm, coiling the length around his wrist to ensure he would not lose his hold on it again.

Suddenly a new sound filled the enclosure. Gunfire. Bobby

looked up, Delaney was racing across the small steel span towards her, but it wasn't him that was shooting. On the walkway, Baducci had put his weapon back to its original configuration and was now firing bullets blindly into the swamp only feet behind Hernandez.

"Jesus!" Hernandez said, as the bullets hissed into the mud, sending small gobs of it flying into the air.

"He ain't gonna help you now," Delaney yelled from next to Bobby. "Hold on!"

Delaney pulled hard on the rope, yanking Hernandez forward, and then he and Bobby in unison hauled Hernandez in hand-over-hand. All the while Baducci continued to fire into the swamp behind him.

"There!" Cookie yelled again. Bobby looked up. The first puglion's back broke the surface again, this time only ten feet away from Hernandez who was now reaching up from below the steel walkway. Delaney was on his knees, reaching through the bars to pull him up. It was only seconds, Bobby knew, before the aliens would strike.

In security, the young guard's shaking hand was moving closer and closer to the touchpad that would re-activate the containment field. "Wait for it." Wyatt said under his breath, just loud enough to be heard. "Wait for it."

Delaney was leaning over, yanking Hernandez up by the belt on his pants. His head and shoulders were now on the walkway, his arms flailing wildly in a vain attempt to get some kind of hold. Bobby reached down and grabbed him with a locking grip around the wrists and pulled as hard as she could, a superhuman effort fuelled by fear and adrenaline. With a great heave, Hernandez was pulled clear of the swamp and the three of them fell back onto the walkway.

"Now!" Bobby yelled.

"Now!" Wyatt said to the guard who hit the flashing interface with lightning speed.

The water below the walkway erupted as the reptilian aliens

launched their attack, the two creatures breaching clear of the water. Bobby flinched as two sets of massive jaws snapped at the three of them and then flinched again as the containment field sent a barrage of blue sparks flying just inches away from her face. The two enormous creatures fell away, repelled, and sent great showers of spray out over the swamp as they crashed back into the dark water. Bobby, Delaney, and Hernandez all lay on the narrow bridge, panting heavily.

* * * * *

After she had scaled the perimeter wall of the IZP, she had headed south and taken refuge in Burnham park. It was impossible for an alien of her size not to be noticed and the few joggers in the park that morning had fled at the sight of her and called the authorities, not knowing at the time about the break-in at the IZP. When the police had arrived there was no visible trace of her - but she was still here.

She had climbed up into a tree and spread her slender limbs wide, freezing into place. Rapidly, her color had begun to change, her legs and wing case taking on the mottled hue of the surrounding branches. Within seconds she was invisible to all but the most acute of eyes. Now, under cover of darkness, she decided it was time to move.

She climbed down from the tree, her body taking on its natural black coloration and allowing her to blend into the night. She cleaned her compound eyes with swift, repetitive sweeps of her narrow forelimbs and clicked her mandibles, as if testing the night air.

Despite her size and bulk, she was still capable of limited and somewhat ungainly flight. She opened her wing case, the black carapace over her abdomen splitting in half and rising, exposing the more delicate yet equally black wings below. She tested them once, as if flexing muscles, a clattering sound as the huge rotor like appendages flicked wildly in the moonlight. Then she took to the wing, climbing sluggishly into the Chicago night.

She was immediately disoriented the moment she rose above the tree line. On the ground, the light pollution from the west had only manifested itself as a faint orange cast on the night sky. Now she could see the city and its galaxy of artificial stars.

She flew a couple of faltering circles, trying to make sense of it from her own innate knowledge of constellations and the magnetic fields that she detected, but this was something new to her and she was hopelessly lost.

Far away in the distance, something attracted her. A single bright red flare in the darkness, high above the others, flashing like a beacon amongst the chaotic jumble of light. She righted herself in the air and headed for it.

* * * * *

"So what do I do now?" Hernandez asked. "I've lost all my gear."

"You're not going to do anything. In fact the only thing I want you to do is keep Mason company on the way to the hospital. He could use the moral support and you'd do well to get checked out yourself." Bobby said. "Besides, you're covered in so much filth you're useless to us anyway."

"Whaddya mean?"

"I mean, everything that we're trying to recapture is going to smell you from a mile away. Half of them are going to bolt before we even get anywhere near them. The other half might just come looking for you. You want that?"

Hernandez huffed. Beaten by reason.

"Now go on, get out of here, and if they check you out and discharge you, take a shower, grab some new gear and meet us back at security. We'll debrief there with Wyatt once we're done."

On the visitor walkway, Baducci and Hamilton seemed to have buried their differences, united by the effort to contain the puglion.

"I've seen these things hungry before, but never that ferocious." Baducci said.

"They weren't hungry." Hamilton replied. "I was on the expedition that caught these things. I've watched them up close and I can tell you, if they were hungry, Hernàndez wouldn't have gotten out of there alive." He thought for a moment, trying to explain in his own mind what he had observed. His eyes searched the swamp in front of them. "They're angry" he realized, speaking out loud.

"Angry? About what?"

"You got kids, don't you?" Hamilton asked quickly, excited by his revelation.

"Yeah, a little girl. So what does that have to do with anything?"

"Well how mad would you be if she went missing?"

"I...I...Well, there's no words to describe how I'd feel. I think I'd be angry at everyone and everything." Baducci frowned at Hamilton, still not getting the meaning of their conversation and then it dawned on him what was wrong. He followed Hamilton's eyes out over the swamp.

The two puglions swam together, their backs breaking the surface regularly as they traversed the swamp. It seemed they were engaged in some graceful yet somber dance, their movements exaggerated and slow.

Baducci had never seen this kind of behavior from them before. This wasn't some kind of courtship or mating ritual - and then he got it. They were looking for something. "Oh my God!" he said. "Their baby's gone!"

"Yup." Hamilton said beside him.

Since birth the baby puglion had barely left its mother's side. Baducci watched as the two backs broke the surface of the swamp again. There was no youngling to accompany them. Now the two adults searched the swamp, lamenting the loss of their infant.

"Bobby!" Hamilton shouted. "Check out the overflow sluice."

Bobby and the rest of the team looked over to the far side of the enclosure. The puglion swamp was constantly being aerated with a fresh supply of water which was pumped in underground, but the ever increasing volume was drained by means of a large overflow pipe located under the visitor walkway. From this side of the enclosure, it was clearly visible. Normally, the pipe was covered with a heavy, hinged, metal grate, bolted down on either side, there simply to allow the excess water through and nothing else. Now it was hanging open, the bolts on one side clearly cut away. The adult puglions were too large to crawl through the opening, but the infant could have.

"Where does that go?" Hamilton called over to her.

Bobby visibly blanched. "Straight into the sewer."

* * * * *

She was tiring now, for she had never had the opportunity to use her wings in captivity and the exertion of appendages unused for so long was taking a heavy toll.

At this altitude, the air was much colder and she struggled against the buffeting winds, but she was close now, the blinking red light ahead of her, enticing her through the darkness.

Suddenly, a huge gust caught her and carried her forward, smashing her against glass which shattered under her weight and allowed her to fall through.

She landed badly, one of her rear legs folded awkwardly beneath her and she struggled to stand. The limb was broken and useless, but the injury was not life-threatening. Her seven other legs could adequately support her weight and allow her to move.

It was warm here. She raised her head and looked up at the cone of glass that towered above her, beyond which flashed the red light which marked Chicago's tallest building for the air traffic flying in and out of O'Hare skyport. Around her, industrial-sized air conditioning units belched out heat, laboring hard to cool the gargantuan tower beneath. This was a good place to rest and prepare. Soon she would need to eat, and after that, find a host.

CHAPTER 8

Bobby stood on the walkway above the vandalized grate. "They must have had some pretty serious hardware to cut through this thing," she said. A set of muddy footprints led away from the scene of the crime. "Looks like whoever did it got away, too."

"Who said they were alone?" Fairchilds asked.

"You'd have to be pretty friggin' nuts to take that containment field down, then climb down there with no protection and break that thing open," Delaney added.

"It makes no sense," Bobby said. "On the face of it, it looks like they knew what they were doing. The break-in and sabotage of the systems seems so well planned—and yet at the same time, the people that broke into the animal enclosures seem to have no clue what they were up against."

Baducci looked at the backs of the breaching adults. "I hope they got a meal out of it," he muttered quietly, "That might have been some compensation at least."

* * * * *

As soon as Wyatt had learnt about the missing puglion, he had called Travis over and told them he was going to dispatch his team of rookies. Sure, the mantor was still loose and dangerous, but the police and local Earth Alliance forces were out in the city in numbers and both of them had units in the air. He could not afford to wait any longer in the hope that the mantor would show its face. The puglion took precedence now.

Chicago's sewer system comprised thousands of miles of sewer pipes, and in some places it was over three hundred and sixty feet underground. They needed to catch the puglion fast because if it was lost to them, subsequent searches would be like looking for the proverbial needle in a haystack.

"I'll tell them," Travis sighed, after learning of his team's assignment. "But they aren't going to be very happy about it."

"Neither would I," Wyatt said. "But given my lack of personnel and resources right now, I don't have a lot of choices. I've called someone from the Department of Sewers, they've agreed to meet you and get you into the system. The police are also going to supply us with a personnel carrier so you can transport your whole team over there. It should be arriving soon."

"Chauffeur driven to the sewer. How nice." Travis managed a grin. "Guess I'd better go and break the good news to my boys."

* * * * *

The young man stepped out of the darkness and into the small pool of light cast by the street lamp. He wore sneakers, a pair of baggy blue jeans and a loose-fitting leather jacket covered with patches which paid testament to the poor allegiances he had made in his short life. He had been a member of many gangs over the years. Now he had his own crew—the Eighty-niners. A baseball cap sat at an angle on his head. He chewed gum and oozed attitude.

"Hey asshole!" He called into the night. "You out here?"

This was the place. The pre-determined meeting spot where old grievances were finally going to be laid to rest and, if all went to plan, he would leave to rule the precinct with his own particular brand of street law, consisting of primarily terror and intimidation.

When he had taken control of the Eighty-niners, or rather, inherited it due to the untimely death of the gang leader, murdered in a drive-by shooting, he had staked their claim to this neighborhood. He knew it would anger the rival gang who also believed their rights extended to these streets. It was they, he was sure, who were responsible for the hit.

Over the past five years, there had been casualties on both sides as the tension and anger between the two gangs had festered and fed upon itself. Fatal shootings and stabbings had followed - and those victims had been the lucky ones. Some gang members had been left maimed and mutilated after severe beatings, and forced to live the rest of their lives as cripples. They had been forgotten quickly by their so-called friends, now that their ability to do anything, let alone inflict harm on another human being, had been stolen from them. Tonight, all that was going to come to an end and he would cast his sphere of influence even wider.

"Yo!" he shouted again. His hands were thrust deep into his jacket pockets, one of them caressing the handle of the switchblade it found there, one of the instruments of his success. There was no answer from the darkness.

He hated the "DB's"—the Demon Bloods—they had no respect, a fact that had just been made all the more apparent to him. No regard for the unwritten rules of the streets.

"Chickenshit," he muttered under his breath as he turned to leave.

"Yo!" The voice came from behind him. "Where you in such a hurry to get yo sorry ass?"

He turned back. A second figure stood in the street now, illuminated in a cone of light from a second street lamp two lights down. It was as if the very lamp had spirited the man there to stand in its own drop of yellow glow.

The figure's features were concealed in a shadow cast by the peak of his cap. He wore the same kind of clothing and his body language communicated the same brash, cocksure attitude. They were brothers in all but their misguided convictions. "You come alone?" The figure asked. "Like we agreed?"

"Yeah."

"You's lying man!" The figure threw an accusing finger at him.

"Why you say that? Why you dissing me like that?"

"Wha…? Me? Me dissing you?" He was clearly agitated, pacing on his lit stage, gesticulating aggressively. "You's the one disrespecting me, man. You's lying!"

"You come alone, then?"

The figure stopped as if seriously considering the question, then broke out into a quiet chuckle. "You think I'm stupid," he said to himself. "That's it. You think I'm a dumbass. You think I'm stupid?" The last time it was a rhetorical question.

He half looked over his shoulder, raised his hand, and with an exaggerated gesture, clicked his fingers. Two other figures stepped into view either side of him. "No, I didn't come alone, yo' stupid ass. I got's me some insurance and I ain't dumb enough to think you didn't do the same. That's why I know you's lying.

"My boys here, they found your men hidin' out in them trees. They took care of 'em too."

The first thug felt a knot of fear tighten in his stomach. He had brought other members of his gang to help him kill this punk. Sadly, he wasn't smart enough to think the same deception could be used on him. Now his bluff had been called and his genius plan was crumbling in its execution.

He looked at his opponent's cronies. One was a short, barrel-chested thug with a shaven head. His scalp had been tattooed and now his head was covered in a series of blue lines, intricately drawn into whorls and patterns reminiscent of the marks borne by the ancient indo-pacific warrior tribes. He wore earrings and had a pierced eyebrow, the lamplight reflecting off both his head and the stud that poked out of his face. He was stocky, bordering on overweight, but he used that weight as a weapon and his large, chubby hands looked like they could crack ball bearings.

The other kid, in contrast, was lean and tall. He wore a hooded top under his jacket and the hood was pulled up and over his head. Under the lamp, his face was completely hidden in darkness, the hood forming a cowl in which there was nothing but a black void. It was if the Reaper himself had come to collect.

He swallowed nervously, feeling the switchblade in his pocket again for some reassurance.

"I'm going to kick yo' sorry ass!" the other thug shouted and made as if to move towards him, the other two in tow.

There was a sound from out of the darkness. The three men stopped in their tracks. There was the sound of movement, quiet at first, and then louder.

"I thought you said you took care of 'em?" the gang leader said to reaper man.

The hooded head turned towards him. "We did. That ain't them. They ain't comin' back."

He looked to his other cohort who nodded his agreement, a hint of apprehension in his eyes.

The sounds were louder still and coming from multiple sources. Whatever was causing them was getting closer.

The gang leader's shoulders slumped, defeated, as he finally realized what was going on. "Fuck it man!" He said angrily. "I knew you's couldn't be trusted. You bought your whole stinkin' crew didn't you's? Huh?"

He hadn't. He didn't understand what was going on around him - around them all - but here was an opportunity to gain the upper hand. A broad, knowing smile broke over his face. He allowed them to believe the lie.

"Yo piece o' shit," the gang leader muttered. The three men had now formed a defensive circle, each of them looking out into the darkness. The gang leader had his own wicked-looking knife that he jabbed out at his invisible enemies, stalling the inevitable. The bald gang member had put on a vicious looking set of knuckle-dusters and now massaged the hand that wore them with his other hand, cracking knuckles as he did so; and reaper man had produced a machete, previously concealed in the leg of his pants, which he waved menacingly in the air with a degree of skill that proved he was familiar with the weight of it in his hand.

The young man watched with a certain degree of amusement as his three enemies slowly circled in the spot of light like animated figures on a miniature carousel. They shuffled on the balls of their feet, preparing themselves for the coming fight. It never occurred to him to fear for his own safety.

Without warning, the three men were suddenly engulfed in a mass of fur as five huge bodies leapt out of the darkness. There were screams, briefly, but the aliens knew to go for the throat, and the muffled cries died with the men.

He watched, stunned by what he had seen, unable to make sense of it. Out of the darkness, more of the strange creatures appeared to join the feast and he stood there, rooted to the spot, mesmerized by animals that he could not explain or find a name for in his limited bank of knowledge.

As if sensing it was being watched, one of the creatures looked up at him, its long tongue licking its already bloody nose. It was only when those dark, soulless eyes fell on him that he was galvanized into action.

He turned and ran, abandoning the cone of light that had once given sanctuary from the dark but which now left him exposed. Already he could hear pursuit, the sound of the alien's hurried breathing and a horrible scratching noise as claws struggled for grip on unfamiliar asphalt.

Instantly he knew it was hopeless; he could hear it gaining on him fast. He reached into his pocket and found the switchblade again, pulling it out quickly. He pressed the button on its side and saw the glint of moonlight on metal as the blade flicked into position. He went to turn to defend himself but it was already on him, a pair of immensely strong jaws clamping down on his forearm, splintering bone in one crushing bite. The knife fell from his hand, clattering on the street. The end was quick.

The new, young, alpha male of the gashoks raised his head to the night sky and called to the single moon.

There was a new pack in town.

* * * * *

"How come we get all the shitty jobs?" Smith complained.

"Yeah. Literally!" Argyle agreed next to him.

Travis shook his head and shrugged. "Trust me, it certainly wasn't planned this way, but this needs to be done."

Others in Travis's squad nodded their heads, reluctantly accepting what was being asked of them. Understanding the necessity of their task.

Travis looked across at Helen. She had come down to the lower gallery and sat in a vacant chair. She looked lost and alone in this place. She sipped from a drink that one of the security guards had been gracious enough to get for her, obviously feeling the same pity for her that Travis did now. He didn't want to leave her here. He could use her help, but then he didn't want to ask her to go down into the sewers with him. She just didn't look like the sort of person who would be agreeable about that kind of thing.

She looked up at his approach, pinpointing him by sound alone.

"I have to leave," he said. "You'll be safe here."

She looked surprised. "Where are you going? I thought you brought me here so I could help."

"I did..." He ran a hand through his hair, frustrated. "But I...I can't ask you to do this."

Her lips set in a thin line. "Are you making decisions for me again, Mister Jacks? I thought we'd gone over this."

"Okay, look. It's the sewer. We have to go down into the sewer system..."

"I'll go with you."

"...Something's been released straight into the sewer system and…"

She laid a hand on his arm, halting his rambling.

"I said," she said, quietly. "I'll go with you."

Travis looked at her with a frown. "You will?"

"Uh-huh" A small smile broke out over her face. Travis couldn't help but think she looked kind of cute. He looked her over once, realizing she wasn't really dressed for the occasion.

"Okay then. But we need to get you some gear." He looked up at the rails above them, knowing that Wyatt was up there somewhere, poring over the map and monitoring the news feeds. "Wyatt! Helen's going to come with us. I just need to get her some basics."

Wyatt's head appeared over the gallery rail. "Are you sure, Miss Swift? It could be dangerous down there, and…what with your disability and all."

"I'll be fine. It will be good to do something, to know that I'm helping. Besides, I've got this lump to look after me."

A flush of color came to Travis's cheeks and Wyatt smirked, although the look in his eyes when he turned them on Travis asked a host of unspoken questions. He didn't want Travis putting any of his team in jeopardy with some ill-conceived idea - to him the woman's usefulness was still questionable. Aside from that, he didn't want the death of a civilian on his hands either. The team already had their hands full with the puglion. They didn't need the additional responsibility of her safety to worry about. He wasn't accountable to the zoo in any sense but he still had a moral obligation to the people around him, whether they were in his charge on not. Travis nodded and patted his hands in the air to silently reassure him.

"Okay then, but don't waste too much time down in storage. I want your boys ready. Your ride's here."

* * * * *

Travis hadn't gotten much for Helen, just a basic change of clothes, a pair of boots and a helmet, not that any of the technology wired into it was of any use to her with the exception of maybe the com link. Besides, Travis suspected that her "gift" was going to enable her to "see" more underground than any of the team with their fancy cameras and visors.

To be honest, he was secretly relieved when she had agreed to come with them. He knew Wyatt was skeptical about her skills, but he had experienced them firsthand and knew that she had gotten him out of a tight spot already today. He suspected that she may well do it again before this episode in Chicago's history was over, even perhaps save his life or the life of one of his team members. But most of all, Travis was relieved that she had come with them because, deep down, he was scared. He was really afraid, and he wanted all the help he could get.

Sure, he had been on missions before, but those had always been with fully qualified ULF teams where every man and woman knew their job and did it without question. They were also out in the field, where they knew their equipment worked, free from man-made magnetic fields and frequencies. Now he was about to venture out with a team of sixteen new recruits, some of whom he wasn't even sure he was going to graduate from the program, into an environment for which their apparatus was unsuitable and where their targets had an infinite number of places to hide and would behave unpredictably. It was one thing to live in Chicago, it was another to go hunting there. There were just too many variables to hope that everything would go according to plan.

* * * * *

The cop placed his finger on the touchpad of the side of the armored personnel carrier and a double set of sliding doors opened quickly, revealing an empty but still impressive weapons rack hidden in the side of the vehicle.

The APC was waiting for them outside the stores building, directed there by Wyatt, no doubt so they wouldn't have to go back to the security complex. It was an ugly, nondescript vehicle; a giant black hulk on wheels with the word "POLICE" emblazoned on each side in huge white letters.

"Okay, let's go," Travis said.

Each team member relinquished his quad-sys gun to Travis before entering the back of the APC and taking a seat inside where Helen was already waiting. Travis in turn handed the guns to the cop, who placed them in the gun rack. When they were finished the cop closed the doors with another touch and climbed into the driver's side. Travis elected to ride shotgun beside him, which drew a look of vague contempt from the other man.

Travis looked behind him to the small open window which separated him from the rest of his team in the back. He couldn't help but think how young so many of them looked.

The cop engaged the drive and the APC lurched away. Even to a passenger it was obvious that the thing was built like a tank and probably just as heavy. Travis looked across at him. He was a mean-faced man and he looked miserable, like someone had just woken him up from the best dream he'd had in decades. He wore a helmet, with a clear visor pulled down over his entire face. Travis could also see that he was wearing body armor.

"Taking no chances, huh?" Travis asked.

The cop shot him another look of contempt. "I'm a cop who drives an APC. What do you think my average day is like?"

The two of them spent the rest of the trip in silence.

* * * * *

After the incident at Reptile Mountain and the loss of two men, Bobby had re-jigged the squad so they went into the northern quadrants of the zoo as two teams of seven.

As before, they ran an overlapping pattern but now they exercised a little more caution which was not solely attributable to the darkness. The puglion attack had brought the inherent danger of their job into sharp focus in the minds of each of them. The aliens were deserving of a little respect.

It wouldn't be long now. It had taken them the entire day to complete the sweep of the zoo, such was its size, but soon they would be done. Only a couple more hours of concentration and then they would reach the monorail station at the northernmost tip of the zoo and they could ride it back in safety.

A couple more hours of concentration, that was all. This was no time to let your guard down.

* * * * *

Travis's team rocked and bounced in unison as the APC trundled along. It seemed to the sixteen young recruits that the vehicle had managed to pick out every bump and imperfection in the road since they had left. They weren't used to traveling like this; the suspension in their own HVs or the city's skytrack provided a much smoother ride. Another huge jolt drew muttered curses from the rear of the vehicle.

Smith, who was sat right behind the partition, pulled himself up to the small dividing window. He poked his face through. "Can't this friggin' thing fly? We're getting mashed back here."

The cop never took his eyes off the road and sighed heavily, as if Smith was a small child with whom he was already losing his patience. "It's an APC. It's not meant to fly. It's meant for driving into suburban war zones and mowing down lawbreakers."

Smith and Travis shared a look, not sure whether the cop was joking. Travis nodded toward the back of the truck with his head, indicating that Smith should just give it up and return to his seat. "We'll be there soon."

Smith slumped back into his seat. "Let's hope so," he muttered under his breath. He looked across at Helen, sat opposite him in the darkness. He wondered what the meek, small woman was doing there with them. She hadn't said a word to anyone since they had left the zoo. In the darkness her eyes could be seen as two pinpricks of light, reflecting what little light there was in the back of the vehicle, but Smith was under no illusion as to her ability to see. He had seen, as had the others, when Travis had helped her into the back of the vehicle, and he guessed, from the careful steps that she took, that she was blind. "And what the hell's she doing here?" he whispered to his colleague next to him, venting some more of his angst.

"I'm here to help," she said quietly.

"Oh yeah? How's that?"

"I'm going to help you catch this…puglion thing."

Smith laughed. "You! You can't help us. You're blind."

"I don't need eyes to see." she said.

Smith laughed again. This time it was more of a derogatory snort. "Don't need eyes to see," he muttered, looking around the truck at the other team members to see if they shared his amusement. In the darkness he could see a couple of other faces break into smiles.

Helen sat forward quickly, bringing Smith up short. The smile disappeared from his face and he looked genuinely worried about what she might do next.

"You didn't shower this morning, did you?"

"Wha…w…what? He looked at her as if she were crazy.

"You didn't shower this morning."

"Yeah…yeah, I did." He said with a smirk to hide his embarrassment, looking again at his teammates to see if he still had them on his side.

"No. You didn't. You know what I think? I think you got a call this morning to come in as quickly as you could because there was an emergency at the zoo. You didn't think anything of it. You just jumped up and put on your uniform, or your suit or whatever it is you call it and you came in as fast as you could because that was the right thing to do. But you didn't shower.

"You know why I know this? Because you're giving off a bad smell so strong I can almost taste it. I can almost see it. It's like a....color....hanging in a cloud around you. If I were one of your teammates I'd be worried about going down in that sewer with you because you leave a scent trail almost as clear as an atmos-skipper leaves a vapor trail on re-entry."

Smith's mouth worked but no words came out.

"But don't worry, Mister Smith. That's right, it's Smith, isn't it?" she continued. "You're in good company. Five other people in the back of this truck didn't shower either, four used soap and the other six used an unidentifiable mixture of popular cleaning products." She sat back in her seat, finished.

The team said nothing. They just sat in stunned silence and shared uneasy glances in the darkness.

* * * * *

It was easier traveling up here. Across the rooftops.

On the ground, the mantor had a top speed of approximately forty miles per hour when it ran on all fours, but the ground was home to things. Many things. Things that moved and rolled and rumbled and hooted. There were hundreds of creatures that appeared to communicate by rendering ear-splitting screams at a pitch that hurt the mantor's sensitive ears and fuelled the alien's natural aggression with an insane fear and rage.

The kill this morning had been partly a result of that. The mantor had been confronted by things that it did not understand and which terrified it. For despite its aggressive tendencies, it was capable of feeling fear. Fear was a necessary component of the "fight-or-flight" instinct that seemed to be a universal reaction across inter-species boundaries, terrestrial and extra-terrestrial; and when the HV had come out of the darkness and caught it unawares, all the mantor had understood was that something with two large, bright white eyes was coming for it. In the alien landscape that was the city of Chicago, the mantor had decided in a split second that it did not know in which direction to flee and so had tackled the situation with all-out aggression and attacked. An unfortunate series of events that had resulted in the death of Marty White and his fiancée, Michelle.

As the day had gone on and Chicago had come to life, the mantor had realized that the odds were stacked hopelessly against it and decided to run, but it had to get away from the aliens and the moving things on the ground and so it had taken to the rooftops.

The mantor was now far outside the city center and moving swiftly across the flat-roofed tenement buildings of the suburbs, leaping gracefully from one rooftop to another, and when that was not possible, using the fire escape ladders that, in the darkness of the night, clung like skeletal parasites to the sides of the buildings.

Now, things had settled down, the darkness closing in like an enveloping cloak, and the city was slowing, readying itself for another night. The mantor used the opportunity to rest, huddling up against a rooftop generator to feel its comforting warmth, for with the darkness had come cold and the alien had never experienced a night exposed to the elements and Chicago's crisp, night air.

The mantor's eyelids drooped, exhaustion finally setting in.

Suddenly there was a sound and the alien's eyes flicked open again. It was a high-pitched whine, and it was getting closer. The creature sprung to its feet and immediately saw the source of the sound.

High in the sky, another pair of the bright white eyes came towards the mantor's position. Below them, an intense, bright cone of light oscillated like a giant, white pendulum.

The mantor darted to the edge of the building, rearing up on its hind legs to look down from the rooftop. A row of blue and red flashing lights made slow but steady progress along the street far below.

The creature turned and found that the eyes in the sky were almost upon it. A wind had begun to blow and dust and debris were being whipped up in the miniature storm. The central beam now played over the top of the other side of the building, sending a white disc skittering back and forth across the rooftop.

The alien scrambled to the corner of the roof. The same blue and red lights advanced along this side of the building as well. Looking up, the mantor could see a neighboring building in the darkness, three stories lower but still a significant distance away. Behind it, the white disc continued to dance across the rooftop, stopping briefly on anything that caught its interest. The mantor didn't know what it was, but it instinctively knew that it needed to get away from it.

Dropping to all fours, the alien turned and ran back towards the lights in the sky, at the last minute turning again so hard that it kicked up a spray of loose gravel and almost lost its footing.

"You see that?" The searchlight operator in the police HV asked.

The driver pulled a face. "See what?"

"Like some movement or something? I dunno."

"Probably shadows." The driver mused. "You concentrate so hard looking for something that after a while your eyes start playing tricks on you."

The other man blinked hard twice in an attempt to revive his tired eyes.

In the darkness below them, the mantor bounded at full speed towards the lip of the building, clearing the low wall in a giant leap and then flinging its forelimbs wide, allowing the thin membrane of skin between its waist and elbows to catch a pocket of air and turning what would be a fatal fall into a graceful glide.

The alien landed heavily on the other rooftop and stayed there for a moment catching its breath, feeling its two hearts pumping furiously in its chest. It turned back only once and saw two red eyes in the sky, then it slowly padded away, leaving the noise of search vehicles and police activity behind.

* * * * *

The city's sewerage man was already waiting for them when they arrived. Travis figured the guy couldn't possibly have looked happier to see anyone, a thought confirmed when the other man grasped his big hand in both of his and shook it so hard it made his whole arm convulse.

"Sure am glad to see you boys," he said. "Don't want to be out here a minute longer than I have to be."

Travis smiled faintly.

He reached into a large bag behind him and pulled out a helmet adorned with a large lamp on its front. "Thought you fellas could use some of these."

"Thanks," Travis said, "But we brought some of our own." He reached up under the right side of his helmet and touched a small pad he found there. Two brilliant halogens built into the side of his helmet came alive.

The sewerage guy brought a hand up to shield his face from the glare and turned his head away.

"Oh, sorry." Travis said.

"Nah, that's okay. Figured you guys would be better equipped than us anyway. Just thought, y'know, I'd offer and all that."

"Thanks, I appreciate it, really. Now where are we going?"

"Oh yes. Over here," the sewer guy said excitedly, remembering himself.

It was a ridiculous question. Behind the other man, a large manhole cover lay displaced on the tarmac next to a gaping hole in the road. It was obviously their point of entry, but best just to move things along. Travis didn't imagine working the sewers was a very sociable vocation. Given an audience and a chance, he suspected that this guy could talk them all into a stupor and like he had said, none of them wanted to be out here longer than they needed to be.

"There's a ladder just inside the lip of the hole."

Travis peered into the black void, the two beams from his halogens unable to penetrate the darkness and find the bottom of the tunnel below. He looked again at the other man in his helmet with its feeble lamp. "You guys go down there with those things?"

He shrugged, unable to offer an explanation for what clearly appeared to be madness. "I eat a lot of carrots."

Travis looked back at the hole in the road and couldn't help but be reminded of a gaping maw, ready to swallow him whole, then wondered how close to the truth that might be. He sighed. "Okay, then. Let's get this thing over with." He turned his back on the manhole, then gingerly lowered himself into it until his feet found ladder rungs before further descending into the tunnel.

* * * * *

"How badly was Mason hurt?" Wyatt asked. They'd told him over the link but now that they were here in front of him, he was asking the same questions again, measuring what he knew against the looks of worry and concern in their faces.

"It's bad," Jenny said. "He'll live, but he won't be coming back to work anytime soon. Maybe not ever."

Wyatt nodded thoughtfully. He'd seen enough injuries on expeditions of his own to imagine the kind of wound that would put a man out of action for that long. He looked up quickly, snapping himself out of his own lamentations. "Okay. So what else do we know?"

"As far as we know, the zoo is secure," Bobby said. "That's not allowing for something circling around behind us as we made the sweep."

"Or anything else that decides it prefers its nice warm enclosure versus a night out on the town and attempts to come back," Swarovski added.

"All in all, though, I think you can move through the zoo with a degree of confidence." Bobby finished.

"What about the houses?" Wyatt asked. The IZP had a number of buildings which provided specific environments for certain types of aliens.

"It looks like the doors did their jobs," Bobby said.

Like Reptile Mountain, all the alien houses were accessible only through two sets of inward swinging doors, a safety measure put in place for just this kind of unthinkable catastrophic failure. To escape, an alien would have to be able to pull open a door and most of them weren't equipped with either the anatomy or the intellect to execute such a maneuver. Wyatt sighed, grateful that someone had the foresight to think of the unthinkable.

"We don't think anything escaped, but that's not to say that those things aren't loose inside. Now that security is back up, there's no way anything's getting out, but..."

"There's no stopping them ripping each other to shreds," he finished for her.

He shook his head slowly, his eyes distant, as if seeing the life-and-death struggles he predicted. He cared for the aliens. It was an emotion that he struggled with since, for many of the zoo's denizens, he had been captor and jailer - and those weren't the actions of a caring soul. But it was true. He did care for these creatures. Proximity and understanding had taught him respect—and with that respect had come something akin to fondness. "What about the enclosed environments?"

Shady shook his head. "They were all pressurized enclosures to stop the air from leaching in. Once security went down, they blew wide open. Most of the residents were dead by the time we got there, and those that weren't were in a really bad way and well..."

He looked across at Hamilton who gave only the slightest motion of his arm, not really wanting to bring too much attention to the large gun in his hand; the instrument of their demise. "We put the rest of them out of their misery."

Wyatt slammed his fists down on the desk, startling them all. That was no way for any creature to die. It would have been a painful death—a slow suffocation as the aliens' bodies heaved and spasmed in an attempt to extract the chemicals from the air that they so desperately needed to survive and which were sadly absent from Earth's atmosphere. It would have been like locking a man in a room full of cyanide gas and watching him expire—except that would have been quicker.

Wyatt spread his hands flat and breathed deeply, allowing the anger to pass. "All right," he said, lifting his head slowly. "This is where we're at."

Wyatt drew their attention to the map and explained what he knew. The team gathered around the desk to better see the things he was pointing out. He showed them the locations of different sightings, pointing out the yellow dots of most significance and taking counsel from the others on which should take priority so they could reach a consensus of opinion and form a plan of how to move forward. He told them that he had dispatched Travis's team into the sewer to go after the infant puglion and that the mantor was still loose and yet to be sighted, along with other, significantly dangerous aliens.

"What's that?" Baducci asked. He was pointing at the map, at a circular blue line that contained the ugly red circle centered on Chicago.

"That's the police line." Wyatt replied. "Well, no, sorry, that's the perimeter formed by the police, home guard and local Earth Alliance forces. We believe they've managed to form a complete boundary around the city and are slowly closing in so you guys are going to have some help out there."

Beyond the blue line, a larger amber circle continued to spill over the outer suburbs of Chicago. "However," Wyatt continued, "We're not naive enough to think that perimeter is fail-safe. This amber circle continues to track the possible distance of our fastest escaped alien, the mantor, from the zoo, should it have managed to cross the police line."

Baducci blew out a whistle. The amber circle was visibly spreading. "That's a lot of ground to cover."

"It is." Wyatt sighed. "But let's hope it doesn't come to that."

He looked through the map at the assembled faces. "I know you're exhausted. Some of you should rest. But I have a favor to ask. I need some of you to go out again tonight. We need to start working in the city and you all know this can't wait."

"Are you going to rest?" Swarovski asked.

"No. I'll stay here and coordinate everything as before."

"You know it's important to get this mess cleared up."

"Yes."

"So why would you think we wouldn't think that, too? You want us to rest and yet you won't yourself. When did you start dealing in double standards, Wyatt? No. We all go out again. We all go out again and we keep going out until Chicago and its people are safe. It sucks that we're the only team here to do it but it is what it is." Swarovski looked at the rest of the squad. It was clear that he had spoken for all of them. "We'll catch some sleep wherever or whenever we can, but in the meantime we have a job to do."

Wyatt looked at the faces again. Swarovski had rallied the troops with his battle cry. Where before there had been tired eyes and shoulders slumped with fatigue, now there was a new look of determination in each face and a willingness to motivate.

"Okay." Wyatt said. To be honest, he'd expected no less from them, but he was grateful for their commitment to the task at hand. "At the very least get a bite to eat and a hot drink before you head back out there."

"Besides, who are you to tell us what to do?" Swarovski said angrily, doing his best impersonation of Gruber from earlier in the day. "You don't even work here!"

They all shared a smile.

* * * * *

Travis helped Helen off the ladder, her booted feet splashing in the fetid water that flowed along the bottom of the tunnel.

"Good luck!" the sewer guy said from above them before quickly sliding the manhole cover back into place, locating it with a metallic *thunk*. The guy clearly wanted to be back home and indoors.

The first thing that struck Travis about the tunnel was the

stench. Now that the manhole cover was back in place it seemed to have intensified tenfold. The stink assailed his nostrils and stung his eyes so much that he blinked involuntarily.

He looked down the tunnel. It was about seven feet in diameter, just large enough to accommodate his tall frame. Water and the occasional clump of solid matter filled the bottom of the tunnel. He didn't even want to hazard a guess at what exactly they were standing in.

Travis exhaled and his breath plumed in front of him. "Visor," he said, and as it had done earlier that day, his visor slid down from inside his helmet to cover his eyes. "Thermal imaging camera."

He looked at the feed from the built-in camera. There was nothing to see; he was basically looking at the same scene, just described in a series of cold blues. "Night vision camera," he said, and his feed switched to the second camera on his helmet. This time the tunnel was simply described in a multitude of greens. Unless the puglion was directly in front of them and clear of the water, which Travis was sure would get deeper as they descended into the labyrinth of tunnels, then they weren't going to see it. As he had suspected, for all their hi-tech gadgets, Helen was probably going to be able to "see" more than any of them.

Small black shapes scurried away from them, skirting the water's edge.

"Well, at least it's got a readily available food source down here." Travis noted.

"Rats." Helen said.

Travis nodded. "Uh-huh."

"Jesus fucking Christ!" Smith said behind them. "Are we all here? We are all here right? Nobody died and started decomposing on us, did they? Jesus. What the hell is that smell?"

"Methane," Torres informed him. "Same stuff that you fart out of that fat ass of yours."

"What are you? A biologist?"

"Zoologist actually. University of Texas." Torres gripped the middle two fingers of his hand with his thumb and waggled his index finger and pinkie at Smith. "Go Longhorns!" he said. "Best College Powerdisc team in the country."

"Whatever."

"Actually, it's not just methane. That bad smell is probably more attributable to hydrogen sulfide and indole and some ..."

"Dude. I'm standing in four inches of shit, breathing in an intolerable stink. I don't need a freakin' lecture."

"He's a little bit antsy." Travis said to Helen.

"I noticed."

* * * * *

Stephen Gruber strode into his apartment, throwing his suit jacket over the back of a large armchair. He went to the kitchen and poured himself a drink before returning to his living area.

He took a sip, loosening his tie with his free hand. "Screen" he said. "News Channel One."

The wall screen illuminated and a news anchor was relaying the latest news about the break-in at the IZP and what concerned citizens should do.

"News Channel Two." Again the main story was the IZP. Gruber skipped through the news channels. All were covering the IZP. He raised his eyebrows. Not bad for a day's work.

He skipped through a few more channels until he found a newscast replaying his press conference from earlier. He listened to himself speak, mouthing the memorized words as he watched.

Gruber smiled. He didn't look half bad, some might even say handsome. He didn't like the way that camera angle had caught his double chin, but all things considered, it had gone pretty well. Apart from the timing, all was going pretty much to plan.

Gruber wrestled with his tie again, pulling a face of distaste. He hadn't noticed it before, but it was uncomfortably hot in his apartment. There was no thermostat to check, since the building's artificial intelligence program was supposed to be monitoring every apartment and maintaining the temperature. Gruber ran his fingers over his forehead. They came away damp with sweat.

"Damn AI's," he muttered. That was the problem, the AI's weren't truly intelligent, they just ran learning sub-routines. For the building's computer to be truly intelligent it would have to be self-aware, and while the computing companies had the means to build such things, nobody had the guts to do it for fear of incurring the wrath of the civil liberties groups. He could almost hear them now, *If we give control to the machines then we acknowledge a greater power*, or, *We'll lose our identity, and ultimately our spirit.* Fools. They were probably the same idiots that wanted to save the city's crumbling buildings. He hated their dark age mentality. AI was the natural progression of things. He wished everyone would just accept it and move on.

Instead, here he was having to call down to the doorman to arrange for a *human* engineer to come out and inspect the air conditioning because their computer was nothing more than a caretaker and couldn't do it for him. He didn't pay a stack load of credits for the best suite in the city to have to deal with crap like this.

"Hello. Mister Gruber. Sir." The doorman's voice came over the speakers in the apartment.

"Oh. I see something still works in this building."

"Is there something I can help you with, sir?"

"Well let's see," Gruber said with a huff. "Can you fix the air conditioning?"

"Well, no, sir. I'm just the doorman."

"No. Just the doorman. Right. Well then, no. I don't think you can help me because I need someone who can fix air conditioning because right now it's at least eighty-six degrees in my apartment."

"Right, sir. You're not the first person to complain about heat issues today, sir. We've had at least two hundred other calls about it."

"Two hundred! Well, what the hell are you doing about it, man? Why haven't you got someone on the job right now?"

"We've called dozens of specialists but, well, the lateness of the hour is an issue and also, no-one wants to come out because of...." The doorman hesitated, remembering Gruber's position.

He didn't want to offend his building's highest paying tenant.

"Because of what?"

"Because of the trouble at the zoo. sir." There was a slight pause and then he added hurriedly. "The earliest we can hope for is tomorrow, sir."

"Tomorrow?" Gruber screamed. "Tomo…Computer, end call." He hung up the link with the doorman.

Tomorrow. That was ridiculous. Didn't anyone have a sense of urgency any more? Didn't anyone want to earn an honest credit any more?

Gruber strode to the sliding doors that led out onto his rooftop patio. He touched the finger pad on the wall and the door slid away, allowing a cool draught in to the apartment. He stepped out and raised his head to the refreshing air, allowing the breeze to play around his neck and the open top of his shirt.

Gruber sipped at his drink as he strode over to his balcony and looked down over the city. As per usual, the buildings stood as black forms with random arrays of lights, but the streets far below were empty. Here and there, an occasional set of lights from an HV could be seen moving across the downtown blocks, but otherwise, Chicago was a ghost town.

He didn't know what was happening on the city's streets down there. He didn't care. He was safe up here and that was all that mattered. He just had to deal with the intolerable heat.

Remembering, Gruber downed the rest of his glass and retreated inside, preparing himself for what was clearly going to be a restless night. He touched the finger pad again, allowing the sliding door to close, but released the pressure before the door was fully shut, leaving a two-inch gap for the cooler night air to come through. He had no risk of burglary up here; there was no way in apart from the front door. At least this way he might get *some* sleep.

Gruber turned out the lights and headed for bed.

CHAPTER 9

Lieberwits honked one more time for good measure. Moments later Wood emerged from his apartment block, pulling on his police jacket as he exited the building.

"Heard you got chewed out by the captain," he said as he climbed into Lieberwits's vehicle.

"Really? Wow. News travels fast. How'd you hear that?"

"I've got friends at Central."

"Everyone's got friends at Central."

"It helps."

"It certainly does," Lieberwits sighed, pulling the HV away from the curb.

"So what's the story?" Wood asked. "Where are we heading?"

Lieberwits never took his eyes off the road. "I've got an appointment with an old friend."

* * * * *

Andy Komicki ran a taxidermy shop in west Cicero. It was an unassuming place and easily overlooked on account of the accumulation of years of grime on the store windows, which seemed to make it blend into the filthy building above. Coupled with that, the windows' protective grilles were permanently locked in place, which gave the distinct impression that the store was closed. It was, Lieberwits thought, maybe just the way Komicki liked it.

Only people who knew him or knew of the store would ever come by.

Komicki had been a small-time crook and still had some dubious connections. In his past he had claimed membership in some of the alien rights groups and it was this, Lieberwits hoped, that would generate some leads if they could convince him to talk.

The taxidermy shop was a front, Lieberwits was sure of it. When asked why he had pursued taxidermy as a profession, Komicki had claimed that if he couldn't stay on the right side of the law by freeing animals, then he would pay homage to the creatures he professed to love so much by preserving them. It was an extremely tenuous case of "if you can't beat them, join them"—and Lieberwits didn't believe it for a minute. Komicki just wasn't that smart, a fact he had proved when he had gotten mixed up with one of Chicago's biggest crime lords.

In recent years, Komicki had been branching out and adding new services to his repertoire. One of these included freeze-drying, which had the advantage over traditional forms of taxidermy of producing extremely realistic results. Nothing biodegradable needed replacing. No organs needed removing. Your furry friend could simply be positioned in a favorite pose and freeze-dried as-was.

The results were so lifelike and so realistic that Komicki started to get inquiries from people about freeze-drying relatives. Never one to turn down credits, he had thought about this new line of work for a matter of seconds before deciding to add this new service to his price list. It was then he had made his mistake.

Komicki's greed often rode roughshod over good sense. When one of Chicago's crime lords had asked him to freeze-dry a body, he had never questioned it, simply taken the money and the job. As it turned out, the body was that of another of Chicago's mob leaders, the victim of a hit ordered by Komicki's client, who planned to display his rival as some kind of macabre trophy and a warning to those who might cross him in future.

When the police had got wind of this, they had been all over Komicki's store like a rash. He had been taken into custody and Lieberwits had been the one to interrogate him, but Komicki wasn't talking and he never did. In the end, Andy Komicki opted to do a short stretch inside for withholding information rather than snitch on his client. After all, he'd seen firsthand what happened when you offended the client. It was probably the only reason he was still alive.

The reality was Komicki was small fry and pretty harmless. If it hadn't been for that turn of events, he may well have stayed under the police radar, but the fact that he'd aligned himself with some of Chicago's big league criminals meant that he now came under much more severe scrutiny—and Lieberwits was surprised just how often Komicki's name turned up.

Lieberwits suspected that Komicki still maintained connections with his alien liberation friends, and that the taxidermy store was simply a means for him to root out and identify animal and alien collectors and pass that information on. A number of individuals with large preserved animal collections had been burglarized and those collections destroyed. It was too much of a coincidence not to put two and two together and come up with four. Problem was, Lieberwits had no proof of Komicki's involvement.

The bottom line was, Komicki was nobody's friend and everyone's fool. He had enemies everywhere and that probably accounted for his somewhat nervous disposition.

* * * * *

Lieberwits pulled up outside the store. Wood gave the place a cursory once-over and pulled a face. "Nice place in a nice neighborhood," he said sarcastically.

"Isn't it?" Lieberwits agreed in same.

They exited the HV.

"I suggest you go around the back." Lieberwits said. "Our

friend here and I have some history. He might not be too pleased to see me."

Wood nodded and disappeared around the corner.

* * * * *

Andy Komicki never looked up when the electronic chime sounded and the figure stepped down the few steps into his store. "Help you?" he asked from behind his counter with a tone that suggested he would do anything but.

"I hope so."

The voice sounded strangely familiar. Komicki stopped what he was doing and lifted his head.

What little light there was inside struggled through the windows in long rectangular shafts tinted the color of muddy water. Scores of dust motes strayed through the beams, betraying just how filthy the inside of the store was. Gloom seemed to inhabit the room like a third presence.

The other figure moved towards him. It was difficult to make him out in the dim light. He wore a long dark trench coat and his features were obscured by the hat tilted forward as he bowed his head. There was something about his walk, though. Something Komicki couldn't quite put his finger on, but…

"Hello Andy," the figure said, raising his head. "It's been a long time."

* * * * *

Aaron Schultz tapped the tailgate of his HV and watched it slowly close and lock.

"You ready?" his long-time friend and diving companion Rob Shapiro said from behind him.

He turned. "Sure. I've been looking forward to this for ages."

"Here. Zip me up." Rob said, turning and offering his back, his arms held out wide.

Aaron grabbed the zip of the dry suit and pulled it horizontally across Rob's shoulders, giving it a few hard yanks to ensure it was fully closed. "You're good. Return the favor?" he said, offering his own back for the same operation.

When both men were ready, they picked up their fins and walked out of the parking lot and towards the beach that banked Lake Michigan.

It was a windy morning, gusts whipping up a chop on the surface. Their entry and surface swim wasn't going to be much fun, Aaron thought as he pulled the seven millimeter neoprene hood over his head and tucked his ears back underneath it. Still, the surface swim would be relatively short and then none of this would matter. They would be underwater and in a different world.

"See you finally stumped up the credits for one, then?" Rob said, indicating the small item Aaron held in his hand.

He looked down at it and smiled. "Yeah. It was a little more than I wanted to pay, but I couldn't resist. I've wanted one of these since the day they came out. I've been itching to try one."

"Boys and their toys," Rob grinned.

Aaron was still gazing at his newest purchase. In his hand he held the latest state-of-the-art, cutting-edge product in diving technology. They called it the human gill. He had christened it his "widget."

The human gill was a narrow, curved, roughly triangular gadget with a mouthpiece. The front looked like it was covered in a fine mesh grill and the mouthpiece was attached to the back. When in use, the curve ran down over the diver's face and under his or her chin to where the base of the triangle provided a wide exhaust port for expelled water from each breath in, and expelled air from each breath out.

It was called the human gill because it was exactly that. Inside the small unit were billions of synthetic nanofilaments which had been produced to mimic the action of a fish gill, namely, extracting oxygen directly from the water. When the diver inhaled, the oxygen was delivered via the mouthpiece and the filtered water expelled through the ventral exhaust port. When the diver exhaled, his breath was blown out through the exhaust port as a series of bubbles.

The product had been in research and development for decades and had taken countless man-hours to produce, but finally it was available to the sport diver and people were raving about it. It had revolutionized the dive industry and opened up a whole new world of diving possibilities. From what Aaron could remember, all the reports on it had been good. All the reviewers in the online forums and the e-zines loved it.

For starters, it did away with the cumbersome scuba tank, giving divers a whole new sense of freedom. You could simply swim with it in your mouth. Secondly, by extracting the oxygen directly from the surrounding water it eliminated many of the problems of breathing compressed air from tanks. No longer did divers need to worry about nitrogen absorbed into the bloodstream and the risks associated with it—the bends. There was also no need for decompression stops. But by far the biggest advantage of the human gill was that the diver was no longer limited by the amount of air they could carry on their back. Dive time, or "Bottom time" had just been increased indefinitely.

"Come on," Rob said, pulling on his cumbersome tank. "Let's get down there before the whole place is swarming with divers."

They were going to be diving the wreck of the *Glissade,* a large tour boat that had been ripped free of its moorings in the great storm of 2237 that had destroyed so much of the western banks of the great lake. She had drifted far from the ruined navy pier, tossed about on the waves like a cork until eventually she had capsized and begun taking on water. She had almost righted herself as she sank, the heavy hull racing to meet the silty bottom, but the relatively shallow depth had not allowed her to rest with any final dignity and she lay on her port side in ninety feet of water.

Aaron strode purposefully into the water, kicking spray out in front of him with each step. Even through the waterproof shell of the dry suit and the undergarments he wore, Aaron could feel that the water was cold. When he was wading in waist-high water, he reached down and secured both fins onto his booted feet. He pulled his mask up over his head from where it had been hanging around his neck and spat into each eyepiece, running his gob of saliva around each lens with his gloved finger before rinsing the mask in the cold water. Aaron secured the mask on his face and looked over at Rob to find his friend already waiting for him.

"Okay?" Rob asked nasally through his own mask.

Aaron nodded, placed his widget in his mouth and lowered his upper body into the water. Together they began swimming out from the shore.

* * * * *

The shock that registered on Komicki's face was almost comical. For the briefest of moments, as he stood there wide-eyed and rooted to the spot, he could have easily passed as one of the displays in the store. In the next instant, Komicki bolted. Lieberwits didn't give chase.

Komicki pulled on the door that gave access to his rear storeroom and work area and found himself staring into Wood's chest.

"My. My. We are in a rush, aren't we? Going somewhere?"

"N…n…n…"

"Here, let me finish for you," Wood said. "No officer. No…. That's exactly right. You aren't going anywhere. So why don't you go back over there and take a seat while the nice detective asks you some questions."

Reluctantly, Komicki turned and was escorted back into his store.

Lieberwits cast his hands wide and shrugged with a mock frown. "Andy. I thought we were friends. Why the sudden animosity?"

"The what?"

"Oh that's right. I'm sorry. I forgot you only deal in small words."

"Screw you."

"Five letters, Andy. That's good. That's really good."

Komicki shrugged off Wood's grip on his arm and returned to behind his counter. Lieberwits saw him reach for something out of sight. He sighed, deeply, then tutted.

"Andy, Andy, Andy. I really wouldn't go for that gun I know you have back there."

"I ain't doing nothing." Komicki protested.

"I *strongly* suggest," Lieberwits said firmly, "that you back away from the counter. I really don't want to send Officer Wood around there to find that weapon that we all know is there, because if I do, then you'll be going down for possession of an illegal firearm and none of us want that now, do we?" Lieberwits gave his best smile.

Komicki thought better of it and backed away, taking a seat on a high stool. "What *do* you want?"

"Just some answers. So let's just keep this nice. Now why did you run?"

"I thought you was someone else," Komicki lied. "I owe some people some money. They're due to collect." That was no lie.

"Why don't you say we forget about that? That's your business and none of mine."

"Look, why don't you just get on with it? You two are making me nervous. People see cops hanging around here, they're gonna start asking some questions of their own. It could be bad for my business and bad for my health. You hear what I'm saying?"

"You're okay, Andy. Officer Wood here is the only one wearing a uniform and, as you noticed, he came in through the back door. I think you're safe for now, but I'm hoping that means we can count on your full cooperation?"

"Whatever," Komicki said angrily. "What is it that you want? I think you were telling me."

"Any of your crazy friends been around here lately?"

"Which crazy friends?" Komicki threw his hands up in exasperation. "Look around, detective. You see the line of work I'm in? I deal with people who want their pets frozen and grandma as a permanent fixture. You want crazy? My whole clientele is crazy!"

"I think you know who I mean," Lieberwits said. Komicki just gave him a blank look.

"All right. Let me put this to you another way. Have any of your fanatical friends been around here recently?"

Komicki shook his head. "I told you. I'm not into that stuff any more."

"But you still have friends within the organizations, don't you? Contacts?"

Komicki laughed. "You think so? You think they'd agree with what I was doing now?"

"Maybe." Lieberwits said. "If it was in their interest to do so?"

"What are you suggesting?" Komicki said angrily.

Lieberwits feigned innocence. "Me? I'm not suggesting anything. Why? What's got you so upset?"

"Nothing." Komicki backed down.

"So you wouldn't have contact with anyone like that? You wouldn't have seen any of them recently? None of them came around here asking for favors?"

"No."

Lieberwits sighed. "Well then I guess you can't help us." He turned to leave. Komicki visibly brightened, thinking he had been let off the hook. "Oh, there is one other thing," Lieberwits added, turning back and causing the growing smile to evaporate off Komicki's face. "These people...the ones you said you owed money to..."

"Like you said, it's none of your business."

"No, you're right. It's not. But I'm guessing they wouldn't be too pleased if you couldn't pay them back?"

"What are you talking about?" Komicki snorted.

"Well, you see, Andy, I checked your record before we came to pay you this visit and these folks...well, they're not the only people you owe money to. You've got a nice little collection of parking fines that the Chicago police would like paid up."

"Aw, come on, man. That's low."

"It is." Lieberwits smiled. "But I'm not above low."

"Come on man," Komicki pleaded. "You see the space I've got to work with." Lieberwits cast another glance around, none too impressed. "I've got to get my stock into my store somehow."

"That's not my concern. What is my concern is that, along with your parking tickets, you have a string of minor felonies that, if I spoke to the right people and pulled a few favors, could get you put away for twelve to eighteen months."

"You wouldn't." Komicki was clearly scared at such a prospect.

"Oh I would." Lieberwits assured him.

"He would." Wood agreed enthusiastically.

"You...you can't! I mean...I mean...If I was away for that long I wouldn't be able to work, and if I wasn't able to work, then..." He trailed off, not wanting to contemplate the possibilities. "You can't!"

"Of course, Andy, all of this is avoidable with a little cooperation. Let me ask you again. You're sure none of the alien rights people came around here?"

Komicki shifted nervously in his place as if considering his options. He looked once at Lieberwits and then at Wood, whose fingers played with the restraining cuffs clipped into his belt. "All right. All right." The words seemed to burst from him. "I'll tell you what I know."

* * * * *

Travis's team splashed their way along the tunnel. Periodically they had passed a ladder which led up to a manhole cover and exit to the street, but they hadn't passed one in a while now.

The filth they were marching through was getting deeper and the tunnel getting wider, to accommodate the increased flow of... Travis didn't want to think about it. If he thought too hard about what was seeping through his socks he was sure he would puke.

His helmet lights sent two converging beams through the blackness, spotlighting an area of the tunnel some fifty feet ahead of them. The view never changed, it was always just the same surface of the filthy water and the dark forms of rats scurrying away along the water's edge. His eyes were growing accustomed to the darkness but he was sure his nose was never going to be accepting of the God-awful stench down here.

Behind him, Helen was coping admirably, it seemed. She was using the curvature of the tunnel underfoot to keep herself on a straight path.

"Anything?" he asked her.

She shook her head.

Behind her the rest of the team trudged along as a jumble of silhouettes, their helmet lights sending giant shadows running across the tunnel walls.

Travis wasn't surprised by Helen's response. While the sewer they were searching was silent, their progress was anything but. The tunnel was acting like a giant echo chamber, amplifying the slightest sound tenfold. Eighteen pairs of booted feet walking through shin-deep water made one hell of a noise. Much as he hated to do it, Travis was contemplating splitting the team up, because if the infant puglion had any sense it would be far, far away from them right now.

Apart from that, two other things were clear, They were moving deeper into Chicago's labyrinth of sewer tunnels—and the smell was getting worse.

* * * * *

Aaron hated that sensation. That first time you dipped into the water and the cold liquid seeped through the neoprene to make contact with your skin before your body had a chance to warm it. It was an unpleasant feeling when it soaked through your gloves and touched your fingers but when water that cold came through your hood it was as uncomfortable as an ice-cream headache.

Their surface swim had been a lot harder than he had anticipated. The chop broke over their heads and shoulders, and making headway through the waves had taken considerable effort.

Aaron stopped and lifted his head out of the water, checking the dive computer on his wrist and the GPS coordinates stored in it. He took the human gill out of his mouth. "This is…it," he said between waves. "She's right below us."

Rob simply nodded, not wanting to say anything, just wanting to get underwater and out of the weather. He gave Aaron a thumbs-down sign, meaning they should descend, and Aaron replaced the gill and returned the sign.

Together, face-to-face, they slipped below the surface.

And the world fell away.

* * * * *

"Some guy came in one day."

"You got a name?" Lieberwits asked?

"No. No name. Just said he was referred to me by a friend…if you know what I mean."

Lieberwits smiled and nodded. "Those friends you no longer have any contact with, no doubt. What did he want?"

"He wanted me to keep an ear to the ground, y'know, listen to people in the store. Then if I thought they were the right kind of people, talk to them and try and scope out if they might be interested in getting involved in an organization like that."

"You get a lot of people in here like that?"

"Not really. Like I said, they don't dig what I do. But a lot of the neighborhood kids come in. They're curious. They find all this stuff kind of freaky and cool."

"He wanted you to recruit for them?"

"Kinda."

"Kinda?" Lieberwits raised his eyebrows. "You get any interest?"

"Some."

"Yeah, knowing the neighborhood kids around here, I doubt they needed much of an excuse to get involved," Wood said.

"Did he say what this was about?"

"Just that they had some big job coming up. They didn't want to use any of their regular guys. They didn't want it traced back to them."

"He say what it was?"

"No. But I'm guessing you've got a pretty good idea, due to the fact that you've come sniffing around."

Lieberwits had to admit, sometimes Komicki wasn't as dumb as he looked.

"I didn't ask," Komicki added.

'That's always been your problem, Andy," Lieberwits said. "That's what got you into trouble in the first place."

Komicki shrugged. He couldn't argue with that.

"So how did this work…this recruiting?"

"I just referred them on. Nothing else. What happened after they left, I have no idea."

"You got contact details, then?" Lieberwits asked.

"Y'know, detective," Komicki said, scratching the back of his head in thought. "I had them around here somewhere, but I lost them."

"Andy!" Lieberwits said, in a tone that suggested the Komicki shouldn't play games with him.

"Come on, man. I've told you all I know."

"The contact details," Lieberwits said flatly, holding out his hand.

"If they find out I grassed I'll be dead meat."

"If you don't hand me those details you'll be going inside, and if I understand you correctly, you'll be dead meat anyway."

Komicki shot him a look of disgust, then moved for the counter.

"Ah! Ah! *Slowl*y, Andy. Slowly."

Komicki touched a pressure pad and a drawer popped open. He rummaged around in it for a while, digging through loose bits of paper, small vials of liquid, data crystals and credit chips. Eventually he surfaced, holding a small black rectangle in his hand. He went to hand it to Lieberwits.

"Here. I'll take that." Wood stepped in and took the data card out of Komicki's hand. "This old fossil won't know what to do with it," he said, indicating Lieberwits and inserting the card into his wrist unit.

"Well?" Lieberwits asked him.

"Just a link number, that's all. And a few letters. ALL."

"ALL?" Lieberwits looked at Komicki.

"The Alien Liberation League," he said with a sigh.

"All right. Thanks, Andy. You've been most helpful."

"What are you going to do?" He looked really afraid.

"Don't worry," Lieberwits said, turning to leave. "Your information will be treated with the strictest police confidence."

"Here." Wood handed the data card back to him. "Have yourself a very nice day."

* * * * *

Aaron and Rob had been diving buddies for years and that was a great thing. Good dive buddies were hard to find and the pair of them had been diving together for so long that now they seemed to instinctively know where the other man was in the water. It made for good diving. They didn't need to worry about their buddy, they could both just get on with what they were there to do, enjoying the dive.

And it had been a good dive. Despite the surface weather, they had enjoyed visibility of up to twenty feet and at fifty feet beneath the surface they had caught their first glimpse of the *Glissade* as it emerged out of the darkness below them.

They had come onto the wreck at the stern, first seeing the railings that had once encircled the passenger viewing platform on the back of the boat and which now sported beards of brown algae swaying gently in the mild current. Considering how long she had been down here, the *Glissade* was still relatively intact.

They dropped over the side onto the deck, seeing seats arranged in neat little rows of six and looking out of place in their new, vertical configuration, waiting for passengers that would never come. There was something eerie about it, like they were looking at the husk of a ship and somewhere above them, the spirit of the *Glissade* still cruised the surface, shiny and new, searching for the body now dead and rusting on the lake floor.

They had swum around the back of the stern and past the huge bulbous end of the boat that housed the anti-grav hover system. The *Glissade* had once given its passengers a ride that was as smooth as skating on ice whatever the weather, hence her moniker. Like most modern boats, she had floated ten feet above the surface of the water. It was only when her drives were switched off that her actual hull came into play and she floated at her mooring like the boats of old.

Once they had swum back up onto her starboard side, they used the railings as their guide, following them up the middle of the ship until the upper decks had started to appear. At one point, Rob had found an open door and encouraged Aaron to follow him inside the wreck but Aaron had refused. He wasn't keen on the idea of wreck penetration, certainly not with something like the *Glissade* that had been underwater for such a long time and whose fundamental structure was starting to fail. It might only take the slightest displacement of water from a fin kick or merely the disturbance created from bubbles to bring rusting decks and bulkheads crashing down and trapping them inside.

Rob had looked disappointed but they had moved on.

Not long after, they had reached the wheelhouse—a misnomer since boats hadn't had wheels for centuries. Most of its windows were shattered, either from the storm that had been the boat's nemesis or from disrespectful divers breaking their way in. On this occasion Aaron had consented to swimming inside with Rob, sending a shoal of resident fish scattering, and the pair of them had enjoyed a few moments pretending to be at the helm of the great ship, albeit horizontally and seventy-five feet underwater. Aaron cast his eyes over the panels and displays, all covered in a fine layer of silt and waved some of it away to see the controls underneath. He couldn't help but be reminded that for all of man's technology, nature and the elements still had a way of besting him.

They had left the wheelhouse and swum parallel to the deck, pointing out features of interest to one another and marveling at the life that had managed to get a foothold on the wreck, using the place as a home.

When they reached the bow, Aaron had turned to Rob and bringing his thumb and forefinger together in a ring had signaled his friend the "okay" sign. It was a question and an answer. "*I'm okay. Are you okay?*"

Rob had wrapped his arms around himself and shook slightly. He was cold. Even with all their thermal protection, the water still sucked heat away from the body at an alarming rate. Aaron checked his dive computer. They had been down for forty minutes. It was time to end the dive and ascend.

Aaron gave Rob a thumbs-up sign and jerked his hand upward. Rob nodded and returned the gesture. Together they came off the wreck.

* * * * *

Travis's decision was made for him when he came to a fork in the tunnel. He stopped, wondering which was the best way forward, peering into the identical voids to try and find something that might indicate which was the better route. He was rewarded with nothing.

"Do you have any inclination of which way we should go?" he asked Helen.

She cocked her head, as if straining to detect something and stood there for a moment before shaking her head. "I'm sorry. I'm not sensing anything."

"Don't worry. I understand. I think this smell has dulled all of our senses."

She smiled, faintly.

"Visor," he said. "Schematic"

On the right side of his visor, the blueprints of the city sewer system were displayed. One of the first things Wyatt had done when he arrived was get access for the ULF teams to the city database so they could download all manner of documents pertaining to the city to aid in the recapture effort. Travis had made a point of downloading the sewer blueprints to his helmets in-built chip the minute he had learned they were heading underground.

"Location overlay and zoom," he commanded.

The blueprint shifted in front of his eye, then zoomed in and showed sixteen faint orange dots aligned in a neat row in one of the tunnels. It was them. He was looking at his team, the radio frequency identification tags in each of their helmets showing their exact location.

But they were faint.

The radio signal was failing this far underground and if they went deeper still, it was likely that he would lose any and all ability to keep tabs on the recruits in his charge. Splitting them up was a risk, but now he had no choice.

Ahead of them, on the schematic, he could see the tunnel split into two parallel tributaries.

"Hey! What's going on up there!" someone shouted from the back of the line after being brought up short.

"We've got two tunnels." Travis shouted back. "If we're going to cover this system properly we're going to have to split up."

With sixteen recruits, him and Helen, he toyed with the idea of forming two equal groups of nine. But they were only recruits and Travis had decided he would be staying with Helen. If he split them up equally, then he'd have one team of nine recruits and another with only seven, Helen and himself. For as much as everyone else doubted her, Travis felt that the latter team would have a distinct advantage with Helen on their side.

"Okay, the first six guys are going to stay with me and Helen and take the left pipe. The rest of you, I want you to take this other tunnel."

He couldn't predict what they were capable of with their limited training and experience, but there was safety in numbers, if nothing else.

* * * * *

"So what was your chat with Harrod all about?"

"Huh?" Lieberwits was miles away.

"Your little tête-à-tête," Wood said. "How come Harrod is so interested in what you're up to?"

"He thinks I've got a vested interest in this case."

"And do you?"

"Not exactly."

"Not exactly? What's that supposed to mean?"

Lieberwits paused before speaking. "I was out there. At the zoo. Five years ago. There was a double homicide and something was all wrong about it."

Wood frowned. "What do you mean?"

"The murder weapon was an antique, and the one of the two dead men was a high ranking official from the CSETI..."

"The what?"

"That's what I said first time I heard it. The Continuing Search for Extraterrestrial Intelligence."

"Think I liked the acronym better."

Lieberwits nodded, then continued. "The other guy was the managing director of the IZP at the time."

"And?"

"The whole thing was a whitewash. They called it as they saw it. Swept the whole thing under the carpet. Case closed."

"Any witnesses?"

"Nope."

"So nobody wanted the desk duty. Who cares?"

"I do." Lieberwits protested. "I'm a cop. I want the truth."

"What makes you so sure they got it wrong?" Wood asked.

"What I saw there doesn't make sense with what the report concluded. It's not a gut thing...trust me, I've had plenty of those too. This was just plain wrong."

Wood raised his eyebrows.

"Look," Lieberwits said. "You might make fun of me for not carrying all the new cop gadgets, but I'm a good cop and I've got good instincts. That whole thing just doesn't sit right with me."

"So you've been fishing around for your own version of the truth ever since, huh?"

"Yes."

"Oh yeah," Wood said with a sigh. "I bet Harrod loves you."

The pair of them sat in silence for a while before Lieberwits spoke again.

"You ever hear of a zoo being a crime scene?"

"No."

"You ever hear of a zoo being a crime scene twice?"

"Never."

"Don't you think that's odd? A little more than coincidence?"

Wood shrugged. "I guess."

"You guess?" Lieberwits shot him a sideways look. "Guessing doesn't solve crimes, Officer Wood."

He reached forward and hit a button on the dashboard and the HV lifted off the street, the wheels thudding into place beneath it as it readied itself for skytrack coupling.

"What are you doing?" Wood asked. "Where are we going?"

"I'm going to find the truth." Lieberwits said. "We're going back to the zoo."

* * * * *

Aaron watched as the wreck of the *Glissade* disappeared from view below him as he slowly finned for the surface. Remembering Rob, he turned in the water to check on his buddy. They were still in fifty feet of water and it would be another twenty feet before they hit the thermo cline which would give his friend some minor relief from the numbing cold.

Rob was maybe twenty feet away and facing him. He looked okay, slowly kicking his way through the water, but probably best to check. Aaron started to raise his hand to signal to him again but froze in place.

Behind Rob, something had moved. It was as if the murky water had coalesced and taken on form, but the scale of it was incomprehensible. Aaron thought maybe his eyes were playing tricks on him, or maybe he was wrong and the thermo cline was deeper than he had remembered, the two layers of water causing a brief distortion in his vision, but now there could be no mistake.

Aaron's eyes widened in horror as a huge head appeared out of the gloom. He tried to shout a warning but his scream was carried on a stream of bubbles until he literally spat the gill out of his mouth.

For the briefest of moments, Rob seemed to be aware that something was wrong and sensing a presence behind him, he began to turn toward it.

Aaron looked down to see his widget spiraling into the depths. It was lost to him. He looked back up just in time to see a huge maw open and Rob disappear as he was sucked in with thousands of gallons of water. Aaron screamed again and precious bubbles escaped past his lips.

He bolted for the surface. His only hope now was a controlled emergency ascent on what little air he had left in his lungs. He kicked as hard as he could and blew out a steady stream of bubbles as he rose through the water.

Aaron broke the surface with a gasp, heaving in his first life-saving breath and immediately began to swim for the shore, pulling himself through the water arm-over-arm as fast as he could. He never looked back, terrified that the monster below might return for him.

When he made it to the beach, he had barely enough strength to pull himself from the water, collapsing face down on the sand while the breaking surf played around his ankles.

He lay there for a long time, sobbing and shaking uncontrollably.

* * * * *

Travis's team of recruits waded along the second tunnel, Andersen on point. "What the hell are we gonna do with this thing if we find it anyway?" he complained. "I mean, it's not like we're just going to rope its tail and drag it out of here."

"We're supposed to contain it." Barron replied.

"Oh yeah? How are we gonna do that? Splay nets aren't going to stop that thing."

"They have grates down here in the sewer." Barron said. "They're kinda like big combs. They use them to control the flow of water or to stop and remove any large solid matter. If they need to, they can drop a second grate over the first which completely seals the tunnel, you know, if they need to do maintenance or something. Look" He pointed up at the tunnel ceiling. They were crossing a join between two tunnel segments and in a small gap above their heads, Andersen could see the bottom of a large metal grate that could be lowered like a portcullis into the sewer pipe.

"How's that gonna help? What are they gonna do when they have this thing trapped then?"

"Don't know. But at least they can figure that out without fear of the puglion roaming freely around the sewer system."

"That's ridiculous," Andersen said. "That's the dumbest plan I've heard yet."

"Will you stop complaining?" McDermott yelled from the back of the line. "All I used to hear from you in basic training was you whining, 'Same shit, different day, Same shit, different day.' At least you're out in the field now, actually doing something."

"Yeah," said Cauldfield. "And look on the bright side. At least down here it's different shit, every day."

Andersen huffed and continued on.

* * * * *

Travis struggled through the thigh-deep filth. Realizing something was amiss he stopped. He could not hear the sound of the others behind him.

He turned and found Helen in his lights some thirty feet behind him. She had stopped and now steadied herself with one hand against the tunnel wall, the other hand pressed against her forehead. Argyle had come up behind her. "Sir, she doesn't look right."

Travis walked up to her. "Helen, what is it? Are you okay?"

She waved off his concern with a hand.

"Is it the smell?" The stench had become overpowering.

She shook her head as if trying to clear her mind. "No." She said. "I just got an overwhelming sense of something. Another presence."

"You felt something?"

She nodded. "It's close."

* * * * *

Andersen slowed in his tunnel and held up a hand, motioning for the others to stop. "Shhh."

"What is it?" Barron asked.

"Don't you understand the meaning of 'shhh'?" Andersen snapped at him.

"Sorry."

"Don't be sorry. Just shut up!"

Andersen scanned the tunnel ahead, the spot from his helmet lights describing a slow circle. His right hand played nervously over the butt of his quad-sys gun. "You hear something?"

Barron came up next to him and listened for a moment, then shook his head.

Andersen had never taken his eyes off the tunnel ahead. "There!" he said. "You hear that?"

Barron squinted into the darkness, straining to hear. Yes! There was something. A high-pitched squealing, and now that his ears had tuned in to it, it was clearly getting louder. "Yeah," he nodded slowly. "I hear it."

"Yeah, well, whatever it is, it's coming this way. Get ready, boys!" Andersen shouted to the others behind him. "It's time to prove ourselves."

The squealing was now clearly audible and getting louder with each passing second. In the distance there was movement. Andersen squinted to make it out but it seemed to be just beyond the range of his helmet lights. "What the hell...?"

Whatever it was it seemed to fill the tunnel, but there was nothing identifiable about it. Andersen peered at it harder and soon his lights did a better job of illuminating the mass that raced towards them, reflecting off hundreds of tiny eyes. Now he could see it for what it really was.

"Rats!" he said, watching in horror as the black tide of life swarmed towards them.

There were hundreds, maybe even thousands of them, racing down the tunnel. They clawed their way along the walls and swam through the filth, climbing over one another and pushing others under the surface in their individual bid to get ahead. Their squealing and squeaking was now almost deafening in the close confines of the tunnel. Within seconds they were among the men.

"Get them away from me!" Barron screamed. "Get them away from me!"

McDermott stood calmly at the back of the line. He wasn't afraid of rats. He knew the rats were more afraid of them, which was why the rodents had previously been scampering away down the tunnel.

He couldn't explain it. "Why are they run...?"

He stopped, not wanting to finish his thought process out loud. He found his own answer before finishing the question.

CHAPTER 10

Now that his veterans had completed the preliminary sweep of the zoo, Wyatt dispatched the keepers out to the enclosures of their usual charges. There they could monitor the exhibits that had remained and prepare to handle the return of the escapees.

Bobby, Chris and the rest of the ULF team were now out in the city, mopping up what they could. A number of Chicago's citizens had managed to restrain and hold some of the less dangerous aliens that had stumbled onto their property. Among them was seven-year-old Katie Whittler, whose talking point at today's show-and-tell was something she had found in her backyard, which was certainly of other-worldly origin and had caused widespread pandemonium at Jefferson elementary school. Wyatt chuckled to himself, remembering how the teacher who had called it in had told him how the little girl had thrown a tantrum when they had taken the small grontauk away, stamping her feet and bawling, "I found it! It's mine!" Now these helpful citizens were just waiting for the ULF team to arrive and take away their unexpected visitors.

In addition, the city's law enforcement had done their part, and now a line of police transporters was queuing up at the staff entrance, their caged interiors housing some of the most unusual captives they had ever carried. Interspersed among them were the armored vehicles from the security firms who had also thrown hardware and personnel into the capture effort.

Wyatt looked at the map and ran a hand through his hair. He breathed a big sigh. For the first time since this debacle had begun he was beginning to feel some semblance of control. Now he was able to remove some of the yellow identifiers from the map as the team called in what they had recovered and the keepers updated the zoo's inventory of exhibits as aliens were returned. He wasn't able to match the rate of new sightings, but at least he no longer felt like it was exponentially running away from him.

Gruber had been no help whatsoever. From the time he had sauntered in that morning, he had basically shut himself in his office. On the one occasion Wyatt had passed by his door, he had heard Gruber on his link, singing the praises of his ULF teams - even though there was really only one out in the field. This in itself was unusual for Gruber. Normally he showered his praise on his zookeepers. After all, they were the ones who looked after the aliens and maintained them in such a condition that they could be shown to the paying public. The trappers rarely got a mention. Gruber normally seemed to regard them as one step up the evolutionary ladder from catfish, his mentality apparently being that if these men and women were prepared to risk their lives in such a fashion, then they clearly didn't care much for their own lives and therefore neither should he.

Now, though, the trappers were his salvation and he could not speak highly enough of them. He was still using this disaster as a massive PR event, which was absurd and wrong on so many different levels.

* * * * *

Andersen never stood a chance. The puglion struck with such ferocity and speed that he was dragged under the surface of the water before he had even uttered a cry.

The attack sent Barron sprawling and rats flying everywhere. When he surfaced, Barron was gasping and in a blind panic. Every man had his Achilles heel, and it seemed that Barron's was rats—something he should have maybe expressed before embarking on this venture. A pair of the large black rodents sat on his shoulders while others fell away from him. He fumbled with his quad-sys gun, ratcheting the barrel around to select a different firing mechanism. "Burn them! Burn them!" he mumbled to himself like a madman, oblivious to the fact that his friend and colleague was no longer with them.

* * * * *

Lieberwits took the zoo exit from the skytrack and reconfigured the HV as he piloted it down to street level. Within moments they were back at the staff entrance of the zoo, and at the tail end of a long line of armored vehicles.

"What the hell is all this?" Lieberwits activated his police light and pulled around them, driving along the wrong side of the street until it narrowed and he could go no further. At the gatehouse there was access for only one vehicle so security checks could be performed, and now the pair of them found themselves sitting behind a large police transporter.

Lieberwits honked his horn. "Come on!" he yelled. "I don't have all day!"

In the back of the transporter, something threw itself against the steel bars visible through the two small square windows, and gave an impressive display of teeth and talons.

"Okay." Lieberwits said meekly, re-evaluating his position. "I can wait."

* * * * *

Ahead of him there was chaos in the tunnel. Like Barron, the others were panicking. Fumbling with weapons or turning to run. Their helmet lights sent shadows running everywhere and cast bodies in sharp silhouette, and their cries of terror just added to the bedlam.

McDermott had been stunned, both by the speed of the attack and the size of the infant puglion. He didn't think it was possible, but the thing had clearly grown in just the short time it had been down here.

Cauldfield bumped into him as he pushed past, snapping him out of his trance. McDermott looked up to see a look of abject terror on the other man's face.

"Come on, man!" Cauldfield screamed. "Let's get out of here!"

McDermott turned back to look at the others ahead and his lights fell on Barron. He could see Barron's lips moving as he chanted his own mantra and then Barron looked up and McDermott could see the madness that consumed him.

For a moment the world stood still.

It seemed like everything came to him in that instant. He saw Barron's gun configured for the flamethrower. He was once again acutely aware of the stench. He realized they were standing in a potent gaseous mixture.

"No!" McDermott screamed.

And he knew that they were all about to die.

Without a second thought McDermott took a deep breath and dove into raw sewage.

Barron pulled his trigger and they were engulfed in flame.

* * * * *

"Sir?"

Wyatt looked up at the interruption. One of the security guards stood across the table from him.

"Sir. Our man at the gatehouse says there are some people here to see you."

"Who are they?"

"Police officers, sir. A Detective Lieberwits and an Officer

Wood."

Wyatt nodded. "Send them up. They're harmless enough."

* * * * *

Lieberwits wheezed as he pulled himself up the stairs to the upper gallery.

"Got answers for me already, detective?" Wyatt asked.

Lieberwits smiled weakly, catching his breath. "Sadly, no. No answers. But I do have some questions for you, if you don't mind."

Wyatt shrugged. "Sure. What can I do for you?"

"You weren't here last time I was here, were you?"

"When was that?"

"Five years ago. The last time this place was a crime scene."

"The shootings?" Wyatt asked.

"Yes. The shootings."

"I was an employee here, if that's what you mean."

"Why don't I remember you?" Lieberwits asked, fingering his bottom lip.

Wyatt cast his mind back. Mannheim and Leonardson had been found dead at almost exactly the same time he and his crew had arrived at the moonbase. "I was just on my way back from an expedition. One from which I was never expected to return."

Lieberwits frowned.

"It was a set-up. We were expendable." Wyatt offered by way of explanation.

"Who sent you on such a trip?"

Wyatt laughed. "One of your corpses. Mannheim." He paused for a moment. "I heard he got messed up pretty good."

Lieberwits nodded. "It wasn't pretty."

Wyatt nodded thoughtfully. Lieberwits could have sworn he saw a brief look of grim satisfaction pass over his features.

"The police never interviewed you?"

"No. I quit on my return."

Lieberwits gave him a look to suggest he should explain further.

"I'm sure you can imagine, we'd all had a pretty harrowing time. I wasn't here after that. I guess the police had no reason to speak to me."

"How did Mannheim know about this place he sent you to?" Lieberwits asked.

"I don't know."

"You don't know?"

"Look, detective. I was a trapper. A lackey. The orders came down from on high. We were always getting sent out to new planets. Our part of the job was simply to suit up and show up. We never questioned where we were going. It wasn't our place to."

Lieberwits changed tack. "But your...what do you call them... your ULF teams. They're not getting sent out so much any more, are they?" It was an educated guess and he was throwing it out to see if anything stuck.

"Well, I don't work here any more, but no, from what I understand the teams aren't going out so often. The zoo isn't acquiring as many new specimens as it used to. So, no."

"Why is that?" Lieberwits asked. "Last I heard, we're still exploring the far reaches of the universe. Aren't we?"

Wyatt nodded. "I don't know the reason, detective. Like I said, I don't work here any more but I know this much. This place is nothing compared to what it was in its heyday." He shook his head, remembering times past. "I don't know," he said again. "They must be low on money or something. I know we used to ask for new equipment all the time and never got it. I'm guessing that's it."

"Really." Lieberwits turned to Wood. "Never would have guessed." He returned his attention to Wyatt. "Do you guys keep records of your expeditions?"

"Yes. I'm sure we do."

"Well then, is it at all possible that I could get a copy of those records, for say, oh, I don't know, the last ten years?"

"It might take a little while, but I could probably get someone to get that information to you."

"If you could. I'd appreciate that." Lieberwits forced a smile. "Oh, and send it to Officer Wood here. He has all the new-fangled gadgetry that handles all that stuff."

An awkward silence descended on the three men.

"Was there anything else?" Wyatt asked.

"Actually, there was." Wood spoke up.

Both Wyatt and Lieberwits raised their eyebrows in unspoken question.

"When I interviewed your security guards here, they said that a section of your perimeter wall had gone down briefly before the intruders got in. Is there any possibility I could go and take a look at it?"

Wyatt thought about it for a moment. "Sure. I don't see why not. I just need to get you guys some protection. Just in case. Come with me."

* * * * *

Travis felt the stagnant air get sucked past his face and instinctively knew what was coming.

"Get down!" he yelled to his team. He turned and grabbed Helen by her arms. "Take a breath," he ordered and then he dove below the surface of the filthy water with her, but not before catching a glimpse of the raging fireball that raced down the tunnel towards them.

* * * * *

Lieberwits and Wood waited by the doors of the security building and watched as Wyatt approached. He carried what looked like three large cocktail forks and waved them outside to join him.

"My ULF team has given the zoo the green light but that doesn't mean nothing's out there. These things are tazer forks. I want you to each carry one. Do you know how to use one?"

Lieberwits eyed the business end of one of the six-foot long poles. "You mean it doesn't come with a manual?"

Wyatt looked at the two wicked prongs. "I see your point."

Lieberwits turned to Wood. "Is he trying to be funny? I thought I was the only funny one around here."

Wood rolled his eyes.

Wyatt couldn't help but smirk a little. This Lieberwits guy was all right.

* * * * *

Travis, Helen and the rest of the recruits gasped for what little air hadn't been consumed by the fire. That need fulfilled, they immediately began to gag and retch.

Above ground, every manhole cover on nine city blocks was rocketed skyward by the force of the explosion, and on Carpenter Street, one of those punched straight through a taxi HV passing above it, killing the driver instantly.

* * * * *

The air conditioning engineer stood in the elevator and whistled a tune as he watched the floor levels tick by into the four hundreds. Just his luck. Last job of the day and he would be working in the tallest building in Chicago.

They called it the Needle. A gargantuan cylinder of steel and glass that dwarfed everything else in the city and made the Sears and Trump Towers look pathetic in comparison. At its peak, an equally enormous cone of blue glass was tipped with a huge antenna. It resembled a gigantic syringe.

He checked his watch. At this rate it was going to take him twenty minutes just to make it up to the roof. He could have taken one of the turbo lifts which would have propelled him to the top in a fifth of the time, but he'd heard stories of people coming out at the observation deck with bleeding ears. He was sure they were urban myths, but why take the chance? Just in the time he'd been in the standard elevator he'd had to equalize his ears seven times to accommodate for the dropping air pressure. Maybe there was some truth in those rumors after all.

He still didn't understand why they couldn't send a bot to deal with the problem, but he suspected that the tenants of the needle demanded a more personal touch. He shuddered to think how many credits they were paying in rent for this exclusive piece of Chicago real estate.

* * * * *

"This is it." Wyatt said.

The two policemen surveyed the scene in front of them. A large, solid perimeter wall ran around the entire zoo. Inside this a second perimeter fence ran, although it was not really a fence, just a series of containment fields generated between a line of posts.

"This spot right here?" Wood indicated.

"Uh-huh."

Wood stepped away from them and moved to inspect the posts.

"Careful." Wyatt said. "That thing's wound up pretty high. It'll give you a nasty jolt."

Up close, Wood could hear the energy from the field bristling and crackling. He crouched and looked at the first post. Satisfied, he walked to the second and did the same. There was no sign of any physical damage. "It makes no sense," he said quietly to himself.

"What was that?" Lieberwits asked behind him.

"I said it makes no sense." Wood stood and returned to the others. "Why would you take it down and then bring it back up again?"

The two other men thought for a moment. It was a good question.

"To make it look like a blip. A random glitch, so as not to attract attention," Lieberwits offered.

"Besides, once they were in, they were in," Wyatt added. "Getting out is easy."

Wood shook his head. "I've been to enough burglaries to know that people who break in don't take that much care. They smash a window or break a lock because at some point the crime is going to be discovered—it's too obvious to cover."

"You're saying this break-in wasn't meant to be discovered?" Wyatt asked incredulously. "After everything that's happened?"

"Not exactly. You're right, Detective Lieberwits, they didn't want to attract attention in the first moments. They were buying themselves time. They had to get into security to upload the virus. But that said, there's far too much care here to suggest that it was a random break-in by some fanatics."

"What do you mean?" Wyatt asked.

"Your security system is pretty advanced. It has to be, right? These guys knew not only how to take down just a portion of the perimeter fence, but also how to bring it back up again. Not only that, but the virus they uploaded to your system interfaced perfectly with your software and hardware. You can't do that without some knowledge."

"But how would someone know…?" Wyatt stopped asking the question as the truth of what Wood was saying finally sank in.

It was an inside job.

* * * * *

"I'm sorry," Travis said to Helen. Behind her, he could hear the coughs and dry-heaves of the rest of his recruits.

"For what?" She coughed. "For saving my life?"

"No. For getting you covered in shit."

"I'd rather be alive and covered in shit than the alternative."

"Yeah... Well... I'm sorry."

"Forget about it. There are more important things to worry about."

She was right. Travis didn't yet know the origin of the blast but he feared for his other team. All he could hear in his ears from his link was static. "Team one to team two. Do you copy? Over." Nothing. Just the crackle of static that seemed to get worse when he turned his head. "Wyatt? You copy?" Wyatt was supposed to be their liaison with the sewer's master control guys, once they had made contact with the puglion. They would call in their location to Wyatt, who in turn would tell the sewer guys which grates to lower into place to contain the alien. Travis had no idea if any of his other team were capable of responding but Wyatt should be there, at least. Again, just the static.

He suspected that his helmet was now as good as useless to him. They were designed to function in rain, even heavy rain, but they were not meant to be subjected to complete submersion. He'd probably just completely fried the electronics inside it. At least the lights still worked. For now.

"Is everyone all right?" Travis asked. It seemed everyone was accounted for. "Torres? Are you back there?"

"Yes... sir." Torres managed between coughs.

"All right. We need to head back to the fork in the tunnel. Let's go."

Torres gathered himself and then began wading back the way they had come.

* * * * *

He slid his card into the slot and heard the electromagnetic lock deactivate on the roof access door. It opened easily with a push to reveal a very short, gray, barren corridor that ended with a small flight of steps.

He stepped through, sealing the door behind him, and then continued up the steps, grasping the cold, black iron handrail with one hand while carrying his toolkit in the other. As he ascended the steps, he slowed.

More and more of the glass dome was revealed to him as he climbed, and with it, more and more of a stunning cloud-filled sky. He stopped whistling his tune and simply whistled, all thoughts of work forgotten for a moment. "Wow."

A fan on one of the nearby generators kicked in and snapped him out of his awe. He took a look around. He was standing in a maze of machinery. Small nuclear generators, liquid cooling assemblies, industrial-sized air conditioning units. Most of them on a par with the scale of the building itself. For the first time he noticed the noise. That wasn't normal. These were all top-of-the-line machines. Silent runners.

He picked his way through the tangle of metal and piping, trying to pinpoint the sound, careful not to burn himself on machinery or get a blast of hot air from an exhaust vent. It wasn't long before he found the problem. In front of him one of the building's massive air conditioning units was vibrating wildly.

He quickly found and cut the power and the unit seemed to slump in relief. Once more, silence descended on the rooftop environment.

Carefully he removed the side paneling, doing a quick visual inspection of the guts of the machine. At first sight nothing looked amiss. He sighed. More investigation was going to be required—and that was going to mean more work. He looked at his watch and his face brightened a little. At least he could claim some overtime.

He pulled out some tools and began dismantling the air conditioning unit. He hadn't gotten very far when something inside the machine became dislodged and fell past him, hitting the floor with a resounding clang.

He frowned. There should be no loose components inside. Getting down on his hands and knees, he scoured the floor, laying his cheek almost flat against the cold surface. There, beneath the ducts and wiring, something lay on the floor. He pulled a small flashlight out of his belt and illuminated the object, seeing its blue coloration for the first time.

Getting down on his belly, he reached in, straining to grab whatever it was, his fingers playing over its edges teasingly. He shuffled further inside the machine, gaining precious inches, and closed his hand around it, pulling it out triumphantly. Struggling back to his feet, for he wasn't as fit as he used to be, he held it up to the light for a better look. "Glass?" he said. "How the hell did that get in there?"

Had it been regular window glass, the industrial-sized air conditioning unit would have probably chewed it up and spat out the pieces, but this was a solid chunk of glass that weighed maybe six or seven pounds and barely fit in his hand. He looked at it closer. It was maybe two inches thick, its flat surfaces tinting his palm behind a beautiful azure blue whilst the fractured edges and sides were patterned with hundreds of striations, beautiful in their own way.

As if on cue, an unearthly howl sounded in the domed roof, like someone blowing over the top of a tumbler but on a giant scale. It was spooky, and the engineer cautiously walked around the side of the unit, approaching the glass-walled edge of the dome. He walked up to it and touched it, laying his hands flat against the cold surface, looking down at Chicago far below him and then, out of the corner of his eye, he saw the other fragments.

He turned and walked over to them, crouching to examine the huge chunks of clear blue that lay scattered on the floor. Next to him, there was a gaping hole in the roof.

Standing, he peered out of the hole, allowing the wind to tousle his hair while he enjoyed the amazing view. To the west, the sun was already making a slow descent, trading yellow for a hue of orange. Above Lake Michigan, faint fingers of pink crept into the sky. Dusk was falling.

He rested his hands on the thick glass edges that remained in place and immediately removed them, repulsed by a residue on the surface that came away with his hands in long, sticky strands.

Involuntarily, he took a sharp intake of breath. He didn't feel any pain. He was just acutely aware of a sickly sound, like a knife cutting through gristle. Protruding three feet through his chest was a serrated black appendage. Its tip dripped with blood. His blood.

He looked up and behind him and saw a bug-like head with mandibles that clicked and worked together, alien saliva frothing between them.

She was ready to eat.

* * * * *

Torres was just at the tunnel intersection when he spun quickly and brought his gun around. His helmet lights found McDermott, his face pale and drawn and streaked with filth, his eyes wide and afraid. "Jesus, McDermott, you scared the crap out of me!" McDermott shrank under the lights' glare. He was visibly shaking. "Are you okay, man?" Torres asked.

Travis splashed his way to the front of the line. "McDermott! What is it? What happened? Where are the others?"

McDermott shook his head. "Gone. All gone. Barron torched them all."

"Oh, jeez."

"Apart from Andersen. The puglion got Andersen."

"You saw it?"

McDermott nodded quickly, fear flashing in his eyes once more. "It's big."

"I know."

"No. I mean it's gotten bigger. It's real big."

Travis looked down the other tunnel. At least they knew it was down there now. He wondered if they sealed this tributary whether it would give them any advantage—at least make a large portion of the sewer system inaccessible to the alien.

"Wyatt? Are you there? Wyatt? Do you copy?" There was nothing.

"What is it, sir?" Torres asked.

"We can't tell Wyatt which grates need closing." Travis thought for a moment "We've got to be able to seal this tunnel. There's got to be a manual system to shut this thing down if the computer system fails."

Travis played his helmet lights over the walls. He stopped at a deep circular recess in the concrete. Moving to it, he thrust his hand deep inside the hole and felt the square pin hidden in the darkness. "That's it." He said

"But how do we close it?" Argyle asked behind him.

"I have no idea. The engineers must have some kind of crank handle they fit on the end of this to manually wind it down."

"Would have been nice if they'd have told us about that before they sent us down here, don't you think?" Smith snorted. For once, Travis had to agree with him. Someone should get a dressing-down for not supplying them with such a basic piece of equipment.

"What do we do?" Torres asked.

Travis sighed. "Well for now, I'd suggest you lot get out of here. Get McDermott to safety and get back to the zoo. I need you to tell Wyatt which grate to lower into position. You guys know where we are on the schematic, right?"

The recruits all nodded.

"But what about you, sir?" It was Smith.

"I'll stay here and make sure that thing stays down there. We can't afford to have it come back up the tunnel and roam the sewer system again. It could be lost to us for months."

"But sir! ...that's...that's suicide."

"I can take care of myself."

"Besides," a small voice said. "He'll have some help." Helen stepped through the others to stand next to Travis. "I'm staying with you."

"Helen, I can't ask you to do that."

"You didn't. I volunteered."

Just then, Travis's helmet lights shorted out.

"How else are you going to see in the dark?" she said.

Travis frowned at her. How did she do that? He returned his attention to his recruits. "Go. All of you. Now. Before your own helmets start failing. You've got to get to Wyatt and get this grate lowered into place."

The young men regarded him with grim looks. He knew what they were thinking. They were looking at a dead man. They weren't going to see him again. He nodded an okay to them, releasing them of their guilt and allowing them to leave.

"We won't fail you, sir." Torres said.

"I'm counting on that." Travis forced a smile.

Reluctantly, the remaining recruits turned and splashed away into the darkness.

* * * * *

At first Wyatt had quizzed Lieberwits about what he knew; whether he had any leads, but the old detective was playing his cards very close to his chest and surrendered nothing. If he knew anything, he wasn't telling. Now, as they paced their way back to the security complex in response to a call from a very flustered link operator, Wyatt found himself lost in thought. He was perturbed by what Officer Wood had said out at the perimeter fence and what had been insinuated. He couldn't even begin to imagine who would do such a thing or why.

* * * * *

The three men climbed the stairs to the upper gallery slowly, Lieberwits bringing up the rear and puffing as he had done before. On reaching the top step, Wyatt was greeted by an agitated young man.

"Mister Dorren, sir. I'm sorry to have bothered you. He just came in. I didn't know what to do."

"Relax." Wyatt said, "What's going on?"

The young man turned and pointed. There was a figure standing by his table, regarding the city map with a look bordering on vague amusement. Wyatt's face contorted with anger. It was Goddard. The mayor's man.

"I thought I told you to leave!" Wyatt fumed.

Goddard started, unaware that Wyatt had returned. He regained his composure quickly. "Ah! Now, Mister Dorren," he began, fending Wyatt off with a pointed finger, "Let's not be too hasty, shall we?"

"What do you want?"

"Ah, well. You see, Mister Dorren. I considered your words after our last little chat…" Goddard smiled with all the sincerity of a lizard. "…and I realized I might have gotten things a little wrong."

"A little?"

"In hindsight, I agree, it would be foolish to arm convicts and let them loose on the city streets."

Wyatt seemed to calm a little.

"So I'm coming to you with a new offer of help. A new plan."

"Which is?"

"Oh, my. I think you'll like this." Goddard could barely contain his excitement. "I really do think this is brilliant!"

Wyatt regarded him with the same indifference, deflating him quickly.

Goddard cleared his throat. "Ahem. Okay. Well then. Here it

is." He looked around quickly, checking who was in earshot. "We still use the convicts in the recapture effort," he said quietly. "Only this time we use them as..." He leaned in closer, as if the last part was meant for Wyatt alone. "...bait."

Wyatt moved so quickly and punched him so hard that Goddard was flat on his back before he'd even realized what had happened. He sat up, cradling his ruined nose in his hands and looked at Wyatt with something akin to wonder. "What did you do that for?" he managed.

"I told you to leave. Remember?"

"You fuck!" Goddard's pain was rapidly being replaced with anger. He climbed to his feet. "Do you know who I am? I work for the mayor. You messed with the wrong guy! I'll sue you, you miserable bastard! I'll sue you for every credit you've got."

"Really?" Lieberwits regarded him coolly. "And when the story breaks, I'm sure the media are going to have a field day hearing all about how the mayor's office was proposing to use convicts as bait."

Goddard looked at him in horror, like someone who'd been betrayed at the deepest level. His eyes flicked between Lieberwits and Wyatt and back again, and then he turned and marched down the stairs and out of the control room.

Wyatt pulled a face of distaste and shook the pain from his hand. "I'm sorry you had to see that."

"See what?" Lieberwits asked. "You see anything?" he asked, turning to Wood.

Wood pulled a face and shook his head. "You want some ice for that?"

CHAPTER 11

Lieberwits's headlights came on automatically in the fading light. The HV cruised quietly down the street, its two occupants equally quiet, lost in their own thoughts.

Wood's wrist unit beeped, startling them both. He pulled back his cuff and checked it, then raised it to his mouth. "Received," he said.

"What was that?" Lieberwits asked.

"Test message from the IZP," Wood replied. "Just to make sure they're getting through. Don't want to be sending all their confidential documents to the wrong place, do they?"

Lieberwits shook his head. "Guess not." He thought a moment. "Can you pull up records from the CSETI on that thing?"

"I don't know. Maybe. That stuff's classified for a while, you know. I might be able to pull up some declassified records. What are you looking for, specifically?"

"Planet discoveries. The full history. Get the declassified stuff, and if any of it's classified, I want you to get a warrant for the rest." He paused for a while before speaking again. "That was a nice little stunt you pulled back there."

"What?"

Lieberwits pulled a face and did his best impersonation of Wood. "Oh, I wouldn't mind going to look at the fence." His face fell. "What was that all about?"

"It just occurred to me while we were there. That was all. If it weren't for you taking a detour in the first place, we wouldn't have been there. Are you upset?"

"No."

"You sound upset."

"It just came out of left field at me. We're supposed to be partners. I just want to know what you're up to."

"Chasing criminals." Wood said flatly. "And you, pulling years of IZP and CSETI records. What are you up to?"

"Chasing ghosts," Lieberwits said, his voice distant.

A silence descended on the vehicle again as the two men went back to their thoughts, both a little hurt and disappointed by their confrontation and obvious lack of communication.

"So what does a technophobe detective keep in his glove compartment anyway?" Wood said, reaching for the touchpad on the underside of the dashboard.

"Hey! Hey! You stay out of there!"

Wood reached in and pulled out something with a triumphant grin on his face. "A stress ball!" he laughed. He bounced it off the top of the dashboard and caught it in the same hand, giving it a squeeze. "I haven't seen one of these things in years!"

Lieberwits sighed. "Let me guess, you have software for that, right?"

"Oooh," Wood looked at him, feigning hurt, then raked his hand through the air like a set of claws. "Meow."

* * * * *

Gruber placed his palm on the access plate and the door to his apartment slid open. He was greeted with a wall of heat. Immediately his mood changed to one of anger.

Muttering expletives under his breath, Gruber marched into his apartment. He wrestled the tie off his neck and immediately went to his kitchen where he pulled a cold bottle of water from the refrigerator and gulped it down.

"Doorman!" he bellowed and heard the buildings comms system dial the link number.

"Hello?" The voice filled the room.

"I thought you said you were getting this air-conditioning fixed?"

"Ah yes, sir. Mister Gruber, sir. We have someone on it."

"On it? For God's sake, man, it's been all day. What's he doing, repairing it or installing it?"

"I don't know, sir."

"You don't know?" Gruber screamed.

"I mean…obviously the job is taking longer than originally thought."

"Obviously!"

"I'm sure the matter will all be taken care of as soon as is practically possible."

"You'd better hope so," Gruber yelled. "Or it will be your head that will roll." He hung up the link, disgusted, and cast his eyes over to the still-open sliding doors and the tied-back curtain that swayed in the breeze. He was going to have to spend another miserable night in a hot apartment.

* * * * *

Travis shivered. They had been down in the sewer system for almost twenty-four hours now, their bottom halves constantly submerged in the tunnel water, the rest of their clothes soaked from the dive that had saved their lives.

Not only did the water seem to suck the heat from their bodies, the tunnel concrete seemed only to serve to suck the warmth out of the surrounding air. Travis guessed that the hour was getting late, the temperature around them falling fast as night fell above ground. In the pitch-black, Travis could hear Helen's stuttering breaths as her small frame shook from the chill.

"You cold?"

"What do you think?" she snapped back at him. "I'm freezing."

"Sorry."

"About what?"

"About this. The cold. The whole thing. I'm sorry I got you involved."

"I wanted to help. It's not your fault,"

"Yeah, well. It doesn't stop me feeling bad about it. Maybe when this is all over I can take you out for a nice dinner or something."

A small smile touched her lips. "Are you hitting on me, Mister Jacks?"

"Oh, no! No. I would never."

She laughed. "For such a big man, you really are a timid soul, Mister Jacks."

"I guess."

"What is it you're not saying to me? I sense a sadness from you. Sorrow."

"Have you always been blind?" He asked.

"Always."

"I guess it's that. I'm sad for you. Sad for all the wonderful things in this life that you will never see."

"What makes you say that?"

"Well, just down here, in this tunnel, I'm starting to get an appreciation of what life is like for you."

Helen thought about his words for a moment. "No, Mister Jacks, you feel sorry for me because I will not experience the world as you do. However, my experience of the world is significantly different from yours, an almost altogether different experience. My world is ten times richer in sound and smell and touch and taste than yours will ever be. I might even suggest that it is you that I should feel sorry for. You rely so much on your sight that you miss so much more of what is around you. You close yourself off from so many other possibilities."

"What do you mean?"

"Here, I'll show you. Empty your mind of thought and cast your senses wide. Just listen. Don't pass judgment on the sounds you hear. Just listen."

He did as he was told, closing his eyes just to focus on his hearing and within a few moments he began to detect sounds that he had been oblivious to before. The quiet sound of slow-moving water. The pitter-patter of rat feet hundreds of yards away, and a haunting melody of drips. Now a smile touched his lips.

"That's just the beginning, Mister Jacks," Helen said, sensing his joy. "With practice you'd be amazed at what you can hear."

He opened his eyes again, having a new appreciation for the woman who stood before him. "We should try and keep warm," he said.

"How do you propose we do that?" Helen asked.

She heard him move and then felt a huge pair of arms encircle her and pull her close

"You're sure you're not hitting on me, Mister Jacks?"

"Oh, no. I would never." He let his head fall down on top of hers. "And by the way, it's Travis."

She sensed him smiling above her and put her slender arms around him in return. She smiled into his chest.

Together they shivered in the darkness.

* * * * *

Now that she was satiated and darkness had fallen, it was time to move.

Slowly, she began to extricate herself from the roof, exiting through the entry hole she had created when she had crash-landed here. Segmented limbs strained against the thick glass, struggling to lift her large frame back out into the night.

After an hour, she finally stood on the conical glass roof of the building, held there by the fleshy foot pads on the end of each leg that stuck fast to the smooth surface. She waited there awhile, her abdomen swelling and contracting as she composed herself. Then, with slow, measured steps, she began to descend.

* * * * *

Helen was virtually asleep on her feet. It was only Travis's strong arms that kept her upright, although he, himself, was exhausted.

Her head snapped up, catching him under the chin. "Oh! I'm sorry!"

Travis cupped his chin in his hand, rubbing away the pain. "Don't worry about it." He was more concerned with what had made her jump awake. "What is it? What's wrong?"

"I sense it again," she said. "It's coming back."

Travis felt his stomach knot. He had hoped they would have more time. He strained to hear something but there was nothing. Then he remembered Helen's lesson and closed his eyes to focus on his hearing.

From far away in the tunnel came a chorus of squeaking.

* * * * *

Wyatt's head dropped. He lifted it and placed his cheekbone back into the palm of the hand he was using for support. He had repeated the movement three times in as many minutes.

He sat on a tall stool now, struggling to remain focused on the map that hovered over the table next to him. Its marks and symbols appeared blurred and in duplicate to his tired eyes. He'd been awake for almost forty-four hours straight.

"Wyatt!"

"Huh!" Wyatt's head snapped up as he jumped to full alert.

"Wyatt." It was Hernandez. "Dude. You look awful, man."

Wyatt got down from the stool and nodded his agreement.

"I'm sure I do." He offered his hand and the other man shook it before clasping hands as was typical for their close-knit group. "It's good to have you back. Are you all right?"

"I'm fine. A little beaten up and a bit of wounded pride, but otherwise a good shower took care of most of my needs."

"That's good. And Mason?"

Hernandez shook his head. "He's gonna be claiming benefits for a long time. It doesn't look good."

"Shame. He was a good kid."

Hernandez nodded.

"Well," Wyatt sighed. "You'll be pleased to know that the rest of your crew is doing a fine job out in the city."

"I heard. Local news seems to be very supportive."

"Even Gruber's singing your praises."

Hernandez shrugged.

"So I guess you'll be wanting to get back out there with them?"

"That can wait. You gotta get some sleep."

"I'm fine. Really." Wyatt waved off his concern.

Hernandez's face turned serious. "You remember when you were a trapper?"

Wyatt shrugged. "Yeah."

"You remember how your teammates looked out for you and you looked out for them because lives depended on it?"

Wyatt nodded, knowing what was coming.

"I'm looking out for you right now. You're the nerve center of this whole operation, Wyatt. If you fail, this whole thing goes down. I can't allow that. Especially since I know when I go back out there, you're the one that's got my back, and I'm not going to be happy about that if I know you're not on the top of your game. Now what do you say I take over for a little while." Hernandez regarded Wyatt with a look that told him he would be foolish to argue.

Wyatt nodded again, secretly grateful for the younger man's persistence, then passed over his headset.

"Thank you."

The two men spent more than ten minutes discussing the current state of affairs, the indicators on the map and what to do in the event of a new sighting. Once Wyatt was happy that Hernandez could handle things for a few hours, he bade him goodnight and went and found a deserted office with a large sofa. He stretched himself out along its length and was asleep in seconds.

Forgetting that Hernandez had not been present when he had briefed the ULF veterans, Wyatt, in his exhausted state, completely failed to mention Travis and his team.

* * * * *

She was head-down and vertical, stuck against the side of the building as she continued her descent. She walked with a wobbling gait, inching herself forward slowly. It was a deliberate behavior she had honed on her home world that had enabled her to close in on prey without being detected.

Now her forelimb touched a new surface, a large rooftop terrace that jutted out from the wall. Its perimeter was marked by a wrought iron fence and its center was home to a pool of blue water.

She turned and skirted the wall, her left legs walking on the paved slabs, right legs still claiming footholds on the wall.

Her legs lifted and fell in her choreographed walk, and then her foremost limb reached out and touched something smooth. She pulled, expecting to move her large bulk forward. Instead, her limb retracted, the surface sliding easily towards her.

She climbed down fully from the wall and looked at the two dark rectangles in the building in front of her, testing them gingerly with her forelimbs. One was solid and smooth. Her relatively primitive brain recognized it from before. It was the same material that she had just made contact with. The other was a hole.

She moved forward and went inside.

* * * * *

Travis's helmet lights flickered on briefly and then went out.

"Your lights are coming back!" Helen said, seemingly as excited for herself as for him.

"How do you do that?" He asked.

"I'll tell you sometime. I just don't think this is the time."

Helen was right. The squeaking from along the tunnel was getting louder, which meant whatever it was, was getting closer.

"Rats?" Travis asked.

"Yes."

Travis slapped his helmet with the palm of his hand, hoping to get his lights back, but to no avail. "Dammit!"

He reached into his pocket, pulling out a glowstick which he held in his hand and snapped with pressure from his thumb. The mixing chemicals in the small plastic tube illuminated the immediate surroundings with a faint green fluorescence. Travis held the tube up in front of him like a talisman to ward off the approaching evil. He squinted into the darkness. The glowstick was as good as useless to them. As a light source it was pitiful.

Travis switched his gun from his right hand to his left, then reached behind him and began to remove the clubs from his pack.

"What are you doing?" Helen asked.

"Anything. Something that I think will buy us some time. How far away is it?"

"I don't know, but I wouldn't hang around."

Travis pushed the first of the clubs home around the barrel of his weapon and heard it lock with a click.

Helen heard it too. "Are those the same things you used in my apartment?"

"Yes."

"Well let's hope you have better success this time!"

"Agreed."

Travis pushed the rest of the clubs home, then placed the bound bundle of cord in the barrel of the gun's grenade launcher. Satisfied, he readied himself for the puglion. "I'm counting on you, y'know."

"For what?"

"To tell me when to shoot."

"You won't need me to know that."

Travis didn't doubt it.

* * * * *

Wood squinted at the large holo-screen in front of him, the bright white light providing the only illumination in the dark office. He rubbed his tired eyes and checked his watch. It was 3:00 AM.

He hadn't been able to access any of the CSETI's records from his wrist unit, even though it was supposed to be synchronized to CORE, which in turn was networked with local and federal government mainframes, and so he had asked Lieberwits to drop him at Central where he now sat and conducted his research.

He had downloaded as much data as he could find to his wrist unit but as he had suspected, the last five years of the CSETI's records were classified.

Wood typed into the last few fields of his e-warrant request and submitted the file. Tomorrow he would have the necessary means to seize the rest of those records.

* * * * *

Despite its initial encounter, the mantor had quickly learned to travel and hunt by night, scavenging from garbage cans and fleeing when its investigations would cause lights to come on from the nearby houses. Homeowners would open front doors and step outside to see who or what had roused them from their sleep. Sometimes they were armed. Often times they were not, brandishing nothing but a flashlight, blissfully ignorant of the lethality of their long-gone intruder. But the mantor did not seek confrontation or wish to hunt the humans that slept in their beds. It was simply hungry and searching for anything to fulfill that basic need.

The mantor slowed from its run and now padded noiselessly down a deserted street. The alien was now thirty miles northwest of the city and well beyond the shrinking perimeter set up by the police and armed forces. Here the suburban sprawl was punctuated by parkland. Oases of green dotted the concrete and asphalt.

Turning off the street, the mantor stepped onto grass for the first time and immediately stopped, lifting its large paw and retreating before bringing its nose down to sniff the new surface. Experimentally, it patted the grass again, unsettled by the foreign texture. The mantor hesitated before pacing the line of paved slabs that bordered the large play area, a low growl giving voice to its unease. The alien continued to test the grass with a paw until eventually it was satisfied and took its first tentative steps towards the small row of trees on the opposite side of the clearing. Once there, it lay on its belly, dropping the chicken carcass it had salvaged from its earlier foray between its outstretched legs, sniffing it over once more.

After an experimental lick, the mantor started to feed, crunching bone and gristle with one powerful bite.

* * * * *

The sound of the rats was much closer now. Travis held his quad-sys gun in his left hand and waved the glowstick before him with his right. He could see nothing save for himself and a faint impression of Helen close by.

He looked down at his weapon, seeing the four clubs of the splay net loaded and ready to fire, and wondered if his plan would work.

The net itself was useless against a creature the size of the puglion. It was designed to capture small- to medium-sized animals. Once fired, the clubs would fly on their diverging paths, pulling the carefully wrapped net apart between them. Once the net hit the target, the clubs, halted of their forward progress, would then wrap around the specimen, enveloping it in netting and immobilizing it immediately. It was an extremely effective capture method when used correctly. Except he wasn't using it for capture. Not directly, anyway.

The squeaking was much closer now, accompanied by the sounds of splashing water as the vermin swam and climbed over one another in their attempt to escape. Travis shifted in his spot, unsettled by his lack of sight, but knowing that the danger was frighteningly close.

His gut told him to act.

Travis hurled the glowstick as far as he could down the tunnel, watching the small plastic tube and its accompanying sphere of illumination describe a graceful arc away from them. Just before it splashed into the dirty water and was lost to them forever he saw them in the faint glow. A swarm of rodents, no more than twenty feet away from them.

With one deft move, Travis switched the gun in his hands and fired into the abyss. "Come on! Move!" he said to Helen, finding her arm in the darkness and pulling her away.

Together they struggled through the thigh-deep water, willing themselves to move faster. Travis instinctively chanced a glance over his shoulder and the movement of his head caused his helmet lights to briefly flick on. Behind them, in the water, a huge ball of rats struggled to escape the netting.

He said a silent prayer to himself, hoping that he had done enough, when suddenly there was a huge splash behind them as the water erupted and the puglion attacked.

"Come on!" Travis yelled again.

A series of splashes followed, as the puglion's huge jaws worked to maneuver its meal. Then it threw its head back and swallowed it whole. Satisfied, for now, the alien slowly turned and sank back into the water, swimming away from them with casual strokes of its tail.

Travis stopped. "It's okay," he said breathlessly. "I think we're okay."

"What happened?" asked Helen. "What did you do?"

Travis looked at the retreating puglion. "I packed it a lunch."

* * * * *

Gruber rolled over. Even unconscious, his body protested against the heat, causing him to toss and turn. He sighed deeply in his sleep.

He fidgeted again, grasping the top of his sheet and attempting to push it away from him, but the sheet wouldn't move.

From somewhere deep in his mind came a spark of conscious thought. That shouldn't be. There was no reason why he shouldn't be able to push his sheet away. As he began to further process the thought, Gruber slowly blinked awake.

His eyes were well-adjusted to the darkness and as he lay on his side, he could make out the bedside cabinet close to his head and the items of furniture that skirted the wall, the room described in grays, dark blues and black. He sniffed and immediately wrinkled his nose in disgust. Whatever they were doing to the air conditioning, they had royally screwed it up. Something foul was permeating the air.

Gruber grabbed the sheet to flick it away from him. He would sort this farce out once and for all. But again, the sheet would not move.

He turned his head then and found himself staring into a pair of compound eyes only feet away from him. A pair of black, segmented antennae searched the air and a wicked set of mandibles worked feverishly together.

Gruber screamed and tried to push himself away from the abomination but he was held fast. The creature was standing over him, its legs making a cylindrical prison around him and the sheer weight of it on his bedsheet holding him fast.

He felt pressure and looked down to see the alien's abdomen curled up underneath it and probing the sheet, the tapered segment of body heaving and pulsating with the promise of new life.

Gruber screamed again and then fire exploded in his belly as the alien found its mark and injected its precious cargo. He saw his blood spreading over the sheet and then he passed out.

CHAPTER 12

"Here you go, sir." The young link operator put the cup of coffee down on the desk.

"Thanks." Hernandez gave her a quick nod of acknowledgement. "And you don't have to call me sir. It's Juan."

The woman smiled, embarrassed, and left.

Hernandez turned back to the map. It had only been a few hours and already he was getting tired. He had asked for the coffee to counter his fatigue and took a sip of the dark brown liquid, wincing at both its strength and temperature. He had no idea how Wyatt had managed to keep this level of concentration up for so long, but guessed it was because he had a vested interest in making the city safe - his young family.

Hernandez stopped himself. Wyatt's sense of responsibility probably ran a lot deeper than that. Wyatt had worked in the ULF department for years before he had elected to leave. He would know firsthand what most, if not all, of the aliens in the zoo were capable of. It was not just Wyatt's son at risk, it was the whole population of Chicago, and Hernandez realized that was something that they should all be deeply concerned about.

He shook his head, trying to rid himself of the weariness that was creeping up on him and regain some focus when Smith and Argyle and the surviving members of Travis's rookie squad clomped their way up the stairs to join him. To a man, they looked disheveled, exhausted and apathetic. They looked broken.

"Jeez." Hernandez wrinkled his nose in disgust. "What's that stink? Is that you?"

Smith just shrugged and nodded. "Yeah."

"What happened?"

"We got sent into the sewer to go after the puglion."

"Oh, jeez," Hernandez said again.

"You didn't know?"

"No, I didn't know!"

"Wyatt didn't tell you?" Smith was somewhat agitated now.

"No, he didn't tell me." Hernandez could sense Smith's brewing anger. "Look, I'm sure it just slipped his mind. He was exhausted when I relieved him."

"Yeah, well, whether it slipped his mind or not, we need his help now."

"Yeah," Argyle chipped in. "That sucker's gotten big. I mean bigger."

"And Travis is still down there with the civilian. They could be in big trouble. They could be dead, for all we know. We need Wyatt. Where is he?"

* * * * *

Travis's helmet lamps were slowly coming back, electing to stay on more often than off. Occasionally they would flicker and go out, plunging them into darkness again and causing Travis to curse under his breath, but a few good slaps on the side of the head would usually be enough to encourage the lights back into life.

It appeared most of the circuitry in his helmet was drying out since now his comms system was broadcasting a constant hiss of static, which, while somewhat irritating, seemed somehow slightly more reassuring than the dead silence of before.

With his lights back and his ability to see restored, even if it was somewhat intermittent, Travis was mindful of the lesson Helen had taught him. He tried to remain focused on the heightened state of hearing she had enabled him to tap in to. It may well have been why they both sensed danger at the same time.

"You heard it, didn't you?" She asked.

"Yes. I heard something. Sounds like it is still a long way away, though."

She nodded. "What do we do?"

"If it is coming to feed, we run." He didn't know how many hours had passed since their last encounter with the puglion but he doubted it was more than four or five. The alien was feeding much more frequently than he had expected which no doubt accounted for its sudden growth spurt.

"You can't do whatever it is that you did before? Don't you have any more of those things?"

"Nope. Normally we retrieve it with the captured specimen and then get it ready to use again. We don't expect it to get eaten. It was our 'get out of jail free' card and we've already played it."

For the first time, Helen looked really scared.

"You should go." Travis said. "Just go back the way we came. It's practically a straight route. Just keep going until you get to a ladder to get out of here."

"What about you?"

"I'll do what I can." Travis sounded pessimistic. "Besides, I can see it coming now."

"I think I'd rather be blind, Mister Jacks…" She stopped herself. "Travis. I can't see this thing but even I know there is nothing you can do to stand against it. Your weapon is useless to you - the slightest spark is going to cause an explosion down here. What's so important that you have to sacrifice yourself? What is it you think your kamikaze attitude is going to achieve?"

"I'd hoped we could contain it in this part of the sewer. It would make the recapture effort so much easier if we knew which section it was in. Once it goes back past that split in the main pipe, it could go anywhere."

"That's not worth losing your life for, Travis, and now is not the time to be a hero. It may get free run of the sewer system but it is in the sewer. It poses no threat to the people above ground. Others can come and find it at another time."

She was right, of course. Now he knew he could not even fire off a few rounds to scare the puglion away, since just the flash from the muzzle of his gun could be enough to set off a catastrophic chain reaction. If not that, then a spark from a ricochet.

He was clinging to an idea that somehow his efforts could contribute to a greater good, but ultimately the likely result would be his death. He was not afraid of that eventuality, but looking at her reminded him that there were things to live for. "Kamikaze, eh?" A wry grin spread over his face. "Is that what you think of me?"

She nodded. "Among other things."

"Oh? Such as?"

"You're too good a man to die in such a pointless fashion."

Travis felt his cheeks blush with color. "You form opinions of others pretty quickly."

"Sometimes. Sometimes their actions define them for me."

"Anything else?"

"Maybe," she said with a smile. "But you'll never know if you stay down here to meet your maker."

There was a pause and then Helen spoke again.

"Anyway, I need you."

"You do?" Travis felt his heart lift.

"Yes. If I'm going to get out of here, I could use a guide. In case you hadn't noticed, I'm blind."

She offered her hand and Travis took it and together they began to walk back the way they had come.

As Travis splashed through the water, dozens of thoughts raced through his mind. If the puglion was coming back, chances were they wouldn't get to an exit ladder before it caught up with them and they were going to be forced into a confrontation regardless. He knew this, of course. It was why he had elected to stay - to give Helen a fighting chance - but it was not a concern that he wanted to voice out loud. Going with her though only served to put the two of them in danger. By insisting that he go with her, she was putting herself in harm's way.

He thought about her last comment. She was teasing him, of course, she was more than capable of finding her way out of here, even blind, but when he thought about it seriously he realized, for the first time, that he didn't notice her disability any more.

* * * * *

Wyatt jumped awake, then groaned as he remembered where he was.

He checked his watch. 8:15AM. He had slept for a while, but not nearly long enough. It would have to do, though. He lay on the sofa for a moment, collecting himself and his thoughts, rubbing sleep from his eyes.

He dialed home on his com link. It probably wasn't too early to do so. He was sure Alex would be up and giving Kate the runaround already. The link rang twice before she picked up and her face appeared on his small screen. She looked flustered.

"Hello...oh, hi."

"Hey. How are you doing?"

"Good...Can you hang on a minute?"

"Sure."

He could hear her in the background settling Alex down. After a moment she returned, brushing back a wayward strand of hair. "What's up?"

"Nothing. Just thought I should call and see how my wife was doing."

"I'm good. We miss you."

"Yeah. I miss you guys, too."

"Have you slept?"

"A little. One of the other guys relieved me. Basically ordered me to get some sleep." He chuckled.

"That's good." Kate gave a weak smile. "It sounds like things are going well," she continued. "At least from the bits of news I've seen."

Wyatt nodded. "It's not perfect, but I'm pleased with the way things have been going so far, considering what we've had to work with. We've had a lot of help from people we never expected to get help from.

"That's partly why I'm calling. You should be okay to go to your parents now. The perimeter has closed in. Just don't go straight through the city, that's all. I'd take the skytrack out to the end of the old tri-state, then cut up through Addison and keep west of the skyport."

Her face brightened. "Okay. I'll do that. I think Alex will be pleased to see Grandma and Grandpa. It'll be good for him to get a change of scenery."

"I think so too."

"I'll take Furball too. He likes the open spaces out there. It's really the only chance he gets to climb."

"Sounds good."

"Okay."

"Okay."

There was an awkward silence and then Kate spoke again. "Can we expect to see you out there any time soon?"

"I'll try, it's just…"

"I know. You've got to take care of that stuff. Any idea when you'll be done?"

"It's impossible to say, Kate. It could be a couple of days, it could be a week, but I'll come and get you guys as soon as I can."

"All right," she sighed. She sounded resigned to the fact that she was going to be without her husband for quite some time. Alex wailed in the background as if he, too, was dismayed at his father's news. "I gotta go. Okay? I love you."

"I love y…"

But Kate had already terminated the link.

Wyatt sat forward on the sofa and held his forehead, giving his eyes one last rub with the heels of his hands. He sighed deeply, psyching himself up to go and face another day of Chicago's problems. He never expected Chicago's problems to come to him.

* * * * *

Gruber's eyes blinked open. Sunlight streamed through the bedroom windows, bringing a harsh light to the room. He squinted against the brightness and then remembered the horror from the night before.

He went to move and found he was stuck fast. He couldn't even lift a finger. He tried to scream but discovered he couldn't open his mouth, his lips sealed together by hard strands of resin that had set in place. He could just barely breathe through his nose.

His eyes, now wide and afraid, searched the room, just as his thoughts, in similar fashion, searched his mind for an explanation.

He looked down his prostrate body, having just enough vision to see his torso and upper arms encased in organic white strands, and he realized that he had been cocooned in place while unconscious. The alien had cemented him to his bed after its attack and now it...what?

He saw it then. A creature of obsidian black, stationary in the corner of the room. It was standing almost upright, its eight legs folded and stacked in front of it, moving gently in tandem with the slow pulse of the abdomen as it breathed through the spiracles in its body. Occasionally, one of its antennae would twitch or move, but otherwise it was motionless.

Gruber could not tell if it was sleeping or just standing there waiting. And if it was waiting, waiting for what?

He felt something move in his stomach, like trapped gas shifting through his guts, and then there was excruciating pain. Gruber tried to scream again, but all that passed his lips was a muffled grunt. He blinked back tears, terrified, finally understanding what was happening.

He was going to be eaten alive. From the inside out.

* * * * *

The door burst open and Hernandez, Smith and Argyle spilled into the room.

"Wyatt! You gotta come quick," Hernandez said.

"What's the matter? What's going on?"

"These guys say the puglion has gotten bigger and Travis is still down in the sewer."

"What! What happened to the rest of your guys?"

"Gone," Smith said.

"Gone?" Wyatt didn't want to believe what was implied.

"Dead," Smith confirmed for him. "Nine of them wiped out."

"The puglion?"

"No. Barron decided to light up his flamethrower. We didn't know that the air down there was explosive. He torched them all before they could even scratch their asses."

"But…?"

"We were lucky," Smith anticipated the question. "Travis had split us up. We were in a different tunnel." He turned for the door, "Come on, I'll fill you in as we walk. Travis could be in serious danger." He shared a glance with Argyle, "And we promised him we wouldn't let him down."

* * * * *

The four men ran down the corridor and into the security control center. Wyatt bounded up the steps to the upper gallery, taking them two at a time. Smith was right behind him, still talking a mile a minute to get Wyatt updated on everything that had happened.

Wyatt ran around the central table and cleared the city map. He pulled up the sewer blueprints, which now hovered in its place. "Where did you say you were again?"

"Sector green five," Smith said, unconvincingly, looking to Argyle for confirmation. He nodded his agreement.

Wyatt identified the area on the map. "Zoom and resolve." The map homed in on the target area, updating itself so everything remained described in smooth flowing lines.

"Is that them?" Smith asked from across the table, squinting and bringing his face closer to the image.

Wyatt saw it too, now. Two orange spots on the blueprint, so faint as to barely be visible. He watched them for a moment. They were definitely moving. "I think so. Hold on. Let's see if we can raise them on the com link." Smith looked pessimistic. He adjusted his headset mic and spoke. "Travis? Travis? Are you there?"

* * * * *

"…avis…an you…ear m…" Fragments of speech broke up the static.

"Oh my God!" Travis said, instinctively holding a hand up to the side of his helmet.

"What? What is it?" From his tone, Helen couldn't tell if Travis was surprised or relieved, or maybe a little of both.

"It's them. I mean, it's Wyatt. Wyatt! We're here!"

* * * * *

"Anything?" Smith looked skeptical.

Wyatt began to shake his head, and then stopped himself. He pressed the earpiece of his headset further into his ear and with his other hand motioned for the others to be quiet.

* * * * *

"Wyatt! Can you hear me? We're here! We're still alive!"

* * * * *

Wyatt looked up quickly, the fire of excitement in his eyes. "I've got them, but they're faint." He walked quickly to the balcony, looking down over the dozen security staff who were working frantically. "I need this patched through to the speaker system immediately, and crank it up, it's barely audible." He didn't care who did it, as long as it got done.

Wyatt returned to the desk and spoke another number into his com link, waiting while the number dialed.

"Hello. Chicago sewer system master control."

"Yeah. Hi. This is Wyatt Dorren with the Interplanetary Zoological Park."

"Good morning, Mister Dorren. We've been expecting your call."

Thank God. At least they had been briefed. "Hi. I have personnel down in the sewer system right now, sector green five. I'm going to need your help in lowering grates into place."

"Certainly, Mister Dorren. We have green lights on all operational systems. Shouldn't be a problem. Which grates can we assist you with?"

He didn't have the faintest idea. He looked at the map again. Red hashed lines bisected the solid lines of blue designating the sewer tunnels. He didn't for one minute think the water down there was that color. He looked closer. The red lines were clearly grates, but there was nothing on his blueprint to distinguish one from another. "I don't know," he said.

"Do you have him on the line?" the sewer operator asked.

"Yeah."

"Connect me to him. I can help him out."

* * * * *

Travis's elation was quickly extinguished. Behind them what

had begun as just a distant sound was evolving into a full-scale disturbance. The sound of the rats was getting louder. They were running out of time.

* * * * *

"Wyat... We nee...your...elp. Quickly!" Travis's voice filled the control room, which was unfortunate since everyone present could easily detect the anxiety in his voice.

"We're doing everything we can. The sewer people are conferenced in."

"Hello?" the operator's voice came over the speakers. "With whom am I speaking?"

"...avis Ja..."

"I'm sorry?"

"Travis Jacks. His name is Travis," Wyatt impatiently filled in the gaps in their conversation. He ran a hand through his hair, frustrated. He wished she could see their position as easily as he could. She would be able to immediately identify which grate to lower - as it was, they were all blind in some capacity.

"Travis. Are you near a grate?"

"No. We passed...a while back"

Wyatt spun and looked at the blueprint. They were midway between two, but marginally closer to the one they had passed. "Travis. Can you backtrack? The nearest grate is behind you."

"...egative. The pug...is coming up the tun...ehind us. I'm not going to risk go...back just to identify....grate."

"How far apart are those grates?" Wyatt wondered out loud.

The sewer operator heard him. "Half a mile."

Half a mile. That would mean Travis had to cover at least a quarter of a mile through water to reach safety.

"Should I just lower all the grates in their sector?" The operator's voice came again.

Wyatt thought about it for a moment. It wasn't a bad idea. If they lowered every grate in place they effectively stopped anything from moving down there. Then as soon as Travis could identify exactly where he was, they could begin to withdraw the grates to free him whilst keeping the puglion trapped. The problem was, Wyatt didn't know just how far away from them the puglion was and judging from the urgency in Travis's voice, it was close. If he took the operator's advice, he could effectively be locking Travis and Helen in a segment of sewer pipe with the alien, and if he did that he was signing their death warrant. He shivered at the thought. "No. That's not an option," he snapped.

"Okay," the operator's voice remained cool on the link line. "We need to find another solution, then." There was a pause and then she spoke again. "I need you to find a number for me." Wyatt realized she was now talking to Travis. "It should be somewhere high on the tunnel wall."

* * * * *

Travis pushed Helen forward. "Go! Just keep moving!" He stopped and lifted his head, scanning the tunnel wall as Helen sloshed away from him. He saw nothing but bare gray. "I don't see anything. I don't see it!"

* * * * *

"He doesn't see anything."

"I heard. Tell him to keep moving," she said, momentarily forgetting Travis was patched in himself. "I'm sorry. Travis. Keep moving. Keep looking. It will be there somewhere."

* * * * *

Helen was now some distance away from him further up the tunnel and moving fast. Good. If nothing else he could at least try and keep her safe.

Adrenaline coursed through his body. He could feel his heart thumping in his chest. Behind him, the squeaking of rats and the sound of the approaching puglion was unmistakable. Every one of his synapses was firing, telling him to get the hell out of there, and yet there he was, moving slowly, methodically scanning the tunnel walls for a number. "Jesus H. Christ," he muttered under his breath.

His helmet lights caught a flash of something. Something white against the gray. He rushed forward, almost stumbling as the filthy water impeded his progress, then stood and focused his lights on the wall. "I have it! Fifty-one! The number is fifty-one!"

* * * * *

"How does that help us?" Wyatt asked.

"I know which sector of the tunnel he's in," the operator responded. He could hear her working over the link, finger strokes being made on sensory pads that responded with tones. "Which means we can also identify the grates at either end of that section. Green fifty-one and green fifty-two," she confirmed out loud. "Which way is he moving?"

Smith looked at the map. One of the faint orange dots had almost made it to the next grate and safety, the other lagged behind. Regardless, they were both now upstream of the fork in the pipe. He looked at Wyatt. "Upstream. They're moving upstream."

"Upstream. Away from the fork," Wyatt relayed.

"Green fifty-one then," the operator deduced over the link.

They had put the pieces together. The puzzle was now complete. The only remaining factors now in play were whether Travis had enough time…and the distance.

"Get out of there, Travis!" Wyatt yelled into his headset.

* * * * *

"Ge…t of ther…avis!"

What the hell did they think he was doing? Still standing in place gawking at the number on the wall?

Travis was already moving. In fact, immediately after he had relayed the information they needed he continued to forge his way upstream. He had tried to run, but the deep water had resisted his attempt and he continually stumbled. The fastest he could move was at best what could only be described as a jog, albeit a jog with a comical, loping, gait.

He scanned the tunnel ceiling, searching for the telltale black line that would denote the divide between sections and the home of the saving sewer grate. He willed it to appear. Helen was distant now, well beyond the limited range of his helmet lights. He could hear her sloshing through the water far ahead of him. Of more concern were the sounds of squeaking and the rush of moving water approaching from behind.

* * * * *

"Oh crap!" Smith looked at the blueprint intently. "It's Travis!"

"What is? What?"

"The second radio tag! Look!"

Wyatt scrutinized the blueprint. The small orange dot deep in the tunnel was visibly moving which, on this scale, meant it was moving fast.

"He must have sent the civilian woman on ahead." Argyle pointed to the second marker. "She's already safe."

What Argyle said was true. The second dot in the tunnel had already passed through the red hashed line, or in reality, under the grate. It didn't surprise Wyatt that Travis had sent her on ahead and put himself in danger. It was just the kind of selfless thing he did.

* * * * *

"Wyatt. When I tell you, I need you to drop that grate. No questions asked."

* * * * *

Travis's words had come through as garbled fragments. "Sorry Travis," Wyatt said, "I didn't copy. Say again."

"When I say….rop the grate. No questions as…"

Wyatt looked at the blueprint and Travis's identifying marker. He still hadn't passed the location of the grate. "Travis! You're still not clear. You're not safe. Do you copy?"

* * * * *

Travis huffed. Hadn't he just told them not to ask questions? His survival depended on them doing exactly what he told them, exactly when he told them.

Ahead, just at the maximum range of his visibility, his helmet lights were starting to pick out Helen's form as they jumped and swept across the tunnel. He was starting to catch up to her. Of more concern was what was catching up to him.

The puglion was close. Really close. As a one-time trapper, he had an instinct for these things. He felt the hairs on the back of his neck stand up.

* * * * *

"How fast do those grates come down?" Wyatt asked.

"Fast," the operator replied. "Put it this way, you don't want to be underneath it when it happens."

Wyatt rubbed his chin and noticed his hands were shaking.

Across from him, Smith paced the length of the table, agitated and frustrated. Every second, it seemed, he would glance up at the blueprint and quickly look away, not wanting to believe what it was showing. Argyle too looked at the hovering image, only he stared at it intensely as if privately willing the display to change. He was biting his bottom lip so hard it was starting to bleed.

There was nothing they could do.

* * * * *

Travis scanned the tunnel ceiling ahead. There! Clearly a divide between the tunnel segments. Helen was already well past it. "Get ready!"

"Trav…ou're still not…afe!"

"Wyatt! I need you to do this when I say! I don't have time to argue about it! Besides, there's got to be some delay between me and you." He didn't know how much they had heard or understood. Just as long as they understood what they needed to do.

* * * * *

Delay? Wyatt doubted it. That was probably Travis trying to make them feel better about their situation. Travis could be facing the apocalypse and still find something good in it. It was just the kind of man he was.

"Can you do tha…for me?"

"Yes." Wyatt said quietly, resigning himself to fate. "I can do that." He stood, quiet for a moment, then took a deep breath which seemed to galvanize him to action again. "Operator?"

"Yes."

"When Travis gives the signal, you drop that thing as fast as you can. Copy?"

"Understood."

* * * * *

The squeaking of the rats was deafening. The splashing and movement of water, amplified by the tunnel's confines, had become a roar. It was as if the water itself had come alive to pursue him. He was feet away from safety, but if he didn't act now they would almost certainly both perish. "Now! Now! Now!" Travis yelled.

* * * * *

"Now! Now! Now!" It was the first transmission that had

come through from Travis entirely clear and it blasted out of the speaker system so loud that everyone in security started.

"Actioned!" came the operator's voice immediately.

* * * * *

The grate came down faster than Travis expected. It did not look like he was going to make it.

* * * * *

"Closed and locked," the operator's voice came again a moment later, her soothing tone returned. "Is your man okay?"

"Travis?" Wyatt asked. There was no reply. "Travis?"

Silence. Not even the background hiss of static remained.

Travis was gone.

As if on cue, one of the news networks began replaying Gruber's statement from the previous day. Wyatt looked up at hearing the voice, his face contorted with frustration and anger. "Where is he?" he asked. It was now 10:00 AM. "Has anyone seen him today?" The link operators all shook their heads. "So no one's seen him?"

One of the operators spoke. "I think he was working from home today, sir."

Working from home. What was that, code for sitting around on his ass?

He wanted to have it out with Gruber. He wanted to scream at the man and tell him this wasn't all some big publicity stunt. People were dying out there, and now they had just lost another of their own. Travis Jacks. A good man.

Denied even that, Wyatt slammed his fists down onto the desk.

CHAPTER 13

Whether buoyed by the television news' optimistic appraisal of the recapture effort, reassured by Gruber's PR stunt, or simply blessed with stupidity, some residents of downtown Chicago were now beginning to venture out of doors.

Clearly they thought they were safe, believing that the wave of danger had passed and now radiated outwards to the suburbs. Nothing could have been further from the truth.

The cordon formed by the police and Earth Alliance troops was now slowly closing in, concentrating any remaining escapees within its boundary.

Downtown Chicago was right in the center of Wyatt's "hot" zone.

* * * * *

Immediately following the loss of communication with Travis, Wyatt had ordered the sewer operator to close and lock all grates downstream of Travis's last known position in that section of the sewer. He had regained his composure quickly and realized that if the puglion had been closing in on Travis, then if they shut down that section of the tunnel completely, the alien would at least be contained until they figured out what to do with it.

Regardless, the loss of Travis made him sick to his stomach, like he had swallowed a stone and the dead weight just hung inside him, refusing to budge. They had lost another of their people. A good man and a good friend. Wyatt remembered now why he had quit the zoo and Project ULF. He had thought days like this were long behind him.

* * * * *

Wood drove his patroller up to the front gates of the CSETI. A young uniformed officer exited the gatehouse and stepped down the few steps to the asphalt. He had not looked up at the vehicle, just been aware of the approaching presence and had come to greet it, all the while intently studying a handheld unit which no doubt displayed the day's appointments. There was no entry for this unscheduled visit.

Wood toyed for a second with the idea of turning on his siren and scaring the bejesus out of the man but he curbed the impulse. Instead, he lowered the virtual window a couple of inches so only his hat and eyes were visible.

The guard finally looked up, his furrowed brow giving way to a look of surprise at the presence of Wood's black and white at the CSETI.

"Official police business," Wood said, with a curt nod.

The guard immediately turned and signaled another man in the gatehouse to open the gates. The two solid panels jolted awkwardly, and then swung slowly inward with unhurried ease. He turned back and waved Wood through.

* * * * *

Wood cruised slowly along the single-track road that wound a meandering path through lush green lawns to the CSETI complex. It was a beautiful day and the sun caught in and reflected from countless windows and girders on the building. Wood looked at it in wonder. He had seen it before, of course, it was a staple of many a tourist's e-card; but he, like all of them, had never been allowed this close to it. After making its headquarters here in Chicago, the CSETI complex had fast become one of the city's most famous landmarks, originally because of the controversy that had erupted when the site was selected, for it had been the Pioneer Woods forest preserve. Trees that had been spared for centuries were suddenly going to be axed, literally, to make way for manicured lawns and tasteful landscaping. These days, though, it was appreciated for its state-of-the-art architecture. The average Chicagoan had dubbed it "the supernova" and Wood could see why.

At its heart, the main part of the building was simply a huge hemisphere of reflective glass that, depending on the time of day, would appear to be a deep ocean blue or a resplendent gold color. Jutting out from this, gigantic spines of what appeared to be solid glass pointed to the heavens. It was said that these giant needles indicated the exact points in the night sky of the planets and constellations that marked the milestones in mans' voyage to the stars. At night, these enormous spikes appeared illuminated along their entire length, but all they did was draw the light from the main building with a clever fiber optic effect.

A semi-circle of intricately welded steel polished to a silver sheen and leaning at an angle of about thirty degrees arced above and around the entire building, like one of Saturn's rings, encompassing it all.

It was an unquestionably beautiful building, but while others saw an exploding star, Wood could not help but see a dying planet.

The road ended abruptly in a large circular area, clearly designed to facilitate the turning of vehicles. Holo-signs hovered a few feet above the nearby grass, indicating spurs off the dead-end that led to staff and visitor parking areas. At the center of the circle of asphalt was a large round pool and fountain. Twelve foaming jets of water gushed skyward, finally succumbing to gravity and falling back in on themselves. At their center, elevated high in the air, a massive bronze cast of Voyager I paid homage to the small spacecraft that had started everything, mothership to all that now stood behind it.

Wood pulled his patroller to a stop and exited the vehicle. He was sure that the folks at the CSETI would be horrified to have one of Chicago's finest parked right outside their main entrance for all subsequent guests and visitors to see. If nothing else, it might expedite their assistance in his inquiries. They would just want to get him out of there.

He strode across the paved concourse, seeing his warped reflection grow in the building's mirrored doors. As he approached the doors slid open and he stepped inside.

The building was deceptive. From outside, it didn't look that large. Inside, the structure was massive. A reception desk manned by two people looked pitifully small in the gargantuan foyer.

"Can I help you?" A young woman looked up from what appeared to be nothing, obviously using a two-way holo-screen.

"Yeah. I need to speak to someone who deals with archives, historical records. You have someone like that?"

She snorted. "We do, but they are very busy people, Officer…" she squinted, straining to see his badge from across the desk, "… Wood. You'd have to make an appointment. Would you like me to schedule that for you now?"

He could see what she was doing. Keeping the riff-raff, including snooping police officers, away from the scientists and military men and their desperately important work. He had to admit she was good, even if he resented her somewhat. "I don't need to make an appointment. I'm here on official police business."

"Is it something I could help you with?"

Wood sighed. "Miss, I don't have time for this. I need to speak to someone in archives."

She huffed, then went back to looking at thin air. A small smile broke on her lips. "The man you need to speak to is a Doctor Fielding. I'm sorry, but he has already left for the day." She looked up at him. "You'll have to make an appointment and come back another day." Already she had returned her attention to the seemingly invisible display, the police officer forgotten.

He could tell from the twitch of her lips that she was lying. He had dealt with enough liars to spot one. "Really?" He spoke the word slowly with a tone of disbelief. Wood lifted his arm and tapped a command into his wrist unit, wirelessly transmitting his e-warrant to her processor unit.

A look of shock registered on her features. "Oh."

"Maybe you'd like to explain to Doctor Fielding why all his servers and files were electronically interrogated in his absence. I'm sure he'll be thrilled." She looked up at him like a scolded child, guilt written all over her face. "Look, miss, we can do this the easy way or the hard way. I'd rather do it the easy way. Now can I speak to Doctor Fielding, please?"

She tapped the com-link on the left breast of her tunic, cleverly incorporated into a CSETI logo. "Doctor Fielding? Yes, it's the front desk. I have a police officer here to see you...No, I think you should come now...No, I don't know...Okay...Yes...Yes...I'll tell him that." It was clear the call had been terminated. "He'll be right out."

"Thank you," Wood said with more than a hint of sarcasm. He pointed to her badge. "Nice technology. Where can I get one?"

She laughed but there was no humor in it.

After that, Wood found the folks at the CSETI most helpful.

* * * * *

The old gashok was still in downtown Chicago. Weak from loss of blood and unable to capture anything to eat, the crippled alien now sought another easy meal. Being no stranger to scavenging it just had to wait for the right opportunity to present itself.

Unlike humans, predatory aliens were gifted with extraordinary patience. The gashok had waited in this alley all day, and now as the sun had begun to set and shadows grew from the feet of buildings, that opportunity was unfolding.

A young woman passed by the end of the alley. She pushed an anti-grav stroller before her in which an infant cooed and gurgled, clearly enjoying the ride. The old gashok struggled to its feet and, staying hidden within the darkening shadows, began to follow.

* * * * *

Wyatt pored over the map of the city. Sections of Chicago were beginning to look relatively clear of aliens. He reminded himself that "relatively" was the operative word and chastised himself for his optimism. Other parts of the city had a veritable infestation. There was still a lot of work ahead of them.

To be honest, at this point in time he was more concerned for a number of aliens that were out there than the people of Chicago. Many of them were harmless creatures, liable to get themselves killed or injured as they investigated what was to them a foreign world. If not that, then hysterical citizens might take it upon themselves to deal with their uninvited visitors. It had already happened, much to Wyatt's dismay. It wasn't just cats that curiosity killed.

However, dangerous aliens still remained loose. The fact that the mantor had not been sighted at all was troubling. It had either holed itself up somewhere or it had found wooded areas, much like those it frequented on its home world. Wyatt eyes scanned the map once more. If the latter were true then the mantor must have managed to elude the police and troops that were closing in and gotten clear of the city. That in itself was worrying.

Similarly, the gashok pack with a new alpha male would be looking to establish territory. Three victims and a rash of sightings suggested that was happening in the East Rogers Park area of town, but they might still be on the move.

His attention was caught by some movement behind the hovering image. He looked up, allowing his eyes to re-focus, and was surprised to see the civilian woman, Helen, climbing the stairs to the upper gallery. "Oh my God!" he said under his breath.

Quickly, Wyatt moved around the table, rushing to her aid, but as he approached her, he slowed, barely believing his eyes.

Behind Helen another figure climbed the steps. A massive man kitted out in ULF gear, albeit caked with filth. The imposing figure was unmistakable.

"Travis!" Wyatt called. He ran to his friend, hugging him tightly, not caring for his condition or the muck that covered him and reeked so strongly that everyone in security was now wrinkling their noses in disgust. Wyatt pushed Travis away, grasping him by the sleeves and looking him over, confirming to himself that his giant friend stood before him. "What happened? We thought you were dead!"

"So did I, for a minute." Travis broke a grin, showing a perfect set of white teeth in a dirt-streaked face. "That grate came down damn fast. Didn't think I was going to make it. Had to make a dive for it."

"But we called through to you. Why didn't you respond?"

Travis tapped his helmet. "These things. Once they get submerged all the circuitry's shot. I couldn't hear you. I couldn't hear anything."

Wyatt turned his attention to Helen. "Miss? Are you okay?" She nodded but didn't say anything. "Jesus, Travis, every time you walk in here you look worse than the last time."

"Yeah. No thanks to you."

* * * * *

The young woman slowed to a stop and turned off the stroller's anti-gravity field, allowing the flat base of the unit to gently touch down on the ground. Her infant, curious as to why they had stopped, struggled against his retaining straps, trying to peer around at his mother.

"It's okay, Simon," she reassured him. "Mommy just has to make some room in the car."

She opened the trunk of her HV with the touch of a finger on the biometric lock and ducked out of the way as the tailgate rose up. She sighed at the sight that greeted her. "Jeez, we have so much crap in this car," she muttered under her breath. Remembering herself, she brought a hand to her mouth. "That's a bad word, Simon. You didn't hear Mommy say that." She sighed again, and then set about the task of clearing some room in the back of the vehicle.

It seemed to her that she had only been at it a matter of seconds when the scream came that chilled her soul. She knew that scream. It was her Simon, but he was screaming in a way that she had never heard before.

And then came the silence. A silence more horrifying than the screaming.

She quickly stood up and looked around the rear of the vehicle but it was already too late. The child's stroller lay tipped over on one side, the restraining straps torn and bloody. She looked up the street and saw a large furry creature bounding away from her, carrying the limp body of her child. It ran, awkwardly, clearly injured, but even so, she was no match for its speed.

She screamed a blood-curdling wail. Collapsing to the sidewalk, she gathered the damaged stroller to her, hoping to somehow claim back something of what she had lost. "My baby!" She sobbed. "My baby!"

* * * * *

"What about the rest of my boys?" Travis asked.

"They're here. I didn't have the heart to re-deploy them so soon. Not after what they'd been through."

"You should have. It would have kept their mind off things."

"Maybe," Wyatt mused. "Bobby and the guys could sure use

their help."

"How are they, anyway?"

"Fine. I think. McDermott's pretty shaken up, though."

Travis nodded. "Let me go get cleaned up and go see my guys. In the meantime, find something else for us to do."

"You're sure?"

"You know how it goes, Wyatt, you fall off the horse, you get back on it."

"Okay. If you say so. Oh, before you go, come over here, I want to show you something." Wyatt led Travis and Helen back towards the table. He called up the sewer blueprints once more. "I think we have the puglion trapped. This was your last known location." Wyatt pointed at the hovering image. "I ordered all the grates in your section of tunnel to be closed and locked after we thought we'd lost you. If the puglion was close, there's no way it can move freely through the sewer system now."

Travis nodded. "That was smart. Yeah. We heard the grates coming down farther down the tunnel. Wondered what the hell it was at first, but then we guessed that's what you were doing." Travis stopped and thought for a moment. "This is all well and good, Wyatt but now that we've got this thing immobilized, how do we flush it out?"

Wyatt's head snapped up, his eyes locking on Travis, the spark of an idea flashing within them. "That's it!" he said, clicking his fingers so that his hand remained with a pointed finger aimed directly at Travis. "You've got it! That's it!"

"Oh no," Travis groaned. "What did I just say?"

* * * * *

Making the recapture effort all the more difficult was the plethora of places in the city where escaped exhibits could hide. The family of catchidas had taken up residence in the subway and probably could have survived there unnoticed for weeks, even months, had it not been for the fact that one of their number had chosen a most inopportune time to take wing and ended up splattered across the front of a subway car. However, over the course of the weekend Bobby, Chris, and the rest of the veteran ULF team made good progress in recapturing a number of the zoo's escapees. They were aided in their effort by Travis and his remaining rookies, now re-deployed with Hernandez, who brought some much-needed experience to their decimated team and whose presence would no doubt help to calm some frayed nerves.

In the meantime, Wyatt began to piece together his plan that would get the puglion out of the main sewer system.

Wyatt was already aware of the overflow silos located deep underground. When he had first pulled up the sewer blueprints on his display he had spotted them immediately- huge, open, circular tanks scattered underneath the city. He'd asked the people in the sewer's master control room about them - what they were and why they were there - and had learned that the overflow silos were necessary to cope with the increased amount of water from a surge in volume, like that created from a storm, for example. Travis's comment had been the impetus for his idea.

Right now, he was working closely with the sewer operators, lowering grates into place in the system so that only a single downstream route lay open between the puglion's position and the closest overflow silo. The rest of the plan's success relied upon the cooperation of the people of Chicago.

Wyatt threw himself into the work. It kept his mind focused and off the fact that Gruber had failed to show his face at all over the course of the weekend. Gruber had never worked a weekend before in his life, but Wyatt thought that on this occasion he might make an exception. Now, nothing the man did or did not do could surprise him any more. It was clear that Gruber was not going to let the small matter of the city being under siege spoil his weekend.

* * * * *

Wood pulled his HV up outside Lieberwits's house and checked his wrist unit. 09:58 AM. He was early. The detective would be pleased.

He popped the door and climbed out, then strode along the small pathway to the front door, rapping on it with his knuckles.

"Just a minute!" he heard Lieberwits call from inside and then, moments later, the door opened and the older man peered out. "Oh, hey! Come on in." He swung the door wide and stepped aside.

"I got that information for you."

"You had said in your message. They give you any trouble?" Lieberwits closed the door behind him.

"They tried. We soon straightened that out, though."

"Offer you a drink? Coffee? Tea?"

"A glass of water would be nice. Thanks."

"Ah! One of those."

Wood frowned. Lieberwits was already walking away from him down the narrow hallway.

"Purist." Lieberwits called back to him as he disappeared through a doorway. "My body is a temple and all that crap."

Wood just shrugged, then stepped through the doorway to his left and into a small living room. "Nice place," he called out, giving the room a cursory once-over.

"Thanks!" Lieberwits shouted back from the kitchen. "It's not much, but it suffices. What's up? You don't like coffee?"

"Nah." Wood shouted back. "Gives me headaches."

"Nectar of the gods. Don't know how anybody survives without it."

Wood walked through the room, continuing to scan it with his eyes. There was something about it. Or rather something lacking about it. It was sparse. Almost sterile.

Passing through another door, Wood stepped into the dining room. A beautiful mahogany table stood proudly at its center, complete with six matching chairs. A display cabinet stood against the far wall, full of perfectly placed crystal glasses. Again, the room was immaculate. It didn't look like anything had been touched in years.

In stark contrast to the rest of the house was the room off to the left of the dining room. It was a small office, home to only an antique writing desk, a bookshelf and a filing cabinet. Barely any of the furniture was visible, all of it buried by files and loose shuffled papers. Wood stepped inside, lifting the nearest sheet of paper to him and started to read. It was difficult to make out much of Lieberwits's hand written scrawl but three capitalized letters leapt off the page. IZP.

"Here you go," he heard Lieberwits say from the hallway. "Where'd you go?"

"I'm here!" Wood hurriedly replaced the paper, exiting the office just in time to be greeted by Lieberwits, glass of water in one hand, steaming cup of coffee in the other, the latter so strong, Wood could smell it from where he was standing. Lieberwits eyed him suspiciously, then thrust the water at him.

"Missus Lieberwits not home, then?" Wood asked.

The old detective snorted then raised a hand, waggling a naked ring finger in front of Wood's face. "She hasn't found me yet."

"Hasn't found you yet?" Wood chuckled. "What makes you think she should be out looking for you?"

"I don't have time to be married," Liebwerwits said. "Anyway, you're not very observant for a cop, are you? You never noticed?" He goaded Wood with his ring finger again.

"Just because you don't wear a ring doesn't mean you're not married. My father taught me part of being a good cop was assuming nothing."

"Your father was a cop too?"

Wood nodded. "He was. My grandfather, too."

"You feel a family duty to join the force?"

"No." Wood said, shaking his head. "Just seemed like the right thing to do. Seriously, though, you never married?"

"I'm too busy. Besides, you're making a huge assumption that there's a woman out there that would have me."

"Busy with this stuff?" Wood indicated the office with a sideways tilt of his head.

Lieberwits frowned, a brief flash of anger crossing his features. "You stay out of my stuff, you hear? I know what you regular cops are like, always snooping around."

Wood put his hands up in mock surrender. "Hey, I'm sorry. I didn't mean anything by it."

"What is it with you and my stuff anyway?" Lieberwits asked, calming.

Wood shrugged and then buried his hands in his pockets. "Oh! That reminds me." He pulled out a squashed ball of foam. "Your stress ball. I forgot to put it back."

"Ah, keep it," Lieberwits said. "Those things don't work anyway. Come on," he indicated the dining room table. "We've got work to do and I'm interested to hear what you found out."

* * * * *

"Hi, darling."

"Hey, Dad." Kate wrapped a slender arm around her father's neck and hugged him tightly, Alex clinging to her other hand.

They pulled apart and her father squatted down to Alex's level. "How's my big man?" he asked, poking Alex with a finger, causing the youngster to giggle and bury his chin in his chest. "Come on, you. Wroagh!" he grunted as he stood, heaving Alex up onto his hip. "Come on inside. Your mother will be pleased to see you. She's been worried sick, what with all this craziness going on in the city."

She sighed. "It's pretty bad."

"Keeping that man of yours busy, huh?"

Kate shrugged, a defeated look on her face. "What else was he going to do? They needed him. I mean, I get it. Doesn't mean I have to be happy about it, though."

Her father nodded knowingly. "You and your mother should talk. Ask her about the early days of the business, when I was never around. I'm sure she can sympathize. Anyway, come on in and get settled. Your mother cooked your favorite."

"All right dad. Just let me get my bags and Furball."

"Anything I can help you with?"

"No. I'll be fine, thanks."

Her father turned and carried Alex back towards the house and its inviting open door, his footsteps crunching on the gravel drive.

* * * * *

Wood took a sip of water, then bounced the stress ball off the wall and caught it in the same hand. Lieberwits stared at him.

"What?"

"Do you mind?" Lieberwits looked at the ball in Wood's hand, then at the wall and back at him. "Talk about making yourself at home."

"Sorry." Wood crushed the ball in his fist and then released it. It seemed as though something occurred to him then because he repeated the action but this time stared intently at his fist as he released the pressure, this time much more slowly. He did it again, the third time stopping himself in mid-release.

Lieberwits watched the whole episode. "What? What is it?"

Wood shook his head, as if waking himself from his thoughts. "I don't get it."

"You don't get what?"

"It makes no sense. We're still exploring the universe, right? You said so yourself."

"As far as I'm aware."

"So you would think we're exploring outwards in all directions."

Lieberwits shrugged. It seemed a fair assumption. "What are

you getting at?"

Wood clenched his hand again, hiding the ball within his fist. "Assuming we have a single point of origin...the Earth, or the moon, which given the cosmic scale of things can be considered one and the same. Then we start moving outwards..." He began to release his grip, patches of red foam becoming visible between his fingers as the ball expanded. "The further out we go, the volume of space covered increases exponentially."

Lieberwits latched on to the idea. "Which would make you think we'd be discovering new planets at an exponentially increasing rate as well!"

"Exactly!" Wood snapped. "Now what did that guy at the zoo...Wyatt. What did Wyatt say again? That they weren't going out as often as they used to. They weren't discovering new planets as often as before. That can't be right, can it?"

Lieberwits felt his heart begin to race. Had Wood done it? Had Wood discovered the link that he had been searching for all this time? He did not want to give a voice to his thoughts. Not yet. Not until they had proved their theory. "Hold on!" he said. "I'll be right back."

Lieberwits rushed into his office. Wood could hear him rummaging around until finally he came out with a thin black strip which he laid upon the dining room table. It was the holo-screen generator for his computer. While they had been talking, Wood had been uploading all the data from the IZP and CSETI from his wrist unit to Lieberwits's old dinosaur of a computer. It had taken some software modification since the detective's hardware was so out of date, but eventually they had gotten it to work. Now, all the information had been transferred. Lieberwits poked thin air and touched the screen, activating the display. With a few deft finger strokes he had pulled up the two sets of records. The two men stared at the information from opposite sides of the table.

"Okay, look, here is the declassified stuff from the CSETI," Lieberwits pointed it out. "And here are the expeditions sanctioned by the IZP at around the same time."

Wood's eyes flitted between the two. "There's definitely a correlation there. Not necessarily consistent in terms of time frame, but certainly within a few months of the CSETI discovering a planet, the IZP is sending out an expedition to the very same place. Then here..." Wood pointed, "...It just seems to stop."

"What date is that?" Lieberwits could barely bring himself to look. He realized he was shaking.

"Twenty-four-fifty."

"Five years ago." Lieberwits said quietly.

"And look," Wood added. "It's as I suspected, since then the CSETI have reported an ever-increasing number of planet discoveries."

"It's not that they're not discovering new planets as often as they used to," Lieberwits said quietly, as if to himself. "The IZP just isn't learning about them any more." He looked up at Wood. "You're wasted as a cop. You know that?"

Wood's face broke into a boyish grin. "Thanks." He paused for a moment. "Listen, I've been thinking. Why don't we go and do something else?"

"What do you mean?"

"Well, since we met with Komicki I've been working on a little something."

"Like what?"

"I'll show you," Wood said, the smile still on his face. "Come on. I've got a plan."

CHAPTER 14

CORE had scanned their faces and matched them to staff biometrics long before Wood and Lieberwits were even close to the building. Central's computer entity opened the front doors as the two men approached.

"Where are we going?" Lieberwits asked.

"You remember those friends at Central I told you about?"

"Yeah."

"They're cops."

"Well, that's pretty obvious," Lieberwits said, as they approached the bank of elevators, "Seeing as how it's only cops that work here."

Doors parted and Wood stepped inside. "Level U-four," he said.

Lieberwits looked at him questioningly as the doors closed behind them. "U-four?" That was four levels underground. He couldn't remember the last time he'd been to one of Central's lower levels.

The elevator stopped, the doors parting in front of them. Lieberwits looked out onto a dark floor bristling with technology. Figures moved among the blinking arrays and hovering schematics, barely more than shadows themselves. "Like I said," Wood said. "They're cops. Covert ops." He stepped out of the elevator, beckoning Lieberwits to follow. "Come on. There's someone I'd like you to meet."

Wood walked across the large open floor, Lieberwits following slowly behind, his head flicking left and right as he stared at displays and holo-screens displaying data that he could never hope to understand. They stopped at a large U-shaped desk interface, a young man with a look of intense concentration on his face sitting at its center. The other man acknowledged them but held a hand up, indicating that they should wait for his full attention. He pressed a link further into his ear and listened intently, then ran hands over the interface around him with a speed that Lieberwits found incomprehensible. With a tap, the other man saved his recent work and cleared the surface, making his workspace seem like nothing less innocent than a glass-topped desk. He looked up, his face relaxing and breaking into a smile. "Hey, Ed!" he said, offering Wood his hand. "Good to see you again."

"You too." Wood said. "Scott, I'd like you to meet Detective Superintendent Lieberwits. Detective; Scott."

The two men shook hands, Scott's eyes flashing with recognition at the mention of Lieberwits's name. "It's a pleasure to meet you, detective. You're somewhat of a legend down here."

"Why's that?" Lieberwits asked. "'I'm never seen down here. People don't believe I exist?"

Scott laughed, then returned his attention to Wood. "Okay, we got everything you asked for."

"Everything's in order?" Wood asked.

"Yeah. It was all pretty straightforward. That's easy stuff for us. I can go and pick it up now if you want. You want to set up the meeting now?"

Lieberwits looked at Wood, still clueless as to what was going on. "Yeah. Why not?" Wood said. "No time like the present."

"Okay. Follow me." Scott turned and led them to a room in the far corner of the floor. He opened the door and ushered the two men inside. "Lights," he said, and all three of them squinted as the lights came up, the plain, brilliant white room harsh on their ill-adjusted eyes. "I'll be right back," Scott said. He closed the door, leaving Wood and Lieberwits alone in the room.

A long table hosting a lone com-link was the only furnishing in the room. Lieberwits walked to it, turned and leaned against it, folding his arms across his chest. "What's going on?" he asked. "I thought we'd talked about this, about being open with each other."

"I know. I'm sorry. This was...I just thought this was something that I could handle alone."

"What?" Lieberwits asked, a slight hint of anger in his voice. "I still don't even know why we're here."

"After we went and saw Komicki and he told us that the Alien Liberation League had been recruiting, I thought maybe I could pose as someone interested in getting involved, y'know, infiltrate the organization."

"And?"

"Well, when I thought about it a bit more, I figured, the job is done. They might not be recruiting any more."

Lieberwits nodded. "So now you think that approach might not work."

"Exactly."

"So where do I fit in with all of this?"

"Well, we need to meet with these people somehow. We're never going to be able to get close to them if they suspect we're cops."

"I'm still listening."

The door popped open and Scott stepped back into the room. He was carrying two cards and a reader. He scanned one of the cards and looked at the display, then handed the card and unit to Lieberwits. "Here you go," he said with a smile. "Say hello to yourself."

Lieberwits looked down at the reader's display. His own face looked back at him from a fake ID. He read the name next to his image. "Winston Samuelson."

"You're a bad man, Mister Samuelson," Scott said, as he

handed the second card to Wood. "City businessman and financial genius who uses his amassed fortune to fund alien liberation groups nationwide. You've got some very dubious connections."

"So we're going to offer to fund their criminal activism," Lieberwits surmised.

"That is, of course, if they turn down your son, Daniel, here," Scott clapped Wood on the back.

"Think of it as a two-pronged attack," Wood said.

Lieberwits huffed. It was the second time Wood had caught him off-guard and he didn't like it, but he had to admire the younger man's tenacity. "All right," he said finally. "Where are we doing this?"

"Right here," Scott said. "Boardroom." The white walls shimmered, two of them taking on the appearance of frosted glass, the remaining two becoming the walls of a top flight boardroom complete with 3D renderings of furniture. Blurred outlines of fictional people passed by the fictional glass walls.

Lieberwits looked around in wonder. "I didn't know we had a sensory stimulus room."

Scott nodded. "We've had it for a while. It's ideal for setting up things like this."

The door to the room opened again and a young woman stepped in carrying some shirts and ties. "I hope you don't mind," Scott said, "I took the liberty of having one of our guise assistants bring you some clothes, just so you look the part if these liberation people want to use vision stream on the link. I doubt they will, they'll want to remain anonymous, I'm sure, but, you know, just in case."

Lieberwits took a shirt and tie from the collection that was offered. Wood did the same. "Thanks, Lacey," Scott said, as the woman turned and left. She gave him a quick smile of acknowledgement.

Lieberwits stripped down to the waist and began putting on the new shirt. "What about call ID? Won't these guys see that the call is from Central?"

"No. We can fix that."

"You can?"

"We're covert ops. We can fix *everything.*" Scott gave a knowing grin and then located the door in the disguised wall. "All right, if you guys are all set, I'll leave you to it." He closed the door behind him, leaving Wood and Lieberwits alone in the room once more.

"You ready to do this?" Wood asked.

"I guess I am now."

Wood called up the number on his wrist unit, transmitted it to the com-link and then removed the unit from his arm, putting it down where it would be out of sight.

The link rang three times. "Hello?" The recipient was answering with voice stream only, as Scott had predicted.

"Hello. Yes...Is this the Alien Liberation League?"

"Who's asking?" The voice on the other end of the line was immediately defensive.

Wood ignored the question. "I heard that you were recruiting. I'd like to get involved, if I can."

"Where'd you hear that?"

"Some friends."

"You heard wrong." There was a click and then the line went dead.

"Well, that went well." Lieberwits sighed.

"We'd expected as much." Wood said. "Right?"

Lieberwits shrugged.

"Recall." The link dialed again at Wood's command.

"Look, I told you we're not recruiting." It was the same voice, obviously recognizing their number.

"Wait!" Wood pleaded. "I said I wanted to get involved. It doesn't necessarily have to be actively."

There was silence on the line for a moment. "What do you mean?"

"We can help you. I mean my father and me. We can help you out financially. Fund some of your future projects."

"Why would you do that?"

"My father has long been sympathetic to your cause. He doesn't believe in alien entrapment and loathes the idea of zoos. The fact that the IZP is here, right in our back yard, grates on his every nerve. He can't support you actively. He's a very prominent businessman and chairman of a large company here in the city, but he'd like to contribute...we'd like to contribute, to your organization....as a silent partner. As a gesture of goodwill, we'd be prepared to make a large initial donation."

"How much?"

"A million credits."

"Transmit the money, then we can talk."

"No." Wood was firm. "We meet first. Then you get the money."

There was another moment of silence. "Is your father there with you now?"

"Yes, he is."

"Put him on."

Wood looked across at Lieberwits, then indicated with a nod of his head that it was the detective's turn to talk.

Lieberwits cleared his throat. "Er, Hello?"

"You want to support us?" the voice asked.

"Yes."

"Why?"

"Well...my son just explained that, didn't he?"

"I want to hear it from you."

"I...Well, I..."

Wood was rolling his hand in a forward motion, suggesting Lieberwits should quit stammering and spew forth whatever first came to mind.

"...I'm opposed to the idea of alien captivity. I don't think we have any right to imprison intelligent life from other planets, in fact I think it's downright cruel. This recent thing with the zoo was you guys, wasn't it?"

Wood frowned and shook his head from across the table. Lieberwits was trying too hard. He was going to blow the whole thing. There was silence on the link line. Wood hurriedly motioned for him to continue.

"I, er, well, anyway, anyway, I like the idea of someone like me being able to support a group such as yours. A group who stand for everything I believe in. A group who take bold actions when necessary." Lieberwits was really getting in to character now. "I've been fortunate to have the financial freedom to invest in matters that are close to my heart and I've supported a number of other alien rights groups. Now I wish to affiliate myself with you but I must remain a silent partner. You can expect major funding for your future activist actions but I, in return, expect complete anonymity."

"You say you want to meet with us? Why?"

"Young man, if I'm about to invest millions of credits in your organization, I want to know who I'm dealing with. Can your people be discreet? I need to know I can trust you as much as you need to know you can trust me."

Wood gave him a thumbs-up from across the table. He'd nailed that one.

There was a long pause. "Hang on," the voice said. The line fell silent. A moment later the voice was back. "Tomorrow. Three-thirty. Room two-oh-five. The Phoenix building. West Monroe Street. Be there. You don't show, we don't speak again." The line went dead.

Wood gave Lieberwits a high five. "Nice work. I can't wait to meet these scumbags." He rose from the table. "Come on. We've got things to do."

"Like what?"

"Like shopping."

"Shopping?"

"Yeah. Shopping. You and I are going to get some fancy threads."

Lieberwits frowned at him again.

"A new suit!" Wood explained. "We're going to get you a new suit."

"I don't need a new suit! I have plenty of suits."

Wood gave him an old-fashioned look. "Nah. You think you have suits. If we're going to pull off being city high-fliers, we need to get you *a suit*."

* * * * *

Alex slurped noisily at his lemonade, clutched clumsily in two hands. Kate helped him place the tumbler back on the low table before the youngster resumed playing with the new toys his grandparents had just given him.

"The yard looks nice, Dad," Kate said, looking through the glass wall of the expansive summer house that extended out from the back of the house.

"Yard" was an understatement. Kate's father had built a hugely successful freight forwarding company which, when he retired, was worth billions of credits. The huge six-bedroom house in which they now sat was situated in the center of four acres of land on the outskirts of Barrington. Kate's parents were doing very nicely, thank you.

"I've been dabbling," he sighed. "In fact, I've been getting into this gardening thing."

Kate raised an eyebrow at him. "Are you joking?"

"No. Really. It's very therapeutic. Just what a man at my time of life needs." He smiled. "And then of course there's the power tools that come with it."

Kate laughed. "I noticed the shed."

"Ah yes. Our latest purchase." He sounded like he had forgotten about it already and Kate had just reminded him. "What do you think of it out there by the side of the house? Your mother wanted it tucked away around the back here but I said it would spoil the view. She thinks it's an eyesore where it is, though, where the 'neighbors' can see it." He snorted a laugh. "Like we really have neighbors."

She shrugged. "It's okay."

"I mean it's practical, right?" He looked at her, waiting for confirmation, an ally in his reasoning. "Right? I can get to the front and back of the house easily and over to the forest over there."

A wooded area bordered the left-hand side of the massive property. For as long as Kate could remember, they had called it the forest, and as a child she had run and played within its boundaries, imagining countless adventures under the dappled sunlight. It was where she had first become interested in plants and bugs and birds and the natural world around her, but it was not really a forest, more a copse of trees.

"I mean, that's where all the damn weeds come from, anyway."

"Dad!" She scolded him, then looked at Alex, the youngster oblivious to the expletive.

"Sorry."

"Here you go, dear." The arrival of Kate's mom in the room was heralded by the clinking of fine china. "Just what you need after your drive. A nice cup of tea." She carefully set the tray down and began pouring. Kate snatched a cookie off a neatly arranged plate and broke it with her teeth, catching crumbs with her free hand.

"I assume the police are all over this?" her father asked.

Kate tossed her head back to better manage a large chunk of cookie. "Not as far as I'm aware," she mumbled through her mouthful. "From what Wyatt tells me, they've got two guys working on it. One regular cop, one detective. Wyatt said it was the same detective that investigated the shootings."

Kate's mother stopped dead, her cup only an inch from her

lips. "Shootings? Did somebody get shot, too?"

"No, Mom, from before. You remember?"

"Oh yes. Terrible. That was awful too." She lifted the cup to her lips and continued drinking.

"But that's crazy...!"

"It was a break-in, Dad! Once they've taken statements from everyone, what else are they going to do? I mean, nobody got hurt. Nobody except the people that did it."

"Not then, but what about the fatalities since?"

"It's not a priority, Dad. People get murdered all over the city all the time, and besides, these are animal attacks, it's not like there's really a crime to investigate other than the break-in. They just don't have the resources to dedicate to something like this."

Kate's father tutted and shook his head. "Makes you wonder what you pay your taxes for."

* * * * *

Lieberwits looked skeptically at the sign above the door. *Outfitters to fine gentlemen for 500 years.* Wood caught his look of apprehension. "Not your kind of place, is it? Come on," he said, yanking on the door. A single bell rang, announcing their arrival. The place was old-school. Classic. Wood took a look around. The store reeked of tradition and old-world charm. "Perfect," he said.

"How do you know about places like this?" Lieberwits asked.

Before Wood could reply a tall, lanky man entered the store from a back room. Lieberwits couldn't remember the last time he had been in a store with a real, live sales assistant.

The man wore black pants pressed to tight seams and a matching single-breasted jacket with coattails that hung to the back of his knees. His white shirt was pristine, sporting a rigid collar and a gray tie with a large knot that lay so neatly around his neck, Lieberwits wouldn't have been surprised if it had been aligned electronically. Completing the ensemble were a pair of plain black shoes polished so well the entire store was visible as a warped miniature caricature of itself on their fronts. He was an elderly gentleman with a thinning amount of gray hair lacquered into place across his forehead, the tracks of the comb teeth still visible and set in place. To the detective, it looked like he had been here every day of those five hundred years.

On sight of them his face fell. Lieberwits guessed at the assumptions he was making about them. They were not his usual clientele. They did not look like the kind of people who had credits to spend in this store. The next thirty minutes were going to be a waste of his time. He was already prejudiced against them. It would only take one question from Wood to confirm the man's worst fears.

"We need something quickly. Off the peg. Classic. Classy. You have anything like that?"

These two clowns were at a tailor's and could not even be bothered to get something fitted. Despite his growing unease about his two newest customers, the assistant tried his best. "I believe we do," he managed through a smile without warmth. "If you would care to follow me, sir," the title laced with such a thick upper-class accent it sounded more like *sah*.

He led them through the store, seeming to glide rather than walk. "Would sir be looking for something single-breasted or double-breasted today?"

"I don't know," Wood said. "What would you recommend?"

"At the present time, sir, we are finding our gentleman customers of the most refined taste prefer to wear single-breasted."

"That will be fine then."

"Something like this, perhaps?" The old man removed a navy suit from a rail and draped it over his free arm, allowing the two other men to see it.

"Mmm." Wood rubbed his chin thoughtfully. "I wasn't thinking quite so plain. How about something like..." He cast his eyes around the nearby rails. "...this?"

The old man's face brightened a little. Maybe his two clients did have a modicum of taste after all. "Ah. An excellent choice, sir."

Wood had selected a jet-black suit with a fine gray pinstripe. The old man moved to the rack, looked Wood over once and began flicking hangers down the rail. "Here," he said finally, pulling one out and handing it to the young officer. "I think you'll find this to your liking." He cast his attention to Lieberwits, looking him up and down longer than was necessary and making the detective extremely self-conscious. Lieberwits looked down at his crumpled flannel suit. Strange, until today he had always felt extremely comfortable in it. Now he felt horribly underdressed. Wood was right. He didn't own a suit. Not a real suit.

The old man fixated on Lieberwits's waist. "Mmmm," he mused, pursing his lips. "Forty," he muttered. He returned his attention to the rack, then shook his head and looked back at Lieberwits. "No. Forty-two," he corrected himself. Lieberwits actually blushed. "Here. Try these," he said, thrusting a clearly more generous fit in the detective's direction."

"Do you have a changing room?"

"Our cloakroom is over there."

* * * * *

Lieberwits struggled into his pants. Not that they did not fit, it was just that for a man of his size, the cubicle was a little small. It was nice enough. Rich oak paneling lined the walls and the bench seat was upholstered with a green velvet cushion that looked ridiculously too low and too small for anyone to realistically use, but the fact remained, it was a small space. Next to him, he could hear the clatter of Wood's hanger in the adjoining cubicle. "How are you doing in there?"

"Good," Wood replied. "This is just the ticket."

Lieberwits slipped on the jacket. It was a fine cut and a good fit. He could feel the difference in quality. A difference that worried him somewhat. "Yeah, speaking of which, I don't see any prices on these things."

"If you shop here, you don't worry about the price."

"So how much are they, then?"

"I don't know."

"Well can't you ask Jeeves out there?" Lieberwits hissed.

"You don't ask in a place like this," Wood replied in hushed tones. "What's the problem anyway? You've got good credit, haven't you?"

"Well...yeah."

"So don't worry about it."

"But I do worry about it. I've still got to pay for this."

"No, you don't."

"What do you mean?

"Expense it."

"Expense it!" Lieberwits was horrified. "I've never expensed anything before in my life. Certainly not a top-flight suit!"

Wood sighed. "You're really not with the program, are you?"

* * * * *

Wood dumped the two sets of jackets and pants on the counter in a disheveled heap. "We'll take them." The sales assistant looked appalled. "And my friend here is going to pay."

"Wha...?"

The old man shot Lieberwits a look of disgust. Maybe he had overheard the Jeeves comment. Lieberwits shut his mouth quickly.

"Oh, and we'll need ties too." Wood turned around. Behind them an ocean of ties lay in rippled waves over a table. He grabbed two, paying no attention to their color or style and threw them on top of the pile of clothes.

The old man began calculating their costs. "That will be fifteen thousand credits," he said with a smug grin.

"Fifteen th...!"

"I'll meet you back in the car." Wood was already heading for the door.

"But..."

"Remember," Wood said, waggling a finger in the air, still walking away from him. "You're going to have the police department and the Chicago taxpayer to thank for this." He opened the door and exited, leaving only the ring of the bell in his wake.

"But I am a taxpayer!" Lieberwits shouted after him.

The old man scowled at him and passed a biometric thumb pad for Lieberwits to ID himself and close the transaction.

"Sorry." Lieberwits mumbled. "But I am."

* * * * *

"That's it?"

"That's it," the young man sighed in confirmation. He pocketed the small recording device.

"Really?" Wyatt asked. "I thought there would be more to it. Lights and a backdrop or something."

"No. This is just a public service announcement. We don't need to flower it all up for something like that. Anyway, it looks good with all the tech stuff behind you. Makes it look official." He smiled. "Don't worry; it'll look good when it goes to air."

"Well, thanks for your time." Wyatt offered his hand. "I appreciate you coming out here."

"Oh. No problem, man. My pleasure. Thank *you* for giving us the exclusive."

Wyatt frowned. "Exclusive? This is going out on all the networks, right?"

"Oh, yeah. No, I mean, thanks for calling us and having us do the shoot."

"It just seemed logical. Channel One. First thing that popped into my head."

The young man smiled. "I'll get this back to the studio. We'll prep it and load it up to our server, then you just tell us when you want it to air. We'll network with all the other news servers, synchronize and transfer it across. Load it and lock it in. Your face will be on every screen in the city and surrounding suburbs."

Wyatt looked daunted at the prospect.

"Hey, cheer up, man. You're gonna be famous!" He laughed, then turned and left.

* * * * *

The mantor stirred, rolled onto its belly and yawned. It stretched its large paws out in front of itself, scythe-like claws extending and retracting. The creature pulled itself to its feet, shook itself and began to pad slowly on all fours through the trees.

The mantor was more settled here, out of the city and among pockets of grassland and wooded areas akin to the habitat of its home world; a habitat in which it hunted and killed.

The alien was well-rested, sleeping the last few hours of the day in preparation for the night to come. Like most apex predators the mantor preferred to hunt by night, its huge yellow eyes well-adapted to the darkness. It was dusk now, an excellent time for hunting, when the creatures of the day grew tired and careless.

The mantor blinked, irises narrowing briefly as they adjusted to the fading light. Soon it would be dark. Pitch dark. There were none of the harsh city lights that hurt the creature's eyes out here. No streetlamps or fluorescent signs. The only light out here came from the moon and stars high above.

In the distance, among the patchwork quilt of grass and isolated roads, small golden squares were visible. Single, isolated homes illuminated from within.

* * * * *

The display next to the buzzer pad for 205 was blank. Neither the detective nor the police officer was surprised. Obviously the Alien Liberation League didn't want to advertise their presence in what was clearly a respectable tower block.

"You carrying?" Wood asked suddenly.

"Do you think I'm crazy?"

"All right. Calm down. Just checking."

Lieberwits gave him a long look. "I told you before, I may be old, but I'm not stupid." He touched the sensor pad and waited.

"Hello?" It was the same voice that had answered the link.

"Hi. Yes. We spoke yesterday. We're here for our three-thirty appointment."

"Hold on."

Lieberwits took a moment to look around the entryway. They must be being monitored from somewhere. He was sure the members of the ALL inside were checking them out, discussing whether to let these two strangers in to their stronghold. He made a point of straightening his tie for the hidden camera. The seconds seemed like hours.

Nothing more was said. A buzz indicated that the door had been unlocked and they should enter. Wood pushed on the door and stepped inside, Lieberwits close behind.

They crossed a grand marble foyer with a high-vaulted ceiling, leather patent shoes click-clacking as they strode across the buffed surface. An impressive chandelier hung high above them. "Who would have guessed this is where they were holed up?" Wood said. Lieberwits could not agree more.

Upon reaching the bank of elevators Wood pushed the call button. Immediately a tone sounded and one of the doors slid open. The two men stepped inside.

"Second floor," Lieberwits told the building's AI.

"You ready?" Wood asked, as the door slid closed, sealing their fate.

"I sure hope so." Lieberwits sighed.

The elevator accelerated, slowed and then stopped, a second tone announcing their arrival. Lieberwits blew out a big breath, psyching himself up for what was to come and prepared to step outside. He was more than a little surprised when the doors drew back.

Two men blocked their exit completely. They were dressed entirely in black, black sunglasses completing the ensemble. One was tall and muscular with fair hair shaved to a crew cut, the other was shorter, bald, and clearly in worse physical shape than his colleague. Obviously he preferred to use his weight as his weapon.

"Excuse us," Wood said, attempting to step out of the elevator. The shorter man placed his palm flat against Wood's chest and shoved him backward.

The two heavies stepped into the elevator, bringing their faces only inches away from those of the policemen. "Close the door and hold at this level," the taller man said.

"What is this? Some kind of welcoming committee?"

"You could say that," the bald man sneered. "Turn around! Both of you! Hands flat against the wall."

Wood reluctantly did as he was told. "Well, I'm not feeling very welcome."

"Shut up!"

The two men did a quick search, patting Wood and Lieberwits down.

"This one's clean," the fair-haired man said, finishing with Lieberwits.

"Yeah. This one too." The bald man finished checking Wood's leg and rose to his full height. He sounded almost disappointed. "All right. Let's go. Follow me."

They exited the elevator and walked the short distance down the corridor in silence, their footfalls muted on the carpeted surface. Then the bald man turned and placed his thumb on a biometric lock pad. Lieberwits looked up. The number 205 hung on the door in neat gold numerals. The door popped open and the bald man stepped inside. The fair-haired man ushered the two policemen in and then followed.

The room was empty save for a single desk and chair at the far end. The walls were painted a neutral off-white, the opposite wall entirely glass with a slatted blind hanging in front of it. The desk had a few small items on it, a clock, a desk tidy with some pens in it and a static link base unit. Behind the desk and to the left, a single door gave access to an adjoining room.

"You!" The bald man pointed at Wood. "Stand here! And you!" to Lieberwits. "Over there!"

Wood and Lieberwits stood six feet apart and four feet in front of the desk. The two heavies retreated to the back corners of the room and stood, statue still, with their hands clasped in front of them.

Silence fell on the room. Wood looked over his shoulder at the bald man who jabbed a finger forward, indicating that he should simply face front.

A couple of minutes passed and then the door to the adjoining room opened slowly. A man stepped through. Lieberwits guessed he was in his late twenties or early thirties. He had short, dark hair and striking blue eyes and it was obvious he kept himself in good shape, even beneath the casual business attire that he wore. He smiled quickly at his two guests, looking at them with a gaze that left both men feeling uncomfortable and somehow violated. He dumped a folder on the desk. "Gentleman," he said. "Welcome. My name is Mister Jones. You've met my colleagues, Mister Jones…" he indicated the fair-haired man in the corner behind Lieberwits. "…and Mister Jones." The bald man in the corner behind Wood nodded at his introduction.

"Keeping it in the family, then?" Wood joked.

The first Mister Jones smiled at the humor. "I assure you, we are not related."

"Fortunately for you." Wood said. Behind him, the bald man snarled.

The grin remained on Jones's face but the laughter in his eyes had gone. He regarded Wood suspiciously. Maybe it had been a mistake to let the two strangers in. He had never seen such gall before. "I assume you gentlemen have ID?"

Wood and Lieberwits both reached for their ID cards. "Slowly!" the bald man said, coming around to face Wood. "Here. I'll take that." He snatched Wood's card away from him, then took Lieberwits's, passing the two cards to his superior.

"I'll just be a moment," the first Jones said. He turned and disappeared into the second room, closing the door behind him. Lieberwits and Wood shared an uneasy glance. Moments later, Jones re-emerged carrying the cards in front of him. He returned them to Lieberwits and Wood and then walked to the desk, turning and leaning against it. He stared at Wood.

"Nice place," Lieberwits said, breaking the silence. "I wasn't..."

"You weren't expecting it. No?" Jones continued to stare at Wood as if lost in thought and then his head snapped to Lieberwits. "No. We get a lot of that. Let me guess, you expected to find us hidden behind some corrugated iron door in the basement of some grungy nightclub. Correct?"

Lieberwits shrugged.

"You've been watching too many movies, Mister Samuelson." Jones brought a hand to his chin and tapped his bottom lip with a forefinger, folding his other arm across his chest. "Samuelson," he said again, thinking. He frowned. "You're an enigma to me, Mister Samuelson. You said you were a major businessman here in the city, correct?"

"That's right."

"And you've been a supporter of many of our brother organizations for some time now, it seems."

Lieberwits nodded.

"So if all that is true and your ID checks out, how come I've never heard of you?"

Lieberwits looked across at Wood. It was clear that their cover was about to be blown. Wood gave him the slightest of nods, letting him know he was ready for whatever was about to come. "Because my name is Lieberwits." Lieberwits palmed his holo-ID, his badge rotating inches above his hand. "Detective Lieberwits."

Instantly both of the heavies mobilized. Wood stayed absolutely still, waiting for his assailant to come to him. At the last minute, he jabbed his elbow back, catching the bald man in his gut and causing him to double over. Wood brought his hand up and found the man's face with the back of his closed fist. The thug fell to the floor, incapacitated.

Wood looked across the room. Lieberwits was going after Jones, who had already decided to make a run for it back to the adjoining room. The fair-haired man was after Lieberwits. "Hey!" Wood jumped across the desk to intercept Jones number two, sending paper and hardware flying in the process. He opened his hand and thrust his palm into the second thug's face with such force that it fractured the man's nose and took his legs out from under him. "Mister Jones" fell heavily to the floor and lay still.

Lieberwits was already next door. Wood could hear the sounds of a struggle. Quickly he entered the room.

The second room was smaller than the first, but again was furnished with a single desk and chair. Along the wall stood a series of data cabinets with flashing green lights indicating them as operational. At the far end of the cabinets, a second door provided an exit back into the hallway. Jones had been heading for the door when Lieberwits had caught up with him, but the old detective had bitten off more than he could chew. Somehow things had gone awry and Jones was now on Lieberwits's back with an arm around his neck. Lieberwits was wheezing and turning red.

Wood covered the room in two strides and, grabbing Jones with both hands, yanked him off Lieberwits. He spun Jones around and threw him headfirst into the cabinets, then grabbed him by his collar and hauled him back to his feet. Jones looked dazed and disoriented; a deep gash on his forehead had started to bleed and he spat a tooth out of a bloody mouth. Wood pulled him close. "Okay, for future reference, nobody touches my dad!"

"Screw you," Jones spat through blood.

Wood pulled his face away in disgust and cast his attention to Lieberwits. "Are you okay?"

Lieberwits nodded. He stood in the corner of the room, supporting himself with one arm against the wall and rubbing his throat with his free hand.

Wood manhandled Jones across the room, then pushed his face into the desk and locked one of his arms behind him.

"I'll sue you!" Jones screamed. "I swear to God I'll sue you."

"For what?" Lieberwits had got his breath back and now moved away from the wall.

"Police brutality!"

"And how about we book you for assaulting a police officer… among other things. You're engaged in illegal activity. Who do you think the judge is going to believe?"

"What do you want?" Jones screamed hysterically.

"The usual. Some answers to some questions."

Jones struggled to look at him from his position on the desk.

"Why'd you do it?"

"Do what? What the hell are you talking about?"

Lieberwits brought his head down level with Jones. "Now is not the time to be playing games with me, sonny. You think you're being smart? You're not smart. We already know it was your organization that was behind the break-in at the IZP. I want specifics. Names."

"I don't know what you're talking about." Jones protested. "I swear to Go…" Wood cranked his arm round a bit more and forced him to eat more desk. "All right!" he grunted. "All right! It was us! We did it!"

"Why?"

"It was a high-profile gig." He gasped through the pain. "It would have been one of the biggest things we'd ever done. Besides, it was too good of an offer to turn down."

"Turn down?" Lieberwits frowned.

"Yeah. You heard me. Someone asked us to do it. It was a paying job. We don't get too many of those."

"Who? Who paid you to do it?"

"I don't know. People like to remain anonymous. You know. Like you." The words were heavy with sarcasm.

"Who was it?" Wood applied more pressure. Jones screamed.

"I don't know who he was. I swear."

"Did you meet with him?" Lieberwits asked.

"Yes."

"How did that happen?"

"He was brought to us by one of our guys. One of our members."

"Name?" Wood demanded.

"I don't..." Wood wrenched Jones's arm higher before he could get out the denial. "Napoli!" he said quickly. "Toby Napoli. Toby brought him to us. The guy said he had this big job for us but they didn't want it to be traced back. Said that we should recruit some people in case anything went wrong. He said he could make it easy for us. Supply us with information about how to get into the zoo."

Wood and Lieberwits shared a glance. Wood had been right again.

"If it was going to be so easy, what did you need the recruits for?" Wood asked.

"Only part of the job was going to be easy. Getting in and out and bypassing the security systems. He gave us all the information we needed. We used our regular guys for that but there were enclosures in the zoo that housed the more dangerous aliens and those needed to be manually broken into or compromised. We knew it was going to be risky. That's what we used the recruits for."

"Did you tell *them* that before you sent them to their deaths?" Wood yanked Jones's arm up further eliciting another tormented scream. "You scum." Wood spat the words at him. Lieberwits placed one hand on Wood's arm and patted the air with the other, cautioning Wood to show some restraint. Jones writhed and groaned and thumped a fist against the desk to try and steel himself against the pain.

"How did this guy have all this information?" Lieberwits asked.

Jones snorted. "I don't know! All I know is he was going to pay us a crap load of credits to do this job and he was going to make it easier for us. You don't ask questions when someone gives you something like that."

"What did he look like?"

"Five-seven. Five-eight, maybe. Brown eyes. Mousy brown hair. Wore a suit. Not that that counts for anything these days."

"Do you think he was a zoo employee?"

"No. Absolutely not."

"What makes you so sure?"

"He was a weasly little guy. Irritating as hell. Breezed in here like he owned the place. He kept going on about the city, how he was a city guy, or the city guy, or something like that."

Lieberwits and Wood looked at each other and simultaneously drew the same conclusion. "Goddard!" they said together.

CHAPTER 15

Since they had made the arrest, three patrollers and a mobile tactical unit had arrived on the scene. Wood led Jones, his hands tied in restraints, back out onto the street. "Here's your perp," he said as he shoved Jones towards one of the other cops. "Take him down to Central and process him."

"What's the charge?"

"Assaulting a police officer. Accessory to murder. That's just for starters. I'm sure we're going to find out a lot more about Mister Jones here, if that's his real name, which I very much doubt."

Wood turned away, glad to finally have Jones off his hands, and saw Lieberwits talking to another detective from the tactical unit.

"Did you get the warrant?" Lieberwits asked.

"Yeah. We have it right here."

"Okay, I want you to seize everything in that room up there. Understand?"

"You got it."

Lieberwits looked across to Wood. "You ready to go?"

Wood nodded. "You wanna go for a drink?"

"Sure. I think I need one."

* * * * *

Lieberwits played with the shot glass, rotating it on the spot between the fingers of one hand. On the ride to the bar he had become more and more withdrawn and Wood was not sure if he was deep in thought or going into shock from their recent attack.

"You okay?"

"Huh?" Lieberwits looked up.

"Are you okay? You don't seem to be yourself."

"Yeah. I'm fine. Just thinking." Lieberwits looked down at his empty glass.

"Another?"

"I think I'll pass if I've got to drive you home, but you go ahead."

Lieberwits caught the barkeep's eye and gestured that he wanted a refill. The man acknowledged with a nod and moments later replaced Lieberwits's empty glass with a full counterpart.

"Thanks," Lieberwits said, so quietly that Wood barely caught it.

"Thanks? For what?"

"For what you did back there. You know…everything."

"Ah. Don't worry about it." Wood waved him off with a hand. "We're partners, right? That's what you said. It's what partners do for each other. Besides, I'm sure you'll get my ass out of a scrape before all this is over."

"Yeah, well, thanks anyway."

"It's like I told our friend back there, nobody touches my old man." Wood grinned.

"Y'know, son," Lieberwits smiled. "I never knew you cared."

Wood gulped down the last of his drink. "To be honest, I care more about that suit." Lieberwits laughed so loudly the other patrons of the bar stopped what they were doing and looked up. "Can you imagine what that old fart's face would look like if we took them back a day later, all torn up?" Lieberwits pictured it and roared with laughter again.

The two men chuckled for a moment longer and then Wood spoke again. "Was that it? Was that all that was on your mind?"

Lieberwits shook his head. "I think you did it. I think you found the answer I've been looking for these past five years."

"Really?" Wood frowned. "Care to enlighten me?"

"Yesterday. At my place. Remember when we compared those two sets of data from the CSETI and IZP."

"Yeah. So what?"

"You know how the recent planet discoveries were quickly followed by an IZP expedition?" Wood nodded. "I think the guy from the CSETI was supplying the zoo with information. Think about it. From the moment both those men died, the zoo's expeditions practically stopped."

Wood pulled a face. "But why? Why would he do that?"

"Dunno. Blackmail maybe?"

"Blackmail? For what? For information about planets? That's pretty lame."

"What if there was money involved?"

"Too obvious. You'd be able to trace that in a second. The zoo is federally funded, right?" It was Lieberwits turn to nod. "So all of their financials are public information. It's all disclosed. It's totally transparent. If you wanted to you could pull up any one of their employees' paychecks."

Lieberwits pointed to Wood's wrist. "That thing of yours. Can it access the city's mainframe? Could it download the zoo's financials?"

"Yeah."

"Well then maybe we should do just that."

"Wouldn't someone have already done that?" Wood asked. "I mean, during the initial investigation?"

Lieberwits snorted. "What investigation? Remember, I told you all of this was swept under the carpet. No foul play suspected. No one made a connection between these guys. Why would they look at their financial records? I mean, c'mon, you're a regular guy, why would anyone care to look at your paycheck?" He downed his bourbon. "Come on."

"Where are we going?"

"My place."

* * * * *

Wyatt looked at the faces assembled around him. They looked tired. Not just tired, exhausted. These men and women, these dedicated few, had worked around the clock to try and keep the people of Chicago safe. Regardless of how committed and dedicated they were, even people like these needed a pep talk every now and then.

"I'd just like to say how much I appreciate your focus on the task at hand. Considering what we've had to work with, the recapture effort is going really well."

He could see some of them brighten. Just the mere acknowledgement of their efforts and a few words of gratitude were enough to lift their spirits.

"However," he continued. "We still have a number of aliens loose and while most of them pose no danger to the public, there are still dangerous animals out there. I've been working closely with the sewer people and believe we have a plan for containing the puglion. You'll be pleased to know that plan does not involve any of you having to go back down there." There was a small cheer from the trappers. "A more pressing issue is that of the gashok pack and that's what I'm assigning you now. All of you.

"Judging from a number of reports and sightings, we've ascertained that the new pack is setting up its territory here." Wyatt pointed to the hovering map, his finger describing a circle.

"How are we going to be able to contain and take down an entire pack of animals?" Delaney asked.

"I was coming to that, but since you ask..." Wyatt paused before continuing. "Right now, the police and Earth Alliance forces are evacuating everyone out of that area, essentially removing a major food source for these animals. Now, located in the center of this district is a school with a fenced and gated recreation yard."

"Is that fence to keep the delinquents in or the kidnappers out?" Delaney asked again. Wyatt gave him a look.

"Thank God for inner-city schools," Bobby commented dryly. "Never thought I'd say that."

"Amen to that," Swarovski said. "God bless America."

"Our plan is as follows," Wyatt continued. "In the first instance we're going to install springs on those gates so they always return to the closed position. Then we're going to chock those gates open and bait the schoolyard."

"Are those gates going to be strong enough to hold 'em?" Shady asked. "Those things will go berserk once they realize they're trapped."

"They're inward-opening gates, so they can throw themselves against them as hard as they like. Once closed, pressure from the inside is only going to serve to keep them closed."

"They'll never go for it," Fairchilds said. "Those things are so twitchy, they'll smell a trap a mile away. They're smarter than you think."

"Maybe, but you'd be surprised what an alien will do when it's starving. We're going to bait that area for a couple of days. Let them get used to it. Have them walk in and out until they get comfortable. Then we'll spring the trap."

"Assuming all that works," Baducci said. "Once we've got them captured, what do we do with them?"

"We're fortunate in that respect." Wyatt said. "The gashoks have been extensively studied. Our veterinarians know exactly the amount of anaesthetic required to bring these critters down." Wyatt turned and popped the catches on a small silver travel case. Lodged within the black foam inside were twenty syringe-like darts, all containing a small amount of golden yellow liquid. "These have been modified so your quad-sys guns will fire them. Once the pack is contained, you guys can pick them off from the safety of the neighboring tower blocks that overlook the yard."

Swarovski sighed and scratched the back of his head. "It's pretty ropey, Wyatt."

Wyatt raised his eyebrows and sighed. "To be honest, everything we're trying right now is pretty ropey, but if it works, we've done our job." He shrugged. "It's the best we've got.

"One other point of concern is the fact that the mantor has not been sighted at all since its initial attack, but we'll cross that bridge when we come to it. Okay, people, this is your assignment, so go to it."

Travis stepped forward, "If I may speak?" Wyatt nodded. Travis turned to face his fellow trappers. "Folks, I'd like to introduce you all to Helen," he said, indicating her with an outstretched arm. "Helen Swift. She'll be coming with us."

Travis felt the questioning eyes of the veterans boring into him. "She's been invaluable to the recapture effort so far, and trust me, you'll want her with us for this assignment. She's going to be the single most important person out there."

The gallery had fallen silent.

"Don't ask me to explain. You're just going to have to trust me on this one."

"What he says is true." The others all turned and Smith suddenly felt very self-conscious as all eyes fell on him. "I mean…I…I mean…What I mean is, I doubted her too. I was wrong. If you won't take Travis's word for it, listen to me. We need to have her along."

"All right. She comes." Bobby said.

Travis nodded his gratitude. "Please show our guest the utmost respect. I'm sure before the next few days are through you'll be grateful to know her."

"All right, people, let's go." Wyatt said

A small smile touched Helen's lips. Travis had finally included her without first questioning her ability or willingness to help. She was finally getting through to him. She sensed him coming towards her, his arm raised out by his side for her to lay a hand on and use as a support and guide. She shook her head and he lowered his arm again, puzzled. She stepped forward, turned to stand next to him and took him by the hand. She smiled again to herself. She didn't need to see to know he was blushing.

* * * * *

"That's it." Wood said.

"Everything?"

"Everything."

"Really?"

"Yep. All the zoo's financial records. Credits and debits, gate receipts, salaries and complete pay histories for all of the seventeen hundred and thirty-one…nope, sorry…seventeen hundred and thirty-two employees."

"That was quick!"

"Not really." Wood looked at his watch. It was 10:55 PM. He rubbed at one eye.

"How long do you think it will take to upload?" Lieberwits asked. He looked much more alert than Wood, but then he was on his third cup of coffee.

"To that sorry excuse of a thing you call a computer? Dunno, couple of hours maybe."

"Well then, let's get to it." Lieberwits slurped noisily at his cup and caught Wood looking at him. "You sure you don't want some?"

Wood shook his head.

"It helps, you know, with the fatigue thing."

"I'd rather be tired that have a blinding headache."

Lieberwits shrugged, then checked his own watch. "It's getting late. You sure you don't want to just let that thing run overnight and we'll take a look at it in the morning? You can crash here if you want."

Wood peered around the corner at the sofa in the living room.

"It pulls out. It's pretty comfortable too." Lieberwits said. "You know what? Maybe that's not such a bad idea."

* * * * *

The mantor's belly growled in complaint. Unlike on its home world, where the alien had favorite prey items and had honed predatory skills to easily catch them, here the targets had proved to be much more elusive.

Rabbits were the most prevalent wild animals in this area, emerging from underground and venturing beyond the protective cover of the trees to streak across the massive lawns and vacant fields. They provided the best opportunity for the mantor to secure a decent meal, but despite stalking numerous animals, hunting had yielded nothing. The terrestrial creatures employed evasive maneuvers that the mantor was unaccustomed to, switching direction with a speed that the alien, with its weight and size, could not hope to match. Hunts had resulted in the mantor being led on a ragged chase back to rabbit burrows and left clawing angrily at earth and leaves. As the night had worn on, so the mantor had grown more tired, more frustrated and more hungry.

Now, as night fell again, the desperate creature stared out across the sprawling estates where scattered lights began to pinprick the darkening landscape. On its escape through the city the mantor had learned where to scavenge, and where there were lights, there was food.

* * * * *

The welding torch crackled and spit. Baducci flipped up his visor and inspected his work.

"How much longer?" Cook said.

"We're getting there."

"Well hurry it up, will you, man? I don't want to be out here any longer than we need to be."

Baducci looked up at him in disgust but Cook stood with his back to him paying him no attention, monitoring instead the other two teams of men stationed beyond the fence at the far end of the schoolyard.

The yard of Williams High School occupied the corner of a downtown city block. The school itself was a somber, gray building and the night did nothing to add to its appeal. From the front corner of the building, a twenty foot-high mesh fence ran along the street and to the corner of the block, before turning and enclosing the far side and finally butting up to an adjacent building on the east-facing street. Three teams of two men covered each exterior corner of the yard, scanning the streets for the newly resident gashok pack. They would provide an early warning to their two teammates working on the yard gates. Similarly, Cook looked out for them.

The remaining ULF team members, veterans and rookies, were stationed in the highrises that loomed above the eight men on the ground, using their higher vantage point to also survey the streets below and give warning if necessary. All the buildings in the neighborhood were vacant, evacuated many hours earlier, and the ULF team had been granted access to all of them. On the opposite side of the street, directly across from the gates where Baducci and Cook worked, the doors to an apartment building stood open. A quick escape route, should they need it.

* * * * *

Kate jumped awake. There was the sound of breaking glass and the distant barking of a dog which could only be Oscar, who belonged to her parents' nearest neighbors, the Fitzroys, over half a mile away.

She threw the bedcovers off and got out of bed, gathering her robe from the back of the door and pulling it on before rubbing sleep from her eyes.

Her door creaked as she slowly opened it. She exited her room and padded quietly along the long landing, stopping to check on Alex, opening the door to his room and peering in.

Alex had managed to scrunch himself up in a corner of his crib. She had no idea how he managed to sleep like that, but sleep he did, his chest rising and falling with each tiny breath that escaped past his lips with a sigh. She smiled to herself in the darkness and pulled the door closed.

Lights were already on downstairs as she descended the stairway to the large foyer. Her father came through the front door, also in his robe and slippers, a large plasma rifle in his hand.

"Is everything all right, Dad?"

He started at the sound of her voice. "Oh, jeez! You made me jump." He clutched his chest with one hand.

"What's going on?"

"It's nothing, sweetheart. Something just got into the trash. Probably a raccoon or something. It's nothing to worry about. Get yourself back to bed."

"You okay?" she asked, a small smirk breaking on her face. She was surprised she had managed to give her father such a scare.

"Yeah, yeah." He nodded. "Just get yourself back to bed."

"All right then." She turned and ascended the stairs.

* * * * *

Helen closed her eyes and frowned. She dipped her head in concentration.

"What? What is it?" Travis asked.

She brought her hands to her head and rubbed her temples. "I don't know. It's jumbled and hard to make sense of. It feels very… primitive."

"It's them. They're coming," Travis snapped. "Yard team?"

"Copy." It was Hamilton.

"You guys need to get out of there. Now."

"Er. We're not seeing anything down here."

Travis looked out of the window of the high rise. "Visor. Night vision and zoom." He picked up Hamilton and Javitz at the far corner of the yard. Neither man was moving.

"Oh, God!" Helen said next to him. She held her head in her hands. It looked like she was in pain. "It's so chaotic."

"Fellas. Trust me. You need to start moving to safety. Now."

"Hamilton!" It was Bobby coming through on the link. "Did you go deaf or just decide to stop following orders? You heard the man. Get the hell out of there!"

"Copy that," Hamilton sighed. "We're moving."

Travis watched as the two men started moving toward the corner of the block where Zee and Delaney were stationed. From outside the school, Fairchilds and Radchovek began moving back toward where Baducci and Cook worked on the yard gates.

"How much time do we have?" Baducci asked.

"I don't know." Travis said. "I just know they're close."

"I just need a couple of minutes. I'm almost done here."

Travis looked back up the street. Hamilton and Javitz had now joined Zee and Delaney and all four men were now retreating from the end of the block and back towards him. Suddenly, some movement caught Travis's eye. The first of the gashoks had appeared from behind the other building where Hamilton and Javitz had been standing only moments before. "I think you just ran out of time."

Cook was looking right at them too. "Let's go!" he said, grabbing Baducci under his arm and yanking him to his feet.

Baducci flipped up his visor. "What the…?"

"No time. Let's go."

Fairchilds and Radchovek were already safe in the open building across the street. "Come on!" they yelled, encouraging Cook and Baducci to cross the short distance. The four other men began running down the street and the pack of gashoks, seeing the flurry of activity, immediately gave chase.

"Oh, crap." Travis muttered from his vantage point. Hamilton and the others were halfway back to the open building but the gashoks had already covered one side of the yard with frightening speed and had now turned onto the street. "Let's go! Let's go!" Travis yelled. In his headset he could hear the squad members already safe in the building shouting words of encouragement to the others now sprinting towards them.

Fairchilds and Radchovek manned the doors to the apartment block, waiting for the others to arrive. Hamilton suddenly appeared around the corner of the entrance, taking the few steps in one giant bound and passing them without breaking stride. Cook held the door to a ground floor apartment open and shepherded him inside.

Behind Hamilton, Zee, Javitz and Delaney quickly followed and Fairchilds and Radchovek closed and barricaded the main entrance behind them.

"Come on! Come on! Let's go!" Cook shouted, gesturing wildly with his arm for the last two men to get in the apartment.

Once inside the eight men sat in a row on the floor, their backs against the wall. Just above their heads, a large window looked out onto the street.

"Are you guys all right? Is everyone safe?" Travis came through on their headsets.

"We're all here." Fairchilds confirmed. The others struggling to get their ragged breathing under control.

The sound of snarling came from close outside as two juvenile male gashoks sparred with each other and Cook brought a finger to his lips and indicated for them all to be quiet. The others held their breath, their hearts pounding in their chests.

In the silence they could hear the sound of one of the aliens sniffing around outside the window and the low guttural purrs of a number of the other members of the pack. Zee tried to crane his neck around and observe the scene outside but Delaney grabbed his jacket and yanked him back to the floor, shooting him a look that told him he should have known better.

"What do we do now?" Javitz whispered.

"We wait." Hamilton replied.

* * * * *

"Morning," Lieberwits said, yawning and rubbing one eye.

"Oh, hey!" Wood was already sat at the dining room table. He looked up from the computer's holo screen. "Good morning!"

"You're perky," Lieberwits said with something akin to disgust. "How long have you been up?"

"About an hour."

"What have you been doing?"

"What does it look like?" Wood gestured to the screen. "Going over our download."

"Anything?" Lieberwits asked.

"You should come take a look. It's interesting, that's for sure."

"In a minute. I gotta get some coffee. You want something?"

Wood shook his head.

Moments later, Lieberwits returned, his steaming cup of coffee in hand. He plodded over to the table, the soles of his slippers scuffing on the carpet, and took a seat next to Wood. "What we got?" he asked before slurping noisily from the cup.

"Well, I decided to look at the zoo's balance sheet as a kicking off-point. You know, see if there are any obvious anomalies, any large sums of money moving, anything like that."

Lieberwits gulped and waved him on. He understood.

"Well, it just so happens that there were. So I decided to cross-reference those with the data we had previously obtained from the zoo and the CSETI." Wood looked at Lieberwits. "There's a startling correlation."

"So look here," Wood pointed to the screen. "Here's a planet discovery logged by the CSETI. And here, a few weeks later the

IZP send out an expedition."

"We knew that," Lieberwits said. "What's your point?"

"I'm getting to that. Now look *here*." Wood pointed to the zoo's financial record sheet. "Five months later, the zoo spends a massive amount on advertising. In the months that follow that, the gate receipts are through the roof."

"So let me understand this correctly. You think that Mannheim was blackmailing the CSETI guy for information so he could send out crews and capture aliens for the zoo. They then spend a load on advertising to get the punters back for another visit to see these new creatures and increase the zoo's profits. What's in it for Mannheim?"

"Well, that would be very altruistic of him, if that was the case." Wood's eyes flashed, "But there's more.

"Shortly after the advertising expenses go out of their account, there's another massive expense. I couldn't figure out what it was at first. It didn't seem to be allocated to any one resource or department. It was just a random, unaccounted-for expense. Then I found it."

"Let me guess," Lieberwits said. "Mannheim's paycheck."

"Bingo." Wood pulled up the data once more. "The amounts tally exactly. Every single time. He'd been paying himself nice fat bonuses from the elevated gate receipts. It had been going on for years."

"But how? The zoo's federally funded. It's a not-for-profit organization."

"In essence, yes, but not exactly. I did some research. The zoo wasn't expected to pay anything back to the city or the state. They had a special agreement. Their profits were theirs to do with as they wished. This Mannheim guy was basically empire-building at the zoo. He was ensuring the zoo's success and securing his position but at the same time he was creaming the profits off the top—and given the amounts he was taking, I'd say the zoo definitely wasn't making any profit. If you get what I mean."

Lieberwits nodded thoughtfully. What Wood was saying made sense. Mannheim had been smart and covered his tracks well. So that was it. That was the answer that had eluded him all this time. He placed a hand on Wood's shoulder. "You're a good cop. Anyone ever tell you that? You'd make your father proud."

Wood looked surprised at Lieberwits's comment. He nodded in gratitude but could find no words in reply.

Lieberwits slumped back in his seat. The weight of five years work seemingly lifted off his shoulders. "That's it?" He stared into space like someone who had just lost something dear to him.

"That's it. Same pattern every time. Logged planet. IZP expedition goes out. Increased advertising expenses. Increased ticket sales. Fat bonus. The time frames vary a little bit from case to case, but once I'd figured it out for one, the rest were obvious.

"Again, it stops dead, exactly five years ago. If you follow the zoo's financials after that..." Wood scrolled down through the data, "...there's nothing spent on advertising and no more bonuses being paid out. The gate receipts have been in steady decline ever since, which may account for the zoo's fall from grace." Wood continued to scroll down through the figures. He frowned. "Hang on a minute. What's this?"

Lieberwits didn't hear him. He was still lost in his thoughts.

"You should take a look at this." Wood looked up. Lieberwits was miles away. "Ed!"

"What!" Lieberwits jumped in his seat, almost spilling his coffee.

"Look at this. What the hell is this?" Wood pointed at the screen. "There's huge amounts going out of the zoo's accounts again."

Lieberwits frowned. "When did that start happening?"

"Er, let's see....about two years ago. Every few months there are credits going out."

"Where's it going?"

"I dunno, but why would they be spending like that when they're already losing money hand over fist?"

CHAPTER 16

"Thanks for the use of the sofa." Wood was pulling on his jacket.

"Where are you going?"

"Downtown. I'm going to go and see what I can find out about this Napoli character. Are you going to be at the precinct later?"

Lieberwits nodded.

"All right. I'll swing by Central, meet you there and let you know what I turn up."

"I'll be in my office. I'll have a dig around and see if I can come up with any leads as to where that money is going."

"Sounds good." Wood left the house and closed the door behind him.

* * * * *

After they had given chase, the pack of gashoks had stayed outside the building that the eight men occupied for a number of hours. Clearly they knew the men were inside, and the humans' scent was still heavy on the air, but as time passed, the gashoks had lost interest and skulked away just before dawn. Regardless, as a precaution, no one had ventured outside for an hour after the last visual contact with the aliens, and not until Travis had been given the all-clear from Helen.

Since their close encounter the previous night the yard team had managed to complete their task and Baducci had finished welding the two massive springs to the gates. Now those gates stood open, held in place by two triangular wedges of wood. All that was left was to bait the yard.

* * * * *

"Sir."

Wyatt turned to look at the link operator.

"It's news channel one, sir. They're just calling to confirm that your broadcast is airing at 7:00 pm on Friday evening."

"What day is it today?" Wyatt asked. He honestly didn't know.

"Wednesday, sir."

Wyatt nodded. "That should be fine. Tell them that's fine."

* * * * *

Swarovski sat in the school building, the muzzle of his gun poking out of an open window. He had a clear line of sight across the schoolyard from here. He raised his head from the gun sight and viewed the triangular blocks of wood in the distance with his own eyes. They seemed ridiculously small compared with the magnified version he had just seen through the telescopic optic, though even from this distance he could see the red pin-prick of his laser guide dancing over the small wooden chock.

Swarovski was a crack shot, a fact he had proved the day of the break–in, when he had wounded the original alpha male of the gashok pack. As a result, this duty had fallen to him. He checked the sight again. It was early yet. The gashoks hadn't even shown themselves since the yard had been baited, but it didn't hurt to be prepared.

He was going to be one of only two trappers whose gun would still be loaded with a regular clip. His task, when the time came, was going to be to shoot the blocks out from under the gates, at which point the springs would slam them shut. In the event of his failure, Chris was stationed in a south-facing apartment of a high rise on the east-facing street. Swarovski peered up at the monstrous building, scanning the multitude of windows in a vain attempt to locate Chris's position. Chris would have an infinitely harder shot but it should not need to come to that. Swarovski was confident of his own ability.

He sniffed and could still smell the rotting meat. His nose wrinkled in disgust. He didn't understand it. He had washed his hands at least three times since they had baited the yard. Maybe his nose had been so offended by the stench that it was reminding him never to subject it to anything quite so wretched again.

Baiting the yard had proved to be more of a challenge than readying the trap. The gashoks keeper at the zoo had driven a small utility vehicle to their location; the rear of it loaded high with meat. He had waited a safe distance away until Helen could give her best affirmation that the area was safe, but when the vehicle turned into the street, Swarovski had muttered a curse under his breath. There was no way they were going to be able to drive it through the gates and into the yard to unload, it was just too big. The vehicle was going to have to be unloaded in the street and the hunks of meat carried into the yard. The task would take that much longer and put more men at risk, but they had no choice.

Some of the meat was fresh, but most of it was already in varying states of decay—just the way the animals liked it. Yes, the gashoks were hunters, but they were also scavengers.

Swarovski had helped with the effort but the foul stink had turned his stomach. In fact it was a miracle that he had not thrown up there and then. Now, as he sat in the school building, his guts were doing somersaults again. Somehow he just could not seem to be rid of the smell. He removed his finger from the trigger and covered his mouth with the back of his forearm to combat the bile rising in his throat. Thankfully, this would all be over in a couple of days.

* * * * *

Wood strode purposefully into Lieberwits's office. The detective looked up at his entrance. "What you got for me?"

Wood looked up where the small office's holo-screen should be. "That thing work?"

"Yeah." Lieberwits ordered the screen to life.

"It's hooked up to CORE, right?"

"As far as I know. Should be."

"All right," Wood huffed. He looked up at the rectangular screen now transmitting pictures. He lifted his arm and pressed a button on his wrist unit, changing the input of the monitor, and then continued to type on his wrist as he began to access the central system. A moment later a still picture appeared on the screen. It was the image of a young man, no one that Lieberwits was familiar with.

"Who's that?"

"*That*..." Wood pointed to the screen, "...is one Toby Napoli."

Lieberwits scrutinized the image further. Napoli looked like a regular guy. A wide grin and a mischievous twinkle in his eye. His face was framed by thick, dark, curly hair that came down to his collar, fashioned in a style that dated the picture somewhat.

Wood seemed to read his mind. "That's an old picture," he said. "Taken from his college files."

"Where did he study?"

"South New Jersey University."

"Anything we should know about that?"

"No. He majored in psychology with a minor in English literature. Seemed he was a model student. It's what he did outside of class that's interesting."

Lieberwits raised his eyebrows.

"Napoli founded and headed the alien rights movement at the college. It's still going strong today. Turns out he's still pretty active himself. He's got connections with many of the alien rights groups but he's affiliated most strongly with..."

"The Alien Liberation League." Lieberwits finished for him.

Wood nodded. "The very same."

Lieberwits fingered his bottom lip. "Interesting."

"That's not all. It gets better." Wood pulled up another image file. Again the photo was dated, but Lieberwits recognized the face immediately.

"Goddard."

"Admittedly a bit younger, but yes, our friend Mister Goddard."

"What's their connection?"

"They were college roommates. Seems they became good friends. Still are, in fact."

Lieberwits's eyes narrowed as he regarded the photo. "What are you up to?" he said quietly to himself.

"Huh?"

Lieberwits looked up at Wood. "Goddard. What's he doing? Where does he fit in all of this? Why is someone from the mayor's office involved with the alien liberation crazies and why is he so keen to help with the recapture effort?" He returned his gaze to the picture. "You're playing both sides," he said to Goddard's image.

Lieberwits snapped out of his thoughts. "I need you to do something for me."

"What?"

"Look for any connection between the mayor's office and the zoo. It doesn't matter how tenuous it appears, I don't care. I don't care if two of their respective employees are related or bumped into each other on the street. Whatever you can find. Anything and everything."

Wood raised his eyebrows. Lieberwits made it sound easy. In fact what he was asking for was an enormous amount of work.

* * * * *

It was uncanny how Helen knew, Swarovski thought as he watched the gashoks feeding. Right now, only seven veterans, Travis, Helen, and two of Travis's rookies watched the schoolyard. Four vets and four rookies had been formed into a squad of eight and Wyatt had re-deployed them into the city to deal with a number of sightings and alien reacquisition. It made sense. There was nothing they could do here except sit, watch and wait. Besides, for those rookies, being in the field with some of the vets would be some of the most invaluable training they would get. There was very little that was dangerous out there for them now, so they could use the time to get some hands on-training from some of the best trappers he knew.

Travis had been right to bring Helen along. She had been one of their greatest assets in this recapture effort. As Fairchilds had rightly stated, the gashoks were twitchy, nervous animals and if they caught sight of any of the squad, or indeed anybody baiting the yard, it may well have blown the whole operation, or if not, at least set them back to square one. Swarovski shuddered at the thought. The fewer times he had to handle that rotting meat the better.

When the eight trappers of the new unit were out on the street, readying themselves to leave, Travis had called through on their links to tell them that Helen was sensing something. Again, nobody on the ground or scanning the streets from high above had seen or heard anything, yet Travis was insistent that the pack was approaching and that they needed to get inside and out of sight. Within a minute of the squad finding safety, the gashok pack had appeared. They had been apprehensive, walking only a few paces at a time and raising their heads to sniff the air. Swarovski hoped it was the foul stench of the meat they could sense, and not the scent of humans carried on the cool breeze.

They had continued down the entire street like this until they had reached the yard gates where, as one, they had turned.

Initially, none of them would enter the schoolyard, even

though a veritable feast, by their standards, lay waiting for them not sixty feet away. Many of the aliens paced past the entrance and along the wire fence, regarding the meat with hungry eyes but suspicious of such an easy offering. Others stood by the gates, snapping and snarling and clawing at the unfamiliar asphalt.

Eventually a large female had braved the yard. She entered cautiously, taking only a few steps to begin with, then raising her head to test the air once more and cast a cautious look around. Something had spooked her and she had bolted for the gates, stopping there with the rest of the pack to stare back at the mound of meat. Her hunger was a powerful motivator, though, and soon she was back in the yard, moving closer and closer to the bait.

This had continued for some time, but with each return visit the female became less intimidated by the situation and advanced closer to the food.

After what had seemed an age, she approached the stinking mass, sniffing tentatively at first but then quickly snatching a hunk of meat and bolting for the gates once more.

Immediately upon exiting the yard, others in the pack had begun to give chase, fighting the female for her prize. In the quiet of the night, the street was filled with the sound of alien barks and growls and the occasional yelp as one of the younger gashoks discovered that they would do well to wait their turn or go fend for themselves. Swarovski had sighed to himself as he had watched them squabble and fight. It had seemed so petty and ridiculous when so much food was still there for the taking.

Tonight was a different affair. The original female had shown none of the caution she had exercised the previous night and had walked straight into the yard, picking a huge chunk of bone and gristle which she bit down on with vigor. Interestingly enough, tonight she had also elected to stay in the yard while she ate, ensuring that her meal remained her own. Three or four others from the pack now joined her. They were all clearly mature animals and showed some of the same caution that she had the night before, but now there was safety in numbers, and the overriding pang of hunger had dispelled any fear they might have had.

For the remainder, though, the yard still posed some kind of danger. They continued to stay outside, regarding the feeding few with hungry, envious eyes. Another day of starvation would end that, Swarovski thought, as he counted them. Fourteen. Fourteen aliens that tomorrow, hopefully, would be recaptured and heading back to the zoo.

* * * * *

"You're here late."

Lieberwits looked up. It was Wood again. He shrugged. "I could say the same about you."

"You got a minute?"

"Yeah. What's up?"

"I think I've found something."

"In one day? That was quick."

"Yeah, well, I decided to work from the top down. It's easier numbers when you're dealing with the top of the pyramid. Anyway, seems like it was a good idea." Wood looked back to Lieberwits's holo-screen. The detective was keeping up to date with his news, as per usual. "Can I borrow that again?"

Lieberwits gestured to it with an open palm. "It's all yours."

Wood began typing on his wrist unit. "Bear with me," he said under his breath. A moment later a new image appeared on the screen.

"What's that?"

"A video file, taken from a major fundraising dinner held here in the city." Wood pressed a button on his wrist and the clip began to play. Lieberwits watched as a "who's who" list of Chicago's rich and powerful networked and schmoozed. The recording was clearly amateur, the footage shaky and poorly filmed.

"Care to clue me in?" Lieberwits asked.

"Wait a minute." Wood had never taken his eyes off the screen. Now he stood poised with his arm up, his other hand ready to press another button on his wrist unit. "There!" he said, stopping the clip on a freeze frame.

Lieberwits's eyes scanned the still image. "Help me out here. What am I looking at?"

"Right here." Wood said, pointing to the screen. He reached up and circled an area of the picture with his finger, bringing it to highlight.

Wood had selected two men standing in the background. They were both dressed in dinner jackets, each clutching a glass of champagne. One of the men was leaning forward, straining to hear something over the sound of the other partygoers as the second man spoke directly into his ear. Lieberwits recognized him immediately. He was well known to the people of Chicago. "The mayor?"

"Correct." Wood confirmed. "And the other guy is Stephen Gruber, managing director of the IZP."

"When was this shot?"

"Funny you should ask that," Wood said with a grin. "Two years ago."

* * * * *

"Sir?"

Wyatt looked up at the link operator.

"I've got the sewer people on comms. They say they've got a red light."

"What the hell does that mean?" Wyatt asked.

The link operator shrugged. "I don't know. Do you want me to put them through to you?"

He nodded. "Yeah, yeah. Whatever." Wyatt really did not want to speak to whoever was on the other end of that line. A red light never meant anything good. A red anything never meant anything good. He huffed and ran a hand through his hair preparing himself for another problem.

* * * * *

"Do you think the mayor is involved somehow?" Wood asked.

Lieberwits shook his head. "N…" The denial stuck in his throat. His eyes glazed over as his thoughts went elsewhere. "When's the next mayoral election?" he asked.

"In a few months. Why?"

A small smile touched Lieberwits's lips. "I think we know where that money's going, don't we?"

"Do we?"

Lieberwits nodded. "Yeah. But at this point I just don't know why."

* * * * *

"Get me news channel one on the line," Wyatt said to one of the link operators.

* * * * *

The young intern sat in front of the bank of monitors with his feet up on the desk. Behind him, droids hovered and smaller bots scuttled across the floor, both inserting telescopic arms into banks of hardware, jacking into servers and adjusting playlists as news files were downloaded to the channel's CPU from across the world. The intern sighed. He was redundant here. Everything was automated. Everything was run by the machines, but like automated systems everywhere, it needed a human overseer just in case something went wrong.

Nothing ever went wrong.

To be honest, if something did, he wasn't sure he'd be able to do anything about it. They'd shown him, of course, when he'd first taken the job a couple of months ago. Emergency procedures and backup plans and everything he was supposed to do. God forbid the news went off the air for even a second. But now, if that eventuality ever arose, he doubted he could remember what was required of him.

It wasn't important. What was the worst they could do? Fire him? He was just an intern making some pocket money babysitting some machinery and monitoring the station's output. They sure as hell didn't pay him enough for that kind of responsibility.

He pulled up a comedy channel on one of the screens in front of him and slouched back in his seat, crossing his feet on the desk in front of him. The high-pitched trill of the link made him start. He looked up at the large clock on the wall. 11:37PM. He could not imagine who would be calling him at this time. He pressed a button on the link, activating voicestream only. "Hello?"

"Hello? News channel one?" the voice on the link asked.

"Yes. That's right."

"This is Wyatt Dorren of the Interplanetary Zoological Park. I need to speak to whoever is in charge there."

"Um, that would be me."

"You're in charge?" Wyatt sounded doubtful.

"Well, I'm the only one here, if that's what you mean."

"Oh. I see." The hint of skepticism had not left his voice. "Listen. I need you to do something for me. I have a community broadcast scheduled for seven o'clock tomorrow evening..."

The intern hastily cleared his half eaten dinner off the surface of the desk and looked down at the display on its surface. "Seven o'clock. Seven o'clock," he muttered to himself as his eyes scanned the multiple playlists. It was right there in front of him, highlighted in red. An absolute, hard event, which meant it would take priority over anything else being broadcast. At seven pm, as registered by the atomic clock, the clip would be broadcast, not just on news channel one, he noticed, but across all the networks.

"Yeah. I see it. A multi-point broadcast."

"Yeah, well, I need you to cancel that for me until further notice."

"Cancel? I can't cancel it."

"What do you mean you can't cancel it?"

"I mean I can't cancel it." The intern said angrily.

"I thought you said you were in charge!"

"Yeah, but I'm not authorized to do something like that."

"Well then, who is?" Wyatt was also getting agitated.

"The station manager."

"And when is he in?"

"Tomorrow. During the day."

"All right," Wyatt said, calming. "I need you to pass that message on to him. Tell him not to broadcast that message. Can you do that for me?"

"Yeah I can do that," the young man said with more than a hint of irritation.

"Okay. I really need you to pass that message on. It's important."

"I said I'll do it." He snapped.

"Okay. Thank you."

The intern hung up the link and sunk back in his chair, returning his attention to the screen on the wall. "Whatever, dude," he muttered.

* * * * *

"Travis, it's Wyatt. Come in."

"Yeah. What is it, Wyatt?" Travis said into the helmet mic.

"I've got a problem. I'm going to need your help again."

Travis snorted. "*You've* got a problem? I think all of Chicago's got a problem right now."

"Well, that's true, too, but I could certainly use you again."

"Why? What's up?"

Wyatt sighed.

"Oh, that sounds bad."

"I got a call from the sewer people."

"Oh, that is bad."

"One of their tunnel grates is jammed."

"It's what?"

"It's jammed. They can't raise it now that it's been lowered into place."

"Well, why not? Don't their people maintain those things?"

"I guess not. They said some of them haven't been used in twenty years."

"Oh jeez. So dare I ask where I fit into all of this?" Travis asked.

"That grate is going to have to be manually cranked open. I'm going to need you to go back down there."

"I was afraid you were going to say that." Travis said.

He felt a hand on his arm and looked down. It was Helen. "I'm going with you, too," she said. Through her helmet link she had heard every part of the conversation, as had every other member of the ULF team.

Travis broke his link circuit so he could speak to her privately. "You can't," he said seriously. "The others need you here. Too much time has been invested in this operation for it to fail now. You're important here."

"And you're important to me," she said flatly. "That creature still has free run of that section of the sewer. When you raise that grate, you don't know where it's going to be. It could be right there waiting for you."

She was right. Just like she was always right. Travis sighed, and then opened his comms back to Wyatt. "Wyatt. Do you copy?"

"Copy."

"I'll do it, but there are conditions."

"Shoot."

"Helen's coming with me."

There was silence on the link. Travis guessed Wyatt was mulling it over, seeing the inherent logic in the request. "You cool with that?"

"Okay." Wyatt said.

"Also, we can't just up and leave from here right now. Helen's been invaluable to this operation so far. We need her here at least until the yard is baited tomorrow morning. What's the urgency on this?"

"That's fine. There's no urgency. I've taken care of things on this end. I just need you to get down there at some point and get that grate raised so we can get to work with the recapture of the puglion."

"Okay. We'll stay here until the morning then. Once everything has been set up here, we'll be back in contact."

"Copy that. Thanks, Travis. I'm sorry I had to ask."

"Yeah, yeah." Travis said with a wry grin. "You're gonna owe me a few after all of this. You know that, right?"

"You know I'm good for it." Wyatt laughed.

* * * * *

Lieberwits raised his head from the only bit of space on his desk that was not covered in paper or files. He swallowed once and then tried again when he found his throat dry and his mouth empty of saliva. He groaned to himself and then searched among the reams of paperwork in the hope of finding an old cup with a dribble of something, anything in it to moisten his palate. The clock on the wall read 7:32 AM. Lieberwits groaned again.

He hauled himself out of his chair and spied a plastic cup perched precariously on the back corner of his desk. He picked it up and peered into it optimistically only to find an inch of cold coffee in its bottom, its thin layer of day old skin sticking to the sides of the cup as he tipped it experimentally. Lieberwits put the cup back down. He was not that desperate. Not yet, anyway. He exited his small office and walked across the large open floor to the bathroom on the opposite side of the building.

He filled a basin with water and then bent to it, cupping the cold liquid in his hands and gasping as he splashed it onto his face. When he was finished, he clutched the side of the basin and looked up. Droplets of water clung to unruly eyebrow hairs and he wiped them away with a hand, bringing it down over his face to clear the remaining surplus that ran down his features and dripped off his chin. He took a deep breath as he regarded the man in the mirror.

A life on the force had not been kind to him. It had been a regular paycheck, of course, but that was where the benefits had ended. With it had come stake-outs, late nights, early mornings, the stress of big cases, and a diet of junk food as a result of always being on the move. Lieberwits's attitude towards the work and his own tenacity had exacerbated the toll of all of this. He had gone gray before his time. First the hairs on the side of his head took on the change, then clearly defined patches had begun to appear. Within two years of being promoted to a senior rank he had a full head of silver-white hair which had amused many at Central and earned him the nickname "The Silver Fox"—a moniker which in time proved to be very fitting for the wily detective, whose gut instinct served him well and who had managed to unearth clues to solve some of the most puzzling cases that had gone cold. Now as he looked in the mirror, Lieberwits wondered if those instincts were deserting him. In five years of trying, he had never been able to figure out what had been going on at the zoo. Now it was the young officer, Wood, whose flashes of inspiration and imagination were connecting the dots.

He squinted, asking silent questions of his reflection but receiving no answers, noticing only that the action emphasized the crow's feet around his eyes and deepened the furrows on his forehead. He was getting too old for this game. Maybe Wood was right about other things too. Like settling down. He pondered it for a moment and realized that the thought did not horrify him as much as it used to. He sighed deeply. Contemplating "Mrs. Lieberwits" was not going to get his work done. He turned, took some noisy gulps from a water fountain, and exited the bathroom.

Immediately upon returning to his office, his link rang. Lieberwits activated it and instantly recognized the detective from the other day.

"Detective Lieberwits?" he asked. Clearly the recognition was not mutual. Either that or Lieberwits looked as bad as he felt.

"Yes."

"It's detective Andrews. We met the other day at the offices of the Alien Liberation League."

"Yes, yes. I know."

"I was just calling to let you know that all the files we seized have been uploaded to CORE. You can view them with your biometric login."

"Thank you, detective."

"Pleasure." Andrews terminated the link and his image disappeared from the small screen.

Lieberwits attempted to clear some more space on his desk, then activated his personal connection to CORE, watching as his keypad shimmered into view on the glass surface. He touched his index fingertip into a small area outlined by a white line and waited as the computer scanned his print. Once confirmed as a user, a desktop interface appeared which Lieberwits began to navigate.

Lieberwits saw the shared folder and opened it. Inside were a large number of documents. He sighed and opened the first one. It was going to be a long morning.

An hour later Lieberwits's eyes were hurting. He placed his elbows on the desk and rubbed at them before bringing his hands around his face to massage his temples while he digested all that he had read. Most of the documents had been personal emails containing nothing of interest, but some had detailed the future plans of the Alien Liberation League and projects they were looking to either execute or fund. It had been enlightening to see the lengths they were prepared to go to for their cause, and the outrageous schemes they had hatched.

Lieberwits touched his keypad again, calling up the next document, readying himself for yet more disappointment.

It was another email and he began to skim it like he had all the others, when the letters IZP caught his eye. He stopped and sat up in his chair, bringing his head down closer to the desk so he could better scrutinize the file, not really believing what he was reading.

He could feel the adrenaline rising and his heart begin to thump as his eyes flicked from word to word. When he was finished he fell back into his seat. Now everything made sense.

"Gotcha," he said quietly to himself.

CHAPTER 17

"But why would the Alien Liberation League have a bunch of private emails sent between the mayor and the zoo guy?" Wood asked.

"Think about it," Lieberwits said. "If you're an illegal activist group and someone comes to you saying they've got a paying job from the mayor, you wouldn't believe it, would you? You'd think you were being set up for a sting or something."

Wood shrugged.

"So you'd want some proof. Some proof that the request was legitimate. Goddard is the mayor's monkey-boy. He's the point of contact. He probably forwarded these on to our friend Mister Jones."

"Doyle, actually." Wood said.

"Huh?"

"His real name was Shaun Doyle."

Lieberwits waved him off with the back of a hand. "Whatever."

There was a moment of silence as Wood thought about everything that Lieberwits had just told him. "But why would they do it?"

"They're both desperate men. They saw a way to help each other out."

"What do you mean?"

"Well, as you pointed out, the zoo has been in steady decline ever since Gruber took over. He had no idea about what had gone on there before and couldn't understand what was happening. He needed help from someone who had the power in this city to turn his fortunes around. It just so happened that he met that man at a charity function two years ago."

"The mayor?"

"Correct."

"What does the mayor get out of the deal?"

"I'm glad you asked me that. It's why I asked you up here."

Wood frowned.

"So you can see the final piece of the puzzle fall into place." Lieberwits smiled. "This bit, at least, I can do on my own," he said with a grin. "Now then, do you have those figures from the IZP accounts? The amounts of credits that started going out of the zoo two years ago?"

"Yeah. I have them right here." Wood began accessing his wrist unit.

"All right." Lieberwits flexed his fingers and began a search on CORE. As he did so, it struck him as somewhat amusing that the last damning piece of evidence was something that anybody with a connection to the ether could access.

Wood walked around the desk to stand behind him and peer over his shoulder. "Campaign donations?" he asked when he saw what Lieberwits had pulled up.

"Yep. Accessible to anyone. The mayoral candidates have to disclose all campaign donations. It's supposed to be one of the things that keep the politics clean in this city." Lieberwits's words were laced with more than a hint of sarcasm. "Note that I stress the word 'supposed.' Anyway, have you got a number for me?"

"What? Oh, yeah!" Wood looked at his wrist unit and scrolled through the displayed data. "Okay. Try this. Two years ago. The first payment on June sixteenth. One hundred and twenty-five thousand credits."

Lieberwits scrolled his own document. "June sixteenth. June

sixteenth," he muttered to himself as his eyes scanned the information. "Here!" he said, pointing to his display on the desk. "June eighteenth. A deposit made for exactly the same amount."

"There's your man," Wood said, reaching over Lieberwits's shoulder to point at the donor column of the file.

Lieberwits read the name out loud. "Gruber. S. Gruber."

The zoo guy.

* * * * *

"Travis, we're all set here. You guys can take off." Swarovski coughed over the link. "Thanks for sticking around."

"You okay, Pete?" Travis asked. "You don't sound so good."

"Yeah. It's just that stuff. It turns my stomach. I'll be all right."

"It's a good job you're not coming with me, then." Travis said.

"Yeah." Swarovski began to laugh and then his laugh turned into a hacking cough. "How does the little lady manage it?"

Travis looked down at Helen. "She's a trooper. She can teach us a thing or two."

"Yeah. Well thank her for us. She's all right. You know what I'm saying?"

"Thank her yourself. She can hear everything."

"She can?" Swarovski had obviously forgotten that Helen had been kitted out with a ULF helmet. "Oh crap. She can. I'm sorry, Miss Swift, I didn't mean to…"

"Don't worry about it. You're not the first." Helen gave Travis a playful nudge which caused him to smile.

Swarovski was still bumbling an apology over the link. There was also the sound of laughter as other ULF team members revelled at his embarrassment. "Aw, crap," he said finally. He sighed. "Listen. We're really grateful for everything you did here, Miss Swift. You've been invaluable to us. A great help."

"You're welcome."

"So you take care of yourself and that big fella with you. He's a good man."

"I know." Helen said. "I'll keep him safe." In their room in the apartment block, Helen linked her arm with Travis's. He did not object.

"Are you guys going to be all right?" Travis asked.

"Yeah," Swarovski called back. "We'll just stay out of sight and hold our positions. Now we just gotta wait until those critters show up."

"All right. Well good luck." Travis looked down at Helen. "Are we safe to go?" he asked her.

She cocked her head as if trying to hear something, her brow furrowed as she concentrated. Finally she nodded. "I think so. Yes."

"Okay. Let's go."

He led her to the elevator and then, once they had descended, quickly through the foyer of the building. Just as they were about to exit onto the street, two bodies barred their way. Travis looked into the eyes of Smith and Argyle.

"We're coming with you." Smith said.

* * * * *

"Give me another one," Lieberwits said.

"Uh. All right. October second. Three hundred and twenty thousand." Wood read from his wrist unit.

Lieberwits searched his file. "Uh-huh. Right here. October fifth. Donor was…" His eyes moved across the data. "….Gruber. Another!" he snapped.

"January seventh. One hundred and eighty-seven thousand."

Lieberwits nodded. "Another match," he announced triumphantly. "Here, why don't we try something else."

Wood shrugged. "Okay."

Lieberwits returned his attention to the file. "Let's see. Let's see," he muttered. "Here! April of that same year. Two hundred and fifteen thousand credits." He looked back at Wood. Wood said nothing, just looked up from his wrist unit and nodded.

In all there were nine donations totaling nearly three million in credits.

* * * * *

"What? You can't!" Travis said. "They need you here."

Smith shook his head. "No they don't. Not now that everyone is back. They have plenty of people here. Fifteen qualified trappers and four of our rookies. They can handle it."

"Well there's no point in putting more people in danger than necessary."

"We've been down there. Remember?" Smith said. "If either of you get into trouble then you're done for. You're going to need some help."

"Consider us backup," Argyle said with a grin.

Travis looked at Smith whose mouth was set in a thin, hard line. Arguing was going to be pointless and waste time. The two rookies were determined to go with them. "All right," he said. "Let's go."

* * * * *

"It seems a bit absurd, doesn't it?" Wood asked.

"What?"

"To go to all that effort and then have your name show up on a document that anyone can access."

"Yeah," Lieberwits mused. "But then in some ways, no."

Wood frowned.

"I mean if we hadn't suspected something we'd have never looked at this document. And as for all the people who do look at it, do you think the name S. Gruber means anything to them? He's just another private donor. Before all this kicked off, would you have known the name of the guy running the zoo?"

Wood shook his head. "I guess not."

"Besides, this was probably the only way he could do it. He certainly couldn't make donations from the zoo directly. That would be stupid. And he wouldn't have been able to set up a dummy bank account, biometrics just won't allow it." Lieberwits sighed. "He took a calculated risk, hoping that no one would ever look into it. Unfortunately for him, we did."

"But I still don't understand why they did it," Wood said.

"Really?" Lieberwits raised his eyebrows. "Like I said before, they're both desperate men and desperate men will go to any lengths to ensure their survival. The mayor's popularity rating has plummeted since he was elected. He's failed to deliver on his promises. Do you remember what he said he was going to do if he made it into office?"

"Deal with the overcrowding problem."

"Exactly. He hasn't managed to do that yet. Maybe he saw this as a way."

Wood snorted. "Are you serious? You can't honestly think that letting a few hundred aliens loose on the city is going to put a dent in the population? The fatalities from this thing so far are thirty-something people. At least that's the last I heard."

"Maybe he's thinking longer-term. Right now, the city is in crisis and everybody knows when times are bad the people rally around their leader whether they like him or not. If he handles this well he's almost guaranteed his next term. After that, well, who knows what these aliens are carrying? Diseases. Parasites. Things that the human population has never seen before and has no immunity against. It could be years before we see what the real fallout from all of this is, but the effects could be devastating."

Wood nodded thoughtfully. "That's genius."

Lieberwits gave him a long, hard stare. "You think that's a genius plan?"

"Yeah. Well, no. Well, you know what I mean." Wood stammered.

Lieberwits continued. "As for the zoo, well they're seen as the heroes of the hour. It's all a massive PR stunt for them. The people of Chicago are eternally grateful for being kept safe and they flock back to the zoo in droves to show their support. The zoo's profitable again. Everyone's happy. You were right. It was an inside job. Gruber supplied the mayor's office with the all the security information. Goddard was the go-between. He used his contacts to reach the alien liberation nuts and passed the info on. Once the whole thing goes down, Goddard shows up at the zoo as the mayor's envoy playing all nicey-nice. It makes it look like the mayor's office is rallying to protect the people of the city, and deflects attention away from them. Pretty smart when you think about it. Bottom line is, they set the whole thing up."

"Gruber *did* know," Wood said quietly.

"That's what I just said."

"No! No! No!" Wood began to pace the office. "God! We were so stupid!"

"What?" Lieberwits frowned.

"Remember that first day when Gruber came into the zoo. Do you remember?"

"Yeah. What about it?"

"Do you remember what he said?"

Lieberwits thought for a moment, then shook his head.

"He said he'd contacted the mayor's office the minute he had heard about it on the news."

Lieberwits continued to look at him, a blank expression on his face.

"There hadn't been any news," Wood exclaimed. "The story was breaking right then and there as we were standing with him."

Lieberwits rested his chin in his hand and tapped a finger, thoughtfully. Wood was right. Gruber had incriminated himself from the very first moment and they had both missed it. He spun in his chair. "Well, I guess that leaves only one question."

"What's that?"

"Who do you want to go after? Gruber or the mayor?"

Wood thought about it for a moment. "Let's take the zoo guy. I'm sure the rest of the officers here would love to take down the mayor. Especially after all the cuts he's made to the force."

Lieberwits nodded. "All right, then."

"I'll go file the warrant request right now," Wood said, bolting out of Lieberwits's office.

* * * * *

"You must be the zoo guys."

Travis looked at himself and the others all kitted out in fatigues, helmets and carrying huge specialized weapons. "Whatever gives you that idea?"

Obviously the other man appreciated his humor, his face breaking into a wide grin. He wore navy blue coveralls and had a small backpack slung over one shoulder. In one hand he held a hard hat adorned with a single light on the front, the other he extended in greeting. "Willie Crass," he said, by way of introduction.

Crass was a short, stocky man, probably in his mid-forties. His rounded face was marked with creases that suggested he laughed long and often. He regarded them all with sharp, sparkling eyes. At the sight of Helen and the vacant look in her eyes his face fell.

Travis felt his temper rising. He was surprised at how quickly he was ready to defend her. Crass turned his gaze back to him, asking the unspoken question, and Travis simply shook his calloused hand, gripping it with perhaps more force than was necessary and giving the man a small but discernible nod that told him everything was okay and he should mind his own business.

The other man's smile returned as quickly as it had vanished. "Very good, then. Shall we go in?"

Travis looked up at the monstrous, nondescript structure. He wondered how the city could have built a sewage treatment plant that looked even more unappealing than it sounded. "Please," he said, even though it was the last thing he wanted to do.

It was dark inside and a musty smell hung heavily on the air. Crass locked the door behind them and elbowed his way through their small party in the narrow passageway. On either side of them dozens of pipes of varying widths and colors intertwined in an organized chaos, and it was these that defined the path of their route deeper into the plant. Crass donned his hat, activating the lamp on its front and looked back at them from the front of the line. "This way," he said, beckoning them to follow. The ULF team all activated their helmet lights and dropped in behind him, their footfalls the only sound among the darkness and scattered shadows.

* * * * *

"What is this place?" Smith asked. Other sounds could now be heard. The occasional hiss of escaping steam and the humming of pipes channeling unthinkable volumes of water.

Crass smiled, seemingly glad that someone had called upon his expertise. "Most of this building is dedicated to water purification. The water here goes through numerous rounds of filtration and sedimentation, heating and condensation. The mucky stuff stays underground. Speaking of which, we're here."

Crass rounded a corner and stood before what looked to be a massive freight elevator. He pulled back a rickety old door guard and gestured the others inside. Once inside, Crass slammed the door guard back and pressed a button. The elevator jolted heavily, causing Smith and the others to re-assert their footing and steady themselves as they began a slow, smooth descent to what awaited them below. Crass smiled and chuckled to himself like a man finding humor in his own jokes.

The elevator was a crude affair, nothing short of a cube with shorn-off sides. The four sighted occupants watched as the shaft passed by, itself nothing more than a vertical channel carved in the rock, which allowed every layer of earth and rock striation to be observed as it rose from their feet past their eyes and disappeared from view. To a geologist it would have been a fascinating ride through hundreds of thousands of years of this part of the earth's history, but to those riding the elevator now, it simply provided a distraction; an interesting sideshow to keep their minds off the danger they had agreed to face. The minutes, and the elevator shaft, passed intolerably slowly. An awkward silence fell upon them; partly because the ULF team was focusing on the task ahead, but partly due to the fact that none of them had much to say to the funny little man who had agreed to be their guide. He seemed to be very much content with his own thoughts as he stood to one side of them, humming something barely audible over the sound of the elevator.

After twenty minutes, the elevator came to a sudden halt, again surprising Smith and Argyle, who grabbed each others shoulders for support.

"This is it," Crass said as he slid open another door guard, identical to its counterpart high above. "Follow me." He stepped out, beckoning the others to follow. "Come on. It's still a ways yet."

Smith and Argyle stepped out behind Crass. Travis could see from their scything helmet lights that they now stood in a tunnel wide enough for the five of them to stand abreast of each other. He offered Helen his hand and began to follow.

It was cold down here, Travis noted. His breath condensed in wispy clouds before him, given a ghostly life as it was lit by the two beams of light that cut through the darkness from either side of his helmet. A chill passed over him, causing him to shiver involuntarily.

Occasionally, pinpricks of white could be seen in the darkness, but they would vanish as the group approached and the owner of the eyes would skitter away, disappearing into cracks and imperfections in the tunnel walls that now provided a home. There was also evidence of industry down here. Along the tunnel walls lay numerous abandoned vehicles, hulks of rusting metal in various states of disrepair; dismantled hardware and small mounds of unidentifiable components.

"What is all this stuff?" Travis asked, hearing his voice echo away down the tunnel, repeating his question.

"The tunneling gear," Crass replied matter-of-factly as if the answer was obvious. "They left it down here. They had to bring all that stuff down in the elevator you just rode in, then assemble most of it down here. As I'm sure you'll appreciate, this isn't a tunnel in the truest sense of the word. It doesn't surface anywhere. So once the job was done the only way to get all this stuff back out was to break it down and take it all back up. The contractor decided that wasn't cost–effective, so they just left everything down here."

"Really?" Travis asked. "Who was the contractor?"

"Oh, I don't know," Crass said. "There's probably a record of it somewhere, but this was all done a long time ago. I know this much, they made enough money off this job to buy all their equipment again and then some."

"Where did all the earth that they tunneled out of here end up?" Argyle asked.

Another smile broke out on Crass's face. "Funny that you should ask that. A lot of it went to reclaiming land along the western shores of Lake Michigan after the great storm. Much of it lies directly under the zoo. Without this tunnel, the zoo wouldn't exist, or at least it wouldn't stand where it is today."

Argyle pulled a face, seemingly impressed.

Ahead of them, a faint orange glow permeated the darkness and an ominous rumble began to fill the air. "Almost there," Crass said.

Five minutes later the small group emerged from the end of the tunnel. Travis, Smith and Argyle stood with their jaws agape as they surveyed the scene before them. "No...way." Smith muttered to himself.

"Impressive, isn't it?" Crass said over the thundering sound of falling water. Travis looked at him and saw the wonder mirrored in his eyes. Even for Crass this place still inspired awe.

Before them was a colossal cavity. Travis could not even begin to comprehend how a void this large could exist this far underground, let alone under the streets of one of Chicago's outer suburbs.

"Count yourselves lucky," Crass shouted. "Very few people ever see this."

Travis's eyes took in the scene again. In front of them, an enormous silo dominated the space. A single metal ladder, which looked ridiculously small against the giant backdrop, ran up one side of the silo and looped over its rim, suggesting that the ladder also ran down inside the gigantic drum. "You guys go in there?" he yelled.

"Once we drain it." Crass said. "Someone's gotta go in there and make sure it's cleaned out." He shrugged, as if that was explanation enough.

"You guys don't get paid enough." Travis offered.

Crass shrugged and gave him a look that told him he agreed with him.

"How much can that thing hold?"

"This one services all of the southern side of Chicago and can handle storm surge for up to a week. Thankfully it's never come to that, but put it this way, it can hold more than enough for what you guys have in mind."

Travis nodded, although he was not entirely sure what "his guys" had in mind. Whatever wheels Wyatt had set in motion, he had not included Travis in those plans. All Travis knew was that he was here to get a grate in the sewer lifted, and that was the extent of his role in the operation.

The whole area was floodlit, four massive arrays of lights reflecting off the walls and bathing everything in an earthy red glow.

"How…?"

"We can light this area, since it's pretty well ventilated. There are shafts in the rock that run to the surface and we use the heat from the pipes you saw up there to create strong convection currents that draw the air away. It means the gasses down here don't reach dangerous levels."

For the first time since they had stopped Travis noticed the breeze at his back. He looked up, seeing what looked to be a huge sewer pipe running high above and overhanging the rim of the silo. It was clearly the only point of entry into the main sewer system. "How the hell do we get in there?"

"Come on," Crass said, "I'll show you."

They walked around the base of the silo. After a few minutes, he brought them to a halt at the base of some rickety-looking scaffolding. Travis gave it a skeptical look. "Let me guess, this hasn't been serviced in twenty years, either."

"Something like that," Crass said, reaching in to find a loose hanging cable with a keypad at the end of it. He typed in something and a noise from high above reverberated around the massive chamber.

Travis looked up. The sewer pipe was now directly above them and the scaffolding climbed up the side of it and beyond, almost reaching the faraway ceiling. From the center of the scaffold array, something descended toward them.

A second, smaller elevator came to rest beside them and Crass shepherded them inside, pressing a button on the wall of the open-faced car and sending them up. Travis watched as the sewer pipe drew closer, then passed by and beneath them before they came to a sudden stop.

In front of them, a narrow metal gantry ran above and alongside the giant pipe. Crass stepped out. "This way."

Travis followed. The sound of falling water was much louder up here. Crass had turned right and was walking away along the gantry; Travis took a brief look left.

Below him he could see the end of the sewer pipe. A torrent of brown water poured out of the end of it and fell into the silo far below, sending a foamy white spray across the surface of the sludge that had already collected in the giant tank. From his perspective, it was difficult to tell just how far away that surface was, but Travis guessed it must have been more than a hundred feet.

He turned back. Smith and Argyle were already following Crass. Helen waited patiently. Travis took her arm and guided her forward, the narrow gantry barely wide enough for the two of them.

Up ahead, Crass had turned off the main walkway and onto a small metal gangplank that extended further out over the pipe. He turned back and looked surprised to see Travis and Helen so far behind, huffing his disappointment. It seemed he was tiring of his charges. Once the two of them had caught up, he began to speak. "Here is where you'll be going in," he said.

Travis looked over the rail. On top of the sewer pipe stood a short, wide, vertical cylinder, like a spur that had been pruned before it had time to grow.

"What? We just jump in?"

Crass brought up a finger to silence him. "Uh-uh. Wait. I think you'll like this." He reached down to a control box attached to the once-shiny rail and pressed the large grimy green button on its face. Once again, they were forced to look up as something descended from above, not noticing that the gangplank beneath them was slowly extending out to make contact with the vertical sewer pipe.

"All right!" Smith exclaimed. "Now that's what I'm talking about."

"Would have been nice to have had those things before," Argyle said glumly, taking a rather more pessimistic view.

In front of them now hung a new section of gantry fashioned in the shape of a giant letter E. In the two cutout areas two small identical vehicles were cradled. The whole thing swung gently from two giant chains, which disappeared into gloom high above. The vehicles were small, comprised of a slim base unit with a padded top which was clearly meant to be stood upon, and a front section which rose upward to a narrow neck and sprouted two handle bars.

"These are our patrol and maintenance vehicles. Officially they're 'riders.' We call them 'sludge riders.'" Crass smiled at his own humor again. "We use these to survey the tunnels."

Beneath each rider was a hemisphere of smoked glass. "What's that?" Argyle asked, pointing to one of them.

"Ultrasound. We use it to detect cracks in the tunnel walls."

"Are they anti-grav?" Smith asked, clearly excited at the prospect of not having to get his feet wet again.

"No. For the ultrasound to work, the vehicles have to be in contact with the surface of the waste water. It provides a medium for the sound waves to pass through. They're jet powered. They have a small, highly controllable jet underneath that sucks the water in and shoots it out the back. It makes them highly maneuverable. Remember, we have to turn these things around in a narrow tunnel."

"So are they fast?" Smith was determined to get something good out of the deal.

"Supposedly they have a top speed of forty miles an hour but we've never had a reason to push them to that. When we're looking for cracks we run them at six miles an hour. Anything above that and the ultrasound starts to give us false positives."

"What's their power source?" Travis asked. "How can you run something like that down here?"

"Internal battery. It's a push button start. No electronic ignition. We can't have any sparks down here in the tunnels."

"We know." Travis said.

"We found that out the hard way." Argyle added, sounding particularly sore.

"Yes. I heard something about that." Crass said. "I am sorry for the men you lost. We do appreciate the effort you are making."

There seemed nothing more to add to the conversation. Travis sighed deeply before stepping on to the new gangway. He turned and helped Helen across and then headed for the second, more distant rider. Smith and Argyle followed. Crass watched them all in silence.

Travis and Smith had designated themselves as pilots, with Helen and Argyle holding on behind.

"The right handle is your throttle," Crass explained. "You'll find the brake in front of your feet on the base panel. I suggest you adopt a surfing-like stance. It helps with control and balance. They're really only designed for one person so you passengers will need to lean into the bends too, otherwise you'll throw the whole thing off and control will be difficult. You need to start them up. You're going to be hitting moving water so you'll want them at least to be idling when I lower you in. It's the green button between your handle bars."

Travis pressed it and felt more than heard the small rider cough briefly beneath them but otherwise there was no sound. "Is it running?"

Crass nodded. "All right. If you folks are ready…" He turned to activate the control that would lower them into the pipe. "Oh! I almost forgot." He slipped the backpack off his shoulder, unzipped it and dug around inside. "Here," he said, pulling out a Z-shaped piece of metal. "You're going to need this." He reached over and handed it to Smith, who in turn passed it across to Travis. "That's the manual crank handle. Good thing I remembered that, otherwise the whole thing would have been a wasted effort!" He smiled again but this time his humor was wasted on Travis and the others. The smile faded quickly. "All right then. Good luck." He turned and pressed a button and lowered them into darkness.

* * * * *

Swarovski released his grip on his gun and sat up straight, arching his back to get a good stretch. He sighed deeply. It was hard work, concentrating and remaining focused for so long. He looked out of the window at the sky. Dusk was upon them, the first stars winking into view above the horizon. Night was beginning its spread across the daylight blue like dark water. It would not be long now, he told himself.

Bobby must have had the same thought for her voice came through on his link, startling him. "All personnel. All personnel. Recommend we maintain a comms silence beginning immediately."

"Copy that, Bobby," he said. "Agreed."

Now he needed to be more alert than ever.

* * * * *

It took a little while for Travis to get accustomed to the rider's controls. As Crass had said, they were highly maneuverable vehicles, but what he had failed to mention was that they were highly sensitive too. Even the slightest touch on the handle bars seemed to send them swerving dangerously off-course and towards the sewer pipe walls. Now, at last, he felt like he was getting a feel for it. He opened up the throttle a little more and began to make some headway against the filthy brown water that swept past them. Behind him, Smith seemed to be having far less trouble. His biggest challenge was trying not to rear-end Travis and Helen, who were traveling at a much more pedestrian pace than he would have liked.

Up ahead, Travis's helmet lights picked out a lowered grate closing off a fork in the pipe, the wider main pipe veering off to their left. Travis adjusted for it and continued upstream.

* * * * *

Swarovski could feel his heart thumping in his chest. It had begun almost immediately after the pack of gashoks had come into view.

They were beyond the fence at the far end of the schoolyard. As on most other nights, they had elected to come down the east/west running street and then turn onto the road that ran along the front of the school and the tower blocks in which most of the ULF team were now positioned. Once they turned onto that street they would be lost to him, his angle of view turning the wire fence into a solid silver wall. He would just have to wait until they began nosing into the yard, and then all the responsibility would fall to him.

He noticed that his palms were sweating. He wiped them hurriedly on his fatigue pants before blowing on them and taking up his gun. He thrust the butt of the weapon into his shoulder, tipped his head right, then left, to release any built-up tension in his neck, and lowered his head to the gun sight. Swarovski blew out one long breath and froze into place.

* * * * *

"Do you think it's much farther?" Smith asked. They had passed a number of closed grates and been forced to make a number of turns as they forged their way farther upstream. This pipe was significantly wider than the one they had been in when they had first encountered the puglion, the filthy water passing by in a strong, steady current.

"I don't know." Travis called back. "But we'll know when we get there." His helmet lights shone on another lowered grate directly in front of them. For a moment he thought they had arrived at their objective. The pipe should, after all, dead-end in front of them with a lowered grate, but a turn of his head lit up more pipe off to his right, the grate forcing them into an almost ninety-degree turn. Travis slowed the rider to a stop and turned to face the new stretch of pipe. He looked back at the second rider carrying Smith and Argyle. "We're certainly not there yet," he said, indicating the new pipe with a nod of his head. Travis opened up the throttle of his rider once more, sending him and Helen further into the sewer system and leaving a wake of brown spray.

"Ugh! Disgusting!" Smith complained.

* * * * *

Swarovski reached up slowly and turned on his laser sight. "Easy, Pete," he said quietly to himself as he tried to keep the gun steady and not send the small red dot dancing over the asphalt in the distance. The gashok pack had been feeding for a while now, and he had waited for them to get settled so that their attention was completely focused on the bait that had been laid for them; but he did not need to take chances and screw the whole thing up for everyone. Not now.

* * * * *

McDermott and Torres watched the pack of gashoks from the seventh floor of the high-rise directly opposite the schoolyard. It was nothing if not an education in the behavior of pack animals. What had first begun as a few hungry aliens snatching bites at a pile of free meat was now turning in to a full-blown feeding frenzy. Animals snapped and snarled at each other or fought over the same hunk of rotting flesh. Even to the untrained eye there was a clear hierarchy. The larger, more dominant males were eating their fill, while the females and cubs skulked around them in a larger circle, fighting for scraps or looking for an opportunity to snatch a bite of meat for themselves while avoiding the wrath of their elders.

The amount of bait had been significantly reduced since the pack had first entered the yard. Soon it would be gone, and with it, their opportunity to recapture these aliens. McDermott wanted to call through the link to anyone and find out what was going on but continued communication silence had put paid to that. He wondered what Swarovski was waiting for. He lifted his head from his gun sight and stared down at the aliens in the yard. "Something's wrong," he said quietly to himself.

* * * * *

Swarovski shifted in place, readying himself to squeeze off the first shot. Pandemonium would break out in the yard as soon as he fired, of that he was sure. He would need to fire the second immediately after.

He took a breath and held it, not wanting the movement of his chest to affect his shot. His finger tightened on the trigger.

And then he felt the hairs on the back of his neck stand up.

Slowly, he turned his head and looked back to the doorway and stairwell beyond. He could see nothing beyond the doorframe, the stairs shrouded in darkness, but there was something alive in that void. Something that regarded him with hunger and alien loathing. "You sly old dog." Swarovski said.

He was not far wrong.

CHAPTER 18

"Thirteen!" McDermott exclaimed.

"What the hell are you talking about?" Torres said, looking up from his scope.

"Thirteen! There's only thirteen of them!"

Torres looked at him blankly.

"Were you not paying attention during pack trapping class? They drummed it in to us like a mantra. 'Count the aliens. Count them again. Then count them again.' There's thirteen of them out there right now!"

"And?"

"Jeez." McDermott spat out the word. "You're not listening to me, are you? You don't get it."

"No, I don't get it!"

McDermott looked at him, exasperated, wondering if he should explain things further. Deciding it would be a waste of precious time, he bolted past his teammate and headed for the stairwell.

"Where are you going?" Torres yelled after him. He could hear McDermott's booted feet on the stairs already. "Aw, crap!" Torres got up and began to give chase.

* * * * *

Swarovski had no idea what had led the alpha male to him. He could only think that it had been the smell of the rotting meat on his hands. Despite being extremely careful and thoroughly washing his hands after each baiting of the yard, even he was convinced he could never completely remove the foul stink. The alien's presence now seemed to bear testament to that fact. He had left a scent trail to his location over the course of the past three days and the gashok had followed it.

A low growl emanated from the darkness, two eyes now visible as pinpricks of light. Swarovski did not move, just slowly replaced his safety catch with his thumb. He knew he had a fight for his life on his hands, but the others could still salvage something from the operation, if the trap could be executed as planned. A stray or accidental shot from his gun would spook the animals still in the yard and ruin the whole thing.

The alpha male stepped through the doorway and revealed itself to him. Its lips peeled back in a sneer, its crushing set of teeth on full display.

* * * * *

McDermott slid more than ran down the stairs, the heels of his feet barely touching the front of each step. Above him, he could hear Torres in pursuit. "Fourteen!" he yelled.

Torres looked over the handrail and into the stairwell. He could see McDermott's hand flashing in and out of sight as it gripped the rail below. The other man was already two floors beneath him. "What the hell are you talking about?"

"There's fourteen of them. There's only thirteen out in the yard right now. Swarovski's in trouble."

Finally, Torres understood.

* * * * *

"This is it," Travis said, idling his rider so it could hold position in the swirling current. In front of them the sewer grate barred their way. Smith pulled his rider up alongside it. "Seemed like a long way, didn't it?"

Their journey had seen them navigate numerous twists and turns in the tunnel, and in the darkness they had lost all track of time.

Smith nodded. "It did. It was. Now can we just get this done and get out of here? I'd just gotten to the point where I'd forgotten how much I disliked it down here."

Travis turned to Helen and she flinched away from him, sensing the heat from his helmet lights on her face. "Sorry."

"It's okay. I just wasn't expecting it."

"Is it safe?" He asked her.

Helen turned her head to one side and closed her eyes. She nodded. "Yes."

"Here. Bring that thing over." Travis motioned to Smith, suggesting he pull the other rider up so the two vehicles were touching. "Argyle. You're going to need to come over and take control of this. Helen can't do it by herself."

Smith carefully piloted his rider alongside until the two of them bumped gently together. He reached across and grabbed a handle bar on Travis's machine, ensuring they maintained contact. Argyle readied himself to step across.

"All right," Travis said. "Let's do this."

"Wait!" Helen reached up and touched the back of his shoulder. "There is something. It is distant, but it's there."

"Are you sure?"

She nodded again.

"All the more reason to do this quickly and get out of here." Travis stepped off the rider and into the swirling sewage. Not for a moment did he imagine he would be out of his depth. He disappeared under the surface, emerging again some ten feet behind them, coughing and spluttering. "Help!" he managed.

Travis's helmet lights blinked twice and went out. He removed the helmet from his head and tossed it away, knowing that it would be useless to him now. It bobbed twice on the surface before gently rolling and disappearing forever.

"I'm coming," Smith yelled. Argyle had made the transition and was already piloting the other rider for Helen.

"What about us?" Argyle asked.

"You just stay here and look after her. I've got Travis." Smith put the rider into a tight turn and pulled away, going after his mentor before he was swept away downstream.

* * * * *

The slightest of smiles touched Swarovski's lips despite the seriousness of his predicament. There was a cruel irony here. It had been his actions that had brought them to this. His bullet that had elevated the animal that faced him to its current status among the pack.

Now it had returned to challenge him.

The alpha male padded slowly towards him, its low growl never ceasing.

Swarovski had to move. The thought terrified him. He knew that the moment he so much as flinched the gashok would attack, but the longer he waited, the more the alien advanced on his position; and each passing second reduced his ability to defend himself.

He spun around and the gashok launched itself into the air, pouncing with frightening speed. Swarovski had just enough time to get his gun around, straight-arming it in front of him with both hands before the creature hit him, its jaws clamping down around the barrel of his weapon only inches from his face. It snarled and shook its head violently, almost ripping the gun from his hands and pushing him back with the ferocity of its attack.

Swarovski used the creature's momentum to his advantage, rolling down onto his back and lashing out with his feet. His boots found the gashok's belly and the kick sent the animal flying over his head. He heard the gashok yelp but that was immediately followed by skittering claws as the creature righted itself behind him. He had no time.

Swarovski kicked out again with his legs, popping himself out of his prone position on the floor and bringing himself to his feet in a single, gymnastic maneuver. He grabbed the muzzle of his gun in both hands and turned to face the gashok, swinging the weapon around like a baseball bat, the butt describing a wide circle.

He made contact the first time, striking the gashok hard across its snout and snapping the creature's head away to one side. It stayed there for a moment, as if stunned, and then it slowly turned its head back to him, its growl seeming somehow deeper and more menacing. Swarovski looked into its eyes and found a new hatred there.

The creature licked the top gum along the left side of its face as if experimentally touching its wounds. And then it came for him again.

* * * * *

McDermott came off the bottom stair and ran through the lobby of the building. He yanked back on the breech bolt of his gun, ejecting the tranquilizer dart, not caring as it flew out of the weapon and clattered on the floor. He reached into one of the many pockets on his pants, slowing as he retrieved a spare clip for his weapon. Inserting it into the bottom of his gun, he banged it home with the palm of his hand and set off again.

Torres arrived in the lobby just in time to see him disappear out the front doors.

* * * * *

"I've got you," Smith said

Travis tried to pull himself on to the rider again and almost succeeded in upending it and sending Smith into the water.

"Whoa! Easy!"

"It's no use. I can't get up. This current is too strong."

"Just hang on the back, there! I'll tow you back."

* * * * *

Chris blinked hard, twice. His eyes had grown tired from squinting down the barrel of his gun and viewing the world through a cross-hair.

His attention was caught by a commotion at street level. Someone was outside the building directly across from the schoolyard and was now running down the street. As one, the gashoks turned and bolted for the open gates.

"Shit!" He returned his eye to the gunsight and started shooting.

* * * * *

"Are you okay?" Helen asked as Smith pulled up alongside them.

"Yeah," Travis replied. "Just a little shaken up. I wasn't expecting that. How are we doing?"

"No change. It's still there, but distant."

"Good." Travis looked up at Smith. "Get me closer. Take me right up to the grate."

Smith did as he was asked, pulling them up to the slatted metal grille close enough so that Travis could reach over and take hold of it. "Shine your helmet lights over here," Travis said. Smith and Argyle obliged. "Do you see it?"

"See what?" Argyle asked. "What are we looking for?"

"A circular hole in the pipe wall. It's where the manual crank pin is located."

The pair of them scanned the surface of the wall but there was nothing.

"Maybe it's submerged," Smith offered.

"I was afraid of that," Travis said. "But I think you're right." He began to feel blindly under the water.

* * * * *

Torres ran out into the street to find thirteen vicious animals bearing down on him. He brought his quad-sys gun up and roared defiantly as he prepared to spray them with a hail of semi-automatic fire. Instead, a single, pathetic tranquilizer dart left his weapon with a pop and flew harmlessly between two of the creatures.

"Oh shit!" Torres said to himself. In his haste, he had totally forgotten that he was armed only with a tranq. He let his gun fall to his side, his shoulders slumped in defeat, resigned to the fact that certain death raced towards him.

Something whined past his head and then one of the chocks disappeared in a cloud of splinters, slamming one side of the gate shut. There were sparks on the asphalt in front of him and more missiles buzzed past him. For a second, Torres couldn't comprehend what was happening and then he realized that Chris was firing from the building opposite and he had put himself directly in the line of that fire.

Torres dropped his gun and fell to the floor. He curled up in a fetal position, covered his head with his hands and prayed that Chris could make the shot. Either that, or his end would be swift.

* * * * *

Travis was almost at full stretch. His fingers had a tentative hold on the grate; his other hand still probed beneath the surface.

"I think I've got it!" he said suddenly.

He reached inside his jacket and retrieved the crank handle from a deep pocket, being careful not to fumble it. If he dropped it now it would be lost to them forever and this whole exercise would be a waste of time.

Slowly, carefully, Travis fitted the handle onto the pin and then began to heave on it, pulling it towards himself. Nothing happened. He tried again, grimacing with the effort. Again nothing.

"This isn't going to work, is it?" Smith said.

Travis looked up at him. "Thanks for your optimism."

"No, I mean, seriously, there's no way you're going to get that thing to move while you're hanging off it at full stretch. Your weight is just compounding the problem."

"Well, come on then, wise-ass, what do you suggest?"

"I don't know. You're going to have to hold on to the grate lower down, though, if you want to have any hope of it moving."

What Smith said was right. Travis knew it. Carefully he moved his hand, pulling himself back toward the grate a little and shifting it down while there was no tension in his arm. Soon he was neck-deep in sewage, both hands under the surface; one clutching the grate, the other firmly clasped on the crank handle. "All right, here goes nothing," he said.

Travis took a breath and pulled, knowing that the action would force his head under the surface. He tried not to think about it, just focused on his effort and the task in hand. It was no good. The grate was stuck fast.

He surfaced and coughed out his held breath, trying desperately not to retch.

"Come on, Travis," Argyle said. "Let's get out of here. We tried. The fact that this thing is down here is not our fault. If it dies down here, that's not our fault either."

Travis gave him a hard look, his discomfort forgotten for the moment. "I'll pretend I never heard that. Talk like that will get you ejected from my training program. The fact that it's here is totally our fault. If it weren't for us it wouldn't even be on this planet, let alone down here. The fact that some crazy people did some stupid things that resulted in it being in the sewer is neither here nor there. It doesn't deserve to die, like many of the others have. These creatures are in our care now. *Were* in our care. We have a responsibility to do everything we can to get it out of here and I will, with or without your help. Are you with me?"

Argyle hung his head, ashamed. He looked up at Travis again and nodded slowly, his eyes distant. Travis's rebuke had clearly rekindled something inside him, the passion that had first caused him to join this specialist group. "We're your backup. Remember?" He smiled weakly.

Travis nodded, satisfied that the other man's priorities had been set straight.

"I'm sorry."

"Forget it," Travis said. "None of us want to be down here a minute longer than we need to be. You're not at fault for saying it out loud." With that, Travis disappeared under the surface again.

* * * * *

Swarovski only just had time to turn away from the second attack. The gashok landed heavily on his back and he staggered forward from the force of the impact, the creature raking its claws across his shoulders.

He craned his head forward. He knew what it was attempting. It was trying to clamber up his back and get to his neck. One bite from those powerful jaws could sever his spinal column and then this fight would be over.

He reached up, trying to grab the gashok's front paws; on the face of it, pure insanity. Claws ripped into his fingers, but he persisted, finally getting a hold and immobilizing the creature on his back. The gashok bicycled its rear legs, raking his calves. Swarovski grunted in pain.

With his head still tucked in to his chest, Swarovski began back-pedaling towards the wall, hitting it at speed and throwing his full weight into the alien behind him. He heard it yelp in pain but could tell there was still a lot of fight left in the animal. His ordeal was far from over. He stumbled forward, desperately trying to hold on to the alien thrashing around on his back, and prepared to throw himself backwards into the wall again.

* * * * *

It was a pure act of will not to vomit. He couldn't throw up, he told himself, because he was submerged, and if he did, he would surely swallow a mouthful of what was causing him to gag in the first place.

Concentrate.

Travis tugged on the crank handle, the burn of spent air in his lungs. With one final Herculean effort, something gave and he felt the grate in his other hand shift.

* * * * *

Torres allowed his forearms to part and peered through the gap between them. Gashoks snapped and snarled at him and he instinctively flinched away from them, bringing his arms back up to cover his head. As he cowered on the street he became aware of something, or rather, the lack of something. The sound of shots had ceased and now he could hear the chain links in the fence clinking as the creatures threw themselves upon it.

Slowly, he peeled his arms away, staring in awe at the thirteen powerful animals that raged beyond the flimsy barrier.

As he slowly rose to standing he began to hear the pops of tranquilizer darts being fired from weapons high above him and saw the colored tufts of the darts as they found their targets.

* * * * *

Travis heaved in a breath, threw up and then heaved in a second. "I think I've got it!" he gasped, spitting away acidic bile.

"Well here!" Smith said quickly, "Grab on, and let's wind that thing up."

"You think you can hold that thing steady?"

"What choice have we got? Come on!"

Travis let go of the grate and took a new hold on the side of Smith's rider, repositioning himself in the water. For a lesser man the task would have been impossible and even Travis, with his size and strength, struggled in the current to turn the submerged crank handle and maintain a hold on the bobbing vehicle. "This is going to take a while," he grunted.

"Yeah, well, we don't have a while."

Travis looked up at Argyle who indicated Helen with a backward nod of his head.

"It's coming," she said.

* * * * *

Swarovski threw himself backward into the wall for a third time, grunting with the impact. The gashok writhed behind him, finally managing to rip a paw out of his grip and slide down off his shoulders.

Swarovski ran then, but the effort was futile and the alien brought him down before he had even managed three strides.

* * * * *

"Get her out of here, would you?"

"No!" Helen protested. "I want to stay. I want to help."

"There's nothing more you can do here, Helen. We know what we need to do..." Travis looked through the slatted face of the grate and into the darkness, "...and we know that thing's coming. There's no need to put more people in danger than necessary."

"But I can still help! I can tell you how close it is!"

"We'll hear it, and when it gets that close we'll know it's time to move." Travis looked up at Argyle. "Go on. You guys get moving."

"No!" Helen cried again.

Argyle piloted the idling rider, looking back and forth between the two of them, an innocent bystander to a brewing argument.

"Helen! Please!"

"I thought you understood! I thought you finally got it. I didn't think I had to prove myself any more, not to you, at least. Why are you being such an ass?"

"Because I care about you!" Travis snapped.

A stunned silence fell over the four of them. "I'm sorry," Travis said quietly. "I never wished to tell you that in such a manner. But it is true. I care about you, Helen. I would never forgive myself if something happened to you."

"Oh, but it's okay for *me* to stay down here with you?" Smith said sarcastically.

"Shut up, Smithy!" Travis shot him a look. "Look, I was hoping when all this is over, if we all make it through this, that we might, you know, still see each other from time to time."

Helen lowered her head, ashamed of her earlier accusation. "I'd like that," she said quietly.

"Look, folks," Smith looked at both of them in turn. "I hate to break up your little soiree here but right now there's a fifteen-foot alien coming down the tunnel towards us and I'd rather be home watching the Grizzlies play on my wall screen."

"Will you go with Argyle? Please?"

Helen thought about it for a moment and then nodded. Travis looked up at Argyle and nodded in turn to him, giving him his permission to leave.

"Hold onto me," Argyle said and Helen adjusted her position

behind him, bringing herself closer so she could wrap her arms tighter around his waist

"As soon as we get this thing up we'll be right behind you."

Argyle nodded and turned the rider around. He gave his friends one long last look, as if he feared he might never see them again, and then gunned the throttle.

Travis looked up at Smith. "I thought I told you to shut up."

Smith cracked his broadest grin.

* * * * *

The gashok was on the back of his legs and had him pinned down. Swarovski rolled over on to his back and immediately regretted it, the alien advancing further up him and making a clear move for the kill.

He brought his bloodied hands up to protect himself and then quickly withdrew them, bunching them up into fists and holding them close to his chest, knowing that if the gashok bit down on them it would render them useless. The creature lunged for his throat and Swarovski rolled again, catching it across its snout with an elbow and knocking its head away.

The gashok recovered quickly, taking a swipe at him with a paw, attempting to rake his face with claws and in the process gouge his eyes out. Swarovski caught the paw inches from his face and with his other hand, grabbed the rolls of loose skin at the creature's neck, attempting to hold the vicious animal at bay and use his elbow as a shield against the other paw.

He looked up and behind him. His gun lay on the floor, well out of reach. Even if he could reach it, he doubted if now he could actually make a bid for it. The gashok was pushing with its rear legs, using the leverage and its three hundred pounds of weight to bear down on him. Swarovski looked back at the animal. Drools of elastic saliva hung an inch away from him and he could feel its fetid breath on his face.

His arms began to shake with the effort and Swarovski knew that he did not have the strength to hold the gashok off for much longer. Slowly, inexorably, its jaws closed in on his throat.

He did not hear the short burst of semi-automatic fire. He just felt the animal go limp and fall against him. He lay there for a moment, breathing heavily, not really comprehending what had happened, the gashok draped over him. Finally, when he had regained some of the strength in his arms, he pushed the dead creature off him, letting it thud to the floor and roll away to one side.

He looked back towards the door. A figure stood there, gun still raised, the butt of it still jammed into his shoulder. Tell-tale wisps of smoke rose from the muzzle. It was one of Travis's rookies. The one they called McDermott.

Swarovski let his head fall back on the floor. "Oh, thank God," was all he could manage.

* * * * *

"Left. Then there's a right up ahead."

Argyle's helmet lights picked out the bend in the tunnel as Helen had predicted. "What? Did you memorize the route or something?" he asked her.

"Something like that."

"Really? How'd you do that?"

"It's not memory. Not really. I don't know how to explain it, but being blind has its advantages. It frees up a huge portion of the brain for other things."

"Other things like your talents, you mean?"

"Yes. I haven't memorized the route but my body has a sense of the motions it experienced on the way in here…left again just up here…and now it seems to know what to expect on the way back. I don't know in my own mind what's up ahead, but innately I seem to know what to expect. Does that make any sense?"

Argyle shook his head. "Not really."

"Like I said, it's difficult to explain."

"Well, you haven't been wrong so far." Argyle opened up the throttle of the rider and accelerated. As far as he was concerned, the sooner he could get them both to safety, the better.

* * * * *

Travis struggled in the water. The sewer grate was now well clear of the surface but three feet of it still hung in the pipe, comb teeth hanging in the cross section giving the haunting appearance of a monstrous mouth bearing down on them; the shape of things to come. The aptness of the image was not lost on Smith.

"Come on Travis. That will have to do. Let's get out of here. That thing's giving me the creeps."

"Almost...there," Travis managed between grunts of effort. "Won't...be long...now."

Over the sounds of dripping water and swirling currents there came another noise. A commotion somewhere in the darkness upstream; a sound consistent with a huge volume of water being disturbed. It was far enough away to not be of immediate concern, but close enough to be heard, and therefore a worry.

"Like I said. It'll do." Smith tore his gaze away from the inky blackness ahead and looked down at Travis. "We're leaving. Now."

It wasn't up for discussion.

"Use that handle to climb up here," Smith ordered.

Travis did as he was told, pushing the handle down a final quarter turn so it hung off the pin in the six o'clock position. Steadying himself with his hold on the rider, he lifted his leg and placed his booted foot where his hand had been only seconds before. With a heave, he managed to lift himself out of the water, using the crank handle as a step to lift his weight. Quickly, he stepped up with his other foot and on to the back of the rider, just as the handle gave way underneath him. He slipped, but Smith had him with one hand in a vise-like grip around his forearm and managed to pull him up the rest of the way. The crank handle was lost to them now. Their work here was definitely over.

"Come on. Let's go." Smith said. He executed a tight turn with the rider and began to pull away.

* * * * *

"*People of Chicago…*"

Wyatt felt the blood drain out of his face. An enormous adrenaline rush made him dizzy and nauseous. He turned slowly, not wanting to believe what his ears told him was true. He looked up. On each of the five screens above him was his own face.

* * * * *

Kate stepped wearily down the grand staircase. It had been a long day and she had just gotten Alex off to sleep. She missed having Wyatt around to help with him. It was hard work doing the parenting thing on her own.

She stopped on the bottom step, her hand resting lightly on the end of the wooden banister fashioned into a giant whorl. She could hear the wall screen from the family room off to her right and see the faint phosphorescent blue glow emanating from the doorway, flickering as the images changed. Her father was no doubt in there, already seated in his favorite chair and scanning the guides to line up his evening's viewing. She could hear her mother still tinkering in the kitchen, cleaning up after supper and finding some last-minute things to do, as was her way.

For the first time all day Kate was alone. She sighed deeply, allowing the tension to leave her shoulders. She let her head fall back and closed her eyes, savoring the relative quiet and enjoying her moment of peace.

"Kate!" Her father called from the other room.

"Ugh!" she groaned. She righted her head, her eyes flicking open.

"Kate!" the call came again.

"What? What is it?" she said, failing to disguise her irritation.

"Come look at this! Wyatt's on the telly!"

* * * * *

Wyatt watched in horror as his recording was broadcast. He knew the script by heart. He'd recorded enough takes to get it right.

My name is Wyatt Dorren and I work for the Interplanetary Zoological Park…

Every word was like a wound.

…As you know, recent events at the zoo have put you, the public, at risk. We are working hard to rectify this situation and the recapture effort is going well.

"Travis! Come in!" Wyatt barked into his headset. "Travis! It's Wyatt! Come in!"

* * * * *

Kate stepped through the door and into the family room. What her father had said was true. Her husband looked back at her from the wall screen. She took in his features, her emotions catching in her throat. Her father turned to look at her. "Are you all right, sweetheart?"

"Yeah," she managed, nodding quickly. She raised a hand and wiped away a forming tear. It seemed like so long since she had seen him. She frowned, making interest mask her ache of loneliness. "What's he saying?"

"Listen."

"In association with the city's department of sewers we are turning to you and asking you to do your part for the city. In short, we are asking you for your help and we need that help right now.

"As a precautionary measure it has been decided to flush the sewer system completely and for that we need your co-operation. I stress, once again, that this is a precautionary measure, there is no cause for alarm but, fellow citizens, I ask you to take a minute right now and go flush your lavatories and turn on your faucets.

"I apologize for the interruption to your scheduled programming and thank you for your co-operation."

Kate folded her arms across her chest. "He's lying."

* * * * *

"Travis. Do you read me? It's Wyatt. Over."

"Wyatt. It's Smith. I hear you."

"Where's Travis?" Wyatt asked.

"He's with me."

"Why isn't he responding?"

"He's lost his helmet. You'll have to communicate through me."

Wyatt sighed.

"What's up?"

"You guys have to get out of there."

"No need to worry about us," Smith said triumphantly, "Mission already accomplished. We're on our way out now."

"You're out of the sewer pipe?"

Smith could almost hear the relief in Wyatt's voice. "No. Not out of the pipe. Not yet anyway." Wyatt's question concerned him. "Why?" he asked slowly. "What's going on?"

* * * * *

"What do you mean?"

"He's lying." Kate said again. "I can spot it a mile away." She looked at her father. "Wyatt's a terrible liar." Her father frowned. "What? You didn't know that about him?"

He shook his head, flummoxed. "But why would he lie about something like that?"

"I don't know," Kate said. "But something's going on."

* * * * *

Travis could feel the rider accelerating, Smith was violently throwing the small vehicle into the turns as they appeared in front of him. "Smith!" Travis shouted. "Smithy!"

Smith pretended not to hear him.

Travis reached up and knocked on the back of his helmet, the other man turned quickly but returned his attention to the tunnel ahead. It was as if Travis had been nothing more than a minor irritant. "Smith! What's the hurry? What did Wyatt say?"

Smith turned again and indicated the ear under his helmet with a pointed finger. "I can't hear you!" he yelled. The rider buzzed beneath them and the sound of the jet spray behind them was louder than previously but not enough that Smith should have difficulty hearing him. Smith was lying. Travis just didn't know why.

* * * * *

Helen's initial euphoria at discovering that Travis and Smith were following them out was quickly replaced with horror when she overheard the rest of Wyatt and Smith's conversation. The two other men, one she cared about deeply, were in grave danger. She wished she had stayed with them now so that she could have guided them all out of the sewer as she had done for Argyle. Yes, she would have been putting herself in danger, but at least they would have stood a fighting chance.

Travis and Smith were now in a race for their very lives.

* * * * *

Travis felt it before he heard it. A deep vibration that seemed to emanate from the earth itself. "What the hell is that?" he said, more to himself than to Smith. His eyes danced around vacantly as he thought, searching for the answer within himself. The vibration was getting worse and with it now came a deep rumble. He could feel air at his back and then his words came back to haunt him.

"...how do we flush it out?"

"Oh, shit!" he said under his breath, realizing what was happening in the pipe behind him. He grabbed a tighter hold on Smith's waist. "Go!" he screamed at him.

Smith gunned the throttle. He'd heard that all right.

* * * * *

"This should be it. It should be just around this bend," Helen said.

Argyle navigated the turn and could see an orange circle in the distance - the open end of the pipe where it discharged into the silo below. He slowed the rider and allowed the flowing water to park the vehicle back in the cradle for him. "Crass!" he yelled, looking up at the open pipe above them. "Crass!"

A face looked down at them from above.

"Get us out of here, will you?"

The face disappeared and moments later there was a clang and the sound of clinking chains as machinery was set in motion. Gently, the rider and its two occupants were lifted from the surface of the water.

"Do you think they'll be okay?" Helen asked.

Argyle shrugged. "I don't know, but I'll tell you this: Smith might be a bit of an ass when you first meet him, but there's no better man to have with you when you're stuck in a tight spot."

* * * * *

At this speed, Smith was practically driving blind. He had only a fraction of a second to react as the twists and turns in the tunnel appeared in his helmet lights. Travis, too, was being forced to react at the last minute, throwing his weight into the turns so they weren't both thrown off-balance and ejected off the back of the rider.

A pipe wall appeared in front of them. It looked like a dead end but Smith remembered the place and the almost ninety-degree turn they had made on their way in. He would have to make a hard left, but at this speed he had no idea if they were going to make it. "Hold on!" he screamed.

He threw the steering controls left and felt Travis shift his weight behind him. The rider leaned low to the water, sending a huge wash of spray against the pipe wall behind. Smith cut the corner as close as he could, the rider sliding across the surface below them, skipping ever closer to the far wall. He gritted his teeth but could see they weren't going to make it. With a sickening bang, the rider struck and began climbing up the curve of the pipe.

There was a crunch as the ultrasound dome shattered beneath them and then the rider was flying along the wall sending a shower of sparks out behind it, the two men momentarily horizontal above the water before the small vehicle slid back down and into the water.

Upon hitting the surface the jet engine kicked back into life, sending them forward with a lurch.

Once again, they were off.

* * * * *

Crass looked across casually at the gantry and cradle system as it lifted out of the top of the pipe. "How'd it g....?" He stopped himself when his eyes fell only upon Helen and Argyle. "Where are the others?" he asked, panicked.

"They're coming." Argyle said.

"Well, why didn't you come out together? Why didn't you wait for them? I'll have to lower the whole thing back down!"

"I don't think they'll be needing it." Argyle said flatly.

* * * * *

"Come on! Come on!" Travis muttered, willing Smith to go

faster. Even if he had yelled, he doubted whether Smith would have heard him. The roar of rushing water was deafening behind them.

They navigated a bend and Travis chanced a look behind him. "Yeah!" Smith whooped, although Travis cared little for his outburst, more concerned with what followed them down the sewer pipe. His eyes widened in horror. Behind them and closing in fast, a wall of water filled the pipe from top to bottom, carrying on its face the puglion, the creature flipping and turning as it tried to right itself against the raging foam which continually engulfed it.

Travis went to scream but then the rider went out from underneath him and he was falling.

* * * * *

Smith made it to the surface coughing and spluttering. He took a quick look around. Travis was nowhere to be seen. "Travis!" he yelled. "Travis!"

A torrent of water poured out of the pipe high above, thundering into the silo. If Travis was caught underneath it, then it could be recycling him below the surface. Drowning him with deadly force.

The rider erupted to the surface next to him, making him start. The vehicle fell lazily onto its side and disappeared beneath the brown water once more.

Travis was nowhere to be seen. Another concern was the fact that the puglion was now in the silo with them. Disoriented and scared, there was no telling what it might do. He had to get out of the water if he was going to be of any help to Travis. He spied the small ladder running up the side of the tank and struck out for it through the swirling waters.

Smith windmilled through the water, head down to speed his progress. When he got to the ladder, he reached an arm up to grab a rung, and a hand gripped him firmly around the wrist. He looked up into the eyes of Travis.

CHAPTER 19

Wood stuck his head around the open door of Lieberwits's office and rapped on the adjoining pane of frosted glass. Lieberwits looked up from his desk.

"Got that warrant," Wood said.

"Okay. Let's go." Lieberwits stood and snatched his hat and coat off the stand, his paperwork forgotten in an instant.

* * * * *

Wood's patroller sped up the ramp of Central's underground car park and launched itself onto the street. Lieberwits braced himself against the vehicle's dashboard. "You know where you're going?"

"Yeah," Wood said flatly.

"Are you going to take the skytrack?"

"No. I'll drive. It'll be quicker."

Lieberwits watched as Wood weaved the black and white through the smattering of vehicles that populated the roads. The way Wood was driving, he didn't doubt it.

* * * * *

"So this is it," Lieberwits said, looking up at the tower. From street level the top of it wasn't even visible.

"Yep." Wood stood by the driver's door as it slowly swung back down. "You ready?"

"As I'll ever be."

The two men crossed the street and entered the building.

They rode the turbo lift in silence, both men contemplating what lay ahead. It was always a strange time, the moments before apprehending a perp. You could plan it out in your head, the knock on the door, the look of shock on the perp's face—whether real or faked - the reading of their rights, or the pursuit when they turned and ran. You could always envision the scenario but it rarely played itself out that way. In fact, in thirty-seven years of police work, Lieberwits had never had an arrest go down exactly as he thought it would. Wood wiggled a little finger in his ear.

"You all right?" Lieberwits asked.

"Yeah, just having trouble with the pressure," Wood replied. He gulped air and the look of discomfort left his face. "That's better."

"There should be laws for folks that live this high above ground. Like, you should need to own a pilot's license or something."

Wood snorted in amusement.

Abruptly, the lift came to a stop and the doors opened. The two policemen peered outside and into a small, carpeted lobby with a door on each side. Lieberwits stepped out of the elevator and turned to the right. Wood followed close behind. The detective knocked loudly on the door and waited. There was no response.

He knocked again. "Mister Gruber? This is the CCPD. May we speak with you, please?" Again, they were greeted with silence.

Lieberwits raised a fist and banged on the door. "Stephen Gruber! This is the police. We have a warrant for your arrest. Open the door or we'll be forced to come in there!"

The neighbor from across the hallway opened the door and peered out at the commotion. Wood shot him a look that saw him hurriedly retreat back inside and close the door.

Lieberwits turned to look at Wood, who shrugged and then returned his attention to the door. Still no response.

"All right!" Lieberwits said, struggling to pull out his plasma pistol from beneath the folds of his coat. "We're going to have to do this the hard way." He spread his arms wide and took a few steps back. "Stand back," he said, sweeping Wood behind him.

Wood looked at him, puzzled. "What are you doing?"

"What does it look like I'm doing? I'm going to break the door in!"

"And when was the last time you did one of these things?"

"I don't know, seven, maybe eight years ago. Why?"

"Because you don't need to break the door in anymore."

"I don't?" Lieberwits sounded genuinely surprised.

"No. You don't."

"Oh, let me guess, that gizmo thing of yours again," Lieberwits said, sarcastically.

Wood nodded.

"You're kidding me!"

Wood shook his head, already tapping something into his wrist unit. "We wirelessly transmit the warrant to the building's AI. It processes it, identifies the apartment we're trying to access and unlocks the front door. Bingo."

"Really." Lieberwits' sarcasm hadn't left him.

"Uh-huh." Wood nodded and gestured to the door with a jerk of his head. Lieberwits turned to look at it, and then turned back to Wood triumphantly when nothing happened. "It takes a minute," Wood said. "It's got to override the biometric locks"

Lieberwits turned back just in time to hear the lock buzz and see the door pop ajar. He raised his gun to his shoulder, holding it in a two-handed grip, then kicked the door in anyway.

* * * * *

Wyatt watched on a monitor as the last of the gashoks was loaded into the enclosure. The animals would be coming around soon and then there would be a whole new round of aggression from them as the males fought again to establish dominance over the remaining group. "That's all of them," one of the gashoks' keepers said.

"All right. Let's fire the enclosure back up."

The keeper nodded and tapped the com link on her wrist. "All personnel, all personnel. Stand clear. Enclosure is about to be armed. Repeat. Stand clear. Enclosure is about to be armed." Finishing the announcement, she turned her attention to a control panel in the keepers' small hut and began pressing a series of keypads. Wyatt could hear a klaxon begin to sound and stepped outside, seeing the red lights flashing atop the nearby posts that marked the perimeter of the containment field. Blue bolts of electricity crackled between them, as if passing over plate glass, and then the invisible field settled and all that remained was the background hum of awesome amounts of power.

Wyatt's com link rang and he tapped his ear. "Yes. What is it?"

"Sir, it's control. Your field team is starting to arrive."

"Okay. I'll be there shortly." Swarovski, he already knew, had been taken to the Hope medical center for treatment, but Bobby, Chris and the others were returning to the zoo for debriefing. He was anxious to see them.

* * * * *

The old gashok hopped awkwardly on its right front leg, its left leg now useless, the paw pulled in to the body giving it the appearance of a stunted limb. The animal had not eaten in days. The pain from its injury made it impossible even to scavenge from the dumpsters it walked among.

A swarm of flies buzzed around the alien's wound, landing on its fur to add their own progeny to the writhing maggots that now infested the gaping hole in its shoulder. Before, when the old male was stronger, it could contract the muscle in its leg, sending a shiver down its side and causing the pestilent swarm to cloud into the air again. Now it could not even do that to gain some respite from its affliction.

Weak from malnutrition and loss of blood, it stopped and collapsed onto its belly, no longer able to support itself on its three good legs. Sirens wailed in the distance as the police and Earth Alliance forces closed their cordon on the city.

The gashok's eyelids drooped, closing over lusterless eyes. The creature fought it, its primitive brain registering that this was something much more significant than mere fatigue. It huffed a tired breath, eyes flicking open as its survival instinct kicked in, but the injury had taken its toll and the drooping eyelids began to fall again, closing, then fluttering open as the alien fought to stay alive. Eventually, the gashok let out one long breath and closed its eyes for the last time.

Among the high rises of the city's central business district, another of the zoo's denizens had come to its final resting place.

* * * * *

Lieberwits and Wood burst into the apartment. Lieberwits spun right, his arms locked out in front of him, pistol held tightly in both hands. His eyes scanned the expansive living space, the gun following his line of sight. "Clear!" he yelled.

Wood had done the same behind him, covering his back and the whole left side of the suite. "Clear!" Wood relaxed a little, straightening from his shooting stance. "Looks like nobody's home?"

"Don't count on it." Lieberwits said. "Keep your wits about y..."

"The doors!" Wood shouted, cutting him off.

Lieberwits looked across to Wood's side of the apartment. There was a massive glass-topped dining table around which stood twelve silver chairs. Behind it, a pair of huge sliding glass doors gave access to the roof terrace. One of them was open; the ribbon blinds hanging in front of it swaying in the breeze passing through the apartment. "You think we've got a jumper?" Wood asked quickly.

Lieberwits turned back. There was an identical pair of doors beyond the living area on his side. They, too, were open to the roof. "No." He shook his head and pointed to the doors. "Look. Mine too. Besides, judging by the ego I think we're dealing with here, I think this guy thinks he is above the law." He looked at Wood. "You know the sort. We can bring him in but he thinks his money and his connections make him untouchable. He's not afraid of us."

"You think he's trying to fake us out? Get us to check outside so he can get away?"

Lieberwits hadn't even thought of that. If that was Gruber's plan, then it was a smart one, knowing that the CCPD cops worked as two-man units. They would cover each other as they conducted the search, and Gruber could effectively play a game of hide-and-seek with them as they moved around the property until the opportunity for escape presented itself.

But Gruber hadn't counted on them. Lieberwits and Wood weren't partners, they were just two cops working the same case, and while splitting up probably broke numerous CCPD protocols, they weren't duty-bound to protect each other in any professional capacity. Lieberwits had no problem with splitting the two of them up if Wood didn't tell. Wood had clearly been working with Lieberwits long enough to know what the detective was thinking. "You want me to check outside?"

"There's gotta be some kind of fire escape out there, right?"

Wood caught the insinuation and grinned. "I take it you're cool with in here?" Lieberwits nodded. Wood headed for the doors and the roof terrace beyond.

* * * * *

"….and that was it." Bobby finished.

"You did a great job," Wyatt said. "Really." He wasn't being generous with his praise. If Bobby's recounting of what had happened out at the school was true, it was a miracle they had managed to salvage anything from the operation, much less capture the entirety of what remained of the gashok pack. "I've spoken to people at the hospital. Swarovski's beaten up pretty bad but they tell me he's going to be all right."

"Thanks to this guy!" Shady slapped McDermott so hard on the back the rookie was forced to step forward.

Wyatt looked at McDermott again, as he had done numerous times during Bobby's debriefing, as his longtime friend and colleague detailed the unassuming young man's heroism. "Thank you," he said. "You not only saved Swarovski's life, but the whole operation."

"Yeah," Bobby agreed. "He's the real hero of the hour."

McDermott shrugged. "It was nothing. I mean, I just did what anyone else would have done. I guess it was fortunate that we'd just done that stuff in training. It was still fresh in my mind."

"Well, regardless, I'd still like to extend my thanks to you." Wyatt shook McDermott's hand. The rookie nodded his acceptance. Wyatt turned back to the others. "It seems like you're not the only one who we owe a debt of gratitude to. Travis picks his recruits well." The rest of the ULF team looked up at the mention of Travis's name. "You'll be pleased to know that Travis and the others are safe. They'll be back soon." There were mumblings among the group and a number of the assembled faces broke out in smiles. "It would appear that Travis and the civilian, Miss Swift, owe their lives to the two recruits who accompanied them into the sewer." He looked at McDermott again. "All three of you will be getting special commendations when you graduate from the program. Honestly, though, I don't know what kind of a zoo we're going to have when this whole debacle is over."

"How are things going?" McAphee was standing over by Wyatt's table and studying the hovering map. "It doesn't look too bad."

Wyatt walked over to join him, the others following and gathering around the schematic. "It's not. We're in the home stretch, that's for sure." A small semi-circle of red on the map spread west from Lake Michigan and encompassed the zoo and most of the central business district. Within it, a handful of yellow sighting markers remained.

"That's it? That's all we've got left to cover?" Hamilton asked.

"That's it." Wyatt confirmed. "Along with you guys, the police and Earth Alliance forces have done a great job locking down the city. We've lost a lot of animals, though, either here at the zoo or out there in the streets. Some were just too difficult to handle and have been exterminated. Others just couldn't survive."

"Do you want us to take over?" Bobby asked.

Wyatt rubbed his chin, looking at the much larger ring of amber that had now spread for tens of miles and covered many of Chicago's outer suburbs. "We've still had no sighting of the mantor. I hate to leave a job unfinished."

"It could be dead, for all we know," she said. "You said it yourself: some of these things just can't survive out there. What are you going to do, hang out here for the next two weeks looking for a creature that could be decomposing in a ditch somewhere? By the time someone finds it there's probably going to be so little left of it they're not going to be able to identify it as roadkill or otherwise." She walked around the table to him and placed a hand on his arm. "You've done a great job too, Wyatt, but we can handle it now. Your wife and son miss you. Go to your family. We can take it from here."

Wyatt looked up at the other men and women. There was a new energy about them. They were fatigued, yes, but the knowledge that their task was so near to completion seemed to have renewed their determination. He could see it in their faces.

"Bobby's right, Wyatt," Chris said. "You've worked harder than most of us, and now you could be wasting time searching for things that just aren't there."

Normally Wyatt would have argued, but to be honest, he was exhausted, both mentally and physically and the thought of seeing his family again was powerful. He nodded. Reluctantly, he pulled the headset from his head. "I suggest you have Hernandez call the shots. He's been here before. He knows what's going on." Hernandez stepped forward and took the headset from him.

After a period of handshakes and hugged goodbyes, Wyatt left to the loud applause and admiration of his peers.

* * * * *

Wood carefully brushed aside the blind with the nose of his gun and tentatively stepped outside. There was a dividing wall to his left, splitting the roof equally between the two penthouse suites. A wooden trellis hung upon it, playing home to a number of climbing plants which had smothered it in a green collage of leaves. Running along the base of the wall, five massive urns also hosted plants of their own. Beyond that, the roof was bare of any attempts at decoration.

There were two large steps at the edge of the terrace, made of the same stone slabs that covered the patio. They led down to a narrow viewing walkway which ran the perimeter of the roof. Beyond that, the only thing saving someone from a fatal fall was a black, waist-high wrought iron railing. It ran the entire side of the roof, turned at the far corner and disappeared out of sight behind the end of the apartment.

Wood turned to his right and trained his gun on the distant corner of the building, ready for Gruber, or anyone else for that matter, should they dare to show their face around it. He sidestepped left, keeping the wall behind him and then stepped his way down to the walkway. He chanced a quick glance over the railing and immediately wished he hadn't. The height was dizzying. He looked again, forcing himself to keep his eyes focused on the side of the building and not the street far below. There was no way off the roof on this side that he could see.

Quickly, he moved back to the apartment building and then, with the wall to his back, he ran to the far end of the roof.

* * * * *

Lieberwits pulled his holo-ID generator out of his pocket in readiness for Gruber in case the other man should walk out of one of the doors ahead. "Stephen Gruber!" he shouted. "This is the police. We have a warrant for your arrest. Come out with your hands up." There was nothing but silence.

The detective walked further into the apartment, approaching a staggered hallway. To his right, the living space had ended and a wall had come out to meet him. To his left, the spacious kitchen was still very much open plan, and the opposite wall of the hallway did not start until farther down.

Lieberwits inched his way forward, keeping his gun trained on the door that faced him, his left hand supporting the butt of his pistol. He stopped. There was a second door in the short wall ahead of him to his left, but there was also a third door in the wall to his immediate right.

He transferred the pistol to his left hand, keeping it pointed ahead of him. Without looking away from the door at the end of the hallway, he blindly reached down and grabbed the handle.

* * * * *

Wyatt watched the door of his HV swing down into place and heard the pressure seal lock, silencing the sounds of the day outside. He let his head fall back on the headrest and closed his eyes, taking a moment to appreciate the peace and quiet. It was the first time he had stopped in a week and a half.

He raised a hand and rubbed the tension out of the opposite shoulder, surprised at the knots of muscle he found under the skin, then repeated the procedure on the other side, grimacing at the discomfort it caused him. He sat up, circled his shoulders forward to loosen them further and then slumped back into the seat.

Had it really only been eleven days? It felt like forever ago that he had got the call to come in. His body seemed to agree.

He realized that he still wasn't relaxed; his myriad thoughts creating anxiety, tension and worry that hunched his shoulders and left furrows on his forehead. He closed his eyes again, allowed his shoulders to fall, breathed deeply and within seconds he was asleep.

* * * * *

Wood stood at the corner of the building, his back to the wall, his weapon clutched to his chest. From here, he could see some of the end of the roof, the end of the rectangular pool and the steps that led down into the inviting water, and beyond, a collection of vacant seats occupying a semi-circular outcrop of patio encircled by the rail.

He flicked his head around the corner, using the split-second to quickly scan for danger before ducking back for safety. He saw nothing from the preliminary look and mentally readied himself to turn the corner. He took a breath and spun, adopting a crouching stance, his weapon locked out in front of him.

There was nobody on the roof.

* * * * *

Lieberwits opened the door quickly and swung the arm holding his weapon to point inside and cover the new room. Racks and racks of clothes greeted him. He had opened the door to a massive walk-in closet.

He stepped inside cautiously, turning to his left. This was as good a place as any to hide. "Stephen Gruber," he said, by way of warning. "This is the police. I urge you to come out. I am armed and will use deadly force if necessary to defend myself." Lieberwits looked for signs of movement but there were none.

He took a moment to look around. This was not a closet. This was a whole other room. It must have been ten feet wide and twenty-five feet long with racks of clothes stretching from one end to the other. Not only that, but there were multiple racks going up into the vaulted ceiling, somehow controlled by a rotating mechanism that would swing whichever was needed down into a reachable position. Suits, shirts, ties, jackets. Everything was here in abundance. It seemed Gruber's extravagance was not only limited to real estate. Lieberwits shook his head and tutted.

He stepped forward and towards a second door at the far end of the closet.

* * * * *

There were two sets of the same sliding glass doors set in the wall to Wood's right. The first was closed. The second, like the others in the apartment, was open. With his back to the wall, he inched his way towards the first.

As before, Wood took a quick glance inside but could see little through the reflective panes of glass. He turned and cupped his hand against the glass, creating the smallest sliver of shade he could manage, to peer through. It was a bedroom, with doors providing access to presumably an en suite bathroom and the hallway inside. To Wood's relief, it was empty.

Wood ran past the glass doors and to the central block of concrete, slowing as he approached the second set of doors. Again he turned and cupped his hand to the glass, making a small window on the world inside. Carefully, he leaned across and looked through.

It was another bedroom. As his eyes surveyed the scene, it looked to Wood like there was someone in there; the lower part of a body or something was visible at the foot of the bed, but the rest of the view was obscured by a large dresser that stood just inside the window against the near wall.

Wood turned away, placing his back flat against the exterior wall. "Stephen Gruber!" he shouted. "This is Officer Wood of the Chicago city police department. I need you to come out with your hands where I can see them." He turned, still using the wall for cover, and pointed his gun at the open door. He noticed that his hands were shaking ever so slightly.

An eternity seemed to pass and yet no one stepped out of the doors. There was not even the sound of movement from inside.

Wood stepped away from the wall and slowly walked around; thinking his distance from the building would give him a wider arc of vision into the bedroom, not banking on the fact that the angle of the sun on the one smoked pane of glass made it as reflective as a mirror. Regardless, no one had shot at him yet and he took that as a good sign.

He continued to circle around until he was facing the open door and looking into the room. The figure on the bed hadn't moved. He frowned, unable to comprehend why someone would so blatantly disobey an order from the police to surrender themselves without at least making a fight out of it. He approached cautiously.

Wood reached the open door and stepped inside. It was a large L—shaped room. The bed occupied the longer length. Beyond the bed there was a mahogany chest of drawers centered against the opposite wall. On its top was a silver tray with three crystal glasses, a tall, slender decanter, and a silver photo frame with a picture of a smiling Gruber in a dinner suit shaking hands with another man dressed similarly. Wood snorted to himself, Lieberwits was right about the ego. On either side of the set of drawers there were doors, one off to the left, and another two, close together and off to the right. None of it was of concern to him. What was of concern was what lay in front of him. On closer inspection, it wasn't a figure at all; more a white, tapered tube that looked like it was cemented to the bed. From this position, he could now see most of it, although the dresser to his right still obscured his view. He took another step inside and for the first time, saw the head that belonged to the body encased in the white cocoon. "Ugh! God!" he said, his tone somewhere between disgust and disappointment. He holstered his weapon and walked slowly around the corner of the room and the foot of the bed, oblivious to the tall bizarre-looking ornament that had previously been hidden, its color matched perfectly to the walls. "You can relax!" Wood shouted to Lieberwits, hoping wherever the detective was in the apartment that he could hear him. "Your stiff's in here!"

Wood stood there for a moment longer, looking at the abomination in front of him. Waiting for Lieberwits's reply.

* * * * *

Wood's call had made Lieberwits start. He hadn't expected it, certainly not from the room beyond the door in front of him. He walked the rest of the way through the closet, holstering his pistol, and reached for the handle.

He stopped. There was a break in the clothes to his right, and another door. His mind began to reel. What if Gruber had somehow captured Wood and was in there right now pointing a gun to his head, telling him to call his partner? What if he was being led straight into a trap? The detective pulled his gun out again and waited.

* * * * *

Wood slowly approached the figure on the bed. The cocoon completely encased the body except for the top half of the head. The mouth was covered but the nose remained unobstructed and open to the air. It was Gruber all right, but there was something very wrong about him. Wood remembered him from their meeting just a couple of weeks ago, a heavy-set man with a portly face that sported jowls, and yet the body that lay before him looked nothing like that. His cheeks were sunken. He looked gaunt. In fact, his skin didn't have the deathly gray pallor that a corpse's would. He didn't look quite dead.

Wood crouched down, bringing his head level with Gruber's,

his eyes taking in all of the other man's sickly features. "What the hell happened to you?" he whispered to himself.

Gruber's eyes flicked open.

* * * * *

Wyatt jumped awake.

He yawned and quickly rubbed his eyes, looking down at his personal com-link for the time. He had only slept for twenty minutes but the brief rest had done wonders for his weary frame. He should call Kate. He reached across and tapped the screen on his link, dialing her parents' number. It was Kate who answered. "Oh. Hi!"

"Hey. It's me. I'm getting out of here. I'm coming home."

"You are?" Her face lit up. "Really?"

"Yeah. They told me to leave, and quite frankly, I wasn't in the mood to argue with them."

"When can we expect you?"

"I don't know. I'll take the skytrack out of the city, then I guess, depending on traffic, an hour, hour and fifteen."

"Great!"

"How's Alex doing?"

"He's fine. He misses you. He keeps asking when Da-da's coming home. Oh look, I'll tell you everything when you get here. Just come home."

Wyatt grinned. "All right. I love you."

"Love you too. Oh, I'm so excited!"

Kate hung up the link. Wyatt grinned to himself again, then touched the ignition pad on the dash and pulled away.

* * * * *

Wood recoiled in horror. His legs back-pedaled but he failed to regain his balance and crashed into the wall and chest of drawers behind him, sending the decanter on its top into a perilous wobble.

Unable to move his head, Gruber's eyes frantically searched

the room. Wood could hear his muffled cries and see a single tear running down the other man's face, and then Gruber's eyes closed tightly against unimaginable pain and his entire body began to convulse.

Wood put his hands behind him and pushed himself up the wall. "Dear God!" He looked at the cocoon. Above Gruber's stomach, something was happening, the white resin turning translucent. Liquefying. It seemed to collapse in upon itself and Wood watched in horror as a pair of scissoring mandibles chewed their way through the sticky mass. He drew his gun again and fired at it, sending a bolt of red plasma sizzling through the cocoon and ending the creature's brief life. And then his attention was caught by something else.

In the corner of the room, something shimmered and turned black.

* * * * *

Lieberwits heard the crash. To him it sounded like a struggle, like a body being thrown against a wall. "Ed? Are you all right?" Seconds later he heard Wood's weapon discharge. He gripped the door handle, steeled his nerves and prepared to face whatever lay in the room beyond.

* * * * *

Wood watched, hypnotized, as the creature slowly, almost gracefully, unfolded each set of legs. There was something frightening and forbidding about its unhurried ease, as if it regarded the human as no significant threat to itself, only to its offspring.

It tipped itself forward, front legs falling on the end of the bed, moving to protect the larvae that it had guarded for so long. It hissed its displeasure at Wood.

He fired at it twice, each shot causing the alien to flinch and recoil, but the plasma did not penetrate the creature's carapace and left no visible mark of its passing. "Oh, crap!" he said to himself, realizing that he had bitten off more than he could chew.

The alien climbed onto the bed, advancing on him with alarming speed. Wood turned and dove through one of the two doors behind him.

* * * * *

Lieberwits was just ready to throw himself into the room when there was a commotion to his right, beyond the second door. Quickly he turned and kicked the door, smashing the lock and sending it flying open. He leveled his pistol at the man he found there and was startled to find himself looking down the barrel of another weapon.

Wood breathed a sigh of relief. "Jesus. Didn't anyone ever tell you it's polite to knock?" He lowered his gun.

"What the hell is going on?" Lieberwits stepped into the new room. It was a bathroom with a huge whirlpool spa, shower cubicle and lavatory to his right and a vanity with twin basins set against the wall to his left. A door stood on either side of the vanity.

"There's something in there," Wood said with a sideways nod of his head, indicating Gruber's room beyond the wall.

"Something? What do you mean *something?*"

"One of those zoo things. It's got Gruber."

"Is he alive?"

"He was, just. I don't think he is any more."

Two feet of black biological weaponry tore through the door, missing Lieberwits by inches. He jumped out of the way, turning to look at the scythe-like limb that had almost impaled him; one side of it a wicked curved blade, the other a serrated saw. "See what I mean?" Wood said.

The appendage wiggled in the door as the alien tried to retract it, the serrations sticking in the inch-and-a-half thick wood.

"What do we do now?" Wood asked. "I fired at it and didn't even leave a scratch." There was a horrible sawing sound as the limb was withdrawn, and then moments later it smashed through the door again, this time sending a shower of splinters into the bathroom. "Do we call the zoo people?"

Lieberwits shook his head. "I don't think we have time." He took a quick look around. "Look on the bright side, though, there's no better place to shit yourself than in the john."

Wood gave him a deadpan look. "That's not helpful."

"Sorry. I just never envisioned my police career ending in a bathroom, nice though it is."

"What do we do?" Wood asked again.

"We need to get it out on the roof," Lieberwits said seriously. "We've got a better chance against it out there than we do in here."

"How the hell do you know that?"

"I don't. I'm guessing. But we've got more room to move out there, we can catch it in crossfire."

"Did you hear me? I said I shot at it and didn't even leave a mark."

"Everything's got a weak spot," Lieberwits said with a grin.

"And how do you propose we get it out there?"

"Well, you can circle around or you can draw it out directly."

"What do you mean?"

The limb smashed through the door again, but this time Lieberwits grabbed it with both hands. "Are you nuts?" Wood screamed at him.

"Go! Now! The other door!"

Wood gave him a long look and then barreled through the other door. He stepped up onto the foot of the bed and cleared it in a single bound, leaping over what remained of Gruber and firing blindly behind him, bolts of red plasma leaving scorch marks in a dotted line across the wall. "Hey ugly!" he screamed at it. "Follow me!"

Lieberwits wrestled with the creature's limb. He could feel it struggling against him, desperate to chase Wood out of the apartment. Eventually it ripped itself free of the door and Lieberwits's futile grasp, leaving the detective with deep gashes across both his palms. "Argh!" Lieberwits screamed, looking at the two surgical cuts in his hands that were already filling with blood. Quickly he ran into the closet, tearing down a shirt to rip into shreds and bandage his hands with. He didn't have time to think about it. He had to go and help Wood.

Wood was out on the roof, and now so was the alien. He was firing at it, but as before, his shots were having little effect on the creature. Occasionally a lucky hit would force it back a step, but otherwise it was making a rapid and purposeful advance on him.

Lieberwits appeared at the open door and stepped out onto the roof. He could see that Wood was in trouble. The young cop was backed up against the edge of the pool and the thing was almost on top of him. "Get in the pool!" he screamed.

"What?" Wood yelled between shots.

"Get in the pool! Bugs hate water!"

"How do you even know it's a bug?"

"Just get in the goddamn pool!"

Wood, realizing he was fast running out of options, threw his weapon aside and did as Lieberwits said, diving into the pool. He surfaced, quickly wiping the water from his eyes, but the alien had halted at the pool's edge and refused to pursue him into the water. As it stood there, testing the surface with its front legs, a blue plasma bolt struck it in the abdomen and rocked it from behind. It spun around on its seven good legs, turning to face its new adversary, and Lieberwits got a good look at it for the first time. He swallowed nervously and felt his mouth go dry.

The old detective took another step out onto the roof, the alien taking several steps towards him at the same moment. He raised his pistol again and squeezed off two more shots, hearing the weapon whine as it recharged. He hadn't fired his weapon on the job since it had been in for service. He hoped to God they had calibrated it as he'd asked.

The alien continued its attack. Lieberwits fired several more times, peppering the creature with plasma. This time the weapon seemed to have an effect, the thing faltering in its advance and then knocked backwards with each subsequent blast. His confidence restored in his weapon, Lieberwits now strode purposefully towards the creature, continuing to keep it under fire, relishing his power as he watched it shy away from his relentless attack.

Suddenly it turned to face him again, crouching and laying itself low against the floor. Its entire back seemed to split open, from its thorax to its abdomen and Lieberwits's heart leapt into his mouth, thinking that it was readying some new kind of biological armament to use against him. Instead, four black wings rose into the air and the creature leapt off the roof and took flight. "Go for its wings!" Wood yelled from the pool, but Lieberwits was already ahead of him, steadying the butt of his pistol with his left hand and tracking the creature as it moved across the sky.

He fired once, and then again, watching as each strike made the alien buck and squirm in the air. Finally, his third shot found its target and he watched as, almost in slow motion, one of the wings splintered away from the animal and the creature began a slow, downward spiral off the side of the building.

Lieberwits raced to the rail. Wood climbed out of the pool and ran to join him. Together they watched as the giant alien's graceful spiraling glide became an out-of-control fall.

A thousand feet below them, the alien crashed into a neighboring building, shattering a window and sending shards of glass falling to the street far below. For a moment it hung there, two feet clutching at the exposed hole in the side of the structure, its remaining legs scrabbling for a hold. Lieberwits prepared to fire at it again, but Wood brought up a hand and pushed the detective's weapon back down. Before it could gain another foothold, the animal's own weight and momentum pulled it off the side of the building and sent it plummeting to the ground.

"Sure hope there's nobody down there," Wood said.

Lieberwits looked at him. Wood's hair was plastered to his head and he was still dripping water, standing in a puddle from his soggy clothes. He laughed, partly at Wood's disheveled state and partly at his own humor. "They're in for a surprise if they are."

Wood laughed briefly but his smile vanished when he saw Lieberwits's hands wrapped in rags and blood dripping from the other man's wrist. "Are you all right?"

"What?"

"Your hands. Are you all right?"

"Oh, that. Yeah. Our friend there left me with a little souvenir. I'm okay."

"What is that, anyway?" Wood was still looking at Lieberwits's hands, and the gun held in them. "That thing packs quite a punch."

"This?" Lieberwits held up the weapon, turning his hand over to look at it nonchalantly. "It's standard issue."

Wood huffed. "Yeah, right. Standard issue. I've never seen anything standard issue fire blue bolts."

"I had it tweaked." Lieberwits winked at him. "Because, y'know," he said, looking down at the alien now far below them, "You never know what you might run in to."

"Well, I'm grateful for your *tweak*. I told you you'd save my ass before all this was over."

Lieberwits smiled. "I'm glad I could repay the debt. Now I never have to see you again." The two men laughed. "What do you say we go back inside?"

"Call the zoo people?"

"That, and a cleaning service."

Together they walked back towards the open door, Wood retrieving his weapon on the way. "I guess Gruber got what was coming to him," Wood said.

"I'm not sure anyone quite deserves that." Lieberwits stepped inside. "Or *that!*"

Wood looked at the bed. Three more black insectoid creatures, each about a foot long, fed on what remained of Gruber. "I don't know," Wood said, "They're kinda cute when they're little."

"You're kidding me, right?"

"Uh, yeah. I'm kidding."

"May I?" Lieberwits asked.

"They're all yours."

Three more blasts rang out in the apartment.

CHAPTER 20

"Mom!" Kate called. She watched Alex as he played on the floor in front of her. "Mom!"

"What is it, dear? I'm right here." Kate's mother entered the sun room.

"Oh. I'm sorry. I didn't know where you were. I just had some good news. Wyatt's coming to join us."

"He is?"

Kate nodded.

"Oh, that's wonderful! You must be relieved."

"I am. He should be here within the hour. I wondered if you'd mind watching Alex for a little while. I wanted to take Furball out to the forest and I'd rather do it now, before Wyatt gets here."

"Of course! Of course! He'll be fine with me, won't you, Alex?" Alex looked at his grandmother. She smiled and returned her attention to Kate. "Go ahead."

"Thanks, mom, I appreciate it." Kate unlocked the glass door that led to the backyard and began to open it. Furball wrapped himself around her shins and nudged the door open further with his nose, bounding through at the earliest opportunity. "We won't be long. Promise," she said, stepping outside.

"Take as long as you want. We'll be fine. Besides, the fresh air will do you good."

Kate smiled and closed the door, Alex running to it and planting both palms against it. "Where mommy going? Alex go too," he pleaded with her not to leave him. Kate pulled a sad face and looked for reassurance at her mother, who waved her away.

"It's okay, Alex. Mommy's just going outside for a little bit. Do you want to play with grandma?"

"Mommy. Want to play with mommy."

"I'll be back in a minute," Kate shouted from beyond the glass. "Be good for grandma." She turned and headed for the small copse of trees on the edge of the property, Furball bounding along at her heels.

* * * * *

"*Skytrack terminus approaching*," the HV's AI announced.

"Wha…?" Wyatt lifted his head off the headrest and opened his eyes. He must have dozed off again, the gentle motion of the skytrack sending him back off to sleep. He hadn't realized just how much coordinating the recapture effort had taken out of him.

He sat up straight in his seat and watched as the tower at the end of the track approached, placing his hands on the vehicle's controls and readying himself for disengagement. The vehicle's turbine fired, started automatically by the AI, and the HV disengaged from the track, Wyatt piloting it down to street level as the wheels rolled out from underneath the chassis and locked into place.

From here it would only be ten minutes to Kate's parents' place. It would be good to see his family again. He pictured Kate in his mind, remembering a happy time and seeing her smile. The mental image brought a smile to his lips. He had missed her, the long absence giving him a new appreciation of her and that which was important in his life; and he realized just how much of it he took for granted. He made a mental note to himself to try and be a better husband and father.

* * * * *

The assembled journalists and crews looked up at the sound of approaching sirens. The mayor cleared his throat, hoping to regain their attention. "As I was saying..." It was hopeless. The sound of the sirens outside was deafening. It was not just one police patroller outside, but dozens.

Already his audience was leaving him, getting up from their chairs and heading for the windows in an attempt to see for themselves just what exactly was going on outside, thinking that whatever it was, it had to be a better story than covering the mayor's weekly press conference. For once, the mayor's weekly press conference was about to get very interesting.

A door at the rear of the room opened with a bang, and a tall, burly cop stood in the doorway. All audiovisual recording devices were quickly thrust in the man's direction, ready to capture the first words out of his mouth.

The cop looked around quickly, self-conscious and not expecting to be the center of attention in a media circus. His demeanor softened. Slightly. "Mister Mayor, sir. You're needed down at Central." It was the most tactful way he could put it without embarrassing the man in public.

"Goddammit, man! What's so important that you interrupt this? Can't you see I'm in the middle of a press conference, here? What's your ID number? I'll see you demoted for this."

Clearly the mayor wanted to be embarrassed in public.

At each door along the sides of the hall a uniformed officer appeared

"What is this?" the mayor demanded. "What the hell is going on?"

"You're under arrest."

"What? That's preposterous! I've never heard anything more ridiculous in my life!"

The first cop nodded to the officers nearest the mayor. "Cuff him."

Two officers moved towards the mayor, who backed away from his podium, sloughing off their arms as they tried to detain him. "Take your hands off me! This is ridiculous! Let me speak to Harrod. I want to speak to Harrod!"

One of the cops managed to grab a wrist. The mayor struggled and quickly found himself face-down on the floor with a knee in his back, his arms wrenched behind him.

After he was secured in wrist restraints, the mayor was hauled to his feet. "I have lawyers!" he screamed at them all. "Good lawyers! You're making a terrible mistake here! I know powerful people!"

The two cops manhandled him out of the conference room and threw him into the back of a black and white.

* * * * *

"Is it nice to be out in the fresh air?" Furball hung upside-down from its tail and gazed at Kate with big orange eyes. The small animal tipped its head from side to side as if experimenting with its new perspective on the world. "You like it out here, huh?" Furball gave her a curious look and chittered something back at her. "Yeah. Me too," Kate said. "I like it out here too, little guy." They had never been able to sex Furball. It was the only one of its kind they had ever captured, but Kate referred to it fondly as "little guy," so for their purposes it was male.

Furball righted itself on the branch and bounded along the limb's length, causing it to bend almost to the point of snapping and sending a collection of leaves into spasm. At the last minute it leapt to a neighboring tree and looked back at Kate as if seeking some recognition for its daredevil antics. Kate laughed. "I wonder, if we talk nicely to Wyatt, whether he'd let us move out here one day?" She turned and looked at the huge expanse of land behind her. She was a country girl at heart. She had done cities, of course, both when she was a student and now, living with Wyatt in Chicago, but truth be told, she was more at home here, in the wide open spaces.

Furball was already climbing the branches of the next tree, oblivious to her musings and thoughts. "Hey! Where'd you go?" Kate called out. A nearby rustle served as her reply. "Well, wait for me. This is a special treat, you hear? I don't want you to go running off without me!" Kate stepped farther into the trees. "Wyatt's coming home. You know that, right? I'd like to be back indoors when he gets here."

There was a sound from above and Kate looked up into the branches, shielding her eyes from the sun that broke through the ceiling of leaves high above. "Where are you?" she asked. A sudden movement to her left made her start. She turned quickly to find Furball upside-down once again and inches from her face. It chittered at her again and she could have sworn that the animal was laughing. "Oh, you think that's funny, do you?" she said with a mock scowl. She grabbed Furball with both hands and gave its fur a vigorous rub, the creature wriggling in protest but at the same time making a contented sound in the back of its throat. "Go on!" she laughed. "Scram!"

Furball hopped from branch to branch, chittering and screeching, clearly enjoying its time out of doors. It jumped to the next tree, running spirals around its trunk in an upward climb before launching itself at the next, gliding effortlessly between the two.

"You're funny!" Kate called after it, laughing. She stopped and the smile dropped from her face. Furball had frozen on the branch and fallen silent. The animal was completely motionless. "What is it, little guy?" she asked, taking a step forward, her foot sweeping through some of the plant debris underfoot. Without Furball's chatter and her laughter, the resulting rustle seemed incredibly loud. Kate quickly realized why. It was the only sound. The whole area was eerily silent.

"Furball. What's wrong? What is it?" Kate slowly approached. Furball still had not moved. "It's okay. Whatever it is, it's okay." She reached up to pet and soothe the animal, but before she had even made contact, Furball's head quickly turned to look at her. There was fear in its eyes.

Wyatt's words came to her in that instant. He had always said to her that the eyes were the key. In all of his years as a trapper the most invaluable lesson he had learned had been to read a creature's eyes. He claimed that ability had saved him on more than one occasion, but she had always dismissed it, thinking of it as one of Wyatt's own personal beliefs rather than a universal truth. Now she understood, and, more importantly, believed.

Furball arched its back, the hair along the entire length of its body standing on end. It hissed, something Kate had never seen it do before, and showed its complement of tiny, pin-sharp teeth. "What is it?" Kate asked again. "What's wrong?"

Furball screeched and leapt into the air a split second before something cuffed the branch, leaving only a stump of splintered wood behind.

Kate screamed.

* * * * *

"Hey! It's me!" Wyatt said.

"Glad to have you with us. Come on in." Kate's father's voice sounded tinny on the intercom.

Wyatt looked up as the gates in front of him swung slowly inward. He drummed his fingers on the HV's controls impatiently, inching the vehicle forward with the motion of the gates, willing them to move faster.

He drove through at the earliest opportunity, the gates still opening behind him after he'd passed through. His eyes traced the long driveway ahead of him, up to the large house at the crest of the rise. He could see Kate's vehicle parked out front.

* * * * *

The mantor appeared from behind the tree and Kate's scream died in her throat. Its yellow eyes locked with hers and time stood still. And then the world came back in a rush of fear and adrenaline.

Kate screamed again. She was paralyzed with fear. The mantor rocked back on its haunches, ready to strike, and then something flew out of the tree and struck the creature hard in its face.

The predator reared up on its back legs, snarling and clawing at its assailant. Furball evaded every strike, scampering over the mantor's head and burying claws in its neck. The mantor roared in pain.

Kate turned and ran, bursting out of the trees and sprinting for the house. "Mom!" she screamed. "Mom! Dad!"

* * * * *

Furball flicked its bushy tail wildly from side to side like a lure, confounding the mantor and frustrating it further, causing the animal to run a ragged figure eight as it snapped over its shoulders at the creature on its back.

* * * * *

"Mom!" Kate screamed again. Tears had begun to stream down her face. "Mom!" she bawled, somewhere between a scream and a sob. Her voice sounded raw with emotion. It didn't sound like her at all.

* * * * *

The mantor bit down on tail and Furball yelped. It flicked its head forward and ripped Furball off its back, tossing the smaller animal some fifteen feet. The predator attacked, but Furball was quick, already on its feet and scampering away on a zig-zag course, heading for the nearest tree.

The mantor jerked its head one way and then another as it tried to follow Furball's path through the brush. It pounced but came up short, clawing at earth and leaves. A second attack yielded the same result.

Furball reached the bottom of the tree and began to climb, quickly maneuvering itself around to the blind side of the trunk and away from the predator which was now upon it, clawing wildly at the tree and removing huge chunks of bark with its attack. The mantor circled and Furball countered, spiraling around as it had done before, always keeping the tree between itself and the other beast. Within seconds Furball was out of reach and safe.

The mantor dropped to all fours and looked out of the small copse of trees, turning its attention to the other prey.

* * * * *

Kate looked behind her and could see nothing but blurry outlines through her tears. She rubbed her eyes and turned to look again. There was nothing. Not even Furball. She began to feel a pang of guilt. She had run with no thought for the animal they had adopted as a pet and that had become part of their family over the last five years. She had just run, assuming that Furball had enough speed and wits and survival instincts to evade whatever it was that had attacked them. She wondered whether Furball had survived or fallen prey to the other alien.

Something exploded from the trees and Kate screamed again. The mantor bounded towards her with giant strides, closing the distance with frightening speed. She looked back towards the house. She was never going to make it.

* * * * *

Wyatt cruised past the house, ducking his head to look out of the virtual window to see if any friendly faces peered out at him. He was disappointed.

* * * * *

The shed! The shed was her only chance. Kate sprinted to it and around to its door. She grasped the handle but the door would not open. "Come on!" she sobbed, trying desperately to turn it again and jostling the door with her shoulder. "Come on!" There was no visible lock on the door, but it was clearly secured.

She could hear the mantor's feet beating out a deadly rhythm as it thundered across the yard towards her. *Think Kate, think.*

There was no biometric pad that she could see. It had to be a voice-activated lock. What combination would her father use? Her birthday! Her father had always used her birthday as a PIN. July Seventeenth. "Seven-seventeen" she screamed, all the while jiggling the handle. The door remained closed. *Calm down, Kate. The lock will never respond to that high a pitch.* She took a quick, calming breath. "Seven-seventeen," she tried again. Still nothing. She felt the panic rising. Now she could hear the mantor's rasping breath over the sound of its deadly pursuit. She had only seconds left. "Oh-seven-one-seven." The door popped open under her hand

Kate ran inside, slamming the door shut behind her. The mantor immediately thudded into the other side. She shrieked, backing away as the alien continued a frenzied attack, causing the door to bow and strain against the bolt. Kate backed farther into the shed, stumbling backwards over tools and other items scattered on the floor, throwing out an arm and luckily finding a shelf with which to steady herself in the darkness.

The mantor fell back from the door and Kate could hear its large feet padding on the grass outside as it paced back and forth, trying to determine the nature of the obstacle it now faced. The creature growled, a low menacing sound, and then fell silent.

Her eyes searched the darkness. What was the creature doing? Had it given up? Was it even still outside? The answers came all too quickly.

The mantor smashed into the side of the shed, sending small pots spilling off the shelves inside. Kate screamed and spun towards the new attack. Almost immediately, the mantor struck again, this time at the rear of the shed, and then again, on the opposite side. The animal was circling, testing the structure for weak spots. Kate continued to spin inside, guessing at the creature's next strike.

Something thudded onto the roof.

Kate looked up. Just the weight of the predator above her was causing the roof to warp and creak under the pressure, vestiges of light breaking through the newly exposed cracks. Her eyes followed the mantor's footsteps as it made its way towards the front of the shed. She looked down. Hanging on the back of the door was a rake, a shovel and a garden fork. Slowly she moved forward, mirroring the creature above her until she stood behind the door. She carefully removed the fork, turning it in her hands and clutching it with a two-handed grip. The mantor was moving again, heading back towards the rear of the shed. She followed, waiting for her opportunity to strike, inching forward, her eyes fixated on the roof. She held the fork inverted in front of her, one steadying hand on the shaft, the other gripping the handle. Her elbow hit something and sent it crashing to the floor. She winced and looked down, seeing broken glass and the glisten of moisture amongst a black slick of liquid. She had given herself away and yet at the same time had given herself the advantage. The mantor had stopped above her.

Quickly she looked back at the roof and then with both hands and as much force as she could muster, she thrust the fork upward. "Take that!" she grunted. The prongs stuck fast in the wood. On the roof, the mantor howled in pain.

Kate pulled on the fork handle, trying to retrieve it and strike again, but her improvised weapon was stuck fast. As she desperately tried to wriggle it free, a rivulet of blood ran down one of its three metal spikes. She felt a small tug and heard the mantor yelp, and then three massive claws ripped into the roof. She screamed and tugged on the handle once more, fear conferring on her a new strength. Wood splintered and cracked and the fork came away, bringing with it a two-foot section of the roof.

The mantor's nose appeared at the new hole, sniffing twice quickly, and then the alien took a look inside. "Get away from me!" Kate screamed, jabbing at it with the fork, but the mantor easily avoided her strikes and began to claw away at the roof.

In attempting to defend herself, all Kate had done was show the mantor what it had been trying to figure out all along. How to get in.

* * * * *

Wyatt pulled the HV to a stop and was about to shut off the engine when something caught his eye. He looked at the structure in front of him. Kate had mentioned something about it in their link calls, he had just never seen it before.

It wasn't the shed that had his attention, though. It was the figure on the roof. It didn't look like Kate's father. In fact, it didn't even look human.

* * * * *

A pool of light now bathed the interior of the shed. The mantor snapped and snarled, occasionally reaching in and swiping at Kate with its deadly claws, and she in turn would prod at it with the fork in a futile effort to defend herself. Then the animal would return to its systematic destruction of the roof.

Kate knew it was only going to be a matter of time before it had ripped enough wood away to be able to get to her. The safety that the shed had represented was rapidly diminishing and she knew she had to get out of there.

She kicked the door open behind her, discarded the garden fork, and ran.

* * * * *

For the briefest of moments Wyatt could not believe what he was seeing. It was nonsensical. *Of all places. the mantor, here?*

As he watched, stunned, Kate burst from the shed, making him jump in his seat. The alien dropped down into the shed from the roof with a feline ease and then quickly emerged in pursuit. Kate's next scream galvanized him into action.

Wyatt gunned the power, sending the HV's wheels into a spin and a shower of gravel out behind the vehicle. Once the tires found purchase, the HV shot forward, striking the small curb at the side of the driveway hard and skipping the vehicle up into the air. Wyatt immediately configured it for flight, the wheels rolling into the chassis before it had even had chance to touch back down.

"Shall I…?" the vehicle's AI began.

"Manual!" Wyatt yelled, "Override safety parameters!" He switched his hands over to the flying controls and aimed directly for Kate.

She was running for the house, the mantor closing in behind her. Wyatt knew the animal well enough to know that it had to be injured. In full health, it would have gotten to her and brought her down already. For the first time he noticed its pronounced limp and realized that was the only thing saving Kate from certain death. He might just have enough time. He slid the throttle control up the armrest and accelerated towards them.

* * * * *

Starving and injured, the mantor was focused on one thing only—its prey. The alien did not notice the HV until it was too late.

* * * * *

Wyatt saw the mantor turn towards him; saw the aggression in its eyes change to fear in a split second, and then there was a sickening thud as the HV collided with the animal.

The mantor's head bounced off the hood and then the creature was gone, disappearing underneath him as he shot past. He pulled back on his controller and stamped on the air brakes, sending the vehicle vertically into the sky on a rapidly decelerating ascent. Just before the HV stalled, he turned at the apex of the climb, allowing gravity to pull the vehicle's nose around and accelerate it back towards the earth, leveling it out at the last minute and flying towards Kate. He pulled up alongside her and popped the door. "Get in!"

She looked at him, dumbfounded, as if noticing his presence there for the first time.

"Get in!"

Spurred into action, Kate clambered inside.

"Shut the door!"

Kate slammed the door shut and then fell into Wyatt's arms,

sobbing. "Oh, Wyatt! I was so scared! I didn't know what to do!" She cried into his chest

He held her tightly, stroking the back of her head. "It's okay. It's over now. Everything's okay."

Wyatt's virtual window exploded inward in a thousand tiny pieces. A clawed paw thrashed viciously, inches from his face. Kate screamed and Wyatt ducked in his seat to avoid being slashed. He threw the vehicle into reverse, launching Kate forward and making her thrust her hands out in front of her to avoid hitting the dash. She let out a shriek of surprise.

The mantor caught the door frame of the HV, and the vehicle's backward motion threw the creature up onto the hood. Kate screamed again, pushing herself back into her seat and then throwing her hands up near her head, her legs straight out in front of her as she tried to push herself as far away as possible in the small confines of the HV. "Restraint!" Wyatt yelled at her. "Put your restraint on!"

She reached behind her, grabbing the two retractable clips she found there, pulling them down and trying to insert them into the clip between her legs. She fumbled with the belt and then her head was yanked to one side. She looked up. Wyatt had put the HV into a flat spin, trying to use centripetal force to throw the creature off. The world slid past in a riot of color.

Wyatt looked at the mantor through the virtual windshield. The collision had seriously hurt the animal. Its bottom jaw hung loose and useless, clearly broken, and its tongue lolled out at one side. Dark patches of blood stained its already dark fur. But hurt or not, the mantor still presented a serious threat.

The animal began to slide away from them and then it reached up, bringing a paw down hard and driving three claws through the hood's light alloy, effectively pinning itself to the vehicle. Wyatt accelerated the spin, but the alien was stuck fast and as he watched in horror, it reached up with its other front paw, repeating its effort and gaining a more secure hold. It was literally climbing up the front of the HV to get to them. Kate still fumbled with her seat restraint, but she could see what it was doing too. "Wyatt! Do something!" she screamed. The mantor reached forward, smashing another clawed foot into the hood.

An enormous bang rocked the vehicle. Red lights came on all over the displays, and the HV coughed and spluttered as something rattled around under the hood. Outside, the mantor roared and jerked its forelimb away and Wyatt could see that its claws were sheared off, a straight, surgical cut across all three of them. The alien fell away and rolled across the front of the HV, still pinned to the vehicle by its other set of claws.

"What's going on?" Kate yelled.

Wyatt's eyes scanned the displays. "We're losing power. The mantor must have damaged the turbine."

"The what?"

"The mantor! That thing outside!"

The HV's spin had started to slow. Wyatt looked out the windshield and saw smoke beginning to emerge from the turbine compartment, escaping the seams of the hood in black, curling wisps. The mantor righted itself and began trying to climb back up the vehicle, reaching pathetically with its now-useless paw. Wyatt looked at it, and then his eyes focused on the copse of trees beyond. "Hold on!"

"What are you going to do?"

"Hold on!" He slid the throttle lever back up the armrest. The HV coughed and did its best to respond. "Come on!" Wyatt muttered under his breath. The vehicle lurched forward, then coughed again, kangarooing them in their seats. "Come on. Just a minute longer." Despite the billowing clouds of black smoke, the HV began to pick up speed.

Kate looked out of the windshield. Wyatt was heading straight for…the forest. She looked down at the mantor hanging over the front of the vehicle and realized what he was about to do. "Oh God!" Her restraint still wasn't secure. "Wyatt! I'm not…" She stopped and returned her efforts to the clips. Talking about it wasn't going to help anyone.

The HV sped across the yard leaving a plume of black smoke behind it. Inside, Kate fumbled with her restraint, her eyes flicking between the clip and the rapidly approaching trees outside. "Come on! Come on!" she muttered to herself. Her hands were shaking.

The mantor straddled the front of the vehicle, rear legs hanging underneath, one front paw lodged firmly in the hood. It desperately continued to try and gain a hold with its remaining clawless limb and then suddenly it stopped, as if becoming aware of the futility of it all and a more serious concern. The creature looked over its shoulder and frantically tried to wriggle free.

Kate pushed her clip home and the world exploded in stars.

* * * * *

"Are you all right?"

"Nuh..."

"Kate? Are you all right?" It was Wyatt. She could hear Wyatt. She rolled her head over to the driver's side but the seat was empty.

"Where are you?"

"I'm here." His voice came again. He sounded distant. Her head lolled back the other way. He was crouched by her open door. "Come on. You need to get out of there." She could barely hear him over the hiss of escaping steam.

"Am I dead?"

He smiled. "No, you're not dead."

"Is that other thing dead?"

"Yes. Yes it is." He looked sad at the admission. "Come on."

Kate reached up and rubbed the back of her neck. "Ah." She grimaced.

"Are you okay?"

She nodded gingerly. "I'll be all right. Just a little sore." Kate hit the release on her restraint and took Wyatt's hand, climbing slowly out of the vehicle. She looked back towards the house.

Her father ran towards them, his plasma rifle held in both hands across his chest. Behind him, Kate's mother walked over with Alex on her hip. "Are you all right?" her father asked.

Kate nodded.

"We're okay," Wyatt said. "Keep Alex away. I don't want him to see this." He walked to the front of the vehicle, its nose smashed against a tree. With the turbine dead, the black smoke had given way to wisps of gray steam that escaped from all around the crumpled hood. In the center of it all lay the upper half of the mantor, the rest of its body lost among the splintered wood and tangled machinery; crushed by the impact.

Kate came to join him and although aware of her presence, he did not turn to look at her. "It shouldn't have been like this," he said, his voice cracking with emotion. "This should never have happened." He stepped forward, fighting back tears, and stroked the mantor's brow. In death, the creature looked peaceful. He looked back at Kate and she could see he was distraught at what he had done. "This wasn't the way it was supposed to end," he said to her.

She nodded her understanding, then offered her hand and led him back to the house. Furball emerged from the trees, running to catch them, and then bounded along at their heels.

* * * * *

The link operator patched into the call. "Hello. Interplanetary Zoological Pa…" She stopped on recognizing Wyatt's face. "Oh. Hello, sir. I didn't expect to see you again quite so soon."

Wyatt managed a weak smile. "Is Hernandez there?"

"Yes, of course. I'll put you through." She made the necessary transfer. "Sir!" Hernandez turned at her call. "I have Wyatt on the link for you, sir."

Hernandez nodded and tapped his com-link. "Hey Wyatt. What's up?"

Wyatt looked serious and drawn and pale. "You can stop worrying about the mantor. I found it."

"You're kidding."

"I wish I was. It was out here, at my in-laws' place."

"Are you serious?"

"I look serious, don't I?"

Hernandez shrugged. "Is it alive?" Wyatt had turned away from the link, his attention caught by something else. "Wyatt. Is it alive?"

Wyatt looked slack-jawed at the wall screen. The sound was muted but he recognized the detective who had come to the zoo. A banner across the bottom third of the picture confirmed his identity as Detective Superintendent Ed Lieberwits.

"Are you all right?" Kate asked him. "You look like you've seen a ghost or something."

"Wha…? Yeah. Yeah, I'm fine. What is this?"

"It's the news."

"Turn it up, would you?"

"*…Lieberwits and another of Chicago's law enforcement officers, Officer Ed Wood, are those credited with breaking the case and bringing those who masterminded the break-in at the zoo to justice. Officers from the downtown precincts swooped on City Hall earlier today and took the mayor into custody…*" The picture cut to images of the mayor screaming at the top of his lungs as he was bundled out of city hall.

"When did this happen?" Wyatt asked.

"I don't know," Kate shrugged. "This morning, I guess. First I've heard of it."

"Hernandez?"

Hernandez looked at him impatiently from the screen on the link's base unit. "Yes. I'm still here. Is the mantor alive?"

"What? No! No. It's dead. Hernandez, are you watching this?"

Hernandez looked up at the set of screens above him. "Watching what?"

"News channel five. Punch it up."

Hernandez muted his other screens and listened to the newscast.

"*Along with those involved in the Alien Liberation League, at least one other member of the mayor's staff has been detained. Also implicated in the plot is the zoo's own managing director, Stephen Gruber…*"

"What?" Wyatt slumped down into a chair. The picture cut to an aerial shot of paramedics loading a trolley with a body bag into the back of a hospital HV.

"*...a search of Gruber's premises found the suspect dead. At this time the Chicago City Police department has refused to release any details as to the cause of death.*"

"Well, that's no great loss." Hernandez's voice came over the link.

Wyatt held his head in his hands. "What are they saying? That Gruber was behind all this?" He ran his hands through his hair and clasped them together behind his neck, looking up at Kate with a pained expression. She had no answer for him.

"It's over, Wyatt," Hernandez said.

Wyatt sighed, still unwilling to accept what he had heard. "What's the news since I left there?"

"Very quiet. A couple of calls. That's all. With the mantor accounted for, there's nothing out there that we'd classify as lethal anymore and with what we've got left to mop up, I'd say another day or two and then we're just going to be following up on leads after that. I'll send someone out to remove the mantor for you."

"Thanks. I'd appreciate that."

"Okay. We'll keep you updated. In the mean time, I suggest you get some rest. It sounds like you need it."

"Yeah. Thanks. And thanks for all that you did out there. You did a great job."

"Don't sweat it. Just doing my job." Hernandez hung up the link.

Wyatt looked back at Kate and shook his head in disbelief. She moved towards him, kneeling on the floor in front of him and resting a hand gently on his arm. "It's over," she said, echoing Hernandez.

He hugged her and held her close for a long time.

CHAPTER 21

Lieberwits looked around his office. It was bare now, free of the clutter that had become part of the furniture. It had taken him days to go through all of it.

There were murmurings among the officers on the main floor. Rumors that the silver fox was calling it quits and hanging up his hat for the last time. They were started by those that passed by and saw the old detective in his office, sorting through papers and packing things in boxes. Lieberwits allowed himself a grin. *Let them gossip.* For once he didn't care that they were talking about him.

Even his desk was clear, save for the two large files that sat at an angle on the corner, and soon even they would be gone. He looked at them, two manila folders gorged with sheaves of paper, hundreds, even thousands of man-hours reduced to these pages of white and yellow and sometimes green, their edges frayed and worn, the entire collection held together by a pair of thick pink rubber bands. That was old-school. Police work was changing, a fact that Wood had demonstrated to him on more than one occasion. This time, Lieberwits didn't think he wanted to change with it. Some of the things Wood had said had resonated with him, struck a chord deep inside of him and forced him to consider his options. Maybe it was time to move on.

He typed the last few words into the document and saved it to CORE, readying himself for what he had to do next. He was just about to log out when the thought of Wood stopped him. Something the young officer had said; *"I'm sure the rest of the officers here would love to take down the mayor. Especially after all the cuts he's made to the force."* The comment now piqued his interest.

Lieberwits had never really been affected by the cuts. Sure, he knew they were going on but at his level in the force they had never touched him directly. There were certainly fewer detectives than there used to be, but that was due to natural attrition and rounds of early retirement. In financial terms, the cuts had never hurt him. But after what Wood had said, Lieberwits wondered if others further down the chain of command were feeling the pinch. He had no idea what a junior officer made for a starting salary. He decided to look it up.

When the figure first came up on his desk interface Lieberwits thought he must have made some mistake. He tried again and retrieved the same document. He checked it for updates but he had the most current file. Lieberwits slumped back in his chair. If that's what they were paying Chicago's finest then it was the members of Chicago city congress who were the biggest crooks in the city. It was insulting. He had no idea how anyone even managed to live in the city on that number of credits, let alone support a family. And they wondered why they couldn't attract good cops! Lieberwits snorted. Wood was a good cop. He deserved better than that.

He shut down the interface and logged out, then gathered up the two files, tucking them awkwardly under his arm. He grabbed the handle on the door and looked back at the room that had been his home for the last two decades. *If these walls could talk…*

Lieberwits closed his office door for the last time.

* * * * *

"What's that pile of shit doing on my desk?" Harrod looked at the two files with something akin to revulsion.

"They're case files, Cap," Lieberwits said.

"I can see that! I didn't ask what they were, did I? I asked what they were doing on my desk."

"Don't worry, they're closed case files. I'll be taking them down to archives in a minute."

"What, and you felt like you just had to come in here and soil my desk with them?"

"No," Lieberwits said. "I came by because there is something I need to give you."

Harrod raised his eyebrows, "And that would be?"

"This." Lieberwits pulled out his holo-ID generator and laid it on the desk. Harrod recognized it immediately and slumped back into his chair. Lieberwits set his pistol down next to his badge. "I'm done, Cap. I quit."

"Why?" Harrod asked, his voice barely more than a whisper, the question almost a plea. "Why now?"

'These two files…" Lieberwits gestured to the bulging manila folders, "…Are the two cases at the IZP,"

Harrod nodded. "I heard what you did. That was good work, Lieberwits, and mighty brave of you to take down the mayor. You sure made a lot of people out there happy." He gestured to the main floor outside his office.

Lieberwits smiled. "Well, the IZP's been haunting me this past five years and it's finally been laid to rest. Now that it's done, I've realized that the force is changing, and it's no place for a man like me."

"What do you mean?" Harrod roared. "I'm not that young myself, you know. What are you saying about me?"

Lieberwits could see through his rare display of humor. "I mean these kids. These young beat cops. They're more into the technology. They're better-equipped to deal with it and as a result, they're just better cops. It's time for me to go."

Harrod nodded thoughtfully. "That's your final decision?"

"It is. I've thought long and hard about it. Don't waste your breath trying to talk me out of it."

"Do you want to work your two weeks?"

Lieberwits shook his head. "My desk is cleaned out. Everything's squared away. I've left no loose ends. I just want a clean break."

"Can we organize a send-off for you, at least?"

"You know me, Cap. I'm not one for all that show and ceremony."

Harrod nodded again. He sighed deeply. "Well if that's it, then there's only one thing left to do." He pushed himself out of his chair and straightened his tunic before saluting. Lieberwits returned the salute.

Harrod stepped forward and offered his hand and Lieberwits shook it, slipping something into his captain's palm. "What's this?" Harrod asked

"It's a data crystal. It's got some expenses on it."

Harrod laughed out loud. "Ha! Expenses. You've never claimed expenses before in your life."

"All the more reason why you should honor it, then."

"All right," Harrod sighed.

"There was one other thing, too." Lieberwits said.

Harrod looked at him. "Go on."

"Well, seeing as how you'll be needing to undertake a round of promotions to fill my position, I wanted to put in a recommendation for the officer I worked with on this case."

Harrod rubbed his chin. "Yes. It was Wood, wasn't it?"

Lieberwits nodded. "He's a good cop. You could do worse than give him a break."

"All right. I'll think about it."

An awkward silence fell between the two men. Harrod noisily cleared his throat. "Well, I'd like to thank you for all your years of service. You're a good man, Lieberwits. I wish you the best of luck."

"Thank you, Captain Harrod."

Harrod shook his hand again and Lieberwits turned and

headed for the door. "Oh, Cap!"

Harrod was halfway back around his desk. "What is it now, Lieberwits?"

"You might want to have someone in plasmatics take a look at that pistol before you reissue it. It seemed to be malfunctioning a little there towards the end."

Harrod eyed the weapon on his desk. "I'll be sure to do that. Thank you."

Lieberwits turned and left. Harrod sat back down in his chair, fingering his bottom lip and wondering what this turn of events meant for his department. After a minute of thought, his eyes fell on the data crystal. He chuckled to himself. "Expenses." He picked it up and placed it on his desk interface to read it.

"Lieberwits!" Harrod roared, but the detective was long gone.

* * * * *

"You're leaving early, aren't you?"

Lieberwits turned at the sound of the familiar voice. "Either that or you're starting late."

"Night shift," Wood said. "Just coming back to finish up some data, then it's home to bed. What's your story?"

"I quit."

"You what?"

"You heard me. I quit."

"What? Why?"

"I'm too old for this game, you showed me that, but I've been doing this for so long now, I don't even know if I can do anything else. Figured it was time I found out."

Wood raised his eyebrows.

"Some of the things you said…you made me think about it, and you made me wonder about what else is out there for me. I got to thinking, you know, maybe Mrs. Lieberwits hasn't found me yet because I just move too fast. Maybe it's time I slowed down. That wouldn't be such a bad thing, would it now?"

"When you said you'd never have to see me again I thought you were joking."

"I was," Lieberwits grinned. "You'll see me around. Besides, you know where I live." Lieberwits offered his hand and Wood took it and shook it firmly.

"Well, it was a pleasure working with you, *dad*," Wood said with a grin.

"You too, son. You too." Lieberwits winked at him. "I put in a good word for you with the captain. I hope something comes of it."

"Well thank you."

"Ah, it's nothing. You're a good cop. You deserve it." Lieberwits donned his hat and clapped Wood on the arm. "Take care of yourself, Ed. Stay out of trouble." He turned and began walking down the sidewalk. Wood watched him go until he could no longer see the detective among the morning crowds.

EPILOGUE

After the recapture effort was complete, the citizens of Chicago returned to the zoo en masse to show their renewed support for one of their most beloved landmarks, but in the months that followed it became apparent to all that what remained of the IZP was not viable.

Between a third and one half of the exhibits were gone, lost, presumed dead, or confirmed dead, either victims of the initial break-in or exterminated on the city's streets. Gate receipts were down, and the federal government elected to pull its funding and stay well clear of the affairs of the IZP.

While Chicago's city congress and the mayor's office tried their best to make up the shortfall, both of these institutions were now under intense media and public scrutiny. In time, the ever-increasing budget to keep the zoo in business grew to be too much for the city to carry. Within the year, the zoo was closed and Project ULF was dismantled. Remaining pockets of the Alien Liberation League hailed this as a moral victory. All zoo personnel and Project ULF staff were required to seek employment elsewhere.

To their credit, the people of Chicago were outraged at the suggestion of euthanizing the remaining aliens at the zoo and it was agreed that those creatures still alive would be allowed to see out the rest of their natural lives. Their care and the upkeep of their enclosures are dependent upon the charitable donations made by the city's more generous citizens.

* * * * *

Some of those donations were put towards the multi-million

credit project to reunite the baby puglion with its parents. The major fundraiser was a large property developer building a super-skyscraper, the foundations of which ran so deep that a tunnel could be run from the excavations to join with the sewer tunnel. In the six months it took to reach the puglion, the alien had grown significantly, living in the silo and flourishing on a plentiful supply of rats.

The members of the ULF squad were hailed as heroes and became minor celebrities in Chicago and the surrounding suburbs. None more so than Travis, who was given the key to the city by the new mayor. In addition, Travis was promised a penthouse suite in the new construction, a suite that would give him a view of the entire city that he had worked so hard to protect. He hopes, if they're still together then, that Helen will move in with him when the building is complete.

* * * * *

Wyatt's friendship with the ULF staff, both old and new, was deepened considerably by the whole experience. They socialize regularly, catching up on each other's lives and helping each other out when they can.

Invariably, when the alcohol starts to flow, they slip back in to "trapper" talk, telling stories and sharing memories of their zoo careers.

Whenever they get together, Wyatt always buys the first round of drinks.

* * * * *

Officer Wood was promoted to detective. He remains friends with Lieberwits, the retiree managing to fill his spare time following Chicago's resident sports teams. He now also tries his hand at virtua-golf.

Lieberwits is still single, maintaining that whoever the future Mrs. Lieberwits might be, she still hasn't found him yet.

* * * * *

Chicago's old mayor was sentenced to five concurrent life sentences with no chance of parole. Goddard was ordered to serve twenty-five years.

Toby Napoli was shot and fatally wounded after a three-hour standoff with police at his Downers Grove home.

Andy Komicki received a five-year suspended sentence and fled the state of Illinois. No one has seen or heard from him since.

* * * * *

As for the creature in the lake…

Lake Michigan proved to be too vast a body of water for any recapture effort to ever be successful.

Occasionally there are sightings of something huge in the dark waters, but each story becomes more embellished and outrageous than the last and the "creature" is fast becoming the stuff of myth and legend, Chicago's very own version of the Loch Ness monster.

A thriving tourist industry has sprung up and for fifty credits you can take an anti-grav hydroglider on a "Mitch" spotting cruise. Their success is debatable.

It is believed by some that the alien has survived, presumably thriving on the plentiful supply of food that the lake has to offer. Others are skeptical. Some refuse to believe it ever existed at all. Memories fade fast.

One thing is for sure, only the ignorant or foolhardy go into the water.

THE END

ILFANTI

Known as an adventurer, the dwarven Council of Elders member Ilfanti is one of the most famous Mages in the realm. Everyone knows his name, and others flock around his charisma. But even Ilfanti is at a loss for why the Mage's Council is ignoring the fact that Zoldex has returned and none are safe as his plans go unchallenged.

The Empress has been kidnapped while in the midst of trying to unite the races. Her true whereabouts are unknown, but her return is vital to the survival of the Seven Kingdoms. The Mages are doing nothing, and Ilfanti can no longer condone avoiding the obvious signs that are plaguing the realm.

Follow Ilfanti as he returns to a life of an adventurer and battles against time to save the Imperium. Experience the adventure and learn if the charismatic adventurer can complete one last mission in time to save the realm.

Ilfanti and the Orb of Prophecy, 0978778278, $19.95
and more to come!

CLIFFORD B. BOWYER
CONTINUING THE PASSION

Continuing the Passion follows the story of Connor Edmond Blake, a best-selling novelist who, after suffering the tragic and unexpected loss of his father decides that the best way to honor the memory of his father is by carrying on the legacy that his father left behind.

Connor's father, William Edward Blake, a Hall of Fame High School Baseball Coach had led his team to numerous state championships. Most of Connor's memories and moments he shared with his father have something to do with and revolve around the sport of baseball. As a former coach himself, of a men's softball team, Connor decides to at least make the attempt to coach a High School team in attempt to honor his father.

Continuing the Passion is seen through the eyes of Connor Blake as he experiences the tragedy of the loss of his father, and his pursuit to help his family find a way to overcome the loss.

Continuing the Passion, 097877826X, $18.95

Stuart Clark

Project U·L·F

Imprisoned for a crime of passion, Wyatt Dorren is given a second chance at life on the Criminal Rehabilitation Program. Dorren becomes the rarest of breeds: an ex-convict who has become a productive member of society, trapping U.L.F.'s–Unidentified Life Forms–from newly discovered planets and returning with them for exhibition at the Interplanetary Zoo. Dorren inspires loyalty and courage in his team members, but nothing from his dark past, or his years trapping dangerous aliens, can prepare him for what's in store now.

Project U.L.F., 0978778200, $27.95
Project U.L.F.: Reacquisition, 0978778286, $19.95
and more to come!

Mike Lynch & Brandon Barr

Sky Chronicles

Since the dawn of time, an ancient evil has sought complete and unquestioned dominion over the galaxy, and they have found...us.

The year is 2217 and a fleet of stellar cruisers led by Commander Frank Yamane are about to come face to face with humanity's greatest threat–the Deravan armada. Outnumbered, outclassed, and outgunned, Yamane's plan for stopping them fails; leaving all of humanity at the mercy of an enemy that has shown them none.

Follow the adventures of Commander Frank Yamane and his crew as they struggle to determine whether this will be Earth's finest hour, or the destruction of us all.

Sky Chronicles: When the Sky Fell, 0978778235, $18.95

ABOUT THE AUTHOR

Photograph by Gene Carl Feldman

Stuart Clark was born and raised in Middlesex, England. He has a BSc. in Microbiology from the University of Bristol and a MSc. In Science Communication from Imperial Collage of Science, Technology and Medicine in London. He moved to the United States in 2005 and now lives with his wife and daughter in New Jersey.